Edward Hoagland was born in New York City in 1932. He graduated from Harvard in 1954 and finished his first novel two years later, devoting the first ten years of his career to fiction. His novels are *Cat Man*, *The Circle Home*, and *The Peacock's Tail*. In the late 1960s he wrote short stories and also a book-length journal of travels in British Columbia, *Notes from the Century Before*. Other direct narratives followed, in essay form. Altogether, he has published more than a hundred essays and reviews, collecting many of these in three books, *The Courage of Turtles*, *Walking the Dead Diamond River*, and *Red Wolves and Black Bears*. He lives with his wife and daughter in New York City, teaching or travelling intermittently and spending his summers in northern Vermont.

AFRICAN CALLIOPE

A Journey to the Sudan

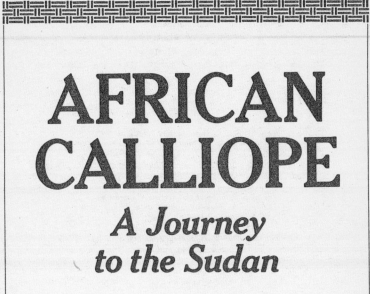

Edward Hoagland

PENGUIN BOOKS

For Alan Learnard,
Elin Paulson,
R. W. Flint,
and for Molly

Penguin Books Ltd, Harmondsworth, Middlesex, England
Viking Penguin Inc., 40 West 23rd Street, New York, New York 10010, U.S.A.
Penguin Books Australia Ltd, Ringwood, Victoria, Australia
Penguin Books Canada Ltd, 2801 John Street, Markham, Ontario, Canada L3R 1B4
Penguin Books (N.Z.) Ltd, 182–190 Wairau Road, Auckland 10, New Zealand

First published in the United States of America by
Random House, Inc. 1979
First published in Canada by
Random House of Canada Limited 1979
Published in Penguin Books 1981
Reprinted 1981, 1984, 1987

LIBRARY OF CONGRESS CATALOGING IN PUBLICATION DATA
Hoagland, Edward.
African calliope.
Reprint of the 1979 ed. published by Random House,
New York.
1. Sudan–Description and travel. 2. Sudan–Social
conditions. 3. Hoagland, Edward. I. Title.
[DT154.75.H62 1981] 916.24'044 80-22897
ISBN 0 14 00.5806 0

Printed and bound in Great Britain by
Cox & Wyman Ltd, Reading
Set in Times Roman

Portions of this book previously appeared in *Harper's*,
The New England Review, and *The New York Times*.

Cartography by Jean Paul Tremblay

Author's Note

This is a travel book, not a book of history, and, for their comfort and convenience, I have changed the names of many people who appear in it. Some are Sudanese citizens. Some are European or American expatriates with careers in foreign aid work to pursue. Only occasionally have I felt a need to alter actual personalities, however.

More often, I have not been strictly chronological. A "gangplank book" will start you right out from the pier on the Hudson River, and, after numerous happenstances, deliver you back to the author's New York City apartment. But this is my second book of travels, and so it has been my pleasure this time around not just to edit my daily diary into an account which remains a journal. I have given emphasis to what I saw by rearranging certain experiences, putting them a little earlier or later than they chanced to occur, or narrating them so that they are not beads on a string. Africa at first can be wonderfully bewildering. Plunge straight in, as befits the age of sudden air travel. Life is a novel.

I had visited Africa before, and chose the Sudan to go back to because of its almost unequaled variety, and because it has seldom been written about. The Sudan must be among the most hospitable countries on earth, but for special kindness shown me during the three crowded months of 1977 that I spent there, I owe a debt to Mr. and Mrs. Alan Williams, Mr. and Mrs. Robert Dirks and Mr. and Mrs. Sterlyn Steele. The excellent newsmagazine, *Sudanow*, published by the Ministry of Information in Khartoum, has helped me keep up with various events since then. For help at different stages of the writing, I would like to thank my wife Marion, Robert Lescher, Joseph Fox, Sono Rosenberg, Suzanne Mantell, Howard Mosher, Eric Robins and Professor John A. Williams.

Finally, I ought to acknowledge the exasperation with which many Africans regard the category of book that mine may fall into. Americans, also, in their early years of independence, were infuriated by what they judged to be hasty, inaccurate, patronizing, rudimentary descriptions of their own nation, written by English diarists like Frances Trollope, Charles Dickens and Harriet Martineau. Although I have tried to avoid such putative faults, a travel book is no substitute for the sort of in-depth work Africans will be producing about their own countries rather soon. In the meantime, the whole continent, and this particular enormous tumbling chunk of it, are in such flux that some of what I saw will be forever changed.

November 1978

Contents

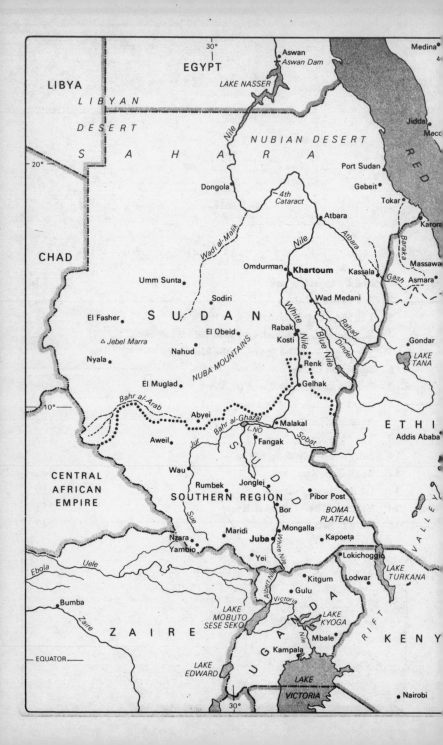

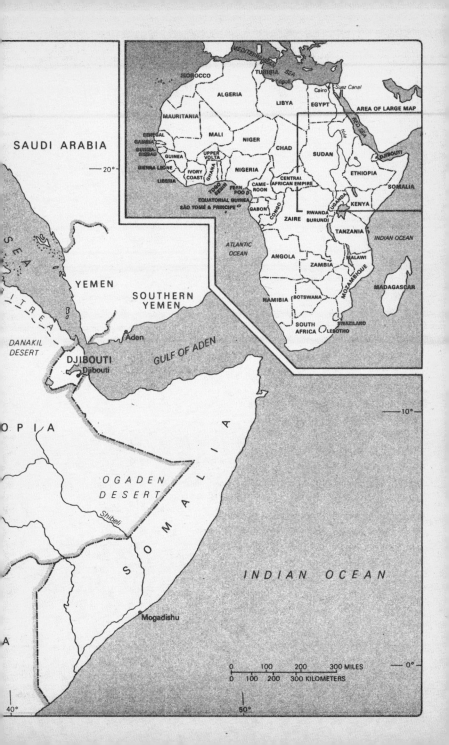

AFRICAN
CALLIOPE

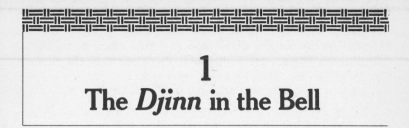

1
The *Djinn* in the Bell

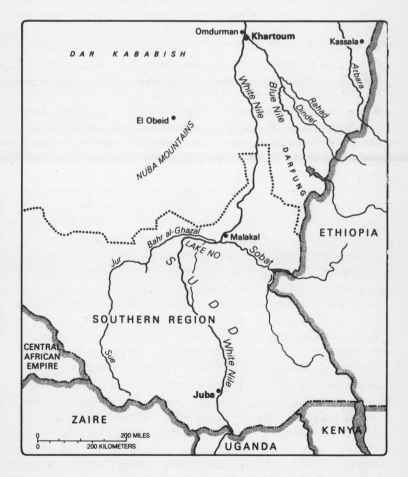

Jimmy Cottle, a roads expert for the U.N., was sitting on the terrace of the Juba Hotel in the Southern Sudan in January 1977, starting to get the feel of his new post. He was a natty, chatty Englishman of the sort with whom you'd share a ploughman's lunch in London, when he might tell you he had "gained a stone to keep in good skin" for his trip. He had worked in Nepal and Rhodesia before this, as well as out in the Australian bush, where the saloons are spaced a hundred miles apart and the local ranchers land their Cessnas on the highway in front and play a lonesome game with a ring suspended from the ceiling which they swing at a nail that sticks out of the wall. He'd camped in godforsaken terrain where the sheep that had drowned in last spring's flood still hung hoisted twelve feet up in the crotches of trees, but where, for lack of water, there would be no sign of either sheep or wildlife again until the rains next spring and he could listen to a truck approaching him for more than an hour before it reached his tent. He was no stranger to isolation and heat, and behind his deceptively lightweight manner and build lurked an energy that was to prove itself here as well.

Juba is the capital of the six provinces of the nearly roadless Southern Region of the Democratic Republic of the Sudan—which altogether is Africa's largest nation, one-fourth the size of Europe, one-third of the contiguous United States. The Sudan stretches across almost a million square miles but has only about seventeen million people, so that from the standpoint of development, one of its problems has been underpopulation. As in many Third World countries, people live from hand to mouth, and the nation's reserves of foreign exchange, though artificially sustained, fell to a low of $18 million recently. But the hope of Egypt and the Arab oil states is that, along the White and Blue Niles, the Sudan will soon become their breadbasket—an urgent idea whenever an American politician has suggested starving them into a framework of policies submissive to the West.

The name originated with the medieval Muslim geographers' term *Bilad al-Sudan*, "Land of the Blacks." In a sense, then, when we call it "the" Sudan, instead of Sudan, we too are saying "the Blacks." Though ethnically one-third of the populace is Arab and Arabic is the lingua franca, this was such a siaving ground around the avenue of the river—and the Arab slavers so liked to tamper with their merchandise under the umbrella of the jolly proverb which says "A woman is like a mare: whatever you put into her you will get out"—that most of the Arabs now also are dark brown or black.

A census undertaken in the mid-1950's on the occasion of independence indicated that a hundred and fifteen different languages, twenty-six of them "major" ones, were spoken in the Sudan, and that the people comprised fifty-six separate ethnic groups, with five hundred and ninety-seven subgroups. "It's a Tower of Babel," said a priest who had preached services in five languages in Juba on Christmas Day. What with the dizzying shifting about that has taken place, and former masters living cheek by jowl with former slaves, in the same village you may meet women veiled to the eyes and women naked to the waist.

In the North, there's sheer bedeviled desert—the Nubian Desert and a southward extension of the Libyan Sahara, both of which are creeping southward into the steppe and savanna land of the central provinces at a rate of two or three miles every year. Even between important cities, such as Khartoum and El Obeid, or Khartoum and Kassala, you drive not on a road but by compass for ten or twelve hours, following the wheel ruts of a previous driver where you can, hoping he knew where he was going and, incidentally, was headed where you are. This is, of course, an age-old adventure, but the cattle herders and camel nomads that you meet are painfully pinched to find grazing lately. The labor of watering the herds from hand-dug wells, which in the Middle East was the first pretext for slavery, has become worse than ever.

But Juba lies right in the heart of the continent, eight hundred miles south of Khartoum by air, or almost eleven hundred along the curve of the White Nile—south of the Mediterranean at Alexandria by two thousand more—and only a hundred miles downstream (which is to say, north) of the Uganda border. It was suggested by some of the British colonial officers that the Southern Sudan might be attached to Uganda instead of being joined with the Arab world, as Idi Amin suggested only recently once again. Ethiopia, Kenya and Zaire are also nearby.

Set on a grassland with thorn trees and mangoes and palms,

Juba is located at just about the inmost crux of the great war-club shape which on the map represents Africa. This Southern Region is home to four million people, and has altogether sixteen miles of tarmac, so that the roadwork is mainly repairing dirt tracks, with a crew of former Anya Nya guerrilla fighters, whom the government did not wish to reintegrate into the army after the civil war, handling the shovels. The seventeen-year war, ending in 1972, by which the blacks of the Southern Sudan Liberation Movement had sought autonomy from Arab Khartoum, cast a paralysis over this part of the nation. Jimmy Cottle himself had just been knocked flat by malaria the last time I saw him in Juba, but he was exuberant because the Canadian foreign aid funding he needed to complete his roads project had just come through.

The British who used to administer the area under the aegis of the Foreign Office were known as "the bog barons" by their supervisors up in the North. It was said to be a situation of "blacks ruled by blues," because they had been enlisted from among the athletes of Oxford and Cambridge—such gentlemen being considered best able to withstand the rigors of the spot. By the Anglo-Egyptian Condominium Agreement of 1899, the Sudan was not officially a British colony, but supposedly jointly ruled, and these hearties were pretty much left on their own by Khartoum, although other Englishmen from the East African colonies would travel to Juba occasionally by railroad, luxury lake steamer and automobile for a pleasure jaunt. Some paused at the Juba Hotel en route north to Luxor and Cairo by paddle steamer, railroad and river felucca —which was the grandest way of ending an African duty tour.

There were the marvelous English walkers, like Dr. J. G. Myers, who in six months as a bog baron collected two thousand botanical specimens as he traversed the territory of the Azande tribe. In one morning he identified sixty-eight food crops grown in a single settlement. And there were the meddlers too, such as his otherwise estimable superior, J. D. Tothill, who in the 1940's, finding the Azandes "amenable to administration," introduced a scheme of forced resettlement and compulsory cotton-growing, to lead to "the emergence of a happy, prosperous, literate peasant community, able by its prosperity to obtain . . . the good things that civilization can bring to the 'Gentle Savage.' " Ten years later, however, Azande society had begun to disintegrate, with malnutrition rampant, and a birthrate steeply declining. In 1955, riots against the "Zande Scheme" helped spark perhaps Africa's most tragic civil war. The war had many other battlefields and many root causes, but a moderate estimate would be that in seventeen years half a million people died.

Nevertheless, in January 1956 the Sudanese by adroit maneuvering finessed freedom from Egyptian control at the same time as they divested themselves of the British—the first of the black African countries to do so. Since then, the flower beds beside the terrace of the Juba Hotel, marked out with the upended brown bottoms of thousands of beer bottles, have gone to seed. But looping, low frangipani trees still drop their fragrant white blossoms. You can journey down the Nile on one of the old boats as far as Kosti, which is four-fifths of the way to Khartoum, if you are willing to spend ten days or so and bring bedbug powder and intestinal pills or your own food and water—the boat I planned to take was two weeks late just getting started. A ruined squash court at the hotel has been brought back into service, and there is talk of rehabilitating the swimming pool by some of the developmental-agency personnel who frequent the grounds in the cool of the evening—Indians and Pakistanis of the sort who make of the United Nations not only a career but a lifelong habitation, and Czech refugees or former residents of French Morocco who somewhere along the line have picked up a Canadian passport as a flag of convenience and now go back to Canada about as often as a Liberian freighter will call in at Monrovia.

And so Mr. Cottle, who had flown in ahead of his wife to settle upon housing and figure out what furniture and foodstuffs she ought to ship down, was lounging watchfully amid the sweetish, weighty, equatorial smell of flowers, garbage, fecal matter, and vegetable saps and syrups decomposing, when three black and white bulls with enormous, lyre-shaped, high-pointing horns were driven up the driveway by a Dinka herdsman with a spear and stick. It was midday. Presently the Arab hotel manager emerged with the Bari cook to have a look at them. They felt the animals' ribs, murmuring an appraisal, and eventually chose one, the manager dickering with the Dinka in "Juba Arabic," as the pidgin dialect of the South is called. The Dinka tied the creature to a tree, where it stood dreaming for a few minutes. Then the cook returned by himself gripping an ax, and, with violently inaccurate blows, hacked off its head, and gradually by stages dismantled the carcass into mashed, five-pound chunks of meat and bone, until the drive was smeared with blood as if after a street accident.

Butchering in the Arab North is accomplished more conventionally in open-air, concrete-floored abattoirs, the customers arrayed around, the meat cut quickly with a knife to order. You notice when it's a camel, for instance, because you see a camel's head lying on the ground. But the Dinkas, Nuer, Shilluk, Baris and other Nilotic Southerners are "cattle people." They marry by a gift of forty or fifty cattle to the bride's family, whose social position is partially established by the size of the herd owned. They drink milk, sometimes enriched with blood tapped harmlessly from the living animal, but eat the meat rarely. Therefore, it's rather from a lack of accustomed savagery that when they butcher even at Juba's central market it looks so brutal.

Many Baris, who were a humbler, riverbank and river-island tribe, less strongly anchored to begin with, have become culturally nondescript. But a Dinka composes songs to and about his cattle, uses dozens of words just to define cowhide color variation and, as a herdsman, to describe the different moods of walking. He will castrate an especially handsome "song bull" to see him grow fatter, believing that his value as a stud is less important than his beauty. As a boy he inherits a "personality ox" calf, according to the color pattern assigned to him among a hierarchy of patterns by the seniority of his mother in the household. He is known by the name for this color pattern and metaphorical names derived from it, as well as by his given name. For example, the oldest son of the first wife of his father gets a "Majok" ox, with a black head and shoulders, white flanks, and black or white hindquarters. Francis Deng, who is a Dinka lawyer and scholar, has listed others: "The Victim of the Arabs," as metaphoric name for a man whose ox is giraffe-colored, an animal hunted more by Arabs than by Dinkas; and "Pollen-grabber," for a man whose ox is yellow and black-striped; "Ambusher of the Animals," for an ox that is lion-colored; "The Shining Stars," for white spots on a dark body; "The Dancing

Head," after the colors of the crested crane, which the Dinkas believe will dance if sung to.

Although his ox stands partly for a fixed social status, the boy trains its left horn to dip down stylishly by tying weights to the tip, pierces both horns to hang pretty tassels from, sharpens them so that it can defend itself (though esteeming the ox's benignity more than a bull's pugnaciousness), and hangs a bell around its neck. When he courts a girl, he comes to her with his ox beside him, so that its cheerful bellowing, along with the clanging of its bell and tossing of its tasseled horns, will serve as an accompaniment to his songs. At a dance he raises his arms above his head as he leaps to make a boastful picture of the tilt of those horns, and at the cattle camps, will die in battle with a lion for the sake of his ox. If a young man disgraces his companions so severely that a beating won't suffice to punish him, they will spear his ox instead.

The Dinkas are extraordinarily tall and thin, as if half their bodies were in their legs. They have small heads and small buck teeth that give their faces an odd, appealing gentleness and fragility, though in their day they weren't bad warriors. They were a powerful nation; two million strong, they are still the Sudan's largest tribe. In skirmishes between clans, they abhorred ambushing each other or killing stragglers, and yet would spear a wounded warrior, lest his friendly ghost follow the man who had shown him mercy forever after. They speared him—that is, unless one of the women of his village, who had followed to assist him and retrieve his spears, managed to throw herself across his body first. She was inviolable, and he became so.

At the cattle camps, which are far from home—rugged living during the dry season, but a life amid their central symbols—the Dinkas recoup their spirits after a personal defeat. Lounging about, fattening on milk, observing the herd and hunting wild meat, a young man composes his best songs, which advertise his wants and idiosyncrasies. As much as by his fighting arm, he makes himself known in the world by the vitality of his songs.

For the Nuer, indeed, a family's herd is part of the collectivity of its lineage, related to the great-grandfather's cattle as a new baby is to the great-grandfather. Through the trading of individual beasts in a complicated fashion, the herd constitutes a part of every family's link with other families, and in religious terms, a direct manifestation of the grace of God. In the time of the ancestor of the clan, "the cow" gave her life for his salvation, and the sacrificial role remains always dormant in cattle, there for either emergencies or ceremonies. "This is why the rubbing of ashes on an ox's back while uttering some short prayer or invocation is a rite which can at any time be performed. . . . They are the means by which men can enter into communication with God . . . the link between the perceptible and the transcendental," suggests the British anthropologist, E. E. Evans-Pritchard.

So few animals are sold commercially or eaten by their owners that the off-take from the Southern Region's six million head is only about five percent a year. Six to eight percent is the estimate for the whole Sudan—versus five times that for U.S. cattle—which is an obvious obstacle to development. Even in the North, a Muslim sheikh, who will die with one finger pointing heavenward to Allah, and feels no need for any mediation with the One God by his hoard of livestock, sees his own sexual potency made manifest in a big herd. They are the bridewealth exacted by him for his daughters, the bride prices that will procure wives for his many sons. And a skinny cow is still a cow to him, just as a tattered dollar would be a dollar. In a nomad's experience, even during a drought, it is better to keep alive as many cattle as he can—no matter how bony—because when the rains finally return, they will fatten. The Baggara Arabs, from the western province of Darfur, walk their market cattle for two months or more—six hundred miles—to sell in Khartoum's sister city, Omdurman, and see them lose one-fourth of their weight from the thirsty ordeal of the desert, en route.

The herds of many Southern tribes were decimated during the war, so that the sort of overgrazing which plagues the North has been postponed. But to demean an ox by harnessing it would be unthinkable to many people. Instead, they cultivate with digging sticks. Dinkas make good townsmen, however, as the Baris do, and with their tribal cronyism have practically monopolized the upper echelon of the Southern civil service. Baris as a group are too ingratiating and manipulatable for such high-level success, though you do hear disgruntled citizens from other tribes—Morus,

Lotukos, Acholis—complain that both the Baris and Dinkas have "sold out to the Arabs."

When a Dinka bigwig goes back to his village to see his parents, he finds that everybody has kept an irreverent perspective on his Juba attainments nonetheless. The hyenas still come sobbing around the hut at night, as he sleeps on a hartebeest skin, and his old schoolmates—to whom a penis is "the horn of the moon, the horn of the buffalo"—drop in to poke fun at him. "Well, you monkey! You black European! You from the Khartoum Ministry! You chief-who's-not-a-chief, can you still eat with your fingers like the rest of us?" A pilot's wife complains that she has "a bird around—not a husband." My friend Jacob Akol, who writes scripts for Radio Juba and who was educated for a decade in Ireland and England during The Disturbances, when he is asked if he wants milk or lemon in his tea, will call out loudly, "Milk is good enough for any Dinka!"

The civil war is euphemistically referred to as The Troubles, The Disturbances, and remains a gingerly subject. Like all African wars, it was scandalously underreported. No one really knows how many people died. The Organization of African Unity is said to have been too young to have acted effectively, although the evidence of more recent tragedies would seem to indicate the O.A.U. could not do better now. A team of foreign doctors who examined some of the Southern refugees guessed that three children out of four were not reaching the age of fifteen. Dysentery, malaria and malnutrition (even as today) were the worst killers, and in one year, according to Anya Nya figures, fifteen thousand out of eight hundred thousand expectant mothers died during delivery in the rebel camps. In one week there were fifteen hundred miscarriages and twenty-five hundred babies stillborn or dead in infancy. During the summer of 1969, eight hundred and seventy-three of three thousand people huddled close to Anya Nya headquarters in the district of Yei died in an epidemic. At Yei in 1955, on the other hand, the Arab district commissioner and his deputy had been burned alive inside their headquarters, and dozens of army officers and Arab merchants slaughtered, up to a thousand in the first massacres across the whole South.

Two periods of parliamentary government in Khartoum—interrupted by a general's six years of military rule—proved unable to end the war. Not until the good offices of Emperor Haile Selassie of Ethiopia and the World Council of Churches and other intermediaries were applied, as well as Gaafar M. Nimeiri's resolve to compromise—in 1972 he was in his third year as Sudan's president—was the Addis Ababa Agreement at last signed. By its terms the Southerners were guaranteed religious freedom, a measurable political autonomy within the region, and the continued use of English along with Arabic as their language of business and bureaucracy.

Africa's boundaries are a hodgepodge of colonial spheres of influence, subdivided often fortuitously, which have invited civil war. Nigeria's, Angola's, Ethiopia's, Zaire's, Burundi's, Mauritania's and Chad's are other examples. The argument can be advanced that it was merely Muslim arrogance that tried to Arabize the animist and Christian South Sudan immediately as independence arrived. There is a strain of absolutism in Islam that reacts to other customs by denying they are customs at all: that any conceivable social or religious basis could possibly exist for women to go bare-breasted, for instance. The Catholic missionaries I met who had worked longest and most affectionately in the Sudan (and who were willing to concede with an austere smile the absolutism of Catholicism) eventually, with reluctance, let drop words such as "fear" and "hate" to describe the Muslim attitude toward Christianity. They said that an ecumenical conference between the faiths held in February 1976 in Tripoli had become "a dialogue with the deaf," that none of the Muslim scholars had familiarized himself enough with Christianity to carry on an educated give-and-take with Catholics who had devoted decades to studying *their* tenets and scriptures. "They think it could corrupt them," said an Italian. "It's just defensive," said an American, "like Catholics facing too many Protestants."

But the new Arab government had also the honest task of attempting to unify a fractured country—an only theoretical nation —after the British policy of divide-and-rule. For many years between the two world wars the (British) Sudan Political Service had actually excluded Arabs from the South, bringing in Greek, Armenian and Melchite-Syrian traders to operate the little grass-roofed crossroads stores instead. The Verona Fathers, an Italian Catholic order, had been encouraged to evangelize the blacks living along the Nile from Malakal south to Juba and beyond. Presbyterian missionaries were assigned certain outposts among the Nuer and Shilluk in the vicinity of Malakal; and numerous extensive Dinka areas away from the river were given over to the Anglicans—while, of course, the Muslim imams were confirmed in their religious regency over the larger portion of the country to the north.

The Verona Fathers, like the Arabs, took a dim view of nudism, but the secular British officials did not. Part of the zest of a stint abroad was to be surrounded by naked men and women. Nudity was "African," and the English, whose intolerance at home and tolerance abroad have been the stuff of legend, were content that tribal variances be maintained. As a consequence, fashionable intellectuals like Mohammed Omer Beshir, who is dean of graduate studies at the University of Khartoum, now prefer to blame the British for practically everything that has gone wrong. The South was kept as an arcadia of primitives, they will tell you, a human zoo—unity prevented between African and Arab. The long bestiality of Arab slaving in the valley of the Nile, the butchery of the recent war itself, are scanted.

The night-black slaves who had passed wholesale downriver to Egypt, Arabia and Turkey may well have had an easier time of it than the Negroes of West Africa who at an earlier stage had crossed the ocean to Anglo-Saxon owners. If they were men, they were likely to be conscripted into Egypt's or Turkey's armies, which offered a path up out of misery. If they were women and bore a prepossessing son to a Muslim master, they saw him accepted as a free citizen to a degree impossible to imagine for a child born of a similar union in North America or Europe. Yet on the Nile and Red Sea during the latter part of the nineteenth and early-twentieth centuries, the British did fight slavery in its every guise and resurrection. In the accounts of traveling inspectors of the 1920's, such as Reginald Davies, who covered twenty thousand miles on camelback and later wrote about it, you find stories like that of the British inspector's kitchen-boy in Nahud, in Kordofan Province, kidnapped by an enterprising Arab unable to resist the temptation of snatching up a ten-year-old blue-black Dinka—just as a sort of speculation—and tucking him into a hollowed-out baobab tree for a few days until the coast was clear. Smaller children were carried in a saddle pouch five hundred miles to where they could be discreetly sold.

Soldiers kidnapped other soldiers and sold them into slavery in the western desert. And you still see the vicious hippo-hide whips that the slaves felt—hippo hide "from the ocean," as a Kababish schoolteacher in Hamrat esh Sheikh, who carried his to class daily, put it to me. The same whips were used for tests of fortitude among the young Kababish in those years, as a circle of ululating wives and young girls watched. The commander of the Camel Corps had to limit the ordeal to six blows for his men. Sudanese Arabs speak derisively of Southern blacks as "slaves" even today and turn apoplectic on the subject of intermarriage. At no level of society do you hear remorse expressed about the institution. Yet many of the present British still seem one-sided here too—three-year men performing some modest technological role, who continue to plump for either the Arabs or the Nilotic tribes, just as their predecessors did under the Condominium, according to whether they had been sent to live among the desert tribes or made swamp barons on the upper Nile.

From a Madi living in Juba you will hear a muttered tale about a raid by "the cruel Arabs" in 1968. The whitewashed mud church of his village was blasted in half by the first armored car that rolled around the bend. Then the gun swiveled to begin demolishing the houses. His parents had stumbled into the bush, yanking the children they could reach with them, to try to sneak into Uganda, which was a three-day walk away. His arm hurts now when he remembers it. A plane strafed them. The Russians, who were assisting the government in Khartoum then, expanded Juba's airstrip to its current size to accommodate their Migs. Afterwards, as he heard, a family of leopards took residence in the ruins of the church.

The war raged perhaps its hottest in 1965, when massacres of several thousand civilians occurred in Juba, in Wau, which is the South's second city and capital of Bahr al-Ghazal Province, and in Rumbek and in Yambio. From a Kakwa: "The Arabs came to my village four times. My father thought that soon we would all be dead. And so he gave me what we had—a little dura [which is sorghum grain], a little money, a bag of papayas, and told me to walk to Gulu [in Uganda]."

In the better-organized Anya Nya settlements, a schoolteacher would have scraped a square of bark from a tree, painted this strip black, and chalked numbers and an alphabet there. And at Makere University in Kampala there was an exile community of Sudanese schoolboys. In Lusaka and Dar es Salaam, as well, and in the Central African Republic and Zaire, white missionaries were sifting through the horde of refugees for candidates to go to college abroad. They were safe enough in Khartoum itself, in the North, but many, many Southern villages had been razed, the dispensaries and schools destroyed, and people on the roads ran the risk of being shot. Because the conflict was in part a holy war, one of the tricks of both armies was to quietly surround a place of worship and kill the self-selected souls inside. It was forbidden to repair a damaged church; sometimes a mosque would be constructed in the next lot. President Nimeiri himself had served in the South from 1959 to 1963, and was helped in seizing power in May 1969 by a revulsion within the officer corps against this utterly futile bloodbath, in which badly trained and equipped garrisons were penned into a series of desolated villages not worth holding, while the Anya Nya controlled the countryside. The very unity of Africa seemed to require that an adjustment be found in this mercurial country, which—Arab in the North and black in the South —was a miniature of the continent.

The expression "the cruel Arabs" kept recurring to me later on in Kababishland, in the deserts of Northern Kordofan, seeing those hippo-hide whips in each man's hand. The Kababish are classic camel-herding nomads descended from a compatriot of the Prophet's in "the island of the Arabs"—which was southern Arabia more than a thousand years ago. They are about as close to being quintessential Arabs as such a hybrid entity as the Sudan can claim. Instead of working for cash, they drive their surplus animals along the Wadi al-Malik, the Valley of the King, a stretch of a great old caravan route between West Africa and the Nubian Nile, to sell in upper Egypt for five or six hundred dollars apiece. Neither have they altered their feudal habits of sheikhly rule; and many of the young men, after the sparse July-August rains, ride off with the breeding herds (*ilbil*) to the Darfur desert near the Libyan border for the frail fuzz of green growth (*jizu*) blossoming there, living almost solely on camel's milk for four or five months, as the camels themselves live on the remarkably moist *jizu,* finding no other source of fluid or food.

It is a proud, spartan existence, and, just so, they are a tribe most hospitable and brave in the profile which they present to strangers. They stay out of the army if they can—indeed, it is the more at-tenuated Arabs who put on a uniform—preferring to war individ-ually over watering points with the Fur, their neighbors to the west, and with the Baggara Arabs, right to the south, for wet areas and standing pools around El Muglad. The Baggara are another tough tribe, hunting elephants on horseback with broad-bladed spears. Though they are possibly outdone by the Kababish, who smuggle in rifles from Libya, the Baggara outfight the Ngok Dinkas, to the south of *them,* for watering spots along the Bahr al-Arab at this dry time of year. (*Bahr* means river.)

One would not want to be a Kabbashi's slave, but to be his guest is princely. A precious scrap of dried gazelle will be produced to make a sauce for the dura polenta for supper, and a bottle of beer, brought from Omdurman by camel, to accompany breakfast. You see his aged, blue, rangy, wire-haired lion dog—though the lions are gone—and his stallion and mare, twin luxuries. One camp, surrounded by a thornbush fence, sits on a lordly knoll. From sunset, and all through one starry night, you watch, at the well at Umm Sunta, a thousand of the nazir's camels watered, the foals suckling, the females sand-colored and white and brown, then all heads and humps against the dark sky. *Karam,* the word both for generosity and nobility, is the core of Kabbashi honor.

And for all of the warring, the way that the life of the African continent chews up even the bitterest memories is characteristic too. It seethes over them like surf sweeping a beach in what by outside perspective might be only an instant or two. There is a velocity to history, new generations rapping on the door. Nearly sixty per-cent of the Sudanese are under twenty years old.

Two bugaboos constitute our preconception of Africa: slowness and savagery. "Sudanese" is the adjective used by the foreign community of Khartoum with a roll of the eyes to convey its despair that anything will ever quite get done right or at better than a snail's pace—but implying the national friendliness, also, the old-fashioned emphasis placed upon honesty and loyalty, which make the Sudanese popular in the oil states, where a good many go. Salaries are five times as high there, and though they are no longer uncorrupted, compared to the Lebanese and Egyptians with whom they compete for jobs, they are less corrupt.

The same days when I trudged across Sharia al-Gama'a (University Avenue), in Khartoum, from a somnolent Ministry of Information to a languid Ministry of Agriculture, trying to make an appointment to make an appointment, but foiled even in this humble aim by the working customs of the place, I had been woken at 5 A.M., when the air raid sirens went off, presumably to keep the soldiery hopping.

The President was living in the middle of Shaggara army camp for safety's sake and commuting to his appointments at the palace by helicopter. Since assuming power in the May Revolution of 1969, he has survived something like fifteen coup attempts. When the Public Security Bureau is in a mood to boast, it indicates there may have been more than that, and the rumor mill reports various lone determined souls storming the palace steps revolver in hand. Three of these emergencies have been noteworthy enough that the government found it more practicable to ballyhoo them than to hush them up. In 1971, Leftist opponents actually held Nimeiri prisoner for three days at General Staff Headquarters, until Sudanese troops stationed along the Suez Canal were airlifted home from Egypt by President Sadat to spearhead a countercoup. Muammar Qaddafi, of Libya—who is now a fiery enemy—chipped in with his support by forcing a British Overseas Airways VC-10 crossing his airspace with two of the coup leaders who were heading for Khartoum to land at Benghazi. He marched them off the plane and later kindly handed them over to the Sudanese for execution, instead.

In 1975 and again in 1976, a coalition that very loosely represented the Right mounted major attempts. In 1976, the fighting continued for a couple of days and more than a thousand people died, with at least ninety-eight more executed in the aftermath. (In

1975, in a "Sudanese" touch, it's said that the leader, Lieutenant Colonel Hassan Hussein Osman, from the country's West, which has sometimes been nearly as restive as the South, made sadly poor use of the two hours when he had possession of the microphone at Radio Omdurman, because he had forgotten to bring along his notes.)

During the winter of 1973—to list some less publicized incidents—Nimeiri's assassination was attempted in Khartoum by a band led by a retired brigadier general; and that summer there were strikes and demonstrations by workers and students seeking a return to civilian rule. In 1974 antigovernment riots occurred in Juba, related to the planning for the Jonglei Canal, which is to drain part of the vast Sudd swamp and winter cattle pasturage on the upper Nile to provide more irrigation water downstream. Also that year, another ineffectual coup attempt was staged by officers in the North, and there were food riots set off when the price of sugar doubled. In 1975 and 1976, apart from the close calls experienced by the President himself, scattered mutinies, due mostly to North-South friction within the army, took place in units stationed at Akobo, Wau, Rumbek and Torit in the South, and in February 1977 a more serious one shook Juba.

Back in 1970, in an action that he much regrets because of the persisting hatred it engendered, Nimeiri waged a mini-war upon the Mahdist Ansar sect, the Sudan's most powerful civilian faction, killing maybe two thousand of them in an attack on Aba Island, their old stronghold south of Khartoum near Kosti on the White Nile. Planes were used to bomb and strafe them, and their venerated leader, the Imam al-Hadi al-Mahdi, was killed as he fled the carnage, just before he reached the sanctuary of Ethiopia along the Dinder River. He was the posthumous son of the storied, gorgeous Mahdi who had wrested the Sudan from the English and Egyptians in 1885, laying siege to and finally killing Major General Charles George "Chinese" Gordon on the palace steps and leveling colonial Khartoum. It goes without saying that some of the old man's followers continue to believe he reached the safety of those wild mountains and lives there still, awaiting Nimeiri's downfall. Nimeiri, however, by dint of decisive exertion and occasional gestures of magnanimity, has stuck in power longer than anybody since Sir

Reginald Wingate, whom Horatio Herbert (later, Lord) Kitchener installed as governor-general after reconquering the Sudan from the Mahdists in 1899.

So, as I sat by the desk of a bureaucrat in the Ministry of Agriculture, waiting for a letter of accreditation to be composed by his clerk—a process which consumed half the day—I had to remind myself that politically the city was a powder keg, and that, apart from conspiracies, a woman sitting outside on the hot sand had held up her dying baby to me.

In the sky a flock of river buzzards was stunting. As we watched them, my companion mentioned bats—the staggered, clever way they flew—opening his eyes to his memories. Bats: I remembered the Dinka boy imprisoned inside the baobab tree, because baobabs were hollowed out first to store water, upwards of a thousand gallons, and the bats of the desert would squeeze through any crevice to reach it. But he was a stocky, rich-skinned man in his late forties, of West African ancestry (no Dinka), and he had grown up in the *jebel* (butte) terrain to the west of the Blue Nile, and had been educated in English in Holland and Khartoum.

Journeying lions and resident leopards hid in the jebels, he said, wherever there was a permanent spring. Also gangs of bandits, periodically, but mainly spirits. He had seen a spirit. With an alarmed laugh he patted his heart. "You see, if I ever die from heart trouble it will be because of that one."

He was with two of his friends from junior secondary school. They had tied their donkeys below, had picked up stones and were climbing after a baboon which they had spotted and which was probably going to lead them to others, if they kept after it. If to only a few, they might kill a young one; but if to many, these would charge them and they might have to run right back down to where they had left the donkeys. They were climbing one of the incisors of Tooth Jebel, as it was called in the local dialect—"like a row of teeth," and a place of considerable mystery. "For our families it was always a question of whether the water from up there would flow out of the rocks and on down to our fields for us to grow a second crop, you know, after the rains ended. There were cliffs and holes and very dangerous places, all sorts of caves and snakes and such things. Trees that smelled like myrrh, and trees that smelled like smelly eggs. We were afraid of the bees and the snakes and the leopards. And bad men were sure to collect and hide in some of the bigger caves whenever the soldiers stayed away for a few years. But they were not as fearful to us as the spirits."

In earlier days the Darfung tribesmen had retreated from Turkish slaving expeditions onto the jebels, where a spear throw was still on some account among the rocks. *Dar* means "abode of"; and in the immensity of the Sudan, just as way over next to Chad there is a province of Darfur, so here in the east near Ethiopia is a land, a history, an epoch—the sixteenth to eighteenth centuries A.D.— and even a *dynasty* of the Fung.* But because my companion's ancestors had been Nigerians who, in traveling overland to Mecca across the Sudan three generations before, hadn't made it home again, a little of the mythology of eastern Nigeria was mixed up with Fung religious lore for him.

The baboon—now four baboons—led them, three boys and two dogs, scrambling up through dry boulders and dom palms, wild fig and toothbrush trees, on up again scrambling over a slope of loose stones, into a rock cut, eventually into the mouth of a large cave, where suddenly they were very much afraid that a whole troop of fierce baboons might be lurking. The baboons they had been chasing escaped, however, by means of an escarpment above them which the boys could not negotiate. They were left with the silent, thirsty presence of the cave itself in front of them. An eagle was wheeling overhead, but it did not come closer, and it was not a djinn.

One boy ("He is now in the People's Assembly!"), after sniffing around the ledge where the sun fell, said the place didn't smell of leopards to him. The dogs, although they were interested, did not act frightened. Together, the three of them tiptoed in just a short distance, then a little farther . . .

"And there was the Spirit of that mountain! We thought he was the biggest Spirit of the biggest mountain that we knew anything

* On the origins of neither the Fur nor the Fung do anthropologists yet agree, though, naturally enough for this tumultuous continent, the former are thought to have moved east-to-west and the latter perhaps west-to-east.

about. I'll tell you what he looked like. He was like a bell, the shape of a big black bell that was hanging from the ceiling. He was horrible, I can promise you. And he moved his sides, as if he was breathing. He may have been seven feet long or eight feet long and four feet or five feet wide, you know, or whatever exactly it was, but he looked gigantic to us. He was making that sound of his breathing, and his sides moved regularly, trembling—regular trembles to how he breathed.

"He was the devil-spirit, certainly. And he lived right in the middle of that mountain. And he was like a school bell or a church bell. We thought we were dead men. He was horrible. We screamed. He was moving as if he was adjusting his *galabieh* [robe]. We threw all the stones we had been carrying. We dropped some. He was shrieking, a very high sound, loud sound. We fell down and screamed and tried to run back. And he swelled up with this most horrible shrieking sound like a—what do you call it in English, a cloth for the grave? And he stretched out over our heads to swallow us—like a bell that was opening its mouth wider to swallow us.

"What he was—let me tell you. He was about a hundred thousand, or maybe ten thousand, bats flying away out of there in just a curtain—like a flapping, screaming curtain, over us, and waving all around us, but not touching us, like we were in one of the folds of it."

He laughed as though to say, you may find it dull to hang around here near Palace Avenue and United Nations Square and the rest of it, but I find it just nice. "Now," he said. "*Inshallah*. I know that there is God! No spirits, no bats!"

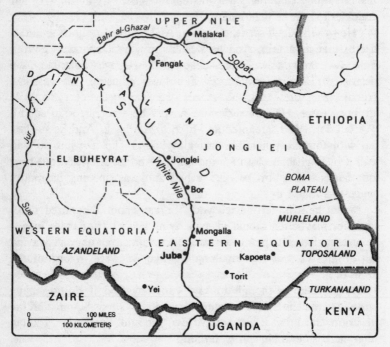

Many of the expatriates you meet in the Sudan have worked elsewhere in English-speaking Africa before they came here—Nigeria,
Zambia, Kenya, Tanzania, Ghana—because although the Sudan
achieved independence sooner than those countries, it was effectively shut off from development for so long by The Troubles. But
first experiences are such a useful avenue of exploration that I am
going to introduce those of another Englishman—whom I will call
Piers Evans, since one must use pseudonyms. He was a building
engineer, fresh out of Bedfordshire, beef-faced, thirty or thirty-five.

He was accompanying a senior consultant named Shorter, who was an expert traveler; Evans himself had not left England before.

The flight from London was uneventful for them, as were the couple of hours by Boeing south from Khartoum over the Nile. At Juba, however, the Sudan Airways pilot proved unable to land. His approach, from a clear evening sky, was too high by a hundred feet. Abruptly perceiving this mistake, he veered up and away for another try. But on his second descent, he was not properly over the tarmac at all. By misreading the pattern of lights on the ground, he had swept in to the right of the runway by a hundred yards, only at the last moment discovering his error and tugging the shuddering 707 into the air, canted like a fighter plane. With all his confidence gone, he flew back to Khartoum, where he wobbled down onto the landing field with difficulty.

Even at midday, for people without reservations the hotel situation in Khartoum is a race in a maze. Evans and Shorter scuttled about till after midnight in humiliating fashion, with the headaches they had gotten on the plane. Out, then, to the airport at dawn: a successful arrival this time.

At the Juba Hotel, Evans quickly picked up a mild case of dysentery because the drinking water comes straight from the Nile—though for about forty cents you can have an orange sweetener added to it, if that will make you feel better. The water system created by the British for seventeen thousand people has deteriorated, while the city has quintupled in size. Occasionally, when fuel is so low that the city's extra pumps can't be worked, a handful of favored neighborhoods receive pure water through the original filtering arrangement and everybody else must lug pails from the river.

But the job was a noble one. Evans was to assist Mr. Shorter, who was visiting a boatyard which had been established with international aid to construct several ferro-cement river launches for swift travel on the branches of the Nile and Sobat during the rainy season, when most roads flood. Between Juba and Malakal the White Nile spreads into the Sudd (which is Arabic for "barrier"), Africa's largest swamp. Twelve thousand square miles are permanently under water, and, seasonally, an area three times that. Half the river's water at this point is lost to evaporation or to the exuberance of the vegetation, which is a great frustration to agricultural planners downstream in Cairo and Khartoum. For the three hundred and fifty thousand people living in daub-and-wattle settlements around the swamp, transport was the problem, and the forty-five-foot boats with fifteen-ton carrying capacity, drawing only three feet, might help.

Also, the Englishmen looked at an experimental brickworks manufacturing an alternative to the traditional crumbly mud bricks of the Nile, which are patted together by hand and baked in the sun or "burnt" slightly harder next to an open fire. Walls built of these are often plastered with cement, for stores and houses of the families who are better off, but, even so, disintegrate all too soon in the equatorial rain. And because the Sudan imports most of its cement—as it shouldn't need to do, with the minerals available for mining in the Red Sea Hills—they wished to experiment with the mix to strengthen it and stretch each bag further. By adding glass fiber or the fiber of a local reed, a coating as thin as a sheet of cardboard might be enough to waterproof and firm up the mud huts most people lived in—mud daubed on stalks of sorghum straw, which can collapse with pathetic results in a hard rain.

They applied cement to a test structure, took photographs, and rumbled about to hearten the British lads supervising at the brickyard and boatworks, and their German counterparts laboring at a small furniture factory that had been set up about the same time under a government-to-government program, linked with a two-man German mission that was restoring the old British teak plantation at the town of Yei. At Yei, another British team was growing pineapples, hoping they could be introduced into the Sudan's economy, and testing improved varieties of peanuts and fast-growing maize. All yeoman-work, and going quite well, if you discounted the cobra and tsetse-fly stories, as well as the fact that by the end of the year the boatyard, which was supposed to be self-supporting, would be in the red by at least $250,000.

Evans was a chunky man, his face already inflamed by the sun, a determined good sport, as the British are, though to me he looked as if he had taken a deep breath and was swimming underwater. He drank loads of tea. "Me tea," he sighed, saluting his cup when he came in for lunch.

Eating fish and meat, he escaped further digestive upset, though the fish can cause difficulties. Nile perch weigh fifty or sixty pounds and, bent over the back of a peddler's bicycle, look like a thick corpse. The manager at the hotel, after buying one, insisted that it be completely consumed before he invested in another. Depending upon the vagaries of appetite of his guests, this might be a week or more, with the refrigeration going off with every power failure in the meantime, and blackouts put into effect nearly every evening to save fuel.

Evans's cohort, Mr. Shorter, was a tireless, optimistic technocrat of the rising British class. He was a bold, brilliant fellow, like the best of the European consultants who flew in and out with an overnight bag, at home wherever the plane put down. Europeans seem always to be on the move in Africa, always a bit too impersonally alert, and always in a hurry; but there are the good travelers, versus the bad.

Cocking his eye like a bird, Shorter visited the Juba Ministry of Transport and Communications, too, because the first of the boats had been fitted with an inboard motor inappropriate to the Sudd, which for hundreds of miles is choked with water hyacinth, papyrus and other debris. The craft had performed dubiously; someone had drowned, and the Sudanese had been doubtful about the idea of a boat floating on a bottom of concrete, in any case. But he'd reassured these ministry officials, rekindled their trust (as he could have done mine), and was briskly preparing his argument to revive the enthusiasm of the funding charity in London, whose interest in ferro-cement boats on the upper Nile had, naturally, flagged along with that of the Sudanese. He was sure that on the strength of his judgment—his flat, unapologetic Midlands accent—they would come round.

We had an Englishman from the World Food Program, distributing sorghum, canned foods, cooking oil, sugar and wheat to four hundred thousand schoolchildren here in the South. Another Englishman was trying to set up a training center for auto mechanics. Also, Dutch veterinarians, Danish horticulturists, German road builders and U.N. experts on local government and fiscal management, rice farming and fisheries matters. One night an Alaska International Hercules C-130 transport plane winged in from Europe, with a deep-throated, savior's roar, carrying the components for a telecommunications reception tower that two technicians from Tennessee were erecting with the help of a Filipino crew. It was a priority flight. The airport was ablaze but the city dark, to lend electricity to the venture until the plane took off again.

These two Americans wore tooled, little-heeled boots, wide-brimmed hats and tousled, cowpoke hairdos. One was almost comically lanky, laconic, unaffable and smooth-shaven; the other, fat, pleasant, with muttonchop whiskers. He claimed that he'd solved the food problem by "living on my flesh" and drinking lots of beer, which he said he strained through his whiskers.

"The food must be good. The flies like it. But never praise a meal for twelve hours."

Just as Evans and Shorter were making every effort to appear unflappable, these two were reliving Dodge City. Both pairs showed up once in a while at Costa's Africa Hotel for a change of diet. Costa was a Cypriot-Sudanese, his wife the same; and the few "true" Greeks left in town—pretty *rentiers,* wistful now, in their empty Greek Club, which had been a famous poker casino—snubbed them because they were half African. Also because Costa had "abandoned the Sudan," as they said piously. He had fought for the Anya Nya as a munitions specialist instead of sitting out the war in Khartoum drawing rental income from the Arab officers billeted in Juba.

Costa was a squat, dynamic cynic, under pressure from the black Sudanese as well, because his blood was half Greek and they would have preferred that he sold his business to an "African." They would shut him down for a day or two because a police inspector had measured the rolls he had bought at the bakery and found them an inch "short." They would jail him for the morning just to get his goat, though that evening he'd be offering a glass of date sherry to his friends, sitting in a metal chair under his tiny grape arbor again.

Costa provided a fairly kindly reception for the international collegium of hippies who staggered into town in famished little bunches, dehydrated from two weeks of the Mahdi's Revenge, traveling on a River Services paddlewheeler up the Nile from Kosti. Burned raw, swollen from mosquito bites, they looked like the Michelin man, as one of them said. Or they might have come overland from Wau—four days on top of a lorryload of dura sorghum, clinging dangerously to the bouncing truck along with thirty-five, forty-five (once sixty-five) other people. Wau itself was a five-day-to-two-week crawl by train out of Khartoum, and they were blanched from exhaustion, as well as sun-red. The fun of begging handfuls of dura porridge and sesame seeds and manioc from impoverished peasants, after they had eaten the two dozen boiled eggs and two dozen oranges they had brought with them, had long since palled. Generally, they looked so blistered and glazed that nobody had the heart to tell them before they had gotten a good night's sleep that they had run into a dead end here in Juba.

Such young souls, in desert boots and traders' beads and granny glasses, with a command of three words of Swahili, five of Greek, four of Arabic, rudimentary French and international English, would be directed to Costa if they could afford to pay $5 a night for a room. He fed them fried chicken and fried eggs, with a side dish of okra. If they had less money, they camped behind the latrines at the police station, and bought finger bananas and sorghum bread and Chinese apple jelly at the market, taking it with five-cent cups of milky tea boiling in a cauldron in front of a tea shop called the People's Restaurant. They had come the hard way from Cairo, but were now to be foiled in their aim of reaching Nairobi by road, because the route doglegged through Uganda, and the Ugandan lieutenant in charge of the detachment at the border was not permitting white people to enter his country, even in transit—only blacks. Still, white tourists were able to pass through freely in the opposite direction, from Nairobi to Juba, as, apparently, his compatriot officer down at the Uganda-Kenya border did not feel the same way.

There were no consular services. The only American I met at the U.S. embassy in Khartoum who had even *been* to the South was the ambassador himself, who had had to lay over unexpectedly in Juba once, after his Sudan Airways plane ran out of fuel while en route to a Unity Day celebration in Wau and couldn't take off again until more fuel was flown in. So you would see a panic supplant the exhaustion in our young travelers' eyes, if they hadn't the $120 for a seat on the Sunbird charter plane that ferried odd parties of elephant hunters, International Labor Organization contractors and Food and Agriculture Organization hydrologists up from Nairobi or back. It meant that somehow they had to beg a seat on one of two missionary planes which also flew to Kenya, or else wangle passage aboard one of the infrequent trucks going privately across the roadless desert between the Sudan and Kenya's Northern Frontier. This is a region of Turkanaland so wild that the administrative and geographic boundaries of the two nations do not coincide.

The Norwegian Church Relief plane, flying from the town of Torit, was usually full. The other plane was piloted by an American named Bowman for an agency called the Africa Committee for the Rehabilitation of the Southern Sudan. Mr. Bowman, too, was often full-up. Though his employers were Christians of the first water—nursing lepers, building schools and the like—he himself was said to be an irascible, impulsive man. At least, the English didn't like him much, because he favored Americans in that last-minute crunch when he was about to take off and a seat turned up empty and seven people were standing around the apron of the field, pleading to go. More puzzling still, he was likely to pick a face that he had never seen before, a frightened newcomer, rather than one of Juba's expatriate habitués who were accustomed to finagling free rides and always knew who was flying where.

Of course, there were a smattering of other planes: a thirty-five-seat Sudan Airways Fokker Friendship that went to Wau and Malakal; a low, gray, snub-nosed, nondescript police plane of Russian vintage; a Boeing 720 for freight, that spent much of its time flying sheep from Khartoum to Jidda—four hundred fifty of them per load—but when that market was flooded, would pick up a consignment of miscellany for our end of the world. The pilot owned it. He was a Floridian with the requisite beard for adventuring in Africa, but also the curious air of insubstantiality most pilots seem to have when you talk to them (considering that you put your life in their hands). His wife was a darling, though. Hillbilly-skinny, hillbilly-rawboned, she was a thirtyish stringy-blonde with a small, friendly, sensitive face, who was a pleasure out on the margins of my life in Khartoum as well. I would notice her in the lobby of the Excelsior Hotel, playing backgammon with her husband before supper, or with a pilot pal of his. Feeling lonesome, I'd be singing "Bicycle Built for Two" or "The Sidewalks of New

York," and she would give me a small hillbilly grin, like that of the girl from Houston I had once been in love with.

Pilots flying north were of no use to our Cairo-to-Nairobi wayfarers, however. They hung about the terrace of the Juba Hotel, hoping to look so winsome that our twin Wyatt Earps, off-duty from erecting the TV tower, would condescend to talk to them. The tower bosses chartered a Kenya plane once in a while to carry supplies, but although they themselves wore their hair at a length that would have fit them for the summer trappers' rendezvous at Ham's Fork in Wyoming in 1834, it developed that they didn't like Prince Valiant or Hindu holy-man hairstyles.

Two Australians had tried to hitchhike to Kenya by way of the Lokichoggio Desert and Northern Frontier sometime before. Each got all gussied up in the standard European red backpack with mountain tent, aluminum canteen, tinned meals, substantial boots. At Kapoeta, the last police post in the Sudan, the officer told them they were crazy; he would not permit it—the Turkana would kill them for their belts alone. But after politely turning back, they had walked around the town and headed by compass into the waterless hundred miles, figuring that in the next day or so a truck would happen along. They walked twelve miles, admired the sunset, built a fire of scrub, heated a bite of food, admired the black tall sky. After stripping to their skivvies, they unrolled their sleeping bags, and, crouching over these, looked up to discover the ghastly apparition of half a dozen warriors with spears held poised above them—men smeared gray with ashes, so that their faces were flatplated like skulls, who let out a death's whoop just as the Australians glanced up. In fact, the Turkana do still kill an occasional white globe-trotter who impresses them as being without any means of defending himself. But these individuals were quite likely Toposas, who war with the Turkana. They let the strangers in skivvies and bare feet light out for Kapoeta again.

Other disaster stories were told on the patio of Costa's Africa Hotel, while our travelers tried to figure out what they should do. It was as much a tradition for them to scare each other as for Evans and Shorter and the Indian and Serbian U.N. technical experts in the $30-a-day rooms at the Juba Hotel to scarf over the dangers here.

A German livestock specialist was said to have headed for his new assignment the slow way, up the Nile from Khartoum—like a man of some imagination—instead of merely flying in. He was sitting on the bow of a barge at night, riding through the Sudd, when the barge hit a mud bar. Although the impact knocked him off, the barge slid free and he was left behind. He swam and waded for five days, until a Nuer fisherman paddling a sycamore dugout chanced to rescue him.

Then there was the Lapland-to-Cape-of-Good-Hope bicyclist who reached Juba, mad and babbling, but with his legs still churning. On, inevitably, toward Nairobi (this was before the arrival of the prickly lieutenant at the Uganda border). His story was that he had tried to cross the Sahara with only sixteen quarts of water hanging from his bike; had found that he needed to "push" a lot because of the sand; and had survived thanks simply to the humanity of passing lorry drivers. Down further south, in a wet hamlet between Jonglei and Bor, among the fishermen along the badlands of the Nile, he had contracted cholera, but had been nursed back to his feet by a Thany woman.

The Africans laughed at all such tales, just as the British diarists in colonial days used to complain that they would, even after watching one of their own tribesmen get swallowed by a crocodile. The same Englishman who noted this lapse might confess, however, that his fear of dying in these grim hinterlands had swelled as he watched, until he too had laughed uproariously at the dark legs kicking in the jaws of the crocodile. A black Kenyan, a business agent for a trucking firm who drank beer with us in the evenings, had heard during November that his father had been murdered in Kampala by order of Idi Amin. At first he shrugged, remarking with a kind of obstinacy that his father had beaten both him and his mother. But at the U.N. Christmas party, when everyone else had forgotten about it, he burst into sobs, crying that his poor father was dead, weeping uncontrollably.

We certainly laughed—at Costa's—telling sad stories and eating paw-paws, which taste like honeydew melons, look like a cantaloupe inside, but contain bitter, bb-sized, black seeds which could serve as "caviar" in a practical joke. Usually an African had rescued the white man from the mess he'd got in, except for a case where a fellow who had lost his money and come down with malaria went and knocked at a white family's door, shivering, his head bursting, and said, *"I'm white. Save me!"*

Now, at this juncture, February 2, 1977—just when Piers Evans had had a couple of weeks to get his legs under him—the anti-aircraft battery at Juba Airport, led by a sergeant named Paul Ponk, mutinied on behalf of the exiled National Front. The Sudanese National Front was then an amalgam of dissident political groups, mainly conservative or religious-purist, but enjoying a spectrum of support because it advocated a return to civilian parliamentary government. The soldiers, augmented by rebels from other units around town, numbered a hundred and fifteen. A mutiny far more widespread had been planned, but the authorities had begun to get a fix on it. Two politicians, Clement Mboro and Joseph Udoho, had been arrested, and, soon thereafter, a scattering of thirty-six men in the military, though none as yet from the air-defense battery itself. The scheme had been for the airfields at Wau and Malakal to be seized also, but, of necessity, the action in Juba was moved ahead, and Wau is four days away by truck, and Malakal two. A messenger could not possibly have reached Wau in time. The messenger for Malakal, a teen-aged boy, was perched on top of the load in a market lorry that overturned on the road.

The Juba mutineers, realizing they must go it alone, shot the eight police plants in their unit (virtually the only casualties the government later admitted to), and, at 2 A.M., lowered their pair of anti-aircraft guns to serve as artillery pieces in a meagerly armed defensive perimeter. The tanks which they ordinarily possessed had already been taken from them. Some were Mahdist Muslims, some Christians—a nucleus from the Nuba Mountains in Southern Kordofan—as well as Dinkas and individuals from other tribes closer to Juba. The promise stirring them was that if they could hold on to the airstrip throughout the day, planes would fly in from the Sudanese rebel camps in Ethiopia, bringing reinforcements, along with officers to lead them. Maybe Sadiq al-Mahdi himself—great-grandson of the great nineteenth-century Mahdi, and nephew of the Imam al-Mahdi, whom Nimeiri's troopers had slain in 1970 near the Ethiopian border after the rout at Aba Island—would arrive. Sadiq was chief of the National Front.

Though only thirty-nine, he was a former prime minister in his own right, and had been slated to assume that office once again by vote of parliament when Nimeiri took power. The province, possibly the whole Southern Region, might rise in revolt, they thought.

Before dawn they sent a tenth of their force to try to free the thirty-eight prisoners, without success. At dawn loyalist troops, with a couple of medium tanks and machine guns and automatics, counterattacked, starting down from the high ground a mile to the south of the airport, where most of the regional ministries and the ministers' new blue-and-white Yugoslav-built houses are. Sudanese make good soldiers. They did well against the Italians in the skirmishes on the Ethiopian border early in World War II. They had fought the British, Turks and Egyptians before that, and they fight hard in their own civil wars.

Firing now in disciplined short bursts, the loyal forces advanced like the two paws of a stalking cat. ("Mostly in an African war they'll kill you with the noise," said my host for that month, who was a Dutchman in relief work.) First one, then two planes could be heard circling, keeping high up. Nobody really knew whether these were planes hired by the National Front or just the weekly bread-and-butter planes from Nairobi bringing Tusker beer to the U.N. folk.

Even a revolt snuffed out, as this one was, furthered the interests of the Front in keeping the Sudan on edge, after the earlier attempts at a coup. All morning there was sporadic firing at stragglers in several districts around town. But by 9 A.M., a rear guard of rebels was protecting the flight of the main bunch twenty miles north alongside the river to the village of Mongalla, where they had previously hidden canoes. Here they crossed, with good covering fire from the opposite bank, and struck out as best they could on foot for Ethiopia, two hundred dry miles away. Some Mandari tribeswomen captured two of them, who asked for water and food, tying them up after they had laid aside their guns to eat. Sergeant Ponk was caught on February 5. A Dinka baby hit in the cross fire died in my Dutch friend's house. Tending another, he remembered Biafra and Bangladesh.

Six people were killed in Torit, when the driver of a truck loaded with passengers inadvertently went through a checkpoint at night.

Talking to his seatmates, he hadn't noticed the pole across the road or heard the order to stop. Mr. Bowman, the irascible and impulsive pilot for the missionary group, was the only expatriate killed. He foolishly attempted to run a series of roadblocks in Juba in his Volkswagen during a lull in the firing to try to "save" his plane, and was shot through the throat. Indeed, he needn't have died, if there had been any blood at Juba's hospital. But the doctors couldn't keep blood, because of the absence of dependable refrigeration, due to a shortage of fuel for the generator. A Swedish well-driller and a nurse riding in the car with him were hit too. Bowman was buried within the week right in Juba's cemetery, and the rest of us in the foreign community quivered superstitiously at the thought, as a Mandari might have done at the idea of being buried over in Oklahoma.

Evans's partner, Shorter, as it turned out, had won an M.B.E. for his demeanor as a district officer for the Colonial Office during the last insurrections before independence on Borneo. He was not martial in manner—only wholly practical. He is said to have dodged into the forest with a handful of true-blue native policemen after the guerrillas overran his headquarters, and to have waged guerrilla warfare on them. At one point (so the gossip ran), he impersonated an entire army with two jeeps, driving forward with his headlights on, switching them off, backing up and driving forward again.

Be that as it may, Shorter shaved at his usual hour, while the fighting crackled past their cottage on the hotel grounds—only taking the precaution of lying on his back on the bathroom floor as he did so. Next morning it seemed to him that one day's work was more than enough time lost. Other expatriates were lining up to book seats on the first Cessna for Nairobi or the first Boeing for Khartoum. They included, incidentally, our Americans from the earth-satellite reception tower, who had been all duded up for weeks for a shoot-'em-up.

But the team from Bedfordshire had come to Juba to complete a job. They got in their jeep, and Shorter badgered his way around the Saladin armored cars guarding the bridge over the Nile. In the hamlet of Gumba, on the other side, he headed for his precious boatyard. Finally he was halted by a soldier with a Bren gun who wouldn't budge. Nevertheless—for a century and more—there has been a special way that a British officer in irregular dress deals with a uniformed, well-armed African. With straight back and squared chest, he merely trots at him. This is what Mr. Shorter did. He charged the man and chased him around the vehicle.

Later, on the afternoon before their departure, we were joking about what they would manage to say about their trip when they got home to Bedfordshire. Would they chat about the battle at the airport, the cobras in the boatyard, the poverty in Malakia, which is Juba's mud-hut quarter? The mutiny had doubtless merited four lines in the foreign press, though the arrests were going to continue for a month in towns throughout the Southern Sudan.

"At a dinner party I say nothing," Shorter remarked. "I talk about bricks, cement, perhaps Mohammedanism. It's easier. You can explain all you like, really—dine out on all the things we've seen here very thoroughly. But they're not going to believe you. It's such a jump. It's just too different."

Evans, with a pot of tea in one hand and a glass of Tusker in the other, did not commit himself. Sunburned, wordless, he had completed the course. He was in good health, drawing deep, relaxed breaths, keeping his own counsel, and may have rattled on volubly when he got back.

3
The Most Ferocious Disease in the World

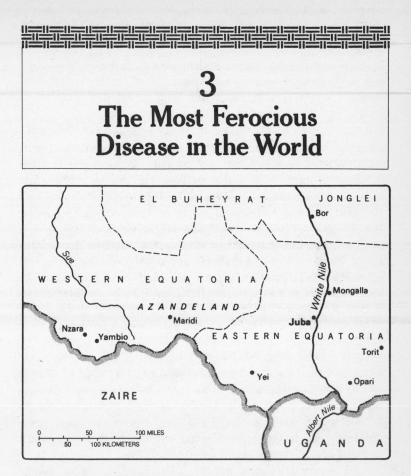

At one moment life has a breakneck pace in Juba, yet again, as in Khartoum, you wonder where *does* the time go. A foreign exchange transaction that would take four minutes to negotiate in London, fifteen minutes in Cairo, twenty-two in Nairobi, twenty-nine in Dar es Salaam and thirty-one in Khartoum will require about forty-five at the Unity Bank on Addis Ababa Street in Juba.

Not within the bank itself, possibly, but subverting the good intentions the nationalized bank is supposed to stand for is a lack of protein and other nutrients, so that at Juba's hospital, for instance, when a person who is regarded as healthy walks in to give a blood transfusion, his own blood count will be only sixty or seventy percent of what would be considered normal for a European. In Europe he himself would be clapped into bed.

The hospital is a flabbergasting proposition—"outpatients" besieging the gate for treatment, soldiers and barbed wire about, a few families of the luckier sick camped semipermanently on the lawn, and yet the wards half empty, a wretched lassitude pervading them. When I took my tour, the patients had no toilet facilities available to them—only bucket latrines. The doctors had the use of an X-ray machine but, because of the Sudan's financial and transport problems, no film to put in it. There was a microscope but no slide-making material; and the refrigerator was almost worthless because of the power cuts, so that, without a supply of stored blood, the only treatment they could prescribe for severe anemia or postoperative debility was bed rest, sometimes for months. Gasoline was so scarce that even when I was being chauffeured in a Ministry of Trade auto, the driver turned off the motor to go downhill. (To blow his horn, he crossed two wires on the dashboard.)

Drugs were also painfully short because of the budget pinch, although a well-to-do patient could send out for them. Physicians on the staff received under $3000 per year; the senior lab technician, less than $2000; a nurse-midwife, $800; the hospital's head carpenter and plumber, $450 each—figures that assume significance because these people could have quintupled their wages by going off to Saudi Arabia.

"We do not resuscitate patients," Dr. Bol Deng, who showed me around, explained quietly. He was a sloping, serious young man, son of the first of one hundred and seventy-five wives of the former Paramount Chief of the Ngok Dinkas, located near Abyei. He had returned here to his own country after seventeen years of school and medical training as a refugee in Italy and England— three brothers and four uncles who had stayed at home having been assassinated by Northerners during the civil war in the meantime. His first task had been to get proper window screening installed in the pediatrics ward, to which he was assigned, and have the inside walls painted, and ditches dug to drain the stagnant pools of water standing outside. With his original Dinka resistance long gone, he had contracted one of the peculiarly virulent strains of malaria that Juba boasts—quite pillproof—which harassed him at night. During the rainy season he went about in Wellington boots to keep from catching bilharzia through his feet and legs.

There was typhoid, meningitis, yaws, hookworm, amoebic dysentery, leprosy, giardiasis, kala-azar, relapsing fever, much pneumonia and tuberculosis, and onchocerciasis (blinding-worm), besides. In Western Equatoria Province, a plague of sleeping sickness seemed to have been aggravated when refugees of the long-suffering Azande tribe resettled themselves after the war in marginal areas of what traditionally had been Azandeland, reinfecting the local tsetse flies with trypanosomes which they had carried across from Zaire. Nine hundred cases had been diagnosed within two years, which probably meant double that number were unreported. But there is not much cancer, for example. When we did see a case—a young woman whose throat was by now inoperably swollen—the nurse had forgotten the word for cancer.

"It's like a human laboratory," said another doctor, a Dane, and one of those troubleshooters who hop about with a shaving kit and change of shirt to the hot spots—"the assholes of the earth," as he put it to me equably.

The fire in this instance was a horrific new virus called Ebola, or (informally) Green Monkey Disease, which had just died down after devouring hundreds of people. Again the Azande of Western Equatoria Province were the prime sufferers. At Maridi's hospital, seventy-six staff members alone had contracted it, of whom forty-one succumbed. Across the border, six hundred miles away, at Yambuku Mission Hospital in Zaire, thirty-nine of the mission staff fell ill and thirty-seven of them died. Much of the Sudan's Southern Region—Juba included—had been quarantined from the rest of the world for two months of the fall. Altogether, by official count, nearly five hundred people were recorded as having died.

Ebola was structurally similar to but antigenically different from another Green Monkey Disease belonging to no previously identified virus group; and the host vectors of both were unknown. This other one had cropped up in tiny outbreaks in South Africa and (transplanted with a shipment of green monkeys from Uganda) in Marburg, West Germany. The symptoms were about the same, and positively Homeric. Five to fourteen days after exposure, a flu-like headache and backache developed. Then high fever, nausea, diarrhea, sore throat and coughing, chest pains and prostration. The eyes and palate reddened. A rash appeared on the skin. On the lips, fissures. In the mouth, "tapioca-like lesions." By now ghost-faced and badly emaciated, often undergoing convulsions, the patients began to bleed from every orifice. They hemorrhaged from the nose and gums, vomited and defecated blood, bled sub-conjunctivally and from the ears and vagina. Pregnant women aborted quickly, bleeding to death. As the walls of their smaller blood vessels gave way, the patients were both bleeding and clotting internally. Although they were in immediate danger of bleeding to death, anticoagulants were given, lest they die first of an embolism.

Among the Azande and Moru villagers, the disease had been spread at funerals by the ceremonial washing of the dead man's body, and other decent respects paid to him. It also sometimes spread when medicine men went about scarifying people with a long pin to protect them against getting sick. But if they visited a government dispensary, the chance of contamination was just as great. Such a shortage of supplies existed that, commonly, the same hypodermic needle was used all day long, on a hundred or two hundred patients, without being sterilized in between. Two kinds of shots were given—chloroquine for malaria and penicillin for respiratory illness—the technician rinsing the syringe and needle in a pan of water as he shifted from one to the other. Although the virus can live on for months in the sick person's semen or other fluids, his blood would be the main point of contact.

Maridi (pop. about 15,000) had 229 diagnosed cases and 117 dead. The epidemic burned itself out in six or eight weeks, after frantic if rudimentary local quarantine arrangements. The hospital soon became an inferno of anguish. There were no more sur-gical masks or gowns or gloves. The staff who had not panicked and fled were all the more susceptible to infection as a result of working double shifts to fill in for those who had. After 59 nurses were down and bleeding, the patients were left unattended in an isolation ward surrounded by a fence. Some of them crept away to lie in makeshift privacy closer to home—perhaps in an abandoned hut where a relative could shove a dish of food within reach. Some, desperately thirsty, crawled under the fence, down the hill, to a spring where the whole neighborhood drew water, collapsing, dying—even drowning—there, a hand found sticking up out of the water, next morning.

The last death in Maridi occurred in November 1976, but two months later a visitor saw bloody syringes and towels from the epidemic still lying around. He saw two people die during his first five minutes in the hospital—one from a skull fracture which the police had inflicted, the other from an undiagnosed stomach ailment—and utter unconcern on the part of the attendants in both cases.

It is hard to convey the sense of hopeless torpor in some of these backcountry towns. The God-soaked fatalism of the Muslim North is not similar. Neither is the atmosphere of discouragement which I had seen before in North American Indian communities. Fatalism and discouragement aren't quite the words to describe the feeling of *removal* these people had. I didn't reach Maridi, or Nzara, the cotton-ginning town where the disease got its start in the Sudan, or Yambuku (Ebola is the name of a stream there), where the death rate was calculated to be ninety percent of those afflicted. Yet listless towns like Yei and Torit, where I did go, could just as easily have been struck by a calamity. They seemed to await catastrophe.

An aghast-looking Bengali showed up in Juba, a smileless, fragile man, a World Health Organization doctor, his hair gone prematurely white as if from all the pestilences he had seen. Also Belgian and British virologists, the latter confiding to me that although the Sudanese wanted it bruited about that the fever had originated in Zaire, they believed it had got started in Nzara and afterwards had invaded Zaire. The Belgians, however—Zaire being the erstwhile Belgian Congo—gave me to understand that, whereas the Zairean government preferred to regard Nzara as the epicenter, *they* considered that this medical honor ought to go to *their* town, Yambuku. One cheerful, brawny Walloon, who had been living off the land and drinking from the brooks judiciously during five years' medical ramblings through Belgian Africa, said he had met a bunch of American big-game hunters who were so scared of the epidemic that they were cooking even bongo stew with Perrier water.

Because of the clamp on publicity, the Belgian had had to fox the Sudanese authorities by telling them he was investigating sleeping sickness, in order to drive here to meet his colleagues. As casual as he was, he had arrived with his jeep's differential busted, and nothing but Zairean zaires to pay to have it fixed. So he was staying at Costa's, blending with the hippies, as if he were one more lost soul trying to find himself through traveling. It was fun to sit next to him to hear how close-mouthed he could be.

He said that several younger African doctors had flown to Yambuku and labored manfully during the emergency, but that the older ones had stayed in Kinshasa. On a hunch, after the end of it, he had bumped three hundred miles along a series of rain-forest tracks through obscure settlements parallel to the known tangent of the disease, and had found that these places, too, had endured a scourge. He drew a few blood samples to prove his point, but, unfortunately, some had deteriorated during the trip. Others, packed in dry ice, he had given to the manager of a little sawmill for safekeeping. But the manager, called away, had felt, rightly, that it wouldn't be safe to either take them or leave them behind intact.

The British investigators put up at the house of a German missionary in Maridi, eating crepes suzette and steak au poivre cooked by his Congolese houseboy and drinking Makassi beer smuggled from Zaire, with a high head on it. Then, in Nzara, by the luck of the draw, they ate scrawny *shamba* chicken with their fingers, Sudanese style, and millet *kissera* (pancakes) in the government rest house. Because of the mutiny at Juba's airport, the team's chief at this point, Dr. Christopher Draper, had to have his pilot circle each landing strip on his trips back and forth, until the soldiers staked out to prevent a repeat performance lowered their guns. A Kenyan who had piloted for him earlier had landed in Uganda on some brief errand and had fetched up in prison.

Dr. Draper, of London's School of Hygiene and Tropical Medicine, has strong features, a bishop's sort of face, with white hair sticking out over a black turtleneck. He speaks Swahili, from a past stint in Kenya, and takes the Londoner's delight in friends with eccentric occupations masked by the sober costumes of convention: a fellow in a bowler hat striding through Oxford Circus with a zoril's skin in his briefcase. His parasite and rodent specialists were catching rats in traps and bats in mist nets stretched across likely openings. The traps vanished; people found them useful. (In a grass hut rats are the bane of existence.) But eventually five hundred animals were collected, drained, ground up and spun through a centrifuge. Serum, liver, spleen, kidney, testes and salivary samples, frozen in liquid nitrogen, were flown to the research establishment at Porton Down, England. Because monkeys are difficult to catch—and, I suspect, from an obstinate objection to the newspaper name, Green Monkey Disease—they did not do any tests on monkeys, though at last report no other lead has been obtained on what the animal reservoir might be.

From the Maridi citizenry, the team extracted nearly a thousand serum or capillary samples, plus plasma from most of those who had been sick from the virus and recovered. Each donor would give his liter of blood, and after the serum had been spun off, his red cells were injected back into him. He was given the equivalent of twelve dollars in cash and twelve dollars' worth of dura grain or powdered milk, though these payments were an unanticipated expense. The people believed the government should pay them compensation, and at first held out on the Britishers to pressure the Ministry of Health.

A Bari from the countryside created a bit of a stir in Juba by walking into the hospital with his sick monkey and asking whether it had caught Green Monkey Disease. Two Arab schoolteachers were driven from Maridi, bleeding from the nose, and "sat in that chair you are in and the one next to it," said Dr. Salama, the director, with lingering nervousness. They died, as did a local farmer, and then one of Salama's nurses. He quarantined forty-five personnel, and snuffed out a siege much worse, he thinks. A doctor from Maridi had been flown to Khartoum to die, before the fearful character of the illness became evident, and a rich merchant took the same route, dying in Omdurman. That fall, Green Monkey fever had seemed for a while the most ferocious virus at large in the world, and when I left Khartoum for America the following spring, travel to Juba was restricted because of rumors of its reincarnation across the border in Uganda once again.

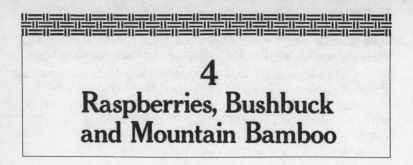

4
Raspberries, Bushbuck and Mountain Bamboo

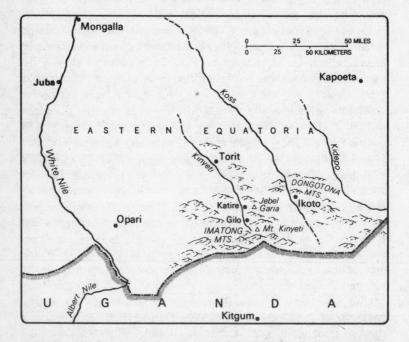

Still, I got more purchase in Juba and the South than in Khartoum. In Khartoum and other Arab towns, family life is lived behind the walls of a compound. If the householder hasn't erected a barricade of mud and dung and plastered stone, he has at least a straw windbreak eight feet tall to cut him off from the common ruck of street existence. As a wanderer, I felt myself cut off. Even if I went to supper at his house, I met only him and his men friends.

I wouldn't claim that the festivities—mainly card games such as whist and quatorze, and beer drinking—that follow dinner in Khartoum are any duller than an evening in an Acholi hut of mud and grass and wattles, down in the Imatong Mountains, which are six or seven hours by car southeast of Juba, verging upon Uganda. With the Acholis, you might play a game of *mancala,* as the Arabs call it, an African cousin of backgammon, with pebbles moved as counters on a board carved into squares. Instead of bottled beer, you drink a piquant, whitish, brownish near beer called *merissa* in Arabic that the women have brewed over the course of a week or so from a combination of sprouted and unsprouted sorghum, buried, dug up and buried again. They call it "White Stuff" in English, and sometimes distill a clear, gin-like strong drink from it, *arak* (or "Strong Drink," when offered to an American). There is nearly always drumming during the evening, on whatever is handy —they don't need a drum. Then, rather quickly, dancing.

Your Arab hosts in Khartoum, or a provincial capital like El Obeid, may dance also—just the men—to a record player, snapping their fingers as loud as castanets. They will have their own arak, unless they are unduly religious, buying it from a woman on the poorer side of town, perhaps a widow who supports herself by the labor of making it, or a married woman who is raising a sum of money to give to her son for a bride price—either sorghum arak, or else one of the variants distilled from bananas, dates, mangoes or honey. In addition, White Label Scotch, in little airline-type bottles, was widely marketed in the North at the time of my visit.

City Arabs will probably have some comfortable overstuffed furniture, built low so that a relative visiting from the desert will not feel he is sitting too far off the ground. They may enjoy the benefits of at least fitful electricity, whereas the Acholis entertain you sitting on a log beside a flickering scrap of fire. It's tiresomely smoky in the Acholis' hut; the family's meat is smoked and stored above the fire. Grass huts have no chimneys, anyway. The smoke streams through the small round dome of the roof almost evenly, like steam, except that it stains the ceiling and walls with greasy, thick, blue-black soot and gives the children pinkeye.

Sorghum merissa, which by itself constitutes many a meal for children and adults alike in the South, by good fortune happens to be rich in protein, ascorbic acid and the B vitamins. But nobody tenders you the platter of tidbits of tomato, meat and cheese that you might get for an appetizer in a Khartoum house—not to mention the feast of kidneys, tripe and roasted and boiled dismembered sheep which would crown such a meal. Neither is the Acholi's courtesy as painstaking, as reassuringly elaborate, as the classical Arab's. And yet the women are with you! Chatting, laughing, dancing, in the social setting of the evening they are not at all a subservient order of being. Even leaving out the pleasing if disorienting circumstance that when they dance they are likely to let their dresses down and tie the sleeves around their waists, they make an immense difference.

My Acholi village was Gilo, with perhaps a hundred souls. They were resettled refugees from the Sudan's war, now living seventeen miles by forest footpath from one of Uganda's most remote borders. I didn't make the walk for fear of being seized as a spy, but used to sit down by a campfire with a pair of smugglers' couriers once in a while—gaunt, shy men in rags, who solemnly shook hands with me. Because they were Ugandans, not Sudanese, and strangers to me, they seemed darker than the Gilo Acholis, though they were Acholis too. They said that Idi Amin was "veddy haarrs. Many people have to fly." Going our way, they carried coffee, tea, factory-dyed shirts and Ugandan Sportsman cigarettes, which are better than the Sudan's Haggar brand. (The Ministry of Industry complains that twelve million cigarettes are imported legally every week, while the country's own facilities manufacture at half capacity.) But as hungry as these smugglers looked, they often wanted only to trade their goods for a load of food; meat cost one-fourth as much here, they said. Otherwise, they carried back items like bicycle tires, white cotton cloth, inexpensive perfume, cans of Flit, and pink chunks of laundry soap—all packed on foot, because the path was too rough for a bicycle.

A larger village might have had a grinding mill, powered by an antique, chuffing donkey engine, from the British era, to save the ladies work. Instead, the women had to kneel, each one on a worn flat rock that she had dragged close to her hut and gradually scraped and pounded into a scooped shape, for about three hours a day. Locking her ankles behind her as an anchor, she ground the dura with a scrubbing, scrubbing motion, pushing and pulling a stone across the grains, half a handful at a time—an exercise as grim as giving artificial respiration. The way she whisked the individual seeds into position with a tiny broom, the way she poured a basketful of ground grain into another basket a dozen times in a light wind to separate the chaff, then soaked and wrapped part of it in wild banana leaves to ferment with wet but partially germinated dura underground—this was stuff for an amateur anthropologist to jot down. But what I watched the most (trying not to be gauche or obnoxious about it), and what rarely appears in my notes, was how her breasts and the breasts of all these women swung.

Some of these people had seen the bright lights of Kampala during the war, perhaps had watched a friend succeed in school there and obtain a job off in Nairobi—and here they were in a rain forest at the ends of the earth, wading in muck for half the year, bundling firewood on their heads, lugging water, cognizant of the fact that they might never see even Juba again unless some Martian like me who had a car found space for them.

Culturally, then, they were "in transition," and the young men had adjusted their method of flirting to how a woman happened to be dressed. If she was wearing a blouse, her beau would touch her on the arm or knee or neck, and take her hand affectionately, appealingly, as Europeans do. But if she was not, he reached playfully, gently for her breasts, as the place most likely to sway her mood. Of course an American raised on pictures of Jane Russell and other "sweater girls" of thirty years ago—already alone now for a couple of months—was going to be affected by the breasts. They weren't always bare, but there was no telling when one might meet them bare. Like the bog barons, who illustrated their agricultural reports on the Southern Sudan with photographs angled to profile the younger women in the fields, and like the Greek, Maltese and Italian trader-adventurers and Austrian missionaries and Arab ivory-hunters who preceded even Samuel Baker to the neighboring Nile, I couldn't get over it.

The Acholi men had shot at Russian MiGs with tommy-guns, had met Israeli secret agents, and the German mercenary Rolf Steiner, while defending an Anya Nya airfield hidden away a day's

walk south of us. But now they were back to the status quo of before, carrying a sisilai-wood bird arrow, with feathers but no metal
head, and a buffalo arrow, with a seven-inch head but no feathers
at the other end. They carried these taped to a six-foot bow, or
else a great nine-foot-long spear. They earned only twelve dollars
a month, planting experimental Dutch potatoes for my American
friend Bob Dirks, who was an agricultural expert for the U.N. We
were all living at a forestry-agricultural project so high up and cold
that the colonial officers in the old days had planted cedars and
cypresses and French eucalyptuses and pines; they had even been
able to stock the Kinyeti River with British trout. A virginal white
man like me could eat native raspberries in the woods, and swim as
naked as Tarzan under the creepers and vines and colobus monkeys
and screaming marsh birds of a "gallery forest," as the books would
call it, of podocarpus conifers and Abyssinian acacias and mountain
bamboos and giant lobelia trees, without fear of catching the grim,
watery disease, bilharzia. Higher up was a cloud forest interspersed
with meadows of bracken fern and blackberries and springy-turfed
heath, at Mount Kinyeti's 10,500-foot crest.

The villagers grew tobacco, corn, sword beans, pumpkins, finger millet and sorghum for themselves in scratch patches in humps
of brushland where the trees had been cut. For meat, at least every
few days somebody would snare a bushbuck with a wire loop
fastened across an animal trail. Bushbuck, except for their horns,
quite resemble small deer. A number of hunters went after them.
One man had rigged a narrow chute of saplings bound together
along a trail, leading to a treadle of sticks tied by vines to a deadfall. The deadfall consisted of five heavy rocks atop six heavy logs.

Altogether, except seasonally, when the stored grain sometimes
gave out, not many people went hungry. The children, nevertheless, had bellies swollen from pinworms and tapeworms. On cold
days they coughed and hugged themselves and couldn't bring
themselves to play. Year round, they cried at night when their fathers had to dig the chiggers out of their bare feet with a razor
blade. Chiggers feel like a splinter and expand with blood, but almost no one in Gilo owned shoes. Everybody wore rags for clothes,
although during the rainy season the temperature sank down into
the shivery forties on these chilly spurs of the mountains, which had

been only sparsely inhabited before the civil war. The best of the village hunters, Ilariyo Oyoo—who was twenty-three but, as a former Anya Nya sergeant, looked as mature as a man of thirty-five —could hardly walk some days because the soles of his feet had split from a fungus disease. He had a shirt but no sandals, whereas his brother Karlo wore sandals but no shirt.

And so to counter their war memories or any memories of the amenities of life at the refugee camps outside Kampala, the women were back to carrying water on their heads and crushing grain for the next meal—like scrubbing laundry on a rock. Nearly always a kite swayed overhead, ready to have a go at the chickens (though, luckily, clumsier at the final moment than a chicken hawk would be). The women had to watch the kites, fling pebbles at them, for want of a more effective weapon; and spent whole days pounding red mud into the walls of their tukls (huts) when the rain eroded them—red mud, because it was black mud that spawned the chigger mites. The ground all around outside had to be kept swept clean of grass and clutter, lest a horned viper crawl in close. Elephants, leopards and buffaloes still lived hereabouts, and just half a decade had passed since an Arab soldier walking down the road might have been a far more dangerous adversary than any of these. So it wasn't for mere pomp and show that when a woman went to market hefting sixty pounds of shelled corn on her head, her husband sometimes stalked in front of her shouldering only his spear.

The younger men were likely to share the load; and the spear-man boldest in manner in fact had a clubfoot—rather as the woman with the milkiest breasts was forced to drag herself around with the aid of two canes because her legs, broken in childhood, had never been set. There was an elderly lady who hiked every year to Jebel Garia, an 8500-foot mountain within sight of us which is boat-shaped at the peak. She climbed to a cave under the boat where the god of the Imatongs, in the shape of a ram, lived with his servant, a snake. She slaughtered a goat for them to eat, and for four nights left out beer for their delectation, while she slept nearby, so that the children of the whole district wouldn't die.

This ritual had become necessary because once, in years gone by, a man whose children were hungry had climbed the mountain and found a honey tree, which he attempted to chop down. Right away his axhead stuck irretrievably, and is still partly buried in the tree. Even so, he brought some of the honey home. However, it was the god of the mountains' honey tree, and for his theft the man and all his family died. The rainmakers of the several villages met. Being soothsayers and chiefs, they figured out what had happened and sent a precursor of the woman from Gilo to make amends. None of them has ever disturbed the axhead, or the dripping combs which surround it, or the bluebottle flies which live there with the bees, or any other tree, bush or tuft of grass in the vicinity. As priestess, our neighbor, because of her holy function, never allowed herself to spit on the ground, but only into her own hands, which she then rubbed in her hair, or many children would have died.

Ilariyo, who was my mentor in the woods, said that thirty or forty miles from Gilo—in a country more arid—lived rhinos, hyenas and lions, and crocodiles and pythons in a swamp near there; none of which we had. On the other hand, people who lived over there hadn't our forest leopards, elephants, buffaloes and vipers. The lore, the myths, the practical techniques of hunting and survival were thus altered within a short distance, not to mention the often conflicting tribal customs of kinship or enmity in choppy terrain split up in medieval fashion between suspicious settlements of Madis, Lotukos, Langos, Laconos, Logirs, Dongotonas, Kakwas and Acholis. These people had been squeezed together within historical times between the then formidable Azande war machine and warlike contingents of Dinkas, Turkanas and Toposas. The Toposas still make such a menacing-looking spear—copper-bound and tapering at both ends—that the Acholis in Gilo employ one in their ceremonies. Also a Dinka dirk sheathed in crocodile skin.

Ilariyo had two pretty wives, who used to sit naked to the waist, combing each other's hair in the sun while their babies nursed. They kept such a healthy fire going that his roof had the blackest thatch. He also had sisters, and a very handsome, statuesque, disdainful sister-in-law, who sold not only merissa and what he called its "sweat" (arak), but, I think, herself. She laid tarpaulins in front of her hut, on which dura in several stages of fermentation was drying. When it was ready to brew, five gallons of the grain would be put into a fifty-five-gallon fuel drum with fifty gallons of water for a night and a day. After that, at ten cents for a quart-sized calabash served to a customer, she would take in the equivalent of about $22 for her barrel of beer. The dura, I calculated, would have cost her about $8, at the inflated rate at which it was sometimes sold this far from Khartoum, though she probably obtained it much cheaper than that by buying either black-market World Food Program sorghum, which was distributed here free periodically to supplement the low wages, or else the locally grown grain.

Tucked in a clean Nairobi *kanga* (sarong), she was thoroughly businesslike, even with Ilariyo, though she let him display her plump smooth arms to me. She sold him two quart bottles of what I later guessed would be about 80-proof arak for $1.25. This is cheaper than the price for the same sort of stuff in Omdurman, but —incidentally—twice what an Omdurman prostitute would charge for her services, or five times as much as the price of a woman in Juba, so easy is the effort of satisfying a man sexually, compared to grinding and fermenting the constituents of his liquor.

Inside her hut the ceiling was richly hung with yellow cobs of drying corn, tied in clusters by the husks. There were also little bunches of short tobacco leaves drying, and a profusion of female clothes tossed about on two or three trunks, an iron cot, a wooden chair. Living by herself, working hard, she was a fat cat in the village—most people slept on rope beds or bark mats on the ground. Yet the way that the children ran close to her hut to play indicated that she was less aloof and stern with them.

Ilariyo told the children I was named "Ted, Son of Hoagland." "Bye-bye," they said, both whenever we met and whenever I left, because the Arabic expression *Salaam* is used to mean Hello as well as Goodbye, and they assumed that Bye-bye was the same.

Ilariyo was guiding me on a series of trips to the salt licks where the buffalo congregated, to elephant forests, and to the marsh where he snared bushbuck ("booshbug") regularly. "Booshbug sleeping here," he said, pointing to a circle of flattened grass. "Bubbalo yeddeday," he said, stuttering a little, pointing at droppings.

I assumed he stuttered in response to my own stutter, which

is a severe impediment to me, as well as perhaps because he knew at least three other languages better than he knew English. I speak only English, and that poorly, so that it is a relief to get into a territory like Acholiland, where nobody expects a visitor to be able to speak the language of the country. (For this reason, Turkey is more pleasant for me to travel in than Italy or France.) These people didn't always perceive that I cannot speak even my own language properly; and when I stuttered in front of the children, there wasn't much danger of their making fun of me, because many of the smaller ones had never seen a white man so close up before and they thought stuttering was the way all white men talked.

The grownups who knew English well enough that I couldn't rely on sign language with them, but had to break into a stutter occasionally, were aware of it as a handicap. It paled, however, before afflictions that they were familiar with, such as elephantiasis and leprosy and filarial-worm blindness, which in the Sudan is communicated by the bite of a relative of our American North Woods blackfly. They didn't mimic my stammer as much as the rural Arabs had. Instead, they were more intrigued by my "strong" sweater and "strong" boots—"strong," as they kept putting it, against the rainy-season cold, the rocks, the chiggers, the soakings they endured. At parties—and we usually ended up at a party after our walks in the woods, because I was so slow that Ilariyo had plenty of energy left over—I felt like a clotheshorse. Somebody might be playing an *opuk,* the so-called African "hand piano," but enormous attention was given over to my boots, jeans, hat and sweater.

"Where do your boots come from? Juba?" a raw-footed old man asked with a natural bitterness that could not be concealed. I said no. "Do you come from the sea?" he asked. "Which sea? The Red Sea?"

Even my eyeglasses were an object of envy. The scholar of the village, Gregorio, the sawmill clerk—who had been christened with an Italian name by the Verona priests, like Ilariyo and so many of the others, and educated by them in English, and who had completed higher secondary school in Uganda during the war and almost won admittance to a seminary—wore glasses with both earpieces broken and one lens cracked. He was a Bari from Juba, nephew of the Speaker of the People's Regional Assembly, but for drunkenness or some further peccadillo he had been exiled to this outpost of progress. When would·he get home to replace them, and how to pay for it? The only swift means of transportation was to cling piggyback to a rare white Tarzan passing through on a long swing by Land Rover, like me.

His wife had been caught thieving and had been sentenced to six months in jail or six Sudanese pounds ($15). He had paid the fine with his savings, rather than hire a housekeeper for their three children for such a period of time. He said she was "a bush girl," and gestured at her, asleep in the sun on a bushbuck skin spread on her grinding rock in the front yard of his tattered board cabin. He himself was "half European, educated as a European, but not a European and not an African either."

We sat talking in two broken camp chairs, he in his brown short-sleeved safari suit. Now, living here in the bush like an African, he said, eventually he had had to marry *somebody*. So he had married this bush girl who, like a child, was a thief, and to whom he had nothing to say and who had nothing to say to him. "Sometimes we have to make a balance between Europe and Africa. We are educated but we have to return home, and then we marry an African girl who has not been to town."

Gregorio owned Gilo's only radio, a dim and doddering instrument which seemed to pulsate from the exertion of gathering the signals emanating from Juba. Whether from the difficulty of hearing, or because the broadcasts themselves were at fault, he had gotten the idea that poor Mr. Bowman had been executed by a firing squad as a foreign mercenary after the mutiny at the airport, and that five other expatriates were also going to be tried and shot. "It is too bad, but it makes no difference. The Europeans, too, will have to die if they took part in a plot like this. All will be shot," he said to me in his soft voice, looking gently my way, for there was some talk in the village that because of my curiosity and note-taking I might be a spy.

"I must descend now," he would say, lacing the bits of string that tied his shoes, going back to his job a hundred yards downhill. Or, "Did you proceed to the Forest Station?" he would ask, of my latest walk. Or, "She greets you," when an old woman waved. Of a small animal skin with yellow stripes on a black back: "This one lives in the ground and cannot be found with many people and walks only at night." When he showed me an arrow: "This is how we fought the Arabs until we got our land." The Bible he called "the Evangelical."

Down at the mill, the drive belt on the steam engine (an actual, leftover, steam-locomotive engine which the British had had hauled for some ungodly distance) had broken and smashed a workman in the face and knocked out all his teeth. One lunchtime we talked about this stroke of fate. Another day, the joke and subject of gossip was that at about dawn the policeman who lived beside the mill had fired three shots at a wildcat which had crept into his hut after the chickens and "became wild to him," as Gregorio put it. It was the smallest of the four kinds of wild cat occurring in Gilo, but everybody who woke up naturally supposed that the war they had heard of in Juba had spread to our hills.

Ordinarily the policeman was not allowed to have any bullets, but he had been issued a few after the emergency, with which to repel a conjectural invasion from the Uganda border by Sadiq al-Mahdi. He would be the first legal officer of the Sudan whom an invader encountered. Usually he had only the rifle—a British .303, from the King's African Rifles, pre–World War II—and no ammunition, because in a manner of speaking, it was the village's gun, and the people were former Anya Nya. One day, before the emergency, he had been kind enough to loan it to Ilariyo when Ilariyo took me on a meat hunt for buffalo. They both decided I'd be safer if Ilariyo hunted with the rifle instead of with his bow, and Ilariyo did have bullets. Before he'd been disarmed at the end of The Troubles, he'd hidden some, and so at a couple of junctures when the policeman had needed a means of defense in facing a husband wielding a spear against an adulterer flailing an ax, he had come to Ilariyo, who had dug up one or two bullets for him, cleaning them off with kerosene.

Unfortunately, on our way to try to kill the buffalo, Ilariyo shot at a red bushbuck, browsing deerlike along the Kinyeti below us. Although he wounded it, it got away and the explosion scared the buffalo herd, as an arrow would not have done. He ran ahead of me just quickly enough to glimpse them as they fled.

Several buffalo had tapeworms; big white cast-off segments gleamed in their stools. And there was a corncob on the path, where a hunter before us had sat and eaten lunch. We looked at a eucalyptus tree whose bark the buffalo and bushbuck had gnawed. An elephant had rubbed moss off another tree eight feet up. We saw a number of places where one or another elephant had forced a solitary path uphill through the undergrowth. On high ground, a half-mile from the buffalo lick we had visited, some of the buffalo had a pawing and rolling spot.

On other walks, the bracken fern and burdock and raspberries made me feel as if I were strolling at home, though the bamboo and Abyssinian banana plants did not. Fifty feet high, in the forks of large trees that were flossy with moss, delicate species of tree ferns grew, and green and brown vines and gray, beardlike lichens hung down. These were gigantic trees, with whole separate levels of epiphytic life sprouting from them. Every so often, up in the crown, a family of blue monkeys ripped through the leaves, leaping, catching and propelling themselves again with feet and hands—a wizened, bald baby clinging to its mother's chest —to get out of Ilariyo's bow's range. Close up, the adults are comely creatures, equipped with white gorgets, full cheeks, grayish backs, and rufous rumps, carrying their tails in a high loop. But Ilariyo fitted an arrow to his bowstring the instant they revealed themselves, so any monkey that had lingered to show its plumage would have fetched up in the pot.

They whistled and chattered once they were at a safe distance, whereas the colobus monkeys had a cry like a frog's croak, amplified. Colobuses are heavier, like decorative, long-tailed, lightboned, arboreal baboons. They have white cheeks, foreheads and beards, and white, long-haired flank ruffs, and bushy white ends to their tails, set off by a contrasting body that is black otherwise. Their long hair apparently acts as a parachute as they sail between the trees, but when they sit on a limb, their splendid tails seem to hang down poignantly, if you are with somebody hunting them.

Bushbuck give a sharp bark of alarm, deeper in pitch than that of American deer—like a German shepherd's, but abbreviated. The ones I handled were dead, with the snared neck bent horribly backwards against the ribs, as the log drag had held it while the legs tugged the body forward. Goat-sized, with goat-shaped horns with three spiral ridges and a white flag of a tail, white spots on the haunches and vertical stripes on the body, they seemed to sigh when Ilariyo released the swollen neck from its circle of wire and the air trapped inside the dead lungs was exhaled at last. The "necktie," as he called it—World War II telegraph wire—had rubbed off a circle of hair, where ants fed on the reddened skin. If the animal had lain for a while, there was gas in the belly too, which Ilariyo forced out by carefully treading on it, first placing the carcass in the river shallows. When I accompanied him, slowing him down, he was likely to leave it there for the time being, weighted with rocks in the cold water, where the meat would keep longer and bushpigs wouldn't smell it. A horde of them might have devoured his catch. Instead, a leopard—a night traveler, like the pigs—found one of the bushbuck we had left, yanked it out of the stream and ate from a hind leg and from some of the organs.

Ilariyo lopped a twig with his *panga* (machete) to remind himself where he had set a snare, leaving me to sit and listen to the birds, while he hurried to thickets further on. He had long feet, all tendons; long shins or shanks, whitened from the wear and tear where the brush just off the path was scarcely penetrable. He'd had three years' schooling altogether, in Arabic, but without that, could convey affectingly by signals the sufferings of an elephant that poachers had killed, whose skull we found. He pointed to the blaze marks on two trees where it had hit its tusks, venting its pain and rage, though at the same time he smiled slightly, because, after all, he might have been one of the poachers himself.

He had a flicking motion with which he dismissed his disappointment when game got away, and handed me his bow to lean on in crossing the footlogs that led away from this bog, which by general agreement among the village hunters had been assigned to him. He said that a leopard skin could bring about $110, nine months' wages, on the black market, and pointed to where a bushbuck had nibbled a charred stick in the ashes of a campfire; and at more elephant tusk and shoulder smudges on some of the trees— no anguish in them—as we went on. Without speaking or glancing around to see whether I was watching properly, he flapped his arms in just the subtle manner of any number of different birds, to warn me which kind was starting to fly up ahead of us.

There was a greater variety and mix of timbre to the bird calls than I was used to, in America. The wading birds, the birds in the brush, and then a whole forest ensemble struck up behind us as we climbed on a slant and descended the intervening ridges on our way home. Usually I'd stop alone and swim in the Kinyeti when we crossed it again before we reached Gilo. I'd see five kinds of butterfly, brilliant blue and iridescent green, drinking at a hole in the sand, and a huge, green-abdomened grasshopper whose wings opened out even more beautifully than the butterflies'—red, purple, black and green.

Cold water, warm sun, no biting flies. Squirrel, mouse and monkey tracks. To hunker naked on a riverbank in the heart of Africa was quite dramatic, if you thought about it—drama, like sex, being primarily in the mind. Because I had worked in a circus many years before, I wasn't afraid of the idea that elephants and leopards might be roaming about within a mile or two, and swam in a deep trout hole with as much pleasure as in a mountain stream in Vermont. Afterwards, I sat for an hour, not thinking or stirring, resting on a log and listening to the water, digging my toes in the sand. Above me in the canopy of trees were birds purposeful in their calling, and birds oblivious-sounding as a pondful of peepers. Jay-like or crow-like calls, and long pretty narratives. A bird with a two-note, bell-toned, knocking rhythm; another with a song like a nasal, high-range oboe. Some displayed their songs as their sweetest and proudest possession; others hacked with them as a weapon. One communicated like a lovely flageolet, endlessly charming; another used wheezy, repetitive, upward whistles. There were birds that sang in a rattling chatter, a minatory, suspicious chirping; and one-note birds; and birds that commanded a grand, waving banner of ten or twelve or fifteen notes. Also, what I took to be cicadas singing.

Once in a while another hunter, silently returning to Gilo, would pass me. As he crossed the little river on a footlog, he averted his eyes politely from my body, but found it more difficult to avoid staring at my boots and other clothing piled together on the farther bank. The one object I think I might have been killed for was those boots. If he was not as naked as I was, he was wearing some absurd and ragged scrap of suburbiana—a plaid sport jacket, a paisley vest—donated by a church group in America.

Though I had had to punch new holes in my belt, as the heat and diet of this drastic continent had slimmed me down quickly toward that frantically ectomorphic archetype which most expatriates in Africa attain soon enough—the *pink spider,* as Juba's black sophisticates used to say, looking at one of us appraisingly—I was never as skinny as one of those hunters.

I was so slow that I prevented Ilariyo from hunting effectively, but if we didn't stumble on a party in progress somewhere on our route home, he was likely to throw one of his own. He was a bony-faced, cheerful, tall man, efficiently muscled, with three tribal cuts on each cheek, and was always the center of a group when talking. His voice was louder, more vigorous-sounding than the others, and like a French horn in its tones. Though not especially "responsible"—not a leader in that sense—he was quick to notice what was going on, a man of action, and of many pleasures, such as his hunting, his wives, his kids, strong drink, and odd chores to be performed that seemed a challenge. He was one of Gilo's solidest citizens, with a full larder of grain set up in a cache woven of sticks and straw upon four poles with tin cans around the base to foil the rats—of which there were a good many, owing to a lack of cats.

Because this was February and the harvest season, not even Ilariyo's numerous family could bring in what grew on the plots he'd cleared across the ravine of the Kinyeti River from Gilo. He and his wives were obligated to play host to the people who had helped them. On other nights, other families with acreage to harvest gave the parties, while Ilariyo's quarter of the village was asleep or quiet, but it was agreed that his guests were more lavishly provided for.

"Just like pombe," he explained to me, when I hesitated at first to drink his beer. *Pombe* is a name for home brew in West Africa, and he assumed that I had traveled widely. In Acholi, he explained to visitors and to people we visited, if they asked, that my stutter was the result of words becoming garbled somewhere between my brain and mouth—pointing to those parts of his own head. I was smart and experienced, nonetheless, he told them, protective of me, picking his teeth with a twig from a toothbrush tree.

He could hold his liquor fairly well, but by 10 P.M. would be drunk—two hours later than most of his guests. From 3 to 6 A.M. the party generally fell into a lull, while people slept on the floor, until it picked up again (at least his parties did) for another two or three hours, whereupon the bell clanged for work to start in the potato fields.

In the chants and dances the women and men answered and stood opposite each other, or else played to each other as coequal groups. The refrains they sang seesawed between them with a sometimes monotonous but seldom melancholy quality: a survivor's sense of the cycle of life. There were no harvest or rainmaking or planting or full-moon songs. Rainmaking was exclusively the province of the rainmakers, who function in the region as what an outsider would call chiefs. At a funeral, however, Ilariyo said, a few traditional songs might be performed, tailored a little to fit the history of the deceased. And certain "grandfather songs" also existed, which theoretically could still be sung if someone went to war, or when hunting, had killed either an elephant, a leopard or a lion: one song for each. What I was seeing were sociable, informal dances, improvised loosely upon established patterns. The women linked hands in a circle inside a circle formed by the men and danced in a reverse direction, while the men clapped the beat. Some of the principal songs were invented and sung by individual men trying to "rob a girl," as Ilariyo said, by publicly shaming a rival suitor, or for the purpose of shining before her and her relatives and their own relatives and friends. Many women sang singly too, no less bold about it, celebrating a husband's excellence or their own charms. Whenever one of the older, fatter ladies started, she immediately moved toward me, seeking to rub her breasts against my chest—presumably she was singing partly about them—whereupon everybody at the party who was already drunk began to cheer delightedly, and everyone who was still sober grew embarrassed, signaling me to leave.

At Ilariyo's, people beat out the time on a skin drum and a gasoline drum, while a one-eyed, one-legged man twanged a hand piano—a wooden box held in the palm which has flat wires attached at one end. Another man tweedled a three-note pipe cut from a bushbuck's horn. C, G, D; C, G, D—gay as a toy-store whistle. At work he blew it also, as when a bunch of villagers were marching back and forth with posts and bundled grass balanced on their heads, to build somebody a new tukl. He walked in front of the file, tweedling and tootling, and made the whole job go easier. Every night, party or not, a veteran Lotuko spearman was paid by the U.N. planting expert, Bob Dirks, to bugle on a great kudu horn in the potato fields to warn the elephants, monkeys, buffaloes, bushpigs, bushbuck and duikers away—a cryptic, loud, distant two-note call we went to sleep to.

Walking slowly, smiling in a kind of rhythmic courtesy, shaking hands with frequency and ceremony, I found I could invite myself into nearly any hut. As color-blind as I'd become, it was only indoors that it really struck me that all these people I was living with weren't just poor, but black. If they sat far from the fire, I couldn't see them, except that, as in the platitudes of old Dixie, the whites of their eyes sometimes shone in the dark. Having been refugees, they still wore donated garments as a matter of habit, employing their animal skins as rugs or blankets and saving their few piasters by not patronizing the Arab (*gollaba*) cloth merchants in the market town of Katire, which was seven miles away—three thousand feet downhill. But these funny blazer jackets, pink shorty nightgowns, scanty nylon sport shirts, Texaco attendants' coveralls, swimming caps, tennis shorts, bras and bathing tops too small for all these nursing mothers had been collected from Lutheran parishioners in Minneapolis, and were inadequate as well as incongruous. We were at six thousand feet, a climate suitable for potatoes in Central Africa, and, all year round, people huddled over the black stubs of a fire and shivered. I wanted to write to the Lutherans of Minnesota to please send winter castoffs.

Where the ceiling thatch met the round wall was a ledge where personal items were stored. A mallet for pounding grain, an adze or other tool, a smoking pipe, arrows, spears, cooking pots, walking sticks, calabashes, clothes. On the floor next to the wall lay a roll of skins—a new one perhaps pinned to the ground, flesh-up, outside—and various woven containers and gourds for food and tins of water and pails of beer. Any meat the family had was hung in strips on sticks stuck into the wall over the fire, which was a handsbreadth wide, burning between small rocks.

It was the women who smoked pipes. They'd buy a jaunty-looking, arabesque clay bowl and make a stem for it, each one raising her own tobacco in a tiny plot, curing it in the smoke of her hut—though several ladies smoked so much they couldn't wait for it to cure, but picked fresh leaves and folded them into the pipe on the old coals. If they were senior wives and no longer troubled themselves to wear a pretty string of beads or copper bangles any more, they'd poke the pipe into their hair when they weren't smoking it. The men preferred to roll a cigarette instead, tearing off a square of newspaper and licking the edge, nursing the cigarette along, pinching it out after a few puffs and then re-lighting it again in fifteen minutes with an ember from the fire.

Once at Ilariyo's I pointed to his baby, who was pounding in the dirt a piece of paw-paw she was eating. Everybody else laughed, because at the same time she had wet the earth under herself, crouching in the doorway, not knowing she was supposed to go outside—which was what they thought I meant. She toddled to her mother, drank some merissa from a bark cup, and suckled too. Ilariyo offered his nipple with a grin.

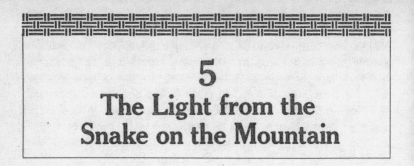

5
The Light from the
Snake on the Mountain

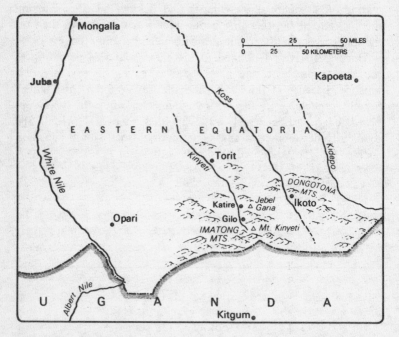

After one has read dozens of explorers' journals, with the books of contemporary wilderness enthusiasts thrown in, it isn't hard to reach the conclusion that the search these individuals have made to find the wildest areas left on earth—a kind of relay race, at best, but a lone compulsion in many cases—was really an attempt, itself, to start over. I'm not speaking of formal anthropology, but of the impetus of so much wilderness trekking and love-of-the-primitive, the wish to go and live in the bosom of raw nature. A fist-fighter lurks just under the surface of a lot of these books. The masochism or sadism, the general tenor of choler, vainglory and self-distrust so often perceptible between the lines makes you suspect that one reason why the author sought so hard for a personal, presumptive site for the birth of man, and a feel for the circumstances of it, was that he wanted to be born again, to reexperience his own birth and thereby possibly straighten himself out— to *do things over*.

So here was I in Gilo, not utterly untypical of all the white people who had roamed Africa before, and waking up each morning to the soft *thump-thump* of a rooster's wings as he stretched them, readying his lungs for a first crow. Then I heard the sound of Attilio's children's painful diarrhea as they squatted in the grass outside. Attilio was the foreman of the potato project, and very progressive. That is, he told them if they didn't wash their hands afterwards, the rats would chew their fingers off. The rats in our thatched roofs punctuated the dreams of nearly all of us at night.

Like Ilariyo, Attilio had two wives. He had married the second during the rather lengthy period when his first mother-in-law, following a common practice, had held her daughter in abeyance at home in a village down the mountainside, along with their first child, until he managed to pay some further installments on the bride price, which was large: something like $250 altogether. Now he had both wives with him, in adjoining catty-corner huts, and was to all appearances a happy man, though other people said that neither woman seemed as cheerful as when they had lived separately, and though he flirted with the wives of other men during the day, when most of the workers were in the fields.

He was a good foreman, however, and stammering boyishly for the moment, would tell me stories of his childhood in the Dongotona Mountains, a twin range somewhat lower than the Imatongs. He was a Dongotona, but had lived with Acholis in a refugee camp during the war, and so spoke Acholi, as well as some English and Arabic. As a boy he had grown up in the town of Ikoto, with people of his own tribe and also Langos, Logirs and Lotukos—each with their own dialect—who spoke Lotuko in common. They had all gotten along, within his and his father's memory, intermarrying, parceling out the traditional hunting grounds. When the Arab troops had come, they had moved higher into the mountains—

Dongotona Mountain itself goes up for 8300 feet—and the Anya Nya had established a skirmishing base nearby to protect them. Like Ilariyo, Attilio was a good provider, but maybe because he had been a refugee instead of a guerrilla fighter, rather than hanging a guinea fowl and the rear end of a bushbuck over the fire twice a week, he reserved the best of the Minneapolis sweaters for his family, and a safe share of the World Food Program dura.

Carla, his second wife, was older than the girl he'd married first, and, of course, had been here in Gilo longer, so she was the dominant one, and had had a chance to have two children. Shortly after the sounds of her son Sebario's diarrhea were over, I'd hear her pull a tuft of grass and, a little tipsy-sounding, walk to her neighbor's tukl to light it, walking back with it blazing, to start her own fire. Like the smell of game curing in Ilariyo's hut, the smell of sour mash ripening at hers for the next beer party was a mark of prosperity, though Attilio did not ask her to cook arak from the merissa, believing that arak was not good for the health of the chest.

When she had settled herself, Sebario—beads around his neck and hips, red and yellow plastic strips around his wrists and ankles —went to suck and wrestle with her breasts. Clearly, one reason why women have two breasts is that their children (and their husbands) have two hands. He really had no other toys, like the other children who were too young to play with a bow and arrow or a hunting stick, except that lately, with the World Food Program shipping in food, his father had nailed four shiny corned-beef cans as wheels to a board for him to push around.

When the sun warmed up, Attilio clanged a chunk of iron hanging in a tree as a call bell to assemble the crew. Bob Dirks, whom I liked more than any of the other U.N. personnel I had met in the Sudan, had been sitting contemplatively in a camp chair outside his straw hut drinking Nescafé since well before dawn, only the glow of his cigarette showing at first. As he said, he was "an equal opportunity employer," because many of the halt and lame of Gilo were among the fifty people waiting for assignments. Several workers had already climbed clear from Katire to get here on time, for the chance to earn eight cents an hour. They were all men, including an elderly fellow with bone points for cheeks and emaciated limbs, who walked on the ball of one malformed foot with the aid of a crutch. But sometimes a number of women came along to collect potherbs from among the weeds that sprang up immediately after the brush had been cleared and burned. Around the village, too, the women plucked wild leaves to flavor their meals, particularly from a honeysuckle-like plant that I found tasty. Once when I was holding a handful of red berries, one of Ilariyo's wives looked up from a wicker basket she was weaving and made a cutting motion with the blade of her hand to warn me I'd fall over if I ate them.

Dirks was chagrined at how low the wages were that he was permitted to pay. But he fought a knock-down battle at the Agriculture Ministry in Juba every month to get at least that much to Gilo promptly. An actual shortage of currency afflicted the Southern Region, as well as the perennial shortfall in foreign exchange. This was said to be because the Arab storekeepers hoarded the cash that they took in and sent all they could afford to part with right to their relatives in Omdurman. Also, on this trip to Gilo, we had been delayed in starting out from Juba by the fact that the payroll clerk had been unable to operate his calculator because of a power failure, and had made a $200 mistake using his pencil. When he had rectified that, the authorizing officer couldn't be located, having gone home for the day. Next morning, the man showed up two hours late, with a hangover, and by the time the error was explained to him and his signature obtained, it was 10 A.M. Thereupon, the second, countersigning official had gone out to have second breakfast, an institution of the country which corresponds to an American bureaucrat's midmorning coffee break and lunch hour combined.

When *he* returned, and Dirks had obtained both his approval and the payroll sack, we—with Dirks's wife, Jackie, along—drove to the bridge over the Nile, only to be turned back by a company of soldiers with a tank and armored car who had been placed on alert. A letter of permission from Juba's police chief would be necessary before we could cross, the captain informed us apologetically. We drove back to the Ministry, and ferried the official who had countersigned the payroll to police headquarters—where the chief, a polite, urbane, stocky man, said he was sorry but that he would need a letter from the regional Ministry for his files. Simply a verbal assurance from the same man who was going to sign that letter would not suffice. The only place where such a letter could be dictated and typed was back at the Ministry of Agriculture, so we returned there. When it was completed, around closing time at 2 P.M., we rushed back to police headquarters—to be told that the chief had left for today.

"Hellacious!" Dirks said; and more under his breath. He used words of that sort in front of ministers, soldiers and police as a delaying action because of his hot temper. When exasperated and tired, he had a way of crossing his *t*'s and dotting his *i*'s, expostulating with extreme precision, even reversing his words—"At all, not" for "Not at all"—to postpone an explosion. Finally he could convert his anger into a kind of comic bombast that got the police laughing. In Gilo, where he was more of a kingpin, if somebody mistook a hacksaw for a hammer, he'd shout, "Can you think of one good reason why I shouldn't kick your ass?" But after flaring up, he eased into an echoic baby talk to conceal his impatience—cadences like those of the television character Huckleberry Hound, until his voice returned to its normally pleasant, Burl Ives tone.

Though Jackie came from Atlanta, and although Dirks talked with that doggy drawl, and in fact had bought a retirement home on a hilltop in Arkansas and lived in it for a year before signing up for what he claimed was this last fling abroad, he wasn't really a southerner at all. He'd grown up in South Dakota, his father a Methodist preacher, and had worked in a Dakota coal mine, after flying as a radio operator in a squadron of B-24s, bombing Japanese targets in places like New Guinea, the Philippines, the Molucca Islands, where he may have confirmed his taste for rough living, during World War II. As a boy he'd dreamed of running off to Peru or New Zealand. Certainly he didn't want to work in a coal mine, so he enrolled at the University of Maryland, where he met his wife and majored in agriculture. They soon found themselves growing rubber at a U.S. aid project in Haiti, thus beginning Dirks's twenty-six-year career as a government expert. In Bolivia and Surinam he experimented with rubber again, and in Libya with apples. He had put in a stint in the Sudan, developing an onion industry;

rice in Nigeria; tomatoes in Ghana. In Ghana the Russians had built a factory for canning tomatoes, but without any commercial tomatoes. Similarly, in the city of Kassala, near the Ethiopian border in east-central Sudan, the Russians had constructed an onion-dehydrating facility, but had not arranged for a project to grow any onions.

This was a decade back, and Dirks, who was with the U.S. Agency for International Development at the time (he still loyally shows an American passport at roadblocks, rather than a U.N. *laissez-passer,* which might be more useful to him), was brought in to produce the onions. The farmers at the new irrigation scheme at Khashm al-Girba on the Atbara River, seventy miles by rail from Kassala, had been Nubians resettled from the extreme north of the Sudan when Lake Nasser backed up behind the Aswan Dam and flooded them out. So they were already familiar with the limousine species of onions which Egypt grows, perhaps the finest in the world. His were a utilitarian California brand—just as Texas short-fibered cotton is supplanting the traditional, luxurious, long-staple Egyptian varieties—and Khartoum was making an accelerated effort with several larger horticultural projects at the same site, which lent momentum to his work. It was one of his successes, as well as for the Sudanese managers who took over after him. Dried onions have just now become one of the nation's exports, which helped persuade him to come out of retirement to try to establish potatoes as another food crop of the Sudan.

Up in that desert he had his adventures, getting back and forth by Land Rover from the capital—no compass the first time, no Arabic, insufficient gasoline and drinking water for a trip of ten hours. The embassy made a practice of reserving the best vehicles and tires for the staff cars that wheeled people around Khartoum, so it was nothing to have to fix five flats on a single trip. He changed that by rolling his bald, broken tires into the office of the Chief of Mission once—though not before he and his driver had broken down for good one night within sight of a vague glow on the horizon. They were lost, but they walked and walked, and at last discovered that the glow was Khartoum Airport.

They'd had a houseboy in those plush days, with two of their children living with them and going to school in Khartoum. The man was a Madi from Torit, the district town forty miles north of where we were in Gilo (though the drive is as slow as the flight of a butterfly). Safe enough in Khartoum, he had been sending his wages to his family in the war zone. But all of a sudden he got word by bush telegraph that his wife, his mother, his father had been massacred in Torit church, along with the rest of the congregation, but that his father—grandfather to his infant son—in crumpling over as the bullets struck, had covered the body of the baby, who was still alive. He excused himself, disappeared for two weeks, and materialized with the baby in his arms, having negotiated a round trip by road and river of two thousand miles, eluding the patrols, skirting around the roadblocks.

Dirks has big ears, gray hair, blue eyes, a thumb of a nose, a busy, boyish push, a constant restlessness. My stutter may have helped me with him, both because of the virtue which farmers attach to slow speech, and because of his own inner seethe. He smoked three packs of cigarettes a day, and on Sunday he and Jackie worked harder than the rest of the week—whitewashing the mud walls inside their hut, putting up screening to thwart the rats, filtering drinking water and so on. She was practical, husky, brusque, and seldom tired of watching Gilo's social life, or Sebario's nightly bath by firelight. She waved with interest at the little kids every mile or two all day long during the hot drive out from Juba, but, naturally, was the one who wanted to get back to Arkansas. They were exaggeratedly American now—*Arkansan*—just as many English with itchy feet who spend their lives traveling become ultra-British. For the U.S. Bicentennial, they had thrown a Fourth of July party in Juba, with two flags and a baseball and bat sent by the squad of marines stationed at the Khartoum embassy, an ambassador's letter, President Ford's message, a bogus communiqué from Queen Elizabeth, some homemade ice cream, and a carton of hot dogs flown in from Nairobi.

Long ago, the British had caused potatoes to be planted in the Imatongs on a small scale to feed their officials, so Dirks found older people who remembered raising them. A few bags of inbred, very poorly specimens were still grown near Khartoum for the expatriates living there. But he hoped to see a good indigenous seed potato created: a hundred and sixty acres' worth in his two chitting

houses by the end of 1977, with which the local farmers could
plant a thousand acres the next year. This would amount to a quick
increment of at least seven thousand tons of food, locally grown.
On these first plots he himself was averaging ten tons per acre with
only a single planting—putting in cabbages and carrots afterwards
—but hoped to be able to combine a March-April, fast-maturing,
Dutch "Amigo" potato, to be harvested in July, with a Kenyan type
planted in August in the same ground and dug out by Christmas-
time. Meanwhile the International Potato Center in Peru (the Incas
freeze-dried potatoes) is trying to develop a tropical white potato
for lower elevations, to go with the yams which are a staple in so
many equatorial countries.

By main strength, Dirks was wrestling this enterprise into existence. It wasn't just the Sudanese who gave him trouble. The U.N.'s
Food and Agricultural Organization itself was experiencing a shortfall in funds, and was threatening to cut his budget from an already incredibly low $14,000 a year to $2,500. The World Bank's
representative in Juba was a tightfisted Scotsman who had amassed
a surplus, but when he offered to beef up Dirks's potato operation
properly with $60,000 in World Bank money, FAO demurred, in
order not to lose the publicity of an expected success. The United
Nations Development Program chieftain in Juba was a rigid young
staffer who had worked close to the seats of power in Vienna and
at the U.N.'s glass headquarters in New York. Presumably he was
getting his ticket punched at this battlefield post in central Africa
for further promotions, but I never met a subordinate who re-
spected him. In Dirks's case, he refused to permit a U.N. road
engineer to design the tote road from the potato fields to Gilo
village, because the man was listed under a different table of organization within the U.N. structure. The engineer came anyway,
on a weekend, to share a bushbuck feast with Bob and Jackie
Dirks and spend the night in the cool air and survey the switch-
backs nicely.

Walking that same day, while they were laying out the road, I
was picked up by Gregorio, the sawmill clerk, who in his super-
visory role was clinging to the back of a bouncing tractor, along
with two other supernumeraries, but carrying a Margaret Drabble
novel I had given him to his woods job.

"You see me naked," he said into my ear above the roar. "But I am an educated man like you."

I was teetering on the slippery fender, holding on so tightly that my hand got writer's cramp.

"He is a very specialized driver," Gregorio shouted as we lurched about the logging path. "He drives like a motorcycle: only on the mountains. Here is where the other tractor tipped over. It hit that stone. The driver of that one is still under medical treatment, but I think now he may be somewhat better.

"In one day you can proceed from here to where King George stayed in the forest," he went on. "And from the roof of Kinyeti Mountain, they say that you can see the zinc shining on the little roofs in Kitgum in Uganda.

"There was some misunderstanding between the forces," he said, referring again to the mutiny in Juba, "and all will be shot."

In fact, President Nimeiri, in an extraordinary grant of amnesty later in 1977, pardoned and released the Juba mutineers and nearly all of his other political enemies, both in the North and South. But under the circumstances pertaining then, in February, my own exploring was causing me to fall under belated suspicion in Gilo. Was I asking so many questions and roaming around in order to plan for a helicopter landing, a radio signaling station, a route for an invading strike force from Uganda?

The policeman, carrying his rifle, wanted to know these things one evening while I was admiring the shipshape peak of Jebel Garia from Gilo's ridge. The citizen who had brought him did the translating—a tough individual who worked in the sawmill, wearing a fez with a sprig of cedar stuck in it, and a down-turning sneer, his lower jaw outthrust by a permanent disfigurement.

He said to me in English that a white man should not be wandering around too much in an independent country. I should need to have a permit to leave the village compound. In Juba Arabic, he suggested to the policeman that he ask me why I was staring at that mountain. Would helicopters land there? The policeman did ask, and he translated the question back to me.

I said no, I watched the mountain because the mountain was beautiful. In a scoffing voice he translated this utterly preposterous attempt at an explanation to the policeman and to the crowd that had gathered. The policeman listened, glanced at the cloud-mansarded mountain, muttered to the man in the fez, and then mildly suggested to me in Juba Arabic—by way of a harsher-sounding translation—that I stay in the village unless the police chief in Katire okayed any particular trip I wished to make. Though I was in no danger of mistreatment here, it was a moment of revelation: to be ignorant of the language and therefore have to depend upon a contemptuous enemy to convey one's every nuance of defense.

A couple of the older women had knelt to me early in my visit to Gilo. They were older in the sense that they were close to my own age, but although, in the African fashion, they had aged much faster than a Westerner would have, one lady—her name was Regina—possessed a wide-faced, even-featured, comely serenity. She was a lovely and intelligent woman, but knelt to me because of some small gesture I had made—handing candy to her children—which, because she had seen few Europeans, reminded her of the Verona Fathers who had taught her and given her communion twenty years or more before. Closing her eyes, clasping her hands, she murmured an old Latin prayer that she remembered. I stepped aside, embarrassed not least because, as an ordinary but now sexually frustrated man, it was an event of significance to me to have a woman of such beauty kneel closely in front of me. Her husband, far from being jealous, however, crossed himself and said "Jesu!" when he saw me. So would several other of the older men, with a certain surreptitiousness—just as a Coptic girl, in upper Egypt, will sometimes lift her sleeve and flash a tattooed cross at you, assuming that, as a Westerner, you, like her, are Christian. Like the fez of my antagonist at the sawmill, it can be a political signal, because such people remember how, in 1963 and 1964, General Ibrăhim Abboud's regime in Khartoum had expelled all the foreign missionaries from the South before gearing up the intensity of the war. The Roman Catholics have been slower to train a cadre of Sudanese to take up the slack since then, but the autonomous Anglican Church of the Sudan, with a black archbishop, three bishops and one hundred and twenty ordained clergy, has surged in membership recently among its old Dinka constituency.

I used to walk down at suppertime to sit with Regina's family at a hissing fire of sticks, placed outside in good weather. Her son Giorgio, who could speak a little angry English and who said that they were Langos, was home briefly for the first time in twelve years, having escaped the war, graduated from secondary school and married, all in Uganda, in the meantime. She took his head and bent it and spit into his hair, and did the same for me, as a blessing, as we shook hands.

There was never much food, so I refused more than a taste, but to celebrate his arrival, she set on the bench a basin of bushbuck stew beside the usual basin of dura porridge, with a basin of wash water alongside, and a calabash of drinking water. The bushbuck was gamy, like wild duck—a winglike shoulder blade awash in a good herb sauce. Though people talked very quietly here and communicated sympathy, agreement or appreciation of a story by soft and frequent utterances of the sound *um,* their glee was evident. From other huts around, you could hear the same subtly modulated murmurs of assent, or perhaps a snatch of song in a woman's voice, a man humming, the startled clucking of a setting hen under the bed. Firelight glimmered through gaps in the thatch. There were other outdoor fires too—men's fires, boys' fires, while they waited for supper to be cooked, and sat outside afterwards again. The straw chicken houses, like the granaries, stood on stilts. "We have rats who are very rascal," Gregorio had said. It was the children's job to find and chase in the last loose birds at night. The stars actually trembled in the black, clean sky.

Regina explained, through her son, about the matter of latrines which the government authorities wanted built—that in a primitive village the custom was that much more privacy should accompany such a private act. It would seem very odd, scarcely thinkable to old-fashioned people, that everybody should crowd one after another into an outhouse to move their bowels, and disgusting that the feces should lie all mixed together afterwards.

The Gilo nurse, like the policeman with his rifle but no bullets, had a needle and syringe but no drugs in his dispensary to inject with them. To my eye, malnutrition was a worse problem than any of the communicable diseases, though in this still largely medieval world, we would hear of a town at some distance in which measles was said to be raging—no medical treatment available. People simply stayed away from there until it had burned itself out.

On many nights, Regina's family contrived to scavenge only a potato apiece to eat. Her husband was older than she was and no longer among the better breadwinners of Gilo. Nevertheless, he had a second wife, eighteen or nineteen years old, who ate at the same fire in the evening, with two young boys with buttons in their ears, and a baby. She lived next door and didn't seem to see as much of her husband as Regina did. She had pretty (scarified) breasts, a heart-shaped face, wide-set eyes and a musical voice. She was going blind, however, and when I met her, she practically knelt as she took my hand in both of hers, laying her face close to it—this not, I think, because of any religious memories, but more in shyness and self-abasement. The older woman, like an aunt or sister, bolstered her confidence enough that when she nursed the baby at the fire, sometimes, as a joke, she "shielded" him from me; "shielded" her boys, too, having told them—as all the children here were told—that I was white because somebody had captured me and peeled off all my skin; that if this same cruel goblin grabbed and skinned them, they would wind up being white like me. It made the youngest cry and hide, but was not a joke personally aimed at me, more one that I was supposed to enter into.

Regina smoked her pipe by the fire. Especially when she had divided her own food with the other woman's children and was hungry, she would pick up a coal with her fingers, put it in the bowl, and crumple a tobacco leaf on top. She had a dog named Lothario, whom she spoke to fondly. A Murle woman, middle-aged and more vociferous—from that warlike tribe—with a brass rifle cartridge pinned into the center of her lower lip, would stop by and pantomime to me how essential the fire was after the sun went down, and the whole long, long routine here of work, cold wind and rain, sparse meals and sleep. The two boys coughed and spit phlegm when the night breeze blew. They had only short pants, not even shirts. Regina pointed to my sweater and remarked upon how very strong it was, and how strong it made me, along with my thornproof jeans and marvelous thick boots. Did such things come from Juba? But no, she said, answering herself in sign language—when I indicated no—goods like that could not have come from Juba.

An old woman without a family, and leaning on a branch, came over once or twice after supper, and shook hands with me politely, offering the Swahili greeting *"Jambo!"* for international flavor (since Swahili is not spoken in the Sudan), instead of the Arabic *"Salaam."* She laughed at the tearful terror of the children when the tale of my being skinned was repeated to them, and asked Regina in Acholi, with the humble humor of the bitterly poor, whether there were any bits of food left over. Most sympathetically and gently, Regina replied that she had nothing to give her tonight; the children had only had one potato each. Perhaps to signify her own hunger, she picked up a coal, took her pipe out of her hair, and lit it. The other woman plucked a green tobacco leaf, seared it carefully at the edge of the fire to dry it a little, rubbed it into a wad between the heels of her hands, and put it in her mouth to suck and chew.

Under the boss of a buffalo skull nailed to a tree lived a family who sold merissa beer to raise a bride price for their son—strictly for cash, no credit—so I could repay hospitality there. A retarded girl whose eye was inflamed by a sty dished it into bark cups or into pails that people brought, measuring carefully, the beer as brown as chocolate but lemony-tasting, with white bubbles on top.

"Quayss?" I was always asked, Arabic for "Are you well?" Then they would say *"Aywa"* to my answer—a word that, spoken slowly, sounds more like the meaning of "yes" than our "yes" does. There were women with babies riding on their backsides, wrapped in a sash, and women who covered their breasts from me, as a foreigner, the way the Arab women in Khartoum sometimes bit the corners of their shawls, seeing me on the street, to cover their nostrils and their mouths. A sapling had been set across a log for a seesaw, but so many kids hung around that, though the children of Gilo were rather a happy lot, with all the playing whenever the weather wasn't cold, there was an underbuzz of wailing and sobbing, as well.

In the beer hut, corncobs had been plastered into the walls as a means of fortifying the mud. Overhead, a season's worth of pumpkin squash was drying, cut into disks and hung along a dozen strings. A man was whittling an H-shaped comb for his wife out of a piece of wood, joking with her as he did so. Another man, a sobersides and very tall, hacked cleverly at a chunk of log, forming a stool shaped like an hourglass.

Regina and her husband led me to meet the arrow-maker of Gilo.

Actually, his brother, in another village ten hours' walk away, forged the arrowheads from slivers of junk metal, but he was fitting them to shafts, which he split from a strip chopped carefully from a log. Apparently he was a man of low status, as blacksmiths among the Dinkas and other Nilotic cultures also are. Hunched up like Hephaestus—from old age, rather than a specific affliction, as far as I could tell—he handed me a slice of corncake. His face was pleasingly contumacious, as a contrast to the overniceness I often met with in the village.

He made hornpipes too—the pipes that warded off wild animals at night, and rendered chores less onerous during the day. These were either Acholi horns, blown from the top like a Coke bottle, with two notes available, according to whether the hole at the bottom was closed, or the Lotuko type, which is sounded like a trumpet, through compressed lips pressed to a slit cut in the side, with the addition of finger holes. We were bargaining so I could acquire one of each. His wife, who was grinding dura on her knees over a stone which she had lugged inside the hut, began holding up a varying number of fingers to strengthen his demands. She kept grinding with the other hand, her breasts swinging as she worked, but soon it was she and I who were doing the bargaining, fingers matched with fingers. When we were finished, he laid my money, after examining the numbers on the bills in the light of the doorway, next to the horns on his workbench. I could pick up my cash again, if I decided I was not satisfied, or the two bushbuck horns to close the sale. Exchanging in this case embarrassed me because, although I'd paid only the equivalent of seven dollars in Sudanese pounds, I thought that by his lights I'd probably overpaid.

At parties, too, I was sometimes embarrassed when, after the other guests had gotten drunk, their courtesy could no longer mask the shock they felt at such a disparity of wealth. A fellow educated at a government school would sidle over in his white government shirt, and in an insinuating, nagging, aggravatedly vexed, soft voice ask me about my clothes, my car, my house and money in America, questions that the others wanted him to ask. Finally, that was what most interested them.

Compared with Latin America or Southeast Asia, Africa has not been one of America's theaters of operations lately. To the Africans even our missionaries were only a subdivision under the British churchmen; and slavery in the United States has remained a peripheral issue, part of a larger mistreatment. The reception accorded an American is therefore conditioned a good deal upon what the British did in the particular country he is in. To his surprise, he finds himself an adjunct Britisher—to snobbish London-educated Africans the Britisher's social inferior, but more English than he might prefer to be. Still, because he doesn't feel personally associated with British imperial history, he is free of the burden of it. At home, not in his lifetime will he be rid of the fear and suspicion that slavery engendered, but in the Sudan, where there was no permanent white settlement and the British trod rather gently after the turn of the century—where, instead, the harshest antipathy was black versus Arab—the vicious circle is broken for him and he can become almost color-blind.

I'd grown so accustomed to seeing many of these people in frazzled Minneapolis housedresses and blazers, I'd nearly forgotten they were Acholis. One day, though, when the snares had been empty and everybody in Gilo was feeling bored and meat-hungry, I stepped out of my hut after a nap to discover about thirty men and boys, down to the age of ten, lounging at the head of the trail that led into the woods. They were next to naked, their bodies polished with sesame oil and castor oil, and held their spears and bows and arrows. All were watching me, either because they knew I would be intrigued by this event and want to jot down something about it, or because they were afraid that I would ask to come along, would break the silence and, by my clumsy movements, spoil the strategy. They planned to drive the bushbuck out of their noon beds, down in the thickets next to the river, and chase them into an ambush. Ilariyo had gone ahead, but here was his chubby, citified, English-popping brother—usually such a chatterbox, from his years in Kampala—and other sidekicks of his and mine, now simply watchful. Shoeless, shirtless, wearing loincloths at best, their shining chests muscular, they didn't smile or otherwise acknowledge that they were acquainted with me. Maybe because they had their dogs with them, I suddenly imagined I might become the object of the chase.

In New York City, of course, I have experienced several spells of extreme irrationality set off not by costume but by color. Just after the crescendo of emotion at the hospital when my daughter was born, for example, as I came home alone in a taxi, I conceived the notion out of nowhere that the Negro cabdriver intended to kidnap or possibly murder me, because he took a route I hadn't expected. We were going downtown, all right, but not via Seventh Avenue, and my voice broke and I shuddered in panic until he stopped and let me out. In Africa it wasn't ordinarily color, but— after a period of weeks of traveling—the wailing music on the radio (old, grade-B movies half remembered), and the stunning heat, which cannot be anticipated from back in the United States, as well as the demoralizing poverty, which blisters the skin of one's neighbors with vitamin deficiencies and has them hopping along on stick crutches, dragging a crooked leg.

Two hours later, the men of Gilo started straggling back. Ilariyo's city brother, glistening with sweat, looked at me without speaking, a red haunch in one hand and his spear in the other. The animals had been divided according to each man's place in the hunt, and although I was interested in observing the butchering process, no-body invited me to watch. I was a little hurt, until, because of the apologetic note in Ilariyo's voice, I realized he was afraid I was going to ask for a dole of meat myself.

Attilio didn't go out on the hunt, perhaps because he wasn't an Acholi, perhaps because he was the foreman. But he was stirred enough by the pull of it to sit down with me, in his white shirt, and tell me about his home village of Ikoto. He said he still sent money there for his family's future—"We marry with cattle"—and against a hunger time. His tribe's name, Dongotona, meant in their language "People who live on the mountain," and he said that in his family's case the mountain was Lomohidang, which, "very big," stood isolated in the Dongotona range. They had shared it with people of other tribes during these latter decades when Ikoto itself had become a trading town and polyglot, and they were not intimidated by the idea of climbing clear to the top or going almost anywhere on its slopes, except for one forest, the Rainmaker's Forest. To this wildwood the Rainmaker repaired once or twice a year, occasionally with another elder, in order to make rain. No animal that lived there or ran there to hide when pursued could be hunted.

His father had grown dura, and cowpeas, whose leaves as well as pods are eaten, and a leafy plant called *tagiri* in Juba Arabic, he said, of which only the leaves are eaten. Also, many forest vegetables and nuts were used. The Kidepo and Koss rivers flank the Dongotonas on the east and west. In their swamps, ten or twelve miles across, live big pythons, which are calm, not dangerous unless hungry, he said, but which certain hunters kill and skin for the merchants in Ikoto, who in turn sell them to merchants in Khartoum or Nairobi. In the Koss are snakes colored like a rainbow, which they don't kill because they believe them inhabited by devils who will kill anybody who injures the snake. Lions, elephants, giraffes, elands, hartebeests, and many smaller antelopes live thereabouts, as well as crocodiles, and three kinds of hyena, one of which is said to be bald-headed, very long, and the most dangerous of the animals sought.

Lomohidang is full of caves, one of which, Attilio has heard, is so extensive that you can walk right through the mountain. Big snakes twelve meters long live in some of these caves. You cannot even see them during the day because they live in black holes, and they are so terribly poisonous that they do not even bite; they only need to exhale upon a person to kill him. They carry a stone inside them which gives a light at night that people can see in the villages around the base of the mountain. They "graze" at night, Attilio said, but not on grass. Instead, they spit out the stone, and its light draws insects, which they eat, and then they swallow the stone again until the next night.

"Insects come around them, and you must stay away. But if you creep up very close and succeed in covering the glittering stone without the snake killing you, the snake may die, and then you may pick up the stone. So there is always the alternative. Either you die or the snake dies."

"What does the snake look like?" I asked.

"Well, we have never picked up the stone."

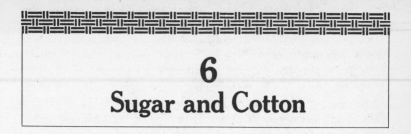

6
Sugar and Cotton

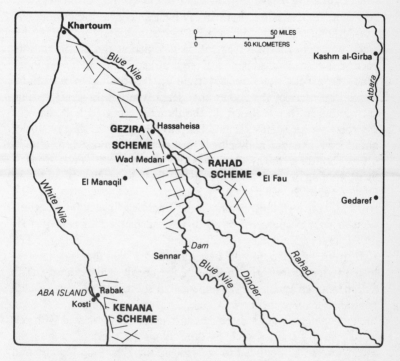

"The Sudan is a useless possession, ever was and ever will be. Larger than Germany, France and Spain together, and mostly barren, it cannot be governed except by a dictator who may be good or bad," wrote General Gordon in one of his many letters, when beleaguered by the Mahdi in Khartoum.

An Arab lawyer, offering me a glass of mango arak, after pouring some in a dish and setting it afire to show how potent it was, asked musingly, "Will we ever be integrated like you? All of the countries that went into making up America maybe weren't less of a mix than our tribes are."

In Khartoum the red tape is attributable to a regime in which too much power has been concentrated too high up (though where else, really, could it be concentrated?), as well as to the affinity for fuss of any assemblage of chums with lifetime tenure in an agency. But in Juba the delays seemed more like a keening of misery, and so struck an answering chord in my own loneliness, besides merely exasperating me. Glum, homely Bari girls in military uniforms with waddly buttocks moved from office to office at the police station, each with a sheaf of papers, although already thousands and thousands of papers were stacked right to the ceiling in pyramidal heaps in several of the rooms the clerks were working in. As one sat waiting for a travel permit, the thought occurred that this was the stage set for some existentialist play. People told shaggy stories about how phenomenally slowly justice was administered, and in several Southern towns there was talk about the Finance Department coming in and performing the first governmental audit in twenty years. In Khartoum, a French girl I knew, after waiting fruitlessly through the morning at the Interior Ministry for a permit, used to walk a couple of miles to the railroad station and just sit on an empty train during the afternoon.

In fairness, I should add that the wonder was that we were allowed to travel so freely, in light of the unrest in the country. The Sudan, though granted independence so soon, has fallen a decade behind states like the Ivory Coast, Tanzania, Zambia and Nigeria in development, and furthermore, instead of being blessed with relatively strong entities such as these along its borders, it had the misfortune to be bounded to the east by the Ethiopian Dergue and Eritrean insurrection, to the south by Idi Amin's monomaniacal autocracy and Zaire's periodical civil conflicts, which pushed refugees into the Juba and Yambio areas, and to the west by crazy "Emperor" Jean-Bedel Bokassa of the "Central African Empire," as well as by Chad, with a lengthy and intractable civil war of its own. In the northwest Colonel Muammar Qaddafi ruled in Libya. One of my Dinka friends pointed out that while it was easy to fault the other nations of the Arab League for ignoring the seventeen-year agony of fighting in the Southern Sudan, so had black Africa; that although the neglect and bigotry of the Arab Sudanese was a good deal to blame for how things stood, the Southerners themselves insisted upon appointing one of their own to any regional position, whether or not he was as qualified as some Northerner who had also applied.

This Dinka was an outspoken man, had friends in jail, and was otherwise knowledgeable. But he said that when you had been looking at the chaos rife in Africa for the past two dozen years, if a benign dictatorship could prevent chaos (and Nimeiri's was benign), then it was better than political democracy with chaos. Nimeiri—and not the intervals of parliamentary government that Khartoum had enjoyed—had brought a measure of democracy to the South. His own hope was that the increasingly permissive sophistication of life in Khartoum, as the city became internationalized, would instill a tolerance among its citizens for Southern customs as well.

Even in Khartoum—not to mention the provincial Arab villages, and cities such as El Obeid—girls in practically all Muslim families are still circumcised between the ages of five and eight, for example, sometimes by the radical "Pharaonic" method of infibulation, in which slices of the labia majora and labia minora as well as the clitoris are pared away by the neighborhood midwife. After suturing is completed, the opening of the vulva will scarcely admit a matchstick, later perhaps a finger. This is to forestall unchastity before marriage, or what might be termed overluxury on the part of married women. At any rate, it focuses a woman's pleasure on the pleasure of her husband. The operation may be repeated after divorce or widowhood, although the complications, inevitably, make painful reading. Marriage between cousins is widely encouraged, for the purpose of consolidating property within the family.

But the hurly-burly of Europeans on the street, European goods in the shops and the influx of tribal peoples from far-off regions do indeed encourage a growing cultural complaisance—which, overall, is what the Saudi Arabians, using the leverage of their petro-dollars, have set themselves to oppose. An Egyptian intellectual could wax ironical on the subject, as it pertained to Cairo— Saudi princes flying in for a dirty weekend with tens of thousands of dollars in hand, creating gambling dens and whorehouses where few had existed, at the same time as King Khalid was urging upon President Sadat an iron return to Sharia law.

But nobody comes to the Sudan for city pleasures. Sometimes you'll see a prince who's bought a falcon. And it is a mark of Nimeiri's generous impulses that, at a time when he needed the backing of no man more than King Khalid, his principal base of support within the country, apart from his old army comrades, remained the educated blacks of the South. Their leaders hinted that they might resume their attempt at secession if Nimeiri were to be overthrown.

A good deal of Kuwaiti money has been invested privately in vast growing schemes next to the two arms of the Nile; also in new hotels, a loan to the railway and an oil pipeline, at commercial interest rates. And through the intergovernmental Arab Authority for Investment and Agricultural Development, $5.7 billion was pledged to a six-year plan for the Sudan. The Saudis were holding out, however, on the sort of powerful infusion of their oil money that would have bolstered Nimeiri meaningfully. He simply hadn't enough funds to give to the North and West of the country what was needed in the way of fundamental amenities, so that they would resent less the special aid pledged to the South. Most days, Khartoum had only a twenty-four-hour supply of gasoline, which was a hardship and humiliation for a capital city. People simply did not believe me when I said that they would see worse privation in Juba.

When you go to El Obeid, a city about Juba's size, the capital of Northern Kordofan Province and the historic railhead for the West, you walk past some modern government buildings and business offices, much middle-class housing and a number of religious edifices—the minarets of eight mosques could be seen from the roof of my hotel, as well as the red-and-white Catholic cathedral. More electric lights were in evidence than in Juba, where the yearly fuel allotment was only two-thirds El Obeid's, a Shell Oil Company executive had told me. There were snappier-looking schools, plenty of cars and Toyota pickup trucks, and three outdoor movie theaters, in contrast to Juba's single dreary emporium. For forty cents I saw *Jaws* under the desert sky.

The *souk* (market), although modestly stocked, was positively crammed with consumer items, compared to Juba's. Aluminum pots, cheap but decorative serving basins, dishware, gas lamps, booths of smithcraft—the blacksmith at work in the back. There were handsome camel saddles carpentered from yellow wood and red-dyed hide; auto parts; Indian perfumes, sandalwood and other types of incense; hair tweezers and straighteners; dried dates, chickpeas, mounds of watermelon seeds and peanuts and de-oiled sesame seeds; garlic bulbs, cinnamon sticks, dried hot peppers, and spices such as cumin and coriander for enlivening the diet of sorghum polenta and pancakes most people lived on. Also, dried tomatoes and okra for making soup; and red carcady leaves, which the Sudanese crumble and add to sugared water for a cooling afternoon drink. The short daggers were sold which Arabs in the deserts of Kordofan wear in a little leather-and-snakeskin scabbard pointing upward from a loop around the upper arm under one sleeve. A sizable community of Egyptian Copts who lived next to the souk presided over the fabric stalls and the sewing machines that are placed separately outside these, whose use you hire, in a second transaction, after making your purchase. And there were Melchite-Syrian merchants and a few Greeks left from pre-Nimeiri days.

It was a lively marketplace, and yet the goods on sale were mainly such as might relieve the monotony of subsistence living. Tourism was unheard of. I could not find a restaurant in town where it was possible to eat with a fork and spoon instead of one's fingers, and was dead to the world for a while, swallowing charcoal pills, after eating tainted fish at a party of some of El Obeid's leading citizens. (I'd forgotten it had taken *me* twelve hours in 100-degree heat on the train to reach El Obeid from the River Nile.) The one time when I took a taxi, going to the airport, the driver ran out of gas and had to pour the contents of a Pepsi bottle, which he said he carried regularly for such occasions, into his tank through a canvas filter. So when I told these people that they were better off than the Southerners, first they took it for granted that they should be—the Southerners being slave material —and then, because they had read so much in the paper about foreign relief and national development in Equatoria, they didn't believe me.

This whole western region, from Kosti on the White Nile to the province of Darfur on the border with Chad, was seriously disaffected. For historical reasons, traditional Mahdist sentiment was thickest here, and the 1975 coup attempt had been western in impetus. But more important, the relative prosperity of El Obeid did not extend more than an hour's drive out of town. The Sahara is blowing south. Sand is burying the clays that were tillable, and the stumpy steppe trees that have furnished house poles and firewood, and some of the wadis where shallow, dry-season wells could be dug by hand. Too many people, too many sheep, camels, goats and cattle are picking at what is left. Already in Northern Kordofan a farmer requires seven times as much land to grow the same quantity of millet as he was harvesting ten years ago. From 1961 to 1973, peanut production per acre fell to one-fifth, and sesame-oil production to one-twentieth, of what each had been. Nevertheless, in the first exuberant decade of independence, the livestock of the province had quadrupled, and has continued to grow, as deep, new boreholes were drilled. Thus, in vulnerable areas the water table was lowered at the same time as the desert crept south.

At Umm Sunta in Dar ("abode of the") Kababish, I was to watch the sheikh's thousand camels watered by starlight—a majestic sight, serving to show that he was still a sheikh, and yet, under the circumstances, no longer a logical spectacle. The offtake from the sheep herds was about fifteen percent, so they, too, brought in meager returns. Around the wells and watering points there was almost no grass left for thirty miles; the animals had grazed the ground bare. Beyond that point, the perennial plants that would best hold in place whatever soil there was had given up the ghost, succeeded by ephemeral annuals. Even desert breeds of sheep and goats must be watered every four or five days in hot weather, so they and their herders engaged in a continuous, nervous, exacerbated shuffle during the nine-month dry season, procuring only water at one end of each thirty-mile trip, and some grass at the other.

The hand-dug wells go twenty, fifty, eighty feet down, lined with stones. The labor of hauling up a small leather bucket sewn of camel skin on a rope laid over a log to water two hundred sheep, and just as soon as they have drunk, two hundred more, then two hundred more, taking them two dozen at a time so that they will not trample each other and the truck-fender watering trough, while the rest, held off by herdboys with sticks, bleat with the misery of a lifelong thirst—this has to be witnessed to be believed. A camel in harness can be made to do part of it. But proud of how hard it is and how tough he is, the herdsman—with his sun-blitzed squint, torn toga and brown-black skin, and slippers to protect his feet from the thorns, who has lived for as long as five months solely on camel's milk, and who laughed a minute ago when, being unused to cars, he slammed the door of your Land Rover on his left hand—admits by suddenly becoming noncommittal that if his life gets much harder he will not be able to go on.

The government can bore additional wells, attach donkey engines to them and possibly set up a transport system so that the shepherds can hustle their beasts to Omdurman without having to drive them for sixteen or eighteen days on foot. But this won't make the grass and trees grow. Commiphora trees, small and spiny, with sticky leaves, which are a forage for camels and cattle, vanish before the hardiest of the acacias do, but it has been estimated that the nomads of the Sudan are uprooting half a billion acacia shrubs every year just for their cooking needs. Though dung is an alternative fuel, as the vegetation disappears there is less dung. When necessary, the custom has been to chop off certain quick-growing species of acacias three or four feet above the ground, allowing the stumps a respite of seven years before cutting them off at the same level once again. But people must cook, and they need a fire for comfort at night, and so they return to the tree stumps too soon, until the roots die—finally even their precious gum trees.

Gum arabic has been the cash crop of Kordofan. It's a knobby, amber-colored resin obtained by scarring the trunks of *Acacia senegal*, an unprepossessing, low denizen of the driest steppe or wettest desert, called by the Arabs the *hashāb* tree. When collected in twisty lumps scraped from the bark, it brings about $35 for a great gunnysack. Ground to a white powder and exported, gum arabic helps to create the foam in beer, the smoothness of ice cream, the chewiness of gumdrops. It is employed in wine making and rubber production, in hair sprays, cosmetics, detergents, adhesives, fertilizers, explosives, in leather-drying procedures and latex coatings. Three-fourths of the world's supply comes from the

Sudan, which earns ten percent of its foreign exchange from gum arabic.

Some gum trees are "wild," though inherited by families who seasonally have camped for generations nearby. Others grow in "gum gardens," on land standing fallow after five years of sorghum-melon-peanut-sesame-hemp cultivation. The trees attain their best yield at about the age of ten, before being cleared away again for food crops. Gathering the gum has been a peasant industry—which for many nations is still the best kind—but because of an ever more urgent need for food along the margins of the desert, the gum gardens are being scanted. In fact, marginal scrub has sometimes been burned, in the villagers' effort to add acreage to cropland no longer sufficient to feed them. Whatever soil the scrub had held down then blows away; more sand sweeps in; dunes gradually form. When you stop your car somewhere at the edge of the desert near a few gum trees, it is only a moment before a shrill voice from way off towards the horizon starts hollering at you, warning you not to lay a finger on one of those trees. Yet, what with the pressures operating, a fifty percent decrease in the harvest was registered between 1970 and 1973.

People starved out of their settlements keep coming back, even from a considerable distance, during the rainy season, in hopes of putting in one last crop. They are demoralized, however; their abandoned houses have become dilapidated. Because they will have no water to drink in crossing the desert unless they wait until the new rains begin, they will probably miss the crucial first showers of June or July that fall on the fields they intend to plant. Therefore they must cultivate skimpily, in haste, not to miss what rainfall is left. Then, most cruelly, a shortage of drinking water may force them to leave before the bulk of their crop is ripe, so that the grain is left for flocks of wild birds like the Sudan dioch to feast on, while they themselves end up with even less to live on as they search for a camping site near a permanent watering center, crushed up against indifferent or inimical neighboring tribes, toward the end of the year.

Amongst a cultivating people, such as the Hamid Arabs, it is not the custom for the men to ride off for whole chunks of the year, leaving the women to manage virtually alone, as the nomad

Kababish, immediately to the north of them, do. So, at the well center, while the men go back to the ancestral settlement to try to wring a last crop of sorghum out of the ground, the family fares badly. Incidents of prostitution and other signs of social disintegration begin to occur. The natural leaders of a village, enterprising individuals, are likely to leave Kordofan altogether, as they read the handwriting on the wall. The rest suffer on, bitterly blaming the government for not helping them, although they can pay no taxes with which a provincial official might be able to finance a program of special services.

The Kababish do not grow anything at all. They buy grain for cash, riding their camels hundreds of miles when necessary to strike a sharp bargain. But now they are forced to range farther and farther north and south with their herds for water and forage, which, besides adding extra harassment to an already hectic life, brings the potential for conflict with various tribes around— the Hamid, the Kawahla, the Berti, the Meidob, the Hawawir— with whom they had almost learned to get along.

So there is a pervasive unhappiness in the steppe and desert country, not only in these western provinces, but among nomads such as the Shukriya Arabs who live east of the Nile, and further eastward still, among the Cushite Bejas in the impoverished Red Sea Hills. Nomad and farmer alike must migrate if conditions get worse, and one needn't be a demographer to figure out where. Though El Obeidians don't know much about Juba, what they do closely observe is the accelerated schedule of investment being poured into major new irrigation schemes in White Nile, Blue Nile and Kassala provinces, at their own latitude, and into the so-called Gezira region (Gezira means island), at the apex of the two branches of the Nile.

The Gezira Scheme—2.1 million acres farmed by ninety-six thousand tenants, just south of Khartoum—has been the very engine of the Sudan's economy. Three-fourths of the country's cotton grows there, in rotation with sorghum, maize, peanuts and other foodstuffs, and cotton accounts for more than half of the Sudan's export earnings. The British began to develop the Gezira immediately after the First World War. By 1925 a quarter of a million acres were already in condition to be watered by pump through canals. But now there are "schemes" planned practically wherever river water flows past a bank of clay or soil: half a million diversified acres at Khashm al-Girba, on the Atbara River; and the Rahad Scheme, alongside the Rahad River, where it is hoped that 850,000 acres can be planted in cotton and peanuts in yearly 150,000-acre increments, mostly with water diverted from the Blue Nile.

The Kenana Sugar Corporation's 80,000 acres alongside the White Nile, a hundred and eighty miles below Khartoum, is supposed to feed a refinery crushing and cooking out 300,000 tons of sugar a year by 1981, in the unlikely event that a series of snafus can be undone as soon as that. Kenana has been hobbled by gap-ridden planning—a threefold increase in the cost of the factory equipment, to $170 million—as well as by shortages of fuel and cement. A cement plant at the town of Rabak, close by, had been slated to produce 100,000 tons a year, but turned out only 40,000, because of a lack of spare parts and fuel for power. This reduced output was mostly sent to other projects by the government, and therefore cement costs went from an expected $38 a ton to $175 for the imported stuff. A shortage of fuel on-site had already slowed the canal work, and the cost of erecting the factory, after its purchase, also shot up, by five times.

There were inevitable but legendary delays in extracting delivered equipment from the Augean bottleneck of Port Sudan and trucking it nine hundred miles across a largely roadless desert, and the whole undertaking was jeopardized—as scuttlebutt had it—because nobody had yet figured out what to do with the 100,000 tons of molasses the mill was going to extrude as a by-product every year. Shipping the molasses out of the country even at cost was not feasible. The selling price of sugar itself meanwhile had declined from $645 a ton, early in 1975, to $170 a ton, in 1977. If the molasses was not simply to ooze into the Nile, some new industry must be created to dispose of it—a feedlot, a rum distillery. A feedlot, as it happens, was just what the Baggara Arabs needed as they walked their cattle from Darfur toward Omdurman, but creating a new industry in the Sudan is like building a new house out of tongue depressors, toothpicks and orange sticks.

Kenana is almost entirely an Arab—principally a Kuwaiti—investment, and so was pointed to with a good deal of malice by the expatriate gossips of Khartoum as another example—like the misdesigned hotels around town that were said to be losing money, and the oil pipeline from Port Sudan whose construction was plagued with fiascoes—of Kuwaiti investing incompetence. At least, so said the British fixers and scouts whom the Saudi Arabians had hired to advise *them*.

The key management was done from London, however, by a flamboyant, controversial businessman named Roland W. "Tiny" Rowland, of Lonrho, Ltd. Ousted as head of Kenana in May 1977, he is described nowadays in Ministry of Information publications as "a dedicated sunbather," which, of course, to Africans has a funny sound. But in 1971, when Nimeiri was almost overthrown by Leftist plotters, and was actually seized and held captive for three days, it was a Lonrho executive jet that flew to Belgrade in the nick of time to pick up his Defense Minister and other loyal officers, who were at a conference, and bring them to Cairo, where, with the help of Anwar Sadat, they tipped the balance. Coup attempts of a sort have been mounted against Rowland at Lonrho, as well, by financiers in the City of London, which may partly explain the friendship that African politicians like Nimeiri who live dangerously have felt for him.

Friendship or no, Rowland had needed to make something like seventy-two trips to Khartoum in five years to get Kenana started. At the scene, I encountered a chattering stew of darting, wiry pommies manning tremendous earth-scrapers (such of the forty-seven as were still in working order), and crazy-bearded Aussies building bland little rows of staff cottages, and irascible Austrians putting in a pumping station, while cursing the Sudanese government for the absence of electrical power they claimed had been promised them months before. Ten thousand wage workers would be employed in the cane fields, and five thousand more at the factory, but for now, these expatriates seemed to be in the majority. I was shown around by a young Yorkshire geologist who said he was here not as a geologist but "as a hustler." He had smuggled in an assortment of flower seeds from England to plant in front of his cottage to make his wife happy.

Ron Colley, the site coordinator, was suspicious that I might turn out to be yet another investigative reporter after "Tiny" Rowland's scalp. A bright, tense, diminutive man, he was persuaded to give me a tour only because a newspaper snoop would probably not stutter as badly and interview him as haltingly as I did. Also, we shared a liking for red-breasted bee-eaters and lilac-breasted rollers. He showed me his nature books.

"And who does he look like, with that nose and that posture?" he asked, swinging his thumb toward the Yorkshireman. "That's right. You don't want to say it, do you? A maribou stork."

Graham Lestro, the cane specialist for Lonrho, looked like an angry Alec Guinness, though away from Kenana he may have looked like Alec Guinness in a happier mood. His father had been a tea planter in India, and he'd grown sugar in Malawi and Zambia. He was leery of me, too, because so many reporters on the subject of Lonrho had "burned the lot"—as circus people used to say when they came to a town where other circuses had preceded them and treated everyone badly. Why was I here?

I said that I was forty-four, and was after experiences and writing matter I had not tried before—much as though he, who looked my own age, were to alter his career by going off to Canada to try growing wheat. He grunted, waving me with irritation into his jeep.

Sugarcane—as he explained—is a perennial grass which itself improves the structure of the soil, just as fallow-field grasses will do. It is plowed up and replanted every four years only to keep production high. The famous dark "cotton soil" of this stretch of the Nile is a viscid, self-mulching clay, ideal for irrigating because it cracks and becomes friable when dry, so that water quickly penetrates to the roots of the cane. But as soon as the ground is sufficiently wet, it seals itself in lovely fashion, he said, as impermeable as a sheet of plastic, and cannot be overirrigated.

Over here alongside the White Nile, too, the soil was laid down by the flooding of the Blue Nile. The White flows more than sixteen hundred miles to Khartoum from Lake Victoria in Uganda, midway down the continent, compared to the Blue's nine-hundred-seventy-five-mile course from Lake Tana in northern Ethiopia. But the Blue Nile falls forty-six hundred feet through many cataracts to Khartoum from a volcanic highland, whereas the White, sliding through swamps and savannas, declines only twenty-five hundred feet. During the main run-off season, from July to October, when floods occur, the Blue carries seven times as much water as does the White (twice as much, averaging for the full year); also, a great deal more silt, which is why it is called the Blue. Furthermore, it is slightly higher at Kenana than the White, and used to be a bigger river than it is, so that geologically its floodplain has dominated that of the White. This is all to the good, because soil of volcanic origin is richer in nutrients than the White Nile's miscellany of humdrum soils. The Blue Nile, nearly incomparably fertile, fed Tutankhamen's Egypt.

"Yesterday's disaster" had been a derailment, Graham Lestro told me. The contractors were squabbling over who was to blame, but the belated question of whether trains or trucks would haul the cane from field to mill remained unresolved.

Flying to Kenana in the company plane, a tatty, ancient DC-3 with air rushing through a crack in the door, the windows rattling, insulation sticking out of the walls, and Anne, the blond stewardess, necking with the co-pilot in the seat in front of me, I had seen that no money was being squandered on frills. The three hundred and fifty expatriates had a "club," as is usual in such dusty climes, and good food in a bachelors' mess roaring with stories of right-hand-thread and left-hand-thread screws while on leave up in Nicosia or down in Nairobi. For what passed as entertainment, that was just about it.

I had visited the Rahad Scheme the week before with the same blend of rueful exhilaration at the expanse of landscape, the scale of operations involved, but also the tender hopes bound up in what was being done—that Sudanese will get enough to eat, that ragged people will earn enough to buy clothes. When set beside the giant machinery at work, the possibility of national bankruptcy and collapse, these hopes seemed incongruously modest. The principal supply canal alone runs for a hundred and thirty miles. At Village 36, which is the irrigation center, I saw fifty-two dragline excavators—cranes put atop crawlers—parked in a row. At Village 10, the repair and storage center, there were a hundred and sixty-four Massey-Ferguson tractors lined up, and sixty-five offset disc harrows, thirty-one Ford tractors, twelve heavier Fiat tractors and forty-six Eversman land-levelers.

At Rahad, which is not an exercise in private capitalism like Kenana, it was the Sudanese who were running scared and the expatriate experts who were relaxed. They, too, had established a club, had inveigled the fanciest chef in all Khartoum to come and cook for them, with the project's plane flying in delicacies regularly, though fewer than ten men were eating his meals. No frenzy, no fear of journalists, no apoplectic, itemized queries telexed from London here. The chief civil engineer at headquarters, in the village of El Fau, was a spade-bearded Briton, not too reticent to murmur his satisfaction at having quartered himself in a grass hut when he had first arrived—nothing but thornbush and sand on all sides; yet now every structure that his eye fell on was his. His friend, a Welshman, said, "Don't tell my wife I'm not lonely." His *beard* looked lonely—like so many of the beards white men wear in Africa—but he claimed, a bit smugly, that "you can find the right lady's company if you know where to look for it" and that he hadn't even bothered going to Khartoum for the last six months.

El Fau is actually an old nomad rendezvous and caravan watering point: fifty mud huts set at the foot of a cluster of jebels. A camel track winds on into the middle of these as if it were entering a mountain range, although at the other side the desert only gets drier. It was a redoubt, however, and maybe the sort of place from which, under the Condominium, a hysterical message at night would rouse the Khartoum telegraph operator: "Send help stop I am surrounded by lions and tigers stop." In one apocryphal instance, Khartoum replied to a station nearby on the Nile: "There are no tigers in Africa." "Cancel tigers stop," came the next message tapped out. "Send help stop I am surrounded by lions and lionesses stop."

Rahad has been funded by the World Bank, the Kuwaitis, the Saudis and other Arab moneys, and by U.S.A.I.D. (fifteen percent)—virtually the only U.S. aid to the Sudan to survive the assassination in 1973 of Ambassador Cleo Noel by Palestinians in Khartoum. Paired oddly with the bearded Britons were a couple of scrunched-up Texans, Bill McDonald of Odessa and W. A. Norman of Sherman. They looked close to what would be retirement age in the United States, but were not about to let me forget their pride in being Texans, nor the antipathy Texans harbor for New Yorkers. They were installing a ginnery designed in Dallas, a 1300-horse-power engine that would gin twenty-five hundred bales in an hour. There would also be three lesser ginneries, and a de-linting plant to produce forty thousand tons of seed for planting each June. Egyptian long-fiber cotton, which had been the Sudan's pride and joy—as in the gauzy taubs that women wear—as well as profitable for the export market, where it goes into fine linens and shirts, does not sell well any more. To combine with or compete with synthetics, cheaper medium-staple and short-staple cottons are used. Here on the Rahad, and in the Nuba Mountains, west of the White Nile, and over along the Atbara and Gash rivers, and on the floodplain of the Baraka on the Red Sea, the winds of change are blowing.

"This is going to be Texas cotton, Texas acala cotton," W. A. Norman said. In the summer it had turned so hot that the cement started to shrink before it had set, within ten minutes of being troweled on, he told me.

"Like in Texas," I said, to flatter him, though for all their fuss, he and his Odessa buddy, with their thin arms and wrinkled hands, looked more like retirees from Tampa, Florida, than broad-brim Texans, and were therefore touching.

Where the Kenana staff had hustled me off-site to the market town of Rabak before nightfall, lest I hear too much gossip, my English and Texan acquaintances here at El Fau invited me to stay and enjoy the French cooking for as long as I wished. I would have stayed, too, except that at the center for land-leveling, at the village of Abushoush, next to the dry bed of the Rahad itself, I had met a peanut specialist named John McWhorter, from Rochelle, Georgia, and was looking forward to having supper with him.

Nominally, a Sudanese was directing each team of foreigners. The supervisor at El Fau, a strapping, vigorous man named Bashir Omer Shakour, was torturedly sleepy when I was brought to his bedside at the mad-dog hour of 3 P.M. I was coughing and blowing my nose from the dust of the road. Shaken awake so that he could play host, he rubbed his furrowed chin and cheeks—all really for nothing, as he knew, leading me to interview the Europeans, whose information would be the only kind a white visitor like me was going to believe, anyhow.

Back in Khartoum, the chief of chiefs for Rahad, Dr. Osman Bilel, had been one of those open-mannered, informally military individuals in whom Americans place ready confidence in the Middle East. His deputy at Abushoush—where I had also arrived at a mad-dog hour—was Sadiq Bedri. Dr. Bedri, a tallish, fastidious, cultivated man, limped from a stroke that he had suffered recently, and, probably as a consequence, he looked discontented, or at least in discomfort, though this did not mar his soft-voiced display of courtesy to me. Nor was it affected by astonishment that I could not speak even my own language properly. The Muslim preoccupation with Allah and His works influences many Arab Sudanese to dwell on and puzzle over any public sort of handicap. But, ailing himself, and educated in the United Kingdom, he passed over my impediment like a gentleman of the old school remembering George VI.

Dr. Bedri was a senior agriculturist from the Gezira Scheme—his father a notable on the High Court in Khartoum at one time. We sat next to each other on the terrace of the new little flat-roofed guesthouse, watching the black-and-white crows whose antics enliven this section of Africa. Red-flowered oleander shrubs sat about in concrete tubs, the only flowers that he could grow, he said, because oleanders are poisonous and the goats leave them alone.

I had heard about riots occurring in the Gezira lately. Though he didn't refer to these, he said the government was preparing to try an incentive system here at Rahad. In place of the Gezira's straight fifty-fifty split, they were going to itemize the charges to each family for water and seed and spraying and ginning the cotton grown, anticipating that a good farmer could not only raise more than his neighbor on the same-sized plot, but might wind up with sixty percent of the proceeds from what he grew. Eleven of his twenty-two acres would be planted in cotton, eight in peanuts, and three reserved for home produce, or fodder for any domestic animals he wanted to keep. At the Gezira Scheme, tenants had been discouraged from raising animals, on the theory that this was an inefficient use of the land. But so many Sudanese are cow-centered or camel-centered by tradition, so used to having sheep and goats loitering outside the door, that such restrictions turned out to be intolerable. Though a man who put all of his children to work on his *feddans* (acres) was going to earn more at the end of the year, if he chose instead to send his sons to herd beasts in the wild-lands beyond El Fau, keeping them at home only during the dry season, he would be permitted to.

Phase One's three hundred thousand acres will include forty-five villages, each with two hundred and fifty families, a few of whom will tend vegetable gardens and citrus orchards full time or manage the tea shops and stores. Every five villages will constitute a "block," with a "block staff," and tenancy will be "compulsory" for the life of the head of the household. I had heard that one of the problems at the Gezira was that too many tenants were picking up and moving to Khartoum or wanting to wing off to Abu Dhabi to seek their fortune. But Dr. Bedri had a headache, to judge by the way he was fingering his scalp—he carried himself like a bottle of liquid that was tipping. He was under pressure from the Agriculture Ministry and President Nimeiri's office, like that which the Kenana project managers were getting from London, and so I didn't ask him what compulsory life tenure on twenty-two acres was going to do to a nomad. Elements of ten or twelve tribes were be-ing displaced: Shukriya, Gaalien, Agalien, Akrien, Gaafria, Kenana and so on. They could enroll or choose not to enroll at the beginning, however, and no serfdom would be perpetuated upon the sons, as is the case in Tanzania's new agricultural schemes.

While being chauffeured about, I had seen a knot of camel riders pointed off toward the horizon. The man had one hand on the rope of his tallest camel, which was carrying a two-story, red-leather howdah, decorated with metal ornaments, tassels and cowrie shells, inside which his wife was concealed. (Her baby, if she had one, would be in the top story.) A boy led another camel, which was so heavily loaded with sheaves of grass for thatching a tukl that it looked like a movable tukl itself. No other grass of any kind was in sight, clear to the skyline. Two smaller children rode on a donkey, and several sheep were running ahead, in the dithery manner of sheep. Four nodding milk goats and a bearded billy stalked in the wake of the parade. Though probably all of them were on a water-ing and roofing expedition, under the circumstances I naturally wondered whether they and several more camelback parties I'd passed were arriving to join Rahad or heading off to escape it. The optical effect was of their walking a yard above the actual ground, however—the ground apparently swamp water—amid a mirage of Alaskan swamp firs and birches. Thorn scrub bushes eight feet high shimmered like sizable trees, and a stake-sided truck traveling ahead of our jeep looked like a helicopter hovering twenty feet off the ground. Besides creating this vision of a marsh alongside the Yukon, the heat shut down the top half of one's brain.

I had been chauffeured to Rahad by a white-haired professional driver named Dafalla who had begun driving for British officialdom during the days of the Condominium, then had motored the Russians around when they exercised considerable influence in 1969 and 1970, and now drove Ford Foundation potentates and World Bank personnel. With frost in his eyebrows and snow in his hair, he resembled a bluntly constructed grandfather woodchuck sitting up in its burrow as he grasped the wheel, yet drove as though this were one activity he would never cease loving to do. He had hit a hundred miles an hour on the hard narrow straightaway leading out of Khartoum, the Sudan's one real highway, and now sped with zest and dispatch over the washboarded roads of Rahad, not as if our lives depended on it but as if life itself were a leaping free-fall. He drove so fast I was sorry to be sharing the front seat with him, yet at the same time wanted to, because of his kindness to me.

After leaving the highway, we had slewed around in the sandy approaches to the bank of the Blue Nile, attempting to reach the ferry crossing. There was no road and no landing—only a deep cut between dunes. We noticed the ferryman napping on the deck of his little craft on the other side, but when we honked he stood up, jumped off the boat and ducked behind a hillock of sand. Most traffic continued from Wad Medani to Sennar, on the same side of the Nile, so we had to wait by ourselves.

Dafalla could have napped too, but, rather, was outraged on a visitor's behalf and interrupted the ferryman's nap with his horn as often as possible for the next hour or two. He had the tireless, perhaps excessive decency of so many Sudanese toward foreigners, which is not just a matter of buying you tea at every tin-walled hut you pass in the cool of the evening. In the bad old era of bandits, it involved the idea that however foolish an adventure a European embarked upon, his guide would lay his life on the line to see him through. This Muslim conception of virtue dates, reasonably enough, to the days when traveling was so risky that a person was paying his hosts a great compliment by wishing to visit their land at all. Once in a while one can still meet a tourist in Khartoum who has been its beneficiary—usually in Ethiopia, now. In the Danakil Desert in Wollo Province, he will say, his Afar camel driver had sat down before three Afar bandits and told them, "Before you rob and kill this visitor to our land you will have to kill me, and afterwards all of my relatives, who will come after you."

A Chinese engineering team had nearly completed a bridge across the river at Wad Medani, which Dafalla tried unsuccessfully to procure a permit for us to use. Nevertheless, we finally went back to the bridge, where Dafalla, after some difficulty, flagged down a truck and persuaded the driver as a matter of honor and courtesy to let us tailgate him, telling the soldiers who guarded the entrance that the wording of his letter of permission included this foreign dignitary as well.

Along the highway the settlements had consisted of boxy, blue-shuttered huts built of mud brick, with many of the local women standing on the pavement, swathed in pink and yellow taubs, their big-tailed sheep following them, nuzzling them, while they waited for a jitney truck to take them to town. Here at Rahad, the huts were more primitive, still round, not square, constructed of sticks and mud instead of mud bricks, roofed with thatch instead of tin, and there were goats and bony donkeys, not so many sheep, because for the moment this was poorer country. No plantings had been carried out yet.

Racing beside the endless spoil banks of the canals, our teeth chattered from the bouncing we did. The land-levelers had not been employed on the roads lately, only on the fields, and so trucks and automobiles alike, driven always flat out, aged about three years in one. The bolts on their motor mounts shook loose from the pounding; their fenders and mufflers fell off.

As well as paying the call at El Fau, we drove fifty miles across the project to Abu Rakham—the brown expanse of Africa spreading everywhere—to see the barrage on the Rahad River where water to provision the canals will be stored: nearly ten million cubic yards, counting what the canals hold.

Barry Morley, the barrel-chested engineer from Somerset who was building the barrage, asked me where else but the Sudan could a cub such as he have charge of five million dollars' worth of contracting, and bring his wife along? It was a V-shaped construction, six gates to channel water into the main canal, and nine more to let it rush down the river course at flood level, if necessary. An extravagant number of laborers were swarming up thin wooden ladders with panloads of cement, or carrying boulders to insert. Ten hours a day, $40 a month—like a scene from the building of the pyramids. England was in recession; there were no jobs for him in England, Mr. Morley said. In Australia, where he had worked, speed was of the essence and damn the cost. But here, with foreign exchange crucially short, one must constantly calculate the effect of shortages of cement and petrol, the mundane foul-ups. Yet it was the sugar project at Kenana, with all of its high-powered expatriates—not Rahad, which was mostly staffed by Sudanese— that was falling way behind.

Drive, drive—the evening sun like an orange balloon on the rim of the sky. Pop, it went down. Dafalla played with the high and low headlight beams, gazing straight ahead, smiling slightly as we dashed by a cluster of people walking in the almost limitless space. He looked not supercilious, but rather as if there were only one automobile in the nation, and this was it.

John McWhorter—the peanut specialist from Rochelle, Georgia —and I didn't do much during the two evenings I spent at Abushoush. We exchanged a few magazines, and watched the white-bibbed crows and vultures circle, chatted about Georgia, ate eggs and bell peppers and cucumbers for breakfast, and chicken, rice and tomatoes for supper. In the refrigerator I discovered a bottle of imported chili sauce and a jar of raspberry jam which some previous tenant had left for the solace of Europeans to come. I shook the chili sauce on everything except the bread—on which I smeared a lot of jam—and, as shaky as I was feeling from sheer loneliness, these were probably more comforting than the French cuisine at El Fau would have been.

McWhorter did not like the Turkish-style coffee we were served, but I did. He was installing a five-ton-an-hour peanut sheller at Village 10, which he said had taken a year to reach the site from the United States. He said that ship captains prefer not to carry cargo to Port Sudan at all because of the jam-up of three dozen ships at the anchorage outside and little or no outgoing cargo. He said he had seen five hundred camels and a baboon at once; had had a night's sleep and some bus rides in London on the way to Khartoum; and was saving these and the rest of his stories for the fish fries he and his family shared with his brother's family in Rochelle. Saturday mornings he and his brother caught blackfish in the Ocmulgee River, and he waxed philosophical about what fish fries could mean in holding a family together.

McWhorter liked these people, but had just had to drive for thirty miles to get hold of a carpenter's level. You would see $300,000 worth of equipment—five sizes of Caterpillar tractor—parked next to a grass hut, and yet no small tool that you might need to fix something, no wrench or scrap of rope or ax or hoe. He said that he could hardly stomach the raw vegetables, but had learned to like the taste of water from a goatskin better than canteen water. The goatskin had looked better and better that first day in the sun. He had ginger-colored hair and a formal, though low-key, manner, and he lived near Jimmy Carter but thought him too liberal to vote for. On the terrace we stretched our heels out after supper and let the chili sauce mix with the jam in our stomachs, just as if we had been to a McDonald's drive-in back home, and considered how lucky we were to be underneath the glittering stars, all expenses paid, so far from New York City and Georgia.

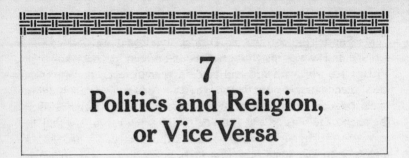

7
Politics and Religion, or Vice Versa

Sudanese Arabs wear white turbans, not the checkered kaffiyehs of the Palestinians and other Arabs with whom Westerners have become more familiar recently. Their galabiehs, too, are usually white, and with an outer cloak and turban, make a costume that is both cool and democratic, indicating the equality of all men in the eyes of God. Business and professional men tend to wear these clothes at least on the Sabbath. They may even help to prevent skin cancer under the desert sun. But to a foreigner, on a bad day—when his own connection to a place such as Khartoum is so tenuous, so entirely self-fashioned, anyway—these "bedsheets" and myriad turbans and the strangers in them can appear enigmatically, ominously the same. You know no one, can no longer distinguish personalities, and you get so keyed up to a particular departure that when the plane is canceled because of a sandstorm, or when a truck breaks down, the riverboat is late, or an imprimatur for travel is withheld by the Ministry of the Interior, the effect can be dangerous.

Unlike a novelist, a journalist is dependent upon where he has stationed himself and what happens to him—what he stumbles upon—and so he is likely to put himself into adventurous situations occasionally, or will push out into the current of a different geography to see where he is carried. Let me see what I run across here, he says, and sometimes has the sense when he gets home—like stepping off an airplane after a shaky landing—of having *walked away from another one*. My discovery may have been obvious that, far from learning something new about the black-white torque that is such a misery in America, here I was freer of it. But the other reason why I had come to Africa, instead of to another southern continent, was that on the contrary, it was not a clean slate, not neutral ground. The myth of blackness, darkness, this "land of sorrow," might be a sounding board. "Before the Congo I was just a mere animal," Joseph Conrad said.

For a writer, what is most endearing about General Gordon besieged in Khartoum is his writing, inevitably—but not so much what he said as the eccentric, incoherent fever of it. "Every morning Sir Evelyn Baring would find upon his table a great pile of telegrams from Khartoum—twenty or thirty at least; and as the day went on, the pile would grow. When a sufficient number had accumulated he would read them all through. . . . There upon the table, the whole soul of Gordon lay before him . . . the jokes, the slang, the appeals to the prophet Isaiah, the whirl of contradictory policies—Sir Evelyn Baring did not know which exasperated him the most," says Lytton Strachey, Gordon's crisp biographer, of Gordon's superior, who was deliberating at the opposite end of the telegraph wire, in Cairo.

Almost any white man traveling in Africa floats close to the surface, but one realizes that the administrative class drifts close to the surface too. A swift, perhaps cursory observer, touching down only briefly, as I did, has his uses in reporting upon such a rapidly shifting scene. The divisions are so drenched in tribal suspicion and regional anger that whatever he says, good or bad, will be disputed by somebody, yet he may have the virtues of beginner's luck and a fresh view. No African knows much about his own special set of adversaries in Africa—not the Arab about the black, nor the radical about the traditionalist chief—or whether there will be a future for him in particular, not to mention what kind of future lies in store for his country.

In meeting high officials, one must bear in mind that somebody —Colonel Qaddafi in Libya, or the Ethiopian Dergue, or some dissident in South Kensington or the Gondar Mountains—would pay to see him dead. Even Bona Malwal Ring, the Sudan's Minister of Culture and Information, cosseted by the English stewardesses in the front of the Sudan Airways plane, after having held up everyone's departure from Port Sudan for two hours while he conferred with sundry officials, seemed to be afraid. Bona is a portly Dinka. A portly Dinka is a contradiction in terms, but good living in the capital has swallowed his chromosomal skinniness in the overburdening of flesh common to so many African statesmen, and to politicians everywhere. He no longer looks like a journalist, either— only like another speech-making general, except for the one redeeming, incongruous touch: little Dinka buckteeth with gaps between them that still mark him as a man born in Bahr al-Ghazal (River of the Gazelle) Province.

Bona was whispered to be "close to H. E." ("His Excellency"), and as the most prominent of the younger Southerners—he was thirty-seven—was a symbol of the nation's reconciliation after the war. More than most of the Arabs in the cabinet, he seemed assured of keeping his job unless Nimeiri himself was overthrown. So, as our plane taxied to the cream-colored terminal building in Khartoum, the yellow-haired stewardesses with their West End accents asked everybody to remain seated while Bona and his less prominent comrade, the Minister of Transport, debarked. Bona, a decent sort of man, wearing as usual a safari suit, walked down the aisle, smiling at several faces he recognized, till he got two-thirds of the way back to the exit at the tail of the plane. Then, about the time he got to me, I saw fear and shyness cloud his expression, unlike any change you might see in the face of an American cabinet minister leaving a plane. Whether because there were too many Europeans—or too many Arabs—on the plane, whether because during the two years he went to college in New York he'd had some experience of being a "nigger"—or was shouted at in Arabic too many times earlier, in Wau and Khartoum, as a "slave"—he looked scared.

I met another minister who had lived in exile in the United States and Britain during The Troubles, and who chronicled folktales from memory and otherwise wrote and thought about the life of his tribe at home, keeping his gaiety and sanity thereby. Nowadays known as an out-and-out optimist, he had dealings with everybody from Idi Amin to Cyrus Vance. When his small son cried to be carried into the American Club in Khartoum for luncheon instead of walking, he growled at him that boys four years old were already herding bulls at home. . . . A man exhilarated, and yet after the novelty of our conversation wore off, a weariness and a sadness settled over his face, an expression of disillusion or dread going beyond the boredom a politician is likely to feel toward the end of an interview. Looking at him, I suddenly remembered that he had just returned from a trip to New York for what a friend of his described as a medical checkup, that he was said to be suffering nightly drubbings from a strain of malaria which, once it is established in the system, is nearly ineradicable, and worse than that, was afraid that he was going blind—a scourge of peoples who grow up along the Nile. None of the honors or perquisites of office could mean much when set beside such a misfortune as that.

President Nimeiri himself has the traditional short ribbing of scars beside the outer corners of his eyes which many Northerners used to receive in childhood from a tribal healer to protect them from the eye diseases of the Valley of the Nile. And there was a Minister of Industry, socialist by inclination, who gained a reputation for antiforeign or "Marxist" arrogance among the American businessmen who visited him, because of his habit of tilting his head toward the ceiling and glancing down his nose at them when he talked. In fact this was unjust; he was only throwing up his head and looking out of the bottom of his eyes to try to see around two cataracts that had formed.

Again and again one meets with a bifurcate reception: the world as it should be, beaming in the fellow's smile; the world as it is, clouding and creeping up behind his eyes. My first arrival in Khartoum had been delayed for several hours while the airport was cleared for Chad's head of state, General Felix Malloum, to fly in to discuss with Nimeiri the invasions staged from Libya during the previous year by dissenting nationals of their respective countries. And when I left, the news of that particular day was that Malloum had just survived an assassination plot by a band of his own officers, who'd shot their way up the front steps of his palace in Ndjamena. Dusting himself off, he flew to Brazzaville almost immediately to attend the funeral of Major Marien Ngouabi—the chief of state of the Congo—who had been shot while eating lunch in *his* palace by four of *his* officers, who gained admittance by means of a ruse. Nimeiri's closest friend among the neighboring presidents, Lieutenant Colonel Ibrahim al-Hamdi, of North Yemen —an unshowy, politically moderate man whom Nimeiri used to fly over and commune with quietly once in a while just for the fellowship that they seemed to have—was successfully gunned down after three years in power by other officers, about six months after this.

The attack on Nimeiri's regime the previous summer—July 2, 1976—had been cleverly timed to coincide with his airplane's touchdown at Khartoum Airport after a three-week visit of salesmanship and placation to the United States, three years after Ambassador Noel's murder. The plotters figured that his guard of troops would be stretched thin and unrehearsed at the airport. Besides, a large welcoming committee could be bagged. The plan went afoul only because Nimeiri's Boeing, flown by an Irishman on loan to Sudan Airways by Aer Lingus, was lifted by a tailwind and landed uncharacteristically early. The President and "the Majors," who have provided the muscle of his government, had a chance to get away in a covey of limousines as soon as they heard gunfire. Because it was the Sabbath, the various lesser bigwigs who were indeed captured were dressed in galabiehs, so they were able to mingle with the crowd of ordinary Arab travelers and save their skins. But rebel sappers did manage to blow up most of the Sudan's precious few Russian MiGs, both there at the airport and at Wad Seidna Barracks air base, ten miles north of the city.

The leader behind this action had been Sadiq al-Mahdi, working from exile, with the military advice of a former brigadier general named Mohammed Nour Saad, who was on the scene. Their force of mixed Sudanese Mahdists and Chadian mercenaries numbered close to a thousand and had been infiltrated from Libya over the course of several weeks. The main attack was concentrated against the Shaggara Armored Corps Command Headquarters in Khartoum South, and at General Staff Headquarters within the central city. The presidential palace and the telecommunications building next to it on the Blue Nile, and the military complex in Omdurman and Radio Omdurman, across the White Nile from Khartoum, also came under attack.

Fighting lasted for thirty hours. Two loyal generals and hundreds of soldiers and civilians died. As in Juba the following February,* Sadiq himself was rumored to be aloft, circling while the initial assault was carried out, ready to land—though other reports had him poised at the Libyan border with a 39-vehicle column of reinforcements. If there had been a nucleus of ranking officers of secret Mahdist sympathies, together with a larger contingent of sympathetic civilian figures, a sustained onslaught might have been mounted, but the coup attempt of September 1975

---

* Actually, it was revealed eighteen months later, during the process known as National Reconciliation, that the attack at Juba was not an operation of Sadiq al-Mahdi's, but plotted by an ally of his, the Reverend Philip Abbas Gabboush, a black Christian leader from the Nuba Mountains, working from Kampala and Nairobi.

had already exposed a number of Nimeiri's opponents, who had been purged or arrested, and it turned out that public sentiment was not sufficiently fed up with the President to support in the streets a coup that had been launched by exiles.

"The Majors" have outranked major generals since the May 1969 revolution which carried Nimeiri to power. Most forceful among them is Abul Gassim Ibrahim, a sidekick of the President from the original Revolutionary Command Council. He has since become First Vice-President, but at this moment was on a tour of the Gezira Scheme, in his capacity as Minister of Agriculture. He therefore took command of forces south of the capital, from as far away as El Obeid in the west, to Gedaref near the Ethiopian border, moving posthaste in the meantime up the highway to join the counterattack with the troops he could collect right where he was, at Wad Medani.

Another of "the Majors," Zein el Abdin al-Qadir, then Minister of Youth and Sport, personally led the charge that retook General Staff Headquarters; and by midnight on that first day, armor and troops from posts several hours north of Khartoum along the Nile had rolled into reserve positions at the edge of the city. From Egypt, Anwar Sadat, in order to assist Nimeiri, as he had during the attempted coup in 1971, airlifted a couple of crack Sudanese battalions that had been stationed on the Suez Canal. All in all, Khartoum had witnessed no worse fighting "in living memory," as a Ministry of Information publication put it.

If they are not too frequent or bloody, coups play a role quite comparable to elections in a good many African countries. Nimeiri's own assumption of office had been bloodless—like that of the Sudan's other military ruler during these years since independence, General Ibrahim Abboud. General Abboud, whose six-year reign (1958–64) proved rather unproductive, was less flexible and energetic than Nimeiri, less responsive to the tribal and regional variety of the nation. Still, he was remarkable because, as well as taking power bloodlessly, he gave it up almost bloodlessly too, bowing to the popular will as expressed through riots by a spectrum of protesters. In an instance of Sudanese good humor, instead of trying to crush the rioters, finally he took his leave.

Abboud was deposed in favor of an elected parliamentary government by a collection of groups calling itself the United National

Front. Though Nimeiri has not faced such convincingly exasperated riots, or given any indication of his readiness to step down peacefully if he did, it must have rankled him that his opposition also called itself the National Front. He would grant no political standing to Sadiq al-Mahdi, though Sadiq had stood on the point of being voted into his second tenure as prime minister by the Assembly when Nimeiri's council of young officers intervened. Every town I visited had a high-walled installation, rivaling in size the soccer stadium, and often right downtown, with a gate of barbed wire, a shuffling populace just visible beyond, and the Prison Service's green flag with a key imprinted on it flying overall.

The President is an impassive-looking, vigorous officer of unpretentious tastes and good intentions. Born in 1930, he grew up fairly humbly in Omdurman, and has a puffy, light-skinned face which can look a little sly, but usually, because of its puffiness and lack of expression, makes him resemble one of that procession of inoffensive prizefighters whom Muhammad Ali in America regularly eclipsed at weighing-in ceremonies by calling himself a "bad nigger," to the delight of the white sportswriters. Despite the half-year spates of preventive detention that were being handed out all too perfunctorily, he was not feared personally at the time of my visit, because he had not permitted an atmosphere to arise which would have allowed torture to become a feature of imprisonment, or imprisonment to result from a mere personal grudge on the part of people in authority. No elite had formed which was above the law.

With certain tribal or individual exceptions, the Sudanese character is one of generosity and pride of a kind that would be humiliated in torturing a prisoner—although a Sudanese businessman had hinted to me that "recently we may be learning something from some of our European and Egyptian friends." Nimeiri had worked to maintain his image of conciliator from the era of The Troubles, and had avoided the sort of self-idolization other African heads of state have indulged in. The officer corps might not have allowed this, anyhow, and it was his "burning determination," he said, that the country's new permanent constitution outlive him. What we in the West may see as an alarming pattern of African dictatorships can, in its more moderate guise, also be described as "role-model leadership." In a nation such as the Sudan, where there is eighty percent illiteracy, a society fractured by sharp tribalism, a subsistence economy possessing no reserves of foreign exchange—statistically one of the dozen poorest countries in the world—where parliamentary democracy has twice since independence been tried to small avail, it is a transition arguably necessary. Nimeiri, who is not venal, and who, though no intellectual, is not a persecutor of intellectuals and gives the impression of unexciting competence, might be just the leader in whom a citizen would see a streamlined version of himself.

Generally, in these countries, it takes a sort of rough consensus among the educated and the military to make a change of government stick—whereupon the out-of-power contingent is not necessarily more bitter when you talk to them than, perhaps, Barry Goldwater or Eugene McCarthy. The army will comprise more of an assortment of personalities than in an industrialized country, where young men of aptitude find other avenues of advancement open to them. But any middle-class Sudanese who has had some part in forming that consensus is well aware that in the West we give a politician two, four, six, or possibly eight years to accomplish some proportion of his promises before booting him out of office. So he has grown restless as Nimeiri's term has stretched beyond eight years. Nimeiri, too, has taken the fun out of it by executing an unusual number of prisoners after the last few failed coup attempts, and by muscling through the People's Assembly a 1976 law permitting unlimited preventive detention. It remains important to the President that his seizure of power be characterized not as a coup d'etat but as the "May *Revolution*," and that General Abboud (whom he had not supported) not be compared to him.

Of course the question is whether the immense new irrigation schemes can fuel the country into solvency before the country loses patience with him—those four-hour queues at Khartoum's gas stations—yet whether they can do so without such haste and tactlessness as to provoke intolerable dislocations. Furthermore, reforms must be introduced gradually, so as to seem evolutionary, in a religious, traditionalist society.*

* Witness the 1979 tumult in Iran.

What Nimeiri tried during the latter half of 1977, after I had left the country, was brilliant. He simply amnestied and released twelve hundred political prisoners, including all of those who had been imprisoned for participating in armed attacks against his government. He also called back from exile Sadiq al-Mahdi and the other conservative former parliamentarians of the National Front, propelling them into the high councils of his own Sudanese Socialist Union party and the People's Assembly, and opened conciliatory negotiations with the Leftist and Communist leaders who had fled to London and to other countries. Abruptly, this tactic lent a fresh breeze to political discussion in Khartoum, palliated many grievances and grudges, and erased the severity which had been clouding the picture people had of him. In the Southern Region he permitted a popular election in which most of the regional ministers, to their astonishment, lost their positions to a new, "clean" slate of politicians. At the same time, by elevating Abul Gassim Ibrahim, the very toughest "Major," to the first vice-presidency, he kept the army with him and made it difficult for any opponent to conceive of gaining an advantage by killing him.

Coup plots had not been uncommon in the decade and a half between independence and the May Revolution. Nimeiri himself had participated in three or four without suffering much for it. He was in trouble in 1957, was suspended from the army for sixteen months at one point, and was arrested again in 1964 and 1966. Instead of being imprisoned, however, when he fell under suspicion, he was usually sent abroad for advanced military instruction. He went to the United States, Great Britain and West Germany, and in 1966 he was given command of the officers' training center at Gebeit in the Red Sea Hills, where—as he prepared for his sudden putsch three years later—he recruited crucial support among the young soldiers passing through his hands.

Even for criminals, the Sudanese penal system has been by custom a lenient one, with home-for-the-holidays and early-release programs. But by executing his opponents wholesale, beginning with an announced figure of fifteen after the Communist coup attempt in 1971 (though his own life had been spared when he was their captive), Nimeiri had upped the ante. Following the 1975 plot by the Right, the number executed was given out as sixteen. After the heavier assault in 1976, ninety-eight were shot by firing squad in the Green Belt just south of the city. A foreign diplomat hazarded a guess to me that the latter number might really be three or four times that. I did believe these figures were sometimes tampered with, having seen how the reporting of the Juba mutiny was managed. Even the stringers for the Western news agencies in Khartoum are government employees, and although the chronology of the action was accurate, the number of rebels acknowledged to have participated was exactly halved and their political and religious affiliation deliberately misrepresented.

Nevertheless, Nimeiri had suppered solemnly with Mohammed Nour Saad, his former comrade from the Revolutionary Command Council who had led the attack on him in 1976 within Khartoum, to hear his thoughts, the day before the sentence was carried out. Such experiences may have helped to cause a change in heart. Whether because of the people he had had shot or the associates who had set their sights on killing him, he has become a more devout Muslim. People who were acquainted with him always mentioned this alteration to me (as did Sadiq al-Mahdi, publicly, upon his safe return); they said he "didn't look himself." Within the past few years he has enforced a public show of abstinence during Ramadan so complete that a traveler must display his foreign passport in order to obtain lunch in a hotel; has shut the brothels and liquor stores of Khartoum; and at one point asked his ministers to sign a pledge that they would not drink alcohol even privately. The draconian, though unlikely, specter was raised that thievery might be punished by chopping off the offender's hand, as in Saudi Arabia and Sharia law, and the police in the Three Towns (Khartoum, Khartoum North and Omdurman) were stopping cars in which a man and woman were riding alone to ask if they were married, or knocking on house doors with the same query.

This sort of practice—which was shortly curtailed—infuriated just the type of middle-class, enlightened citizen whose approval Nimeiri most needed to ward off the Mahdist Right, as well as any threat from officers more to the left or "military" than himself, who may have deplored the way that the Revolution's rhetoric and socialism has been muted since 1971 and the armed forces' weaponry has deteriorated as various Russian military-assistance teams have been expelled.

During the 1971 emergency, according to the London *Times*, Russian advisers tampered with the equipment of a loyal brigade at Shaggara Armored Command in order to immobilize it for the rebels. In 1976, according to *The New York Times*, Russian radar technicians, in support of the Sadiq-Libyan-Ethiopian plot, deliberately left blank a whole swath of the nation between the territories of its enemies, so that planes could ferry arms and dissidents back and forth between Addis Ababa and Tripoli. Tucked into the interstices of the news, there have been a good many hints of Soviet treachery to other erstwhile clients in the Islamic world—Egypt and Somalia—and Arab anger in response.

One reason Muslims take Christianity for granted intellectually is that they believe their religion encompasses it. Jesus, like Adam, Noah, Abraham and Moses, is a prophet to them—Jesus having predicted the coming of Mohammed in John xv and xvi. Some think that Jesus may even return as the true Mahdi at the end of time to cleanse the world. Abraham was "the first Muslim," and Jerusalem the site of Abraham's definitive "submission" (which is what *Islam* means) to God. It is also the site where Mohammed in a vision ascended to Heaven during his period of doubt before the hegira from Mecca to Medina. Gabriel is the Muslim Angel of Truth who called upon Mohammed in a cave outside Mecca when Mohammed was forty years old, instilling in him the strength of a prophet and carrying to him the messages of the Koran, both then and later on. According to some legends, Mecca is the place where God pardoned Adam after he had wandered in the wilderness for two hundred years (Jidda being Eve's burial place). But the itch of rivalry which individual Muslims frequently betray toward Christianity as a senior, or previously dominant, religion cannot be compared with the contempt they feel for the institutionalized atheism of Soviet communism. Somehow the Chinese, whose aid programs, dollar for dollar, are the most effective in Africa—and who promptly stepped in with seventeen MiG-17s to help rebuild the Sudanese air force after the events of July 1976, a full two years before the United States got around to offering a dozen F-5 jets—have escaped the obloquy that attaches to atheism.

To an extent, Nimeiri's measures of religious orthodoxy have been a necessary courtship of Saudi Arabia's king. King Khalid, although a more pragmatic fellow than was King Faisal before him, has insisted that if the Sudan expects to receive the financial buttressing it needs, it must ignore its heterogeneous makeup and adhere more closely to Islamic teaching. After his November 1976 visit, even the soccer lottery was abolished, although six months later a lot of penny gamblers were still waiting for a checkbook response from "petro-Islam."

Because his Saudi bankers continue to see his nation as an arrowhead of the one true religion penetrating Central Africa, Nimeiri has needed to thread a line between escaping bankruptcy and avoiding a resurgence of The Troubles in the South. Faisal, who died in 1975, never did forgive Nimeiri for the early Nasserist language of the May Revolution. Businesses and banks were nationalized, several Soviet economists drew up a five-year plan, and, naturally, a king sitting across the Red Sea felt threatened. Indeed, Faisal walked hand in hand with the exiled Sadiq al-Mahdi for the photographers. But Khalid, and Crown Prince Fahd, who probably has been the acting intelligence in the matter, have quite astutely swung most of "the Arab nation," as they like to call pan-Arabism, away from Marxist-style confrontation with them precisely because they haven't hesitated to mix into roughhouse situations in countries such as Syria and Lebanon, Somalia and South Yemen, which are all stickier to deal with than Khartoum. They have money to spend—in 1977, a reported $300–400 million in wooing the Somalis alone—as well as that inestimable fervor working for them of a religion to which atheism is anathema.

Arabia is still the religious hub of Islam, as Cairo is its cultural center, and what the Saudi leaders want is not merely to perpetuate their monarchy, but to extirpate Soviet ideas altogether. They also wish to win the internationalization of the Old City of Jerusalem, which, after Mecca and Medina, is a holy city to Muslims. The corridor of the Gulf of Aden and the Red Sea, through which Israel's imported oil has passed, is far from Israel's airfields and would be a likely place to apply leverage.

Israel, therefore, has assisted Ethiopia in its fight to prevent Eritrea, the mainly Muslim, formerly Italian colony on the Red Sea, from attaining independence from Ethiopia. Israel in turn makes use of Ethiopian airspace for its flights to Nairobi and Johannesburg, which otherwise would be difficult to route. (Also, the Saudis say, two strategic Ethiopian islands.) The Israelis, too, almost certainly helped the Southern Sudan Liberation Movement with arms and military training during The Troubles. In the latter instance, the Sudan itself had troops facing Israel's on the Suez Canal in support of Egypt, and its civilian prime minister of the time, Mohammed Ahmed Mahgoub, had taken a hawkish lead against Israel at the Arab Summit held in Khartoum in November 1967: no negotiations with or recognition of the Jewish state.

Five years later, however, President Nimeiri became the first Arab head of government to reinstitute diplomatic relations with the United States, broken off after the Six-Day War. In the fall of 1977 he actively politicked in favor of Anwar Sadat's brave initiative for peace, arguing for recognition of Israel, as well. I never heard a Sudanese refer to Israel in ordinary conversation during my stay; it simply wasn't the preoccupation that Libya and Ethiopia were. One reason why the police paid only minimal attention to a Western tourist was that the agents they were watching for would not be scouting for Israel.

In Khartoum, by good luck one morning in March, I stumbled on a bar mitzvah in progress in the humpy old synagogue next to the Egyptian Cultural Institute on Sharia el Kasr (Palace Avenue). This was the first such ceremony in five years—the tallith was mouse-chewed—because only two Jewish families were left in town, and they hadn't had the necessary quorum of ten men to conduct public worship. They'd had no rabbi either, but now a man of some learning, an insurance lawyer, Maurice Aelion, had arrived, a refugee from Eritrea. He told me that while he couldn't read Hebrew with comprehension, he still prayed daily in the language and could remember from childhood how to pronounce the written text, having relearned the meaning of the words for this service by reading translations in Arabic, Italian and English. He had seemed appropriate to the family concerned, and several English tourists whom they took a liking to had wandered into town, which solved the problem of the minyan of Jewish men.

Maybe because of the long delay, nobody had tears in his eyes except the Englishmen and me. However, the boy, whose name was Daniel, was not of an incongruous age. At the party that evening, in his white silk robe, he held his mother's hand to show her that he thanked her. She was plump and sumptuous, in the Levantine manner, and her daughter even more so, and more active, more of an organizer. At least, she was the person who invited me, despite the chanciness of foreign journalists, because I smiled and said my wife in New York City was Jewish.

It was a happy party, with loads of home-cooked delicacies— like an American bar mitzvah, except that the guests seemed a broader ethnic assortment. There was an Egyptian newspaperwoman married to a Sudanese merchant, and other professional and tradespeople of Jewish, Armenian, Arab and Greek ancestry. Not the proverbial melting pot, like a New York gathering, but a pre–Six-Day War, Middle Eastern society of minority communities which wished to remain minorities. Large family-owned businesses and foreign trading firms, such as the men at this party might operate, would have been expropriated in the first phase of the May Revolution, but since then had been returned (along with any debts run up by government mismanagement), so that these families, who had stuck it out during the interim, were doing well again.

Twenty-one Jews of all ages were living in Khartoum, according to Daniel's beautiful sister. This was about one-fourth as many people as in the surviving Jewish community of Cairo, a city ten times Khartoum's size, but down from seven or eight hundred, thirty years ago. I had visited Cairo's central synagogue—they were without a rabbi too, and hadn't celebrated a bar mitzvah in four years —but had gotten the willies there, a sense of tension and ground-down humility absent from this ceremony for Daniel.

Mr. Aelion himself, although a Sudanese citizen, had had the choice, of course, when he had left his home in the besieged city of Asmara, of flying out to Addis Ababa and on to Israel to make a new life for himself, instead of entrusting himself to the Muslim Eritrean Liberation Front and passing through its lines to Kassala, to settle in Khartoum. He was unassuming, down-to-earth, wearing a brown windbreaker at the party. In the manner of the Sudanese, who wish to extend their hospitality to you clear back to your own country, he gave me the address of an associate of his in San Francisco who would be pleased to entertain me. Both he and the girl laughed when I asked if they had had to notify the police before reactivating their synagogue. They'd had the key—an old Christian hermit had been living in a back room writing down his vision of the Book of Revelations all these years in exchange for acting as caretaker—and yesterday, they said, they'd just unlocked the front door and swept out the building. The government had sent a tax bill regularly, as it does for many Christian, but not Muslim, edifices, but they had been able to ignore these. I liked the notion of the apocalyptic mystic who had chosen Khartoum's synagogue for solitude.

In the 1940's, 1950's, 1960's, after Israel's quick conquests, many Arabs must have wondered angrily whether the Jewish communities in their countries now would constitute a fifth column, and must have wanted the satisfaction of revenge upon *somebody* anyway. But it is worth recalling that nowhere in the Arab world during this period, when African and Oriental Jews were migrating in great numbers to Israel, did a religious massacre occur of the Indo-Pakistani variety, or an abortive European-style holocaust. The tactic of Israeli leaders like Golda Meir and Menachem Begin of comparing their Arab counterparts with "Hitler" and characterizing Arab aims as "Nazi" has succeeded enough in the United States that a writer who ventures into the Middle East must make some reference to it. But it was the Jews of the European Diaspora, not the Jews who lived among the Arabs, who were decimated.

Khartoum has a tradition of polyglot coexistence which reasserts itself after a crisis and acts as an undertow against precipitate violence in the meantime. For instance, although many atrocities against Southerners occurred in the provinces during the civil war, in the capital there were very few. Certainly these two spirited Jewish families didn't seem to have been cowed by events of the past decade. When they had lost their property to socialism, so had Greeks, Armenians, Indians, Syrians and Italians. That more of the rest stayed on is probably due as much to the fact that the Jews had a new nation to go to, full of hope and passion, as that they felt themselves under siege.

Now in government circles one hears regret expressed that so many of the Jewish community are gone—a feeling (since the speaker has probably pored over their account books) that they had had more business expertise and yet had been "less grasping," as Mr. Aelion put it, than the other ethnically discrete communities. I'd heard that an emissary had been dispatched to London by President Nimeiri to try to persuade several figures to return and repossess their property. The official who spoke of this expressed the opinion that Jews were better businessmen.

"Why is that?" I asked.

"Oh, they just are," he told me, adding with a sly expression that as a policy it was both "good business and good politics."

At the party, Mr. Aelion remarked with a modest chuckle that compared with other groups, the Jews left here now probably enjoyed "a protected status." This struck me as an overstatement, but not so much so as to try to link Hitler's inferno with Arab nationalism.

After Daniel went to bed, the gathering became less lighthearted. With everybody sitting down to cards and drinks at tables in the courtyard, the scene was like a hundred other patios in the city that evening, except that the women participated. Mascaraed, perfumed, with emphatic hips and bosoms, heavy, hanging, sleek black hair, and stout stomachs, they handled their cards with authority. Although I wasn't as startled as a Saudi Arabian visitor might have been, to my pallid New England eye the whole party began to look a little sybaritic. I was glad the women were present, but their *embonpoint* and strong perfume alarmed me. It was late, people were sleepy, and so a peculiar deadness lay in their glances over the hands of cards. To an American, there was a sense of country-hopping or carpetbagging—of trade-offs, bribery, of coups and civil wars and executions witnessed with the indifference of a stateless person—behind this mix of nationalities and spiritual allegiances. One reason why at first Idi Amin was widely admired in Africa was that he picked his country's Indians as the opening target for his brutality. They were Uganda's merchants and professionals, and, as elsewhere in East Africa—or like the Lebanese of West Africa—were thought to have been bleeding the economy, though in fact they had helped prop it up.

In Khartoum, Greeks tend to be retailers, and Armenians highrollers, hustlers and wholesalers who have the air-conditioning business sewn up, for example. Since the Greeks are the Europeans of

the city, there are several *pensions,* always full, where the lady of
the house, shaking her head with sorrow, will interrupt the stream
of Arabic in the courtyard, silencing everybody with a dainty wave
of her hand, to inform you in charming-sounding French—the
language of choice between Europeans, as she believes—that she
is sorry that she has no room for you and wishes that she had.
She gestures at the dinner table, prettily arranged with flowers,
white pitchers and napkins, and it looks French indeed, though the
food would not be.

The most homelike yet least expensive of the larger hotels in
Khartoum is the Acropole, which is operated with such feminine
attentiveness to the guests' sensitivities that the accommodations
seem better than they are. I couldn't get in because of my constant
comings and goings, but sometimes stayed at the Metropole next
door. It also was managed by a Greek woman, who was more
formal, efficient and "English" in her style. The hotel had once
belonged to a Jewish family, but now was owned by an egg-bald,
pasha-shaped individual who sat wrapped in his toga in the tiled
lobby, drinking Turkish coffee and observing the transactions in the
small bar opposite the registration desk. Less money was made
there, but the activities interested him more. I assumed from his
appearance that he might be a descendant of one of the effendis
who had administered this chunk of the Ottoman Empire before the
Mahdi drove most of them away. He wasn't unwelcoming, but I
never engaged him in conversation because a young man, probably
his son, answered my queries, when I had any, with a jeering
grin, as if his father couldn't understand English and he could
speak as he wished.

Severe though she was, the Greek woman, the owner's junior
by about fifteen years, impressed me at the beginning as possibly
his wife by a marriage of distress. She had a son of twelve who
did not resemble him and whom she kissed on the forehead passionately when he came home from school. But then I heard from
the Eritrean busboys who knocked at my door occasionally because I was a journalist, with a leaflet of propaganda or a shrapnel
scar to show me, that she was a widow still. They disliked her because she took advantage of their being refugees by paying them
only a dollar a day, and in her straight-backed, magazine-reading,

calmly critical way, was a taskmaster not to be trifled with. I thought her handsome, but, by her manner, not somebody I might come downstairs to talk with, instead of running out to catch the Indian melodrama at the Colosseum movie theater, on those evenings when I felt an impulse to throw myself off the balcony in front of my room.

After I had been traveling alone for a couple of months, some days my breath in my throat smelled like burning rubber. My hands shook, or would suddenly twitch as if they were trying to escape from the stumps of my arms; my fingers closed as if catching and gripping them. I've had lots of experience with solitude, and, though I find it easier to bear, like an old lion tamer with his cats, I do still fear it, and find myself slower, less limber in hopping about to deal with it.

Next door to me upstairs, an English commercial traveler was living skimpily on an inadequate expense allowance. Hot baths were not obtainable at the Metropole, which bothered both of us. He felt fretful whenever he thought of his wife and family, worried that a sandstorm might shut down the airport in the middle of the week when he was booked to fly back. The week before, he had scheduled a phone call to Bristol eighteen hours ahead of time, only to discover that at last when his turn came to use the international circuit, nobody was home. He spoke Arabic, from serving with the Colonial Office in old Palestine, but was considerably frailer lately, "less in the swim," as he put it. He had all but abandoned hope of cashing in on his remembered Arabic to accomplish what he had been sent to do—which was to sell a sizable order of textbooks—simply because he hadn't managed to arrange a meeting with the necessary officials.

"I am not a very good commercial traveler," he said with a laugh, on his way to the Sudan Club, the British club in town.

In the heat, I was barefoot, naked to the waist. In the room on the other side of mine, nearly every time I walked past the door, I saw a woman, paper-pale but weighing two hundred pounds, lavishly eye-shadowed and rouged, with reddened lips and glistening sable hair, lying on both elbows across the narrow bed, with her knees bent and her feet twitching slowly in the air. She was waiting for her husband to come home and snacking on chickpeas and watermelon seeds—waiting all day, but waiting only for him, because if I looked twice, she reached out with the heel of her hand and lazily slammed the door, opening it again after I'd gone by.

In the corridors, what with all of the head cloths and body sheeting, there was an awkwardly celibate air of undress. Sudanese women spend a great deal of time adjusting their taubs—that single sweep of cloth they wind themselves up in—which means that in a business office a lady will let you see piecemeal as much of her shape as if she had on European clothes but that in a hotel she may appear to be wearing her nightdress. Outdoors, a respectable or well-to-do man wears a robe or toga over the relatively graceless galabieh. By itself, the galabieh is like a sort of white or gray or brown sack with a hole in the closed end, and four or five small buttons to close the hole around the neck. (Under the galabieh he wears an undershirt and loose, long, floppy drawers.) Without his toga, his turban alone can still lend him a special dignity, but as you see him lounging in his hotel room, the turban is likely to be unwound.

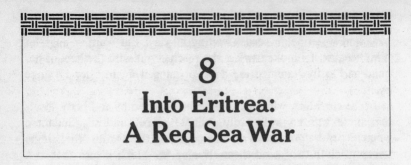

8
Into Eritrea:
A Red Sea War

"These are my golden years, wasted!" a haggard boy named Issayas would say at the Metropole, plucking angrily at his porter's tunic. He had left the city of Keren, in Eritrea, with both a technical-school diploma and a case of amoebic dysentery, for which he still could not afford treatment. In Keren, he claimed, the Ethiopians had killed something like seven hundred and fifty civilians in search operations in 1975, when his father had told him to run for his life. But in the two years since, he had not been able to get word back that he was alive. Like the other Eritreans I met who had been invalided out of the fighting, he couldn't work here legally, and couldn't obtain a passport, either, to leave this one country which harbored a large number of Eritrean refugees—two hundred thousand of them.

"My golden years!" he said, and told me that his father was a priest, but—dramatically—"I don't think any more that God exists!" He slept in the open courtyard with the waiters, who were dark Nubians of the Danagla tribe, located north of Khartoum on the Nile. They were scarred with three vertical cuts in the cheeks, originally possibly a device by which they distinguished each other from their black Southern slaves. The Shaigia Nubians cut their three scars horizontally, and Shaigia women wear a capital "E" lying on its side. A mark resembling the letter "H" is employed by the Ja'alin—though generally now these practices are passing— and several other Nubian tribes used a "T." The Danaglas, in particular, were great slavers, trekking clear to Equatoria and Darfur on the hunt. Like the rest of the Nubians, they were themselves accessible to slaving expeditions roving south from Egypt, and they remain the preferred doorkeepers of Cairo and the house servants of Khartoum.

The Eritreans at the Metropole, who worked in odd juxtaposition with them, were of the Eritrean People's Liberation Front. These young men were much preoccupied with the matter of which rivals they wanted to kill even among the several factions of the insurrection—partisans of either their rivals, the Eritrean Liberation Front, or a third faction, the Eritrean People's Liberation Front—Eritrean Liberation Front, led by the "villainous" Osman Saleh Sabe, who in fact had previously led them. A husky boy named Tsegay, recuperating from a leg wound but whose eyes were going bad would put his hands together to show me how Sabe should be handcuffed for questioning, and then slice at his neck with the flat of his hand to show how he should be killed. I couldn't help sympathizing with Sabe, because the issue that had caused his ouster had been the guerrillas' kidnapping of Western tourists and journalists like me; he had opposed it. Here in Khartoum, however, the threats were mostly just talk. When applying for a passport—a futile process—Tsegay went to the embassy of the hated Dergue itself without killing anybody.

Eritrea is Ethiopia's northernmost province, forty-five thousand square miles of mountains and desert bordering the Red Sea north of Africa's Horn. It is Ethiopia's only outlet to the sea, and the peacetime population has been about two million. The Eritreans' war for independence began with a few skirmishes back in 1962, when Haile Selassie (not for no reason known as the King of Kings) annexed the territory to his own nation, after a United Nations mandate had rather clumsily "federated" it to Ethiopia, with semiautonomous status, ten years before. Between 1941 and 1952 Eritrea had been administered by the British, who took it from the Italians early in World War II. Formerly it had been part of Italian East Africa, the Italians (who coined the word "Eritrea" from the Roman name for the Red Sea) having gained their ascendancy in 1890. For three centuries before that, Ottoman, Egyptian and Abyssinian empire-builders had variously disputed possession of it, and a thousand years before *that,* it was the heartland of the Christian kingdom of Aksum.

Haile Selassie was overthrown in Addis Ababa in 1974 and died a year later. The swiftly radicalized governing Dergue (which is Amharic for "committee") sharply stepped up the Emperor's military campaign to beat back Eritrean secession, but in so doing, only furthered the secessionist cause. Meanwhile, other corners of the Ethiopian empire were coming unstitched, notably the Ogaden region near Somalia; and the Dergue was shifting away from the Emperor's old alliance with the United States and toward the Soviet camp. By assisting Sadiq al-Mahdi against Nimeiri, it had already lost the good offices Nimeiri had been trying to exert to mediate in the Eritrean war so that the refugees, who were an unsettling influence in his own country, could go home.

Besides the Eritreans, there were other rebel groups for the Dergue to reckon with. The Ethiopian Democratic Union was directed by a supposed tiger of a general from the army of the dead Emperor, and was a mix of royalists and social democrats who hoped to overthrow the Dergue, but were not in favor of independence for Eritrea. The Ethiopian People's Revolutionary Party, on the other hand, was Marxist, but believed that the Dergue had betrayed the Revolution by not converting from a junta to civilian revolutionary rule. Therefore they despised both this general and his associates as well as the Dergue, and were neutral toward the Eritreans. They were mainly Addis Ababa intellectuals operating as terrorists within the capital itself. And four additional rebel forces were fighting the Ethiopian army at widely separated localities. The ethnic Somalis, under General Wacko, wished to annex the Ogaden Desert to Somalia. The Afar Liberation Front, in Wollo Province, led by Prince Hanafare Ali Mirah on behalf of his father, the Sultan, were Afars battling for feudal autonomy. The Tigre People's Liberation Forces were Marxists who wanted to set up an independent Marxist state in the province of Tigre, and the Oromo Liberation Front consisted of bands of irregulars in Bale and Sidamo provinces, far to the southwest.

Even down in Juba, however, I'd met Eritrean conspirators, disguised as gospel workers, but shepherding a series of sardonic, shifty-looking agents in and out of town, en route to Kenya and Somalia. Like the ones in Khartoum, they wanted me to write about them, except that in the manner of so many revolutionaries, they would only talk to me if I guaranteed that what I found to say was going to be wholly favorable. For all my curiosity about the guerrillas—the strategy of their raids, their weapons buying, their passionate provincialism—this obsession with killing and ideological purity soon became too much for me.

Then, unexpectedly, a chance turned up to enter Eritrea itself with two newsmen, crossing a dry riverbed at Karora a few days after the town had fallen to the rebels in the first of a domino sequence of victories they won during 1977. The houses had been destroyed beforehand by Ethiopian troops, and there were rumors of mass graves of some of the five thousand civilians who had once lived nearby. The Eritreans, in green fatigues and waving the

Kalashnikov rifles that are ubiquitous in guerrilla warfare, had raised their pretty azure flag with its rosette of olive leaves, and appropriated the trenches and machine-gun sites. They were from the Eritrean People's Liberation Front, and had taken the town while a contingent of the Eritrean Liberation Front that had invested Karora for eight months continued to hold the hills. Nevertheless, they would not permit the ELF partisans to enter now; had fired at them in the flush of victory when they tried. "Comrade," "Brother" came out as every second word, but along the path to the latrine stood a cardboard box heaped with the love letters and family letters of the Ethiopian soldiers they had defeated.

"That's our toilet paper," said our guide, with his fine-boned brown skin, endearing grin, and Afro hair, Chairman Mao's *Thoughts* riding red-bound in his breast pocket.

Izz Abdel—as I will call him—was a Sudanese newspaperman. We also had an English boy along, a would-be free-lance journalist from Liverpool with a brush haircut, who had been teaching English in Omdurman to classes of sixty kids at a time, and was with us to represent the Khartoum stringer for the London *Financial Times,* who had stayed in Khartoum. We drove for a day and night from Port Sudan toward Karora through Hadendowa country. The Hadendowas are Cushites, not Arabs, and by tradition not the friendliest people in the Sudan, even to one another, except for the family bond. Izz Abdel said we ought to have brought a policeman with us for safety's sake, but that because these people associated Land Rovers with government bigwigs they probably would leave us alone. In fact, every time we stopped at a campsite to ask directions across the desert hardpan, the women and children shrieked and ran away, imagining that we might be a team of doctors who proposed to inoculate them.

Our driver, Abdullah—which means "the slave of Allah" in Arabic—was a thin, faithful man with a V-shaped face, scars nicking his brows and forehead. His whispery, musical voice was that of a person raised in the desert mountains, whose gentlest enunciation there might have carried for a mile in the soft air. But he had never been to Eritrea, and neither had Izz Abdel. The latter, a quick-paced, calculating, opportunistic fellow of fifty or more, was just the sort who in America would be a millionaire. As it was, he told me, one way or another, he had earned enough to live on "for twenty years"—nodding to indicate that this ought to be long enough for him. Although in Cairo the souls one sees prostrate in prayer in public places are mostly laborers and the poor, in Khartoum a professor of literature I was talking with grew increasingly restless at nightfall, until he broke off to go outdoors and kneel facing the east. Exactly so, this Khartoum entrepreneur—whose identity I must conceal, yet who at the end of our hectic trip played me a dirty, entrepreneur-type trick—kept stopping the car at dawn, midday, midafternoon, sunset and nightfall to go down on his knees, after first washing his hands and feet with sand.

On our way, we had stopped at the Sudanese army post at Gebeit to visit the Ethiopian prisoners of the battle of Karora, who had chosen to give themselves up to the Sudanese rather than suffer incarceration at the hands of the Eritreans—a saltless, meatless, fruitless imprisonment in caves and a dry wash twenty-five miles deeper into Eritrea from Karora, we were told.

In Gebeit, the Ethiopians' *cook,* at least, was very broad and fat. He had a fire going under a black pot full of water with bits of goat meat and okra floating in it, and was so unfazed by his captivity that he drove us out of his concrete kitchen with a growl and flourish of his fist. The Ethiopian soldiers themselves were skinny, tall, black, mountain-raised Christians with delicate features, who waited now, abashed and timid, under guard in this hot Muslim country—having carried, "like women," as the Sudanese garrison commander put it, several grenade launchers, ninety American M-14 rifles and some twelve thousand rounds of ammunition into detention with them. "A Sudanese company would have held out for a year, and died to the last man, if you gave them that," he said.

Indeed, a wounded Ethiopian we spoke with in the hospital used the same figure of speech. "If a woman has a fight with her husband, she goes to the neighbor's next door, not back to her husband," he explained in murmured Amharic, which was translated into Arabic for Izz Abdel and by him into English for me. "We went in the direction from which there was no firing."

This man, bandaged on one arm, and the Ethiopian in the bed next to his, who had been shot through the mouth, were cowed. They allowed a Sudanese television cameraman to pose them for pictures with a loaned cigarette pushed to the lips of the first and a sarcastic doctor leaning over the second, pretending to listen to his heart. The three Ethiopian officers were not so submissive, although they were in a pitifully precarious position. Their own country would not acknowledge their survival, would not ask for their repatriation, and might well shoot them as cowards if it did.

"We came with our weapons to a neutral country. We are soldiers. We are not prisoners," the captain insisted. And yet the Sudan was no longer neutral, as he realized; it had begun to support the Muslim Eritreans and to hope for the overthrow of the Dergue. "We are not monkeys from the jungle, to be exhibited to white men!" he exclaimed to Izz Abdel, who, like me, was then part of a larger assemblage of newsmen, including British reporters direct from the London *Daily Telegraph* and *Daily Express.* Appealing as an African to the sense of honor of his captors, he consented to see only the Sudanese journalists and a Tunisian—"the Africans," he said, although he allowed a Syrian into the room. "No pictures. No pictures," we heard him say. "We would be signing our death warrants!"

"But this is history! It must be recorded!" the Sudanese cameraman argued, also in English, equally emotionally, until the Sudanese commander, in harsh-sounding Arabic, sided half-contemptuously with the officer.

Gebeit was a little town, reachable from Port Sudan by a stony track that twisted between wild, leopardy, slag-colored hills, with a minaret and water tower standing against the evening sky when we got there. Because the telephone line was down, the garrison was caught almost as much by surprise as were the prisoners when our headlights swept into the central square. Later, the Syrian went home to Damascus; the Tunisian fell in with two Frenchmen who were setting forth to sail around the world but had not yet drunk up the last of their Burgundy; and the London newsmen embroiled themselves—for the fun of it—in a quarrel with the commissioner of Red Sea Province over whether he should furnish his one helicopter for all of us to fly to Karora, and stayed behind in Port Sudan when he did not. But for now, with our cameras or notebooks at the ready, into the common barracks we rushed.

These were privates, sergeants, corporals—ninety-six of them— lying in a two-hundred-foot building, with three weak light bulbs and four water jugs. A jolt of fear went through them. They had been under siege in Karora for eight months. Now, fallen into the clutches of these new but ancient enemies from Islam, they were not yet convinced they weren't about to lose their lives. One man was so startled that he sprang onto his bed and stood teetering there. Every one of them went to a cot, most sidling over and quickly lying down, some on their faces, some masking their noses or covering their heads with a bed sheet so they could not be photographed. For a moment nobody in that long, barren room would admit to speaking either Arabic or English because to do so might involve being quoted. Like Abdullah, these were mountain people accustomed to speaking in hums and clicks and whistles, in murmured whispers, up high in a terrain where they could hear the wings of birds a mile away. The mountains of Ethiopia are much higher, however, and so the very notes of fear and nervousness they uttered amounted to a sort of poignant twitter, ending in silence.

I knew that in Ethiopia repatriated war prisoners at their luckiest were likely to find themselves officially "dead"; no working papers or other identification were given to them by which they might resume their existence. So, as one young man was provoked by the sight of the cameras to break into an anguished remonstration, I began walking the length of the barracks slowly and sadly.

"I have no *need* to be photographed!" he cried, practically weeping—meaning that international law did not require him to submit to treatment appropriate to a surrendered enemy prisoner. Two other Ethiopians also stood in front of the Sudanese and English who were holding cameras, gingerly seeking to keep them back.

"I have no *need* to do this!" the private protested again, as spokesman, in his mission-college English.

I was looking for a face that might show a willingness to talk to me—among these sorrowful, humiliated figures, each stretched out gangling, tense and motionless, as if I were a striped hyena that had got loose in the room. None was in the slightest willing, and gradually, by the time I reached the far end, I had stopped looking and was delaying my steps, closing my eyes in order to try to absorb some memory of the rancid misery. It was tastable, like a mist, and African as well as merely military, so that it did not connect well with my own army recollections.

Since I was not after the same material as the newspapermen, I could join the argument on the Ethiopians' side. The *Daily Express* reporter had been joking as we drove to Gebeit that the commanding general in Port Sudan would have phoned ahead to "paste their fingernails back on." But here we were, after a bumpy ride, including two flat tires, the jackals howling as we'd watched poor Abdullah wrestle with the spares, and nobody would give him a story. "There's no lead," he kept complaining loudly, pushing for an angle, pushing for the sake of pushing, though he didn't want to put anybody's life in jeopardy.

The man from the *Telegraph* was a languid-looking Cambridge graduate who told us he had eaten mangabey monkey on the Congo River, although just now, like his colleague from the *Express,* he felt disgruntled and outflanked because a BBC reporter named Simon Dring had already gotten clear past interviewing these prisoners two days ahead of us, and into Eritrea at Karora, and on for ninety miles to the district town of Nakfa, which the Eritreans currently had under siege. Dring was an intrepid professional, known for his exploits in Pakistan and Vietnam. Once again he was *in there,* as they said a first-rate reporter should be. They were scared the Eritreans might stage a special attack on Nakfa for him to film, and were trying to piece together an account of what was happening from secondary sources closer to Khartoum to telex to London before he got out of Eritrea, in order to take the shine off whatever news and film he had.

"A wink is as good as a nod to a blind man," said Jimmy Brash, from the *Express.* He joked under his breath about "Kaffirs," to see how loud he could say it without being overheard. His paper, or more likely the *Telegraph,* also employed a stringer in Khartoum, a Sudanese newspaperman whom they had brought along to translate for them; and Brash, with the Fleet Street photographer who had been sent from London by the *Telegraph,* enjoyed throwing this fellow up against the fender of the car to frisk him whenever anything went wrong. "Sunburned, are you? This is how we'd do you in Rhodesia." All a joke—calling him "Mo," since his name was Mohammed. Like so many Arab newsmen, "Mo" seemed to be an intellectual *manqué*, a scholar or a poet for whom no job was available beyond routine newspaper work. He couldn't figure out how to deal with this unmannerly roughhousing.

The *Telegraph* photographer was a square-set bloke with a bad back, older, raunchier than the others, a man who knew Morse Code from having been a merchant seaman. He'd had enough adventuring to satisfy him, and when he got tired of hearing about the enterprising Simon Dring, informed us that the only good reporter is a dead reporter. In the car, as we'd bounced to Gebeit— "No cement on your roads, Mo?"—and while we'd waited in the anteroom of the commissioner of Red Sea Province, he had pointed out the window at one of the herds of goats that scavenge everywhere, and said he'd like to pull on a pair of Wellie boots and screw one of those blondies. To roll out such chestnuts was part of being in Africa, and when there was a chance, he skinned off his Hawaiian shirt and exposed his pink-and-white, scantily furred chest to the sun. "Saves going to Monte Carlo."

Inevitably, this confabulation of the British press had not occurred to celebrate a minuscule guerrilla victory in a landscape of candelabrum, dragon's blood and toothbrush trees. Rather, a few days earlier, the Eritreans had released a British contract hydrologist named Ransom and his family from three months' captivity. Unlike a number of previous kidnappings of Europeans and Americans who had wandered into guerrilla territory, there were three children and a pretty wife along, and so the *Telegraph*, the *Daily Mail*, the *Sunday Mirror* had flown in representatives to Khartoum to bid for first-serial rights to the Ransoms' story. But according to Jimmy Brash, who walled his eyes at every discussion of missionary mentality, the *Mirror* man had gotten stranded in Nairobi. Though he arrived prepared to offer £25,000 for this tale out of darkest Africa, Mr. Ransom said no, because he'd already been offered £16,000 by the *Daily Mail* and he had *shaken hands*.

The Red Sea Province commissioner, in Port Sudan, himself a graduate of the University of Manchester, was a somber, ironic man of forty-nine. He spoke with deadly contempt of the Ethiopians who had abandoned their post at Karora. "They didn't want to *die*," he said with a collected relish and ferocity. He seemed coolly bemused by Brash and his two mates as social specimens, when we all sat down to have some tea in his office, but was also alarmed because Brash had drafted a telegram to President Nimeiri concerning the matter of the helicopter. This wire, couched in terms of our being guests of both the President and the nation, was never sent, and only a couple of months later, as it turned out, the commissioner was elevated to a position in the cabinet. Instead of flying, we were told we could go overland to Karora. The Londoners, after the visit to Gebeit, stayed in Port Sudan and interviewed a Sudanese major who had witnessed the final battle and accepted the Ethiopians' surrender.

It's characteristic of traveling in Africa that a little while before I had been told forthrightly by the same Sudanese major that I might well be shot by the Eritreans if I tried to cross the border at Karora. "We have no communications with them. You would have to walk across the river alone, and they have a bunker facing where you would be. They would not know who you are and they would watch you come and decide what to do and it might not be a nice thing. Even we don't know them yet." In any event, I wouldn't be permitted to reenter the Sudan. "It is not a legal crossing point. What you would do if they didn't like you, and how you would get out of there even if they did, I can't say," he had told me with a cool smile. Simon Dring, whose stunt in entering he didn't mention, had employed a daredevil free-lance Sudanese intelligence agent to smooth the way.

But now, after the Londoners' threatened telegram and Izz Abdel's hard sell—invoking me as a correspondent for *The New York Times*, since I was from New York City and because in order to be allowed to go, he needed me—we were rolling. What we lacked was a map. So few roads exist in the Sudan that there are no road guides. No maps of *any* kind at this time were obtainable, except that through special dispensation of the American embassy I'd got hold of a twelve-by-twelve-inch sketch of the nation. Keeping one eye on old wheel ruts, we tilted this around to conform with the course of the sun. Izz Abdel—who was as squat as he was bold, wore a black headcloth, later a white headcloth, and called on Allah frequently—burst unexpectedly into laughter, remembering other adventures on the Uganda border during the Sudan's own civil war. He took over the wheel from Abdullah at the worst spots, as if to show the car who really was its boss. After Tokar, we had no distinguishable roadway to follow.

Tokar, at the delta of the Baraka River, flowing out of Eritrea, is the site of an extensive cotton-growing scheme. Pilgrims to Mecca from West Africa historically have paused here in the cotton fields for a season to earn their boat passage across the sea. We arrived at dark, and it was easy to get stuck in the outflow from the irrigation ditches roundabout or lost among the tractor tracks. For two hours the next morning, we headed out again mistakenly in the wrong direction. The town was spaciously laid out, but so lightless at night that the children needed to wait for the moon to wax to play after the sun went down, and so poor and dispirited that several families had dug mud for their house bricks right from the street in front—pits ten feet wide and ten feet deep which were extremely difficult to see and dodge in a vehicle at night.

Many of these people were Hadendowas, who speak Bedawiye before they learn Arabic, or Bani-Amer, whose native language is Tigré. So when my manipulative companion, Izz Abdel, tried, at the whitewashed Government Club, to procure supper for the four of us by appealing to the obsessive hospitality of Arab culture, he managed to conjure up only a cup of coffee and a glass of orange squash apiece. The members at their card games glared at us suspiciously over one shoulder.

Meeting an Arab peddler leading a donkey in the desert that afternoon, Izz Abdel, in his practiced style, had stepped out of the Land Rover, patting his heart repeatedly, exclaiming, "There is no god but God!"

The peddler, who was a butcher—his animal festooned with goat rib cages and legs—jerked the donkey's halter to bring it to a stop, and placed his right hand on his heart.

"Mohammed is the Apostle of God!" he said.

"Bless the Prophet!" said Izz Abdel.

"Peace be upon him," the peddler answered.

The whole four-part formula had been gone through again, in leisurely, bountifully zestful fashion. Then again, the words for the first time starting to sound a bit slurred, both men dropping their eyes from what I took to be the beginnings of boredom. And then yet *again*—before Izz Abdel inquired about directions to Tokar— by which juncture the fate of the peddler's soul might seem to have been staked upon what he said. But these Hadendowa notables in their white robes did not respond to Izz Abdel's invocations except perfunctorily.

Arabs hoard their women like water in the desert, but the Hadendowa women go unveiled. They do their share of the herding, and will gallop on a camel across the sand like a man when they want to, carrying a wicked-looking cutlass on occasion, which they grip when meeting a stranger on the path—gazing at you with scorn, as though to forestall any incivility. Their tents are frogshaped, constructed of hides and woven mats of goat and camel hair on a stick frame, the large mouth facing east. The men we saw as we drove were dressed in white, with a "fuzzy-wuzzy" hayrick of hair worn as high and proud as a Texan sports his hat. They carried three-foot-long herding poles and narrow-bladed little brushwood hatchets, or one of their definitive, red-scabbarded, immense swords. At the time of the Mahdi, they routed at least one British general with these, and later, in defeat, still charged and broke a British "square," as in Kipling's poem in praise of them.

On the second day, Izz Abdel had Abdullah stop every couple of hours so we could "pass water." Then, "Gentlemen, prepare yourselves!" when it was time to continue again. Black sand alternated after ten or fifteen miles with soft white sand, or thorn-tree savanna land, or brine flats by the sea with saltbush, and the beach beyond. The emaciated, desert-colored dogs darting around the miserable mud shops we passed could muster enough energy to bark but hadn't enough moisture in their bodies to piss successfully when they greeted one another.

George, the journalist from Liverpool whom we had brought with us, was a Communist and had carried his Marx along, a paperback copy of *Das Kapital* to read if we broke down somewhere, or perhaps (it later seemed) to impress the guerrillas with. Though he was sympathetic to the proletariat, and said his father was a lorry driver back home, he kept raging unreasonably at Abdullah for "stupidity" in driving. He claimed he was a pacifist as well, and yet became exultant, bobbing up and down, when the first of what were possibly the Karora Hills materialized in front of us, because that's where the war would be. Izz Abdel acted less sanguine. Apart from not being sure where Karora itself was located, we didn't know where the line of the border lay, and didn't want to cross inadvertently, like a party of "spies."

As we traveled now, to the south and west we generally could see a rough small knot of mountains—not the same ones, apparently—a country where, a century ago, people may have carried gold, poured into hollow vulture quills, from hidden workings to market. We knew that Eritrea was mountainous, but not where it began. George, in the meantime, was trying to argue Izz Abdel, not only into accepting the tenets of Marx, but out of his faith in the existence of God. Izz Abdel, though a broad-minded, worldly man, positively snorted at such folly. "This is the Sudan, my friend. You are not among your bloody atheists in London!"

The Bani-Amer, a tribe related to the Hadendowas but hostile to them, live nearer the border and inhabit thatched-stick, rectangular hovels patched with old tin, with an unbaked clay pot standing outside the door from which water oozes just fast enough to keep the contents cool, and a brush corral attached for the livestock. Our motor startled herds of up to eighty camels, some of them hobbled, and double that number of goats, which had been lying peacefully in the sun, till they lurched onto their feet—all of them the very bulls of the local sheikh. The women in flowing, yellow taubs ran to head off nervous individual beasts.

We suffered another flat, and sprawled under a rock while Abdullah put on the spare and drove the car onto the punctured tire to get it off the wheel. After patching and mounting it again, he inflated it laboriously with a bicycle pump. Once, in Malakal, when flying to Khartoum, I had seen a bicycle pump used to refuel a Sudan Airways jet. In the office building in central Khartoum which houses the U.S. embassy, I'd often ridden up and down for several minutes in the elevator with a CIA type, while we took turns trying to snatch the door open just as we reached the fourth floor, because there was no other way to persuade it to stop. Manual difficulties were therefore a fact of life to all of us, but we were feeling bad-tempered from the heat. In English, which Abdullah couldn't understand, we considered whether in Tokar he might not have woken up before dawn, while we'd napped, and sold some of our gas. The barrel we were lugging in back sounded suspiciously empty when tapped. But we decided not.

We passed a dead camel, bloated up, and several scattered camel skeletons, and a ghastly desiccated donkey carcass, looking almost fossilized, and twisted halfway about as if to plead against a terrific beating as it died—of course, it may only have been protesting the agony of the heat. We also went by single human graves, each with an upright flat stone at the head and foot and a circle of modest-sized stones around. For brief stretches, water would have gathered in sufficient quantity in a slightly soggy area for sorghum to be raised. Then, in other terrain, there was nothing except tan-colored rocky sand relieved every couple of miles by an occasional acacia tree or a few cactuslike, candelabra-shaped euphorbias. At the upper elevations some wild olive trees and cedars grew, according to my copy of an invaluable old volume called *Agriculture in the Sudan*. Miles away and above us, we saw sparse clumps of what may have been these.

"Alexander the Great, you know, could tell when an army that he was chasing was about to give up," Izz Abdel remarked. "That's right. He'd just watch their shit. Whenever he came to a place where they had camped, he walked all over and looked at where they had slept and done their business, and if it was spotted everywhere with runny stuff with blood in it, he knew they would be finished running pretty soon."

I told him that I'd had more troubles with my bowels before I'd left New York, just from jitters at the idea of coming, than here.

"Coming to the jungle," he said. "You're very frank. But so do we when we go to Amsterdam or Edinburgh."

We counted a handful of bananas left, and two oranges and some dry bread. However, we had exhausted both our water and the Khartoum beer we had obtained in Port Sudan. Izz Abdel was a cosmopolite who drank beer when abroad in his own country, but only trusty Khartoum beer, brewed from Khartoum water.

"We will enjoy some *tea*," he concluded cautiously, and directed Abdullah to stop at one of the mud-brick huts roofed with rusty scraps of tin and straw that we encountered every twenty miles or so, where our lorry track forked off from another or simply crossed a camel path. Our host, an Arab petty trader named Yasin Ali Suleiman, reassuringly swore eternal fealty not only to God but also to us. He had thrown a tire on the ground and put a block of salt in it and an armload of sorghum straw for his customers' camels. Three of these were barracked in the yard with their forelegs tied up under them, though they could walk a little on the ball of the knee to reach the fodder or a tin tub of water. The largest was able to get up and stand on three legs and hop along because his owner had bound only one of his knees.

Riding camels are males, whereas the breeding herds we had been passing along the way were mostly composed of females. Although a camel's nostrils can express consummate disdain, it is by a rope wrapped around his nostrils that his rider controls him. Yet controls can't wholly domesticate them, because with their great vigorous necks, mean front teeth, contemptuous lips, menacing grunts and angry groans, camels do hold their own. They haven't even been shaped by the 3500-year experience of man; their long necks and humps are still architectured for living independently in the wilderness. Being so comely and tall—half giraffe and half gazelle—they are undiminishedly free-looking. We could drive all day and never see a wild animal, yet somehow never realize this because we were seeing plenty of camels. These powerful creatures—the grace not sacrificed to strength, the strength not sacrificed to grace—nibbling high twigs in the thorn trees, looked wild enough. And this big one, with his saddle scabbard sticking up as he lay watching us, himself appeared to be sporting the sword.

Yasin Ali, the storekeeper, was a poor man, selling hunks of pink soap, flashlight batteries, cloth cut from a trio of bright bolts, some grain in baskets, perfumes and spices, cooking oil, rope, thin saucepans and stewing pots. Spices are a particular necessity where so many meals consist of nothing but boiled mush. The perfume was a brand known as "Bint of the Sudan" (*bint* meaning "girl"), which is manufactured in Great Britain but advertised by posters of a plump dark girl with naked breasts.

Middle-aged, mustached, Yasin Ali wore an orange skullcap,

just showing underneath his turban, and had a radio, which happened to be playing "London Calling" in Arabic. As we sat with him, he proved his poverty by killing twin baby goats so that his young son could have the mother's milk, though he told us it would be more profitable to raise them and sell them later on. One of the tiny beasts was tied by its foot to a post while he strung up and bled and skinned the other. After offering us a pailful of brown home brew with a gourd floating on top, he sat cross-legged, picking the diminutive ribs out of the kid's chest with his teeth and smiling at Izz Abdel's questions and sallies.

Izz Abdel, like an indefatigable newsman, never stopped angling for information. The Hadendowas in Tokar could shrug and ignore him, pretend not to understand Arabic, and mutter in Bedawiye, but Yasin Ali chatted responsively, Allah all the time as bright as the sun in whatever he said.

Sitting on a mat under another mat propped up on poles, we watched him dip the teakettle into a barrel of muddy water and blow at the coals of a little fire under a broken truck radiator, upon which he set the kettle. This familiar, time-consuming procedure, when you are perhaps thirstier than we were at the moment, and riding on top of a Bedford lorry with a great many local people who have no fear of drinking right out of an irrigation ditch, can become exceedingly frustrating. Everybody else drinks water wherever the truck stops, so it is taken for granted that you have ordered tea only because you are not thirsty. Your tongue scrapes back and forth like a wad of newspaper across the roof of your mouth, but a fire is kindled especially for you and the tea brewed with unhurried courtesy, heavily sweetened as always, so that you burn your tongue from thirsty haste when it is finally ready, and as you drink cup after cup (to the astonishment of your host), all that sugar is a curse.

Yasin had a friend, a tinsmith, an old man with a short white beard, sucking a lime, who showed us a choice of pitchers he had hammered out of red, white and blue soybean-oil cans, a gift of the U.S. people, according to a legend emblazoned on each. Yasin's eldest son, leading a donkey, kept bringing water from a pit dug in a wadi, the water from the waterskins making a peculiar rushing sound, as if the donkey were peeing, when he emptied them into the barrel. Then he'd mount again, sitting straight, tossing a white scarf about his throat, and trot back, his left leg balanced dapperly across the donkey's shoulders. There are these purposeful postures donkey riders assume, the man's weight centered on the creature's shoulder blades, or homey, negligent, comfy styles of slumping over, while perched instead upon its rump. Some people bestraddle the beast, rocking forward impatiently to lend it impetus. Some hang both legs down the same side of its ribs, or cross one leg over the other, casually bumping along, or stick one leg straight out alongside the donkey's neck, with their arms akimbo, or hug themselves —although, really, a fat donkey, as it picks its way nimbly among the stones, looks disconcertingly like a moseying, round-bodied mouse.

"Gentlemen, prepare yourselves," said Izz Abdel, when we had finished our tea. Driving again by the slant of the sun, we saw rain clouds ahead of us over the mountains in Eritrea.

"Are you afraid, my friend?" he asked, glancing at me. While his billing me as a correspondent for *The New York Times* might grease the gears for us somewhat, it would also make me sound like a juicier hostage if the Eritreans were still of a mind to grab and hold a Westerner. Jon Swain, a correspondent for the London *Times,* had only recently been released. Because he was our translator, I couldn't very well prevent Izz Abdel from making any claims he wanted to about me. In fact, he may have begun to believe I actually was a hard-news reporter because of all the notes I took. When we finally got back to Port Sudan, he played me the trick of calling the airport and telling me there wouldn't be a plane for Khartoum for several hours. As soon as I had relaxed and gone into the hotel to wash and change, he dashed with the English boy to catch one that was supposed to leave in fifteen minutes, so they could file their stories quicker.

"Karora," he said, as we pulled up beside a barbed-wire encampment a quarter-mile around. It was Friday, the Sudanese Sabbath. A sentry with binoculars stood on the bluff above, to keep tabs on the Eritreans' activities, but the rest of the detachment of forty soldiers were playing volleyball, laundering their clothes or playing cards. The captain, in his sport shirt, invited us into his tent, where we were given a basin of clear water to drink. Since this was not a commercial establishment, it was socially incumbent upon us to do so. We sat on folding chairs while Izz Abdel explained why we had come. Meanwhile, a dog that was a living skeleton ran inside with two soldiers with clubs stalking and chasing him. He stood with arched back and miserably gaped mouth next to me.

"He is a mad dog who has come out of the hills. They must kill him before he bites someone," Izz Abdel said.

I thought him desperately starved and thirsty, but all of us sat very still while the soldiers sought to maneuver him out of the tent to where he could be safely killed. He must have known that to leave would be to die, but at last they succeeded in forcing him to make a run for it. He couldn't get through the fence, and we heard him yelp. Then as we walked toward the border crossing we saw a private dragging his body to the dump, smiling at us, although the captain shouted that it was a stupid thing to drag a dead dog along in front of an Englishman and an American like that.

Walking down some stone steps, I felt my knees knock a bit. We waited in front of the two-story brick-and-stucco police post in the shade of a big margosa tree, brought as a seedling by the British from India, the police lieutenant in his Sabbath *jibba* said. This was where the British post commander used to meet with his Italian counterpart when Eritrea had been a province of Italian East Africa. They had sniped at each other here at the start of World War II.

The army captain went through the bushes to the riverbank and hailed the Eritrean People's Liberation Front lookout on the opposite side, telling him to call his officer. In due course a stocky figure in olive drab scrambled down the sand slope, about eighty yards away, and crossed. His name, he said, was Sheikh Omer. He was a smoldering, vigorous military man, dark-colored, fortyish, but still alight with pride in the victory that he had won, although he told us that he bore no proper rank, because in a people's army such as his all fighters had an equal role.

Not an individual whose prisoner I would like to have been, the sheikh, who had just recently been dealing with prisoners, cast a cold eye at me. Then, as Izz Abdel talked, we shook hands. I was dressed in a rumpled salt-and-pepper Brooks Brothers summer suit and Oxford shoes, oddly enough, because this trip had been scheduled as a hotel-type press junket from Khartoum to Port Sudan and return (our Information Ministry escorts had washed their hands of us when we set off for the border). But though my strange costume and black briefcase looked incongruous in the setting, they probably acted to convince the sheikh that I was either an American foreign correspondent or, better yet, a U.S. government agent posing as a correspondent. He walked back across the riverbed to radio his superior, who was commanding the siege at Nakfa, for instructions, saying that a decision might take another hour.

In the meantime, the Sudanese captain had sent a pickup truck to bring in the chief of the partisans of the Eritrean Liberation Front who had besieged the Ethiopians here from the crags above but had not managed to crank themselves up to the task of actually overrunning them. Now that the Ethiopians were gone, the Sudanese were bulldozing a supply road to the ELF's new headquarters at a ranch house on the valley floor, about a mile from the EPLF positions.

Bashir Abdul Kadar was the ELF chief, and the Sudanese had known him much longer, and furthermore would tend to favor him because he was a Muslim, and the ELF preponderantly Muslim—armed and supported by Arab countries such as Syria, Iraq, Saudi Arabia and Yemen. The EPLF, originally Christian highlanders for the most part, had split off from the lowlanders of the ELF in 1970 in what began as a religious conflict, ushering in three years of civil war within the Eritrean independence movement itself. About three thousand guerrillas on both sides are said to have been killed. Having been persecuted and driven to the highlands in historical times by the Muslims, most of the Christians of Eritrea had been indifferent at first to the war of independence waged by Eritrean Muslims against Haile Selassie's army of Christians from Addis Ababa. Yet the Dergue in its bombing and ground attacks made so little distinction between the religious affiliations of Eritrean villagers that by the period of my visit, the ELF and EPLF were not killing each other, but merely planning their war strategy separately and holding territory "liberated" from the Ethiopian army in a leopard-spot pattern throughout the province. Each organization boasted its own spots.

The EPLF had ten thousand men under arms, the ELF perhaps fifteen thousand. Both were recruiting more fighters, but the EPLF was better and more boldly led. Its cadres were better educated, intellectually livelier and trendier, more urban and middle-class in origin, and Marxist in theory. They would tell you that the ELF was "tribal," "regional," and "backward," but also "pan-Arab," and thus not truly "national." They claimed *they* fought mostly with captured—which is to say, American—weapons, not brand spanking new Kalashnikovs, such as the Saudis and Syrians had bought and boated to the ELF from Yemen. Both groups included Christians as well as Muslims now, and social democrats as well as Marxists, but the ELF, in answering the accusation that it was pan-Arab rather than nationalist, argued that, on the contrary, the Marxism of so many members of the EPLF rendered it beholden to outside ideologues and foreign powers.

So George, Izz Abdel and I shared a cheese-and-boiled-egg late lunch with Bashir Abdul Kadar on the second-story terrace of the police post. It was a breezy, pleasant spot, with pigeons bustling just above us on the corrugated roof. The Sudanese, after laying out our food, like good marriage brokers, withdrew. Mr. Kadar told us he was thirty-two and had been living as a revolutionary in the mountains for thirteen years. He had become such an ascetic, particularly during the drought and famine of 1975, when the Ethiopians cut off international relief supplies being shipped to Eritrea's civilians, that he allowed himself only one of the eggs and half the cheese that had been placed on his plate. Slender, emotional, idealistic-looking, in the style of a schoolteacher, with delicate Hamitic features and a fragile mustache under his checkered *kaffiyeh*, he didn't alarm me, as had the flat, fearsome manner of Sheikh Omer.

Through his interpreter Mr. Kadar asked why they had never seen a Western journalist before. Why this prejudice? Both George and I laughed uneasily and pointed out that Westerners who had entered Eritrea lately had been detained and, in some cases, had never surfaced again. Why, asked the loquacious interpreter, did America, which had fought its own revolution for self-rule, furnish

the Fascist Dergue with F-5 jets and helicopters to attack them? I
said that the American government had favored Haile Selassie—
true enough—but not the Dergue, and that the arms presumably
were intended to counterpoise the Russian ordnance which was
then still pouring into Somalia.

George, however, elated to be sharing a meal with genuine guerrillas, began to speak of the Imperialist-Oppressors Camp, versus
the Peace-Loving Republics. He wanted them to know where he
stood, and started condescending to me as a representative of capitalism and the Pentagon: "Of course, you *would* believe that."

The Eritreans threw each other an amused glance, to find us
Anglos disagreeing. Without entirely accepting him as a fellow fighting progressive, the translator, who turned out to be the unit's
political officer, launched upon an enthusiastic lecture about the
Socialist March.

I muttered to my colleague that if he'd wanted to get into a
political argument with me, why on earth had he not done so during our many boring hours in the car, instead of waiting till these
precious minutes of the interview? Bashir Abdul Kadar seemed to
feel the same. It was foolishness to harangue this visitor with gray
in his hair and an American briefcase and suit. Interrupting his
assistant, he got him to tell me that many Eritrean revolutionaries
were not Communists at all; that although Somalia helped them
occasionally with passports and other small amenities, they received
no weaponry from Somalia and had their own troubles with the
Somalis—as I already knew. In the wretched fashion of Africa,
these two natural allies against Ethiopia, which stretched between
them, were unable to coordinate their strategy freely. The Somalis
were blood relations of the Issas, one of two inimical Islamic tribes
inhabiting the tiny coastal French protectorate of Djibouti, wedged
between Eritrea, Ethiopia proper and Somalia. But many Eritreans, on the other hand, were tribal relatives of the Afars, who
were outnumbered by the Issas in Djibouti, and lived in danger of
being massacred by them after the French left.

I asked him whether my country's M-14 rifles were of any use
to his men when they collected them from the Ethiopian dead.

"Oh, it is a good rifle, yes," he said, through the interpreter,
smiling at that. "It is a rifle for an army, you understand. It is not

as light and handy when you have to run up the side of a mountain. But what is important is not the rifle that a soldier uses. What is important is the man who holds the rifle. That is why the Eritrean people are winning against the Ethiopians. Not that we have Kalashnikovs. We are fighting for our homeland."

For all of his asceticism, Kadar wore creamy-tan pants and smoked a Benson & Hedges, not the local Haggar brand of cigarette. In a modest way he identified himself as the ELF's commissioner of the Military Bureau for the Northern Front, and a member of its Revolutionary Council. He was naturally embarrassed that his EPLF rivals had come up underneath his machine-gun and rocket positions and, after two weeks' reconnaissance, had taken the town, when he had lain for so much longer in the rocks overlooking it. He had guessed that the approaches must be mined, but when Sheikh Omer, after asking his consent, and with a force only slightly larger than his own—about half the number of the entrenched Ethiopians —launched a creeping assault from the direction of Nakfa, they did not encounter any mines.

Starting four hours before sunset, the sheikh's men had suffered just two wounded, hugging the lay of the land. Although they didn't reach the actual V of the perimeter trench that night, they dug in pressed so close that the Ethiopians the next day sent in four helicopters from Asmara to ferry away their howitzers and other heavy equipment lest these be captured by the Eritreans. The Ethiopians had been supplied by air for months, but judging that the helicopters were going to fly back to evacuate the troops as well, the tough sheikh, in the small hours the following night, dispatched a party to seize the isolated outcrop spur from which the Ethiopians, with a .50-caliber machine gun, had protected their landing pad. They succeeded in doing just this, and so when, around noontime, five Ethiopian helicopters whirled in again to pick up the hundred and fifteen defenders left, they couldn't land. After much frustrated chatter, to which everybody in the valley with a radio listened intently, they flew off. And *that* night the Ethiopians sewed together the white flag with which they had slunk across the river to the old British police post on Sudanese soil where we were now enjoying our lunch.

Fourteen Ethiopian dead and four rear guard, now prisoners,

were left behind. The EPLF Eritreans, after realizing what was up, tumbled into the trenches of the Ethiopians, firing after them, but also shooting at the irregulars of the ELF, who dashed from the nearby ridges where they had witnessed the proceedings, to celebrate the outcome. Indeed, the Christian sheikh now treated Bashir Abdul with blunt contempt, when Izz Abdel posed them for pictures. He almost refused to shake his hand, though this was partly a political punctiliousness. Since I liked the gentler man, seeing him humiliated was painful.

After the picture-taking, Bashir Abdul returned to his enclave and we accompanied the sheikh across the dry river, keeping in his previous tracks in case the Ethiopians at some point had put mines down. Possibly at Izz Abdel's request, the Sudanese army captain tagged along—I think to be sure that we were permitted to return. In the Sudan it is the pattern that you can drive for four arduous days through the desert in order to spend what in retrospect has amounted to only a few hours at a village of naked dancers in the Nuba Mountains, then drive for four days back. But there is generally a suddenness when things do happen, as on a sweltering afternoon when you have phoned the EPLF leader in Khartoum— a number obtained from the *Washington Post*'s Africa expert. You tell the oddly accented voice where you live, and he says he will make inquiries about you. Meanwhile you read *The Plumed Serpent,* uncomfortably aware of the narrow terrace overhanging the courtyard just outside the door, because, like the tightrope walker who must keep moving forward if he is to stay aloft, you simply can't sit still in this hotel for very long; any visitor would be better than none. Abruptly, however, the man appears—pop-eyed, burly, a tough cookie, as unannounced as a commando, so that if you had laid an ambush for him you would be unprepared. The American ambassador, Mr. William Brewer, despite the heat and tedium of his four-year stint in Khartoum, twice a day would make a run for it from his car into the lobby of the embassy building downtown, with his life like a football tucked under his arm, mindful that his predecessor had been shot dead by Black Septembrists on the job.

The EPLF enrolled women in its ranks, as the sheikh said the ELF did not. Several of them, uniformed in baggy fatigues, jumped in the looped trenches to pose with the men for Izz Abdel's camera. The sheikh gestured sarcastically at the Ethiopians' fortifications as he led us around, and at the low buildings which had served as their barracks, holding his nose as if at the stench. A male nurse-midwife who had learned English in school introduced himself, telling me he was a Christian, but here was his best friend, who was a Muslim and fought alongside him. Here was a soldier who admired the communism of Peking, but here was another who liked the Congress of the United States and wished Eritrea to have something like that. "We are many kinds of people," he said, "and we are not paid to fight for our country. The Ethiopians are paid."

Briskly we climbed the spur dominating the helicopter pad to see the big Korean War–type American machine gun whose capture had meant so much. We went, too, to visit the ELF ranch house up the valley, and clambered to *their* best redoubt—although no matter how high we scrambled, always another guerrilla stood up above us waving his Kalashnikov. Bashir Abdul Kadar had changed into a khaki uniform and was lecturing a class of galabiehed herdboys. All told, I was touched, and later did manage to write a squib about the Eritreans for *The New York Times,* so as not to feel that I had imbibed their tea and hospitality under false pretenses.

Within a few weeks, as they had hoped, Nakfa fell. Then, during the spring and summer and early fall, the Eritreans took the cities of Keren, Tessenei and Agordat, until by late 1977, with only their intended capital of Asmara, and Barentu, and the fortified ports of Massawa and Assab remaining in Ethiopian hands, President Nimeiri, in tandem with the Saudis—who said that they were ready to bankroll sufficient weapons purchases to change the character of the guerrillas' war—at last tried to force the EPLF and ELF to merge. They had already coordinated the best sequences of their attack with the rolling offensive of the Somali army and Somali Western Liberation Front in the Ogaden Desert in southern Ethiopia. In fact they had captured ninety percent of Eritrea. This was the period—before the intervention of Russian generals using Cuban troops—when the Dergue was running into disastrous logistical difficulties as it shifted from American to Soviet arms. Both its regular army and the gigantic peasant army conscripted for a Christian holy war against the Muslims were routed.

Afterward, remembering my exuberant hosts at Karora—most of them purist Marxists young enough to be my sons—I thought that what must have pained and bewildered and disillusioned them the most was not that Russian MiGs serviced and flown by Communists had supplanted the familiar American jets serviced by Israeli mechanics that for years had been bombing them. Russia, having been expelled from its port facilities in Somalia, needed a new port, and now Israel was providing cluster bombs for the MiGs. The idea of a cynical and overlapping hegemony of the Great Powers, if they so interpreted it, would not have been a bone to choke on. Rather, the arrival of Cuban mountain fighters, guerrillas like themselves, the heirs of Ché Guevara—guerrillas like the Viet Cong—to garrison besieged Asmara and help defeat their fight for self-rule must have nearly broken their hearts.

By nightfall we were safely ensconced in our Land Rover again, exhausted, relieved, and heading back. Our lights occasionally picked out the white bodies of camels that had been at rest by the side of the path and now heaved to their feet—and once a family of hyenas trotting.

A peculiarity of this part of the world is that the most extreme flip-flops of allegiance are accomplished so cavalierly, without embarrassment. The show of consistency characteristic of Asian, European, even South American leaders—rightists to the Right, leftists to the Left—appears to have no applicability. The Libyans and the South Yemenites, who had supported the Eritreans against the Dergue in 1976, now supported the Dergue against the Eritreans—but through no sudden hope of territorial gain for themselves, and no particular change in the respective positions of either the Marxist Eritreans or the Marxist Dergue.

"We don't have a 'Right' or 'Left' in Africa. Don't you understand that? We are a new continent. That is a concept of you Europeans," Izz Abdel argued.

I pointed out that not even the exigencies of the Vietnam war had allayed the ancient suspicion of the North Vietnamese for China, and yet the Libyans and the South Yemenites had contrived to switch sides like changing a shirt. Did they believe in conspiracies to the exclusion of every other factor in politics?

"They are Communists." He laughed. "No, you are right. We are tribal. It is true, unfortunately. We make alliances that last for a rainy season. But you are mistaken if you think the Libyans will ever love the Ethiopians."

Along about 2 A.M. we got mired in mud. We had bumped down into the trench of a watercourse, following the marks of a wide-axled lorry, and found that the squalls in the mountains had turned the bottom into a baby swamp. Our wheels could neither fit into the truck's tracks nor spin free of them. We could see the fires of two nomad families camped separately against the slopes of a jebel that rose several hundred yards off to our east, and another fire a mile away on the opposite ridge. They were big fires because hyenas emerge at night, scouting for a goat or a camel foal.

Izz Abdel, who could sound ingratiating and self-important in the same breath, had a proverb for every event. He sang a plaintive folk ditty about a beggar boy on a journey who asks for help from anybody within hearing, loud enough so that somebody might come and help us push.

Though his voice carried well, the tribesmen did not respond; only their dogs ran out. George and I, who had remained out of temper with each other, picked up stones to throw at the dogs, but Izz Abdel told us not to. "The tales you hear in London about stoning fierce dogs in the Middle East are wrong. If you stone them, they will run at you."

We had eaten the last of our food, except that by feeling around under the seat Izz Abdel came up with a stray black thumb-sized banana. "Now I am a rich man!" he cried to himself. Rather, he sang it, and gave thanks to God, though we were by no means yet famished.

We had been watching Abdullah dig, George cursing him for slowness again. And we shoved at the vehicle ourselves, in a swarm of malarious mosquitoes, standing in a spongy streambed that quite likely contained the race of snails which harbor the grim trematodes that cause the blood-sapping disease known as bilharzia. My secret feeling was that since Abdullah might already *have* malaria and bilharzia, better that he dig than me. But the longer we stayed stuck, the more mosquitoes bit us. Nor were we entirely eager to see our human neighbors materialize, because this was supposed to be bandit country.

As we struggled with fender and bumper, Izz Abdel loosened up enough to mention politics, as ordinarily he would not.

"Up with Nimeiri!" he exclaimed, grinning because he was being bold with me. "Up with Nimeiri, hey? Straight up to heaven"—it was a code—"and the sooner the better!"

Then our luck changed. Two white figures loomed up on camel-back. Bani-Amers riding home from a dance in snowy robes, they kindly dismounted and lent us a hand that made all the difference.

"No, no," Izz Abdel corrected himself cautiously afterwards, as we bumped on past Tokar at sunrise, aiming for Port Sudan. "He's a good man. Nimeiri's a good man. He has tried to rush a poor country along too fast. That's why things go wrong." He gave a harsh laugh.

9
Around Khartoum

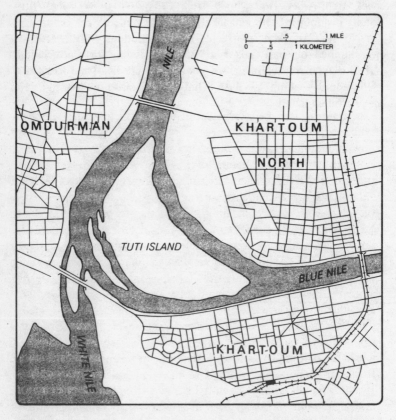

Khartoum is a ship in the sea, the expatriates will tell you, by which they sometimes mean that they are going out of their minds. When they fly back to it from Malakal or El Obeid, El Fasher or Port Sudan, they fall on the cellophaned, wispy airline sandwiches ravenously, as a prelude to civilization itself. Certainly I did that day, guzzling Seven-Up and canned grapefruit, perching on a jump seat behind the pilot in the cockpit of the Boeing, after my muddy pant legs and obvious exhilaration and exhaustion had piqued his curiosity as we sat in the Port Sudan flight office beforehand. He lived next door to the Catholic Club in Khartoum, he told me, when he wasn't at home with his family in Dublin on leave from this job. I asked him if it was a "captain's paradise," but he wouldn't say.

The yellow desert with ash-colored ridges reddened as we flew west, listening to an Alitalia pilot's bemusement at the instructions given him by the control tower in Khartoum. Because his was not the only plane in the sky, he was told to fly fifty miles up the Nile and swing around and back. My new friend, whose name was Larry Smith, was flying at 28,000 feet, so, at 28-times-3-plus-10 miles, he began his own two-and-a-half-degree descent, "as if a moving photograph were activated within your eye."

We discovered we shared several bar buddies in New York, from the Aer Lingus phase of his career. However, I used his name without success at the slave market beside the swimming pool at the Oasis Hotel that afternoon. The commodity was about a dozen single men, each just in from a month or a year alone in the bush. Four British Airways stewardesses lay in deck chairs in a square on the lawn, "London-based," as one of them said. She used the word "we" in speaking of herself, which was confusing because another girl was using the word "one" to describe, plurally, what all of them had done and how they all felt. Their lives were metropolitan; this was a casual stopover for them, a chance for some sun, whereas (speaking for myself) when I blew into town from a visit to Eritrea—or Gilo in Equatoria, or Hamrat esh Sheikh in Kordofan—I not only yearned to lie in a generous lady's arms, I wanted to talk all night and tell her everything I had ever seen or known or done, not only here in Africa but in my whole life, as to somebody loved.

There was certainly a counterfeit element to this emotion, just as my visits to Karora and Gilo themselves had been provisional and quickly wrapped up. But the girls, who might have felt in the mood for such a give-and-take the next evening, back in the rain and cold of Chelsea once again, were not sunning in this sub-Sahel city on their outflight for the purpose of allowing some drifter to pour his haggard, self-imposed loneliness all over them. The one with the pleasantest face was attached for the day to a British pilot with amused, bushy eyebrows and a comfortable belly. Another had clasped both mitts around the arm of a handsome Sudanese, whom she had brought to this small luxury establishment, and whom she presently led off to her room as if he were a jumbo candy bar.

"A man who has a happy family life in Hamburg can have a happy family life here," a German diplomat explained to me, grimacing. His wife sketched camel skulls, bought jewelry and medicated the houseboy. There was everywhere to go and no way to get there—the Komas to visit, for instance, who live on the Ethiopian border in Upper Nile Province and have seldom been visited because the road is open only two months of the year. Or the Murles, who, twenty thousand strong, live to the south of them and, armed with rifles they have borrowed from the Ethiopian Murles, have appropriated much of the Boma Plateau from the local Dinkas, who carry only spears. The Boma Plateau, four thousand feet high, has lots of game and a salubrious climate, once you have crossed the steppe and swampland to reach it. Yet the Murles continue to raid Dinka camps, kidnapping Dinka babies to make more Murles, because their own birthrate, like that of several other Central African tribes, has fallen mysteriously.

North of Khartoum, a visit to the archaeological sites in the Northern Desert was an easier drive, except that a plague of screwworm flies, likely to leave the earnest tourist with larvae embedded in his cheek, had arisen in this region.

I had an American acquaintance who taught at the University of Khartoum and lived in the falling-down Pink Palace, Haile Selassie's residence during his exile from Ethiopia in the late 1930's. He had himself grown up in the court at Addis Ababa, among Christians who might have spit on him if they'd known that he would ever share a meal with a Muslim. His father, a bald white man, had worked for the Emperor, so that as a little boy attending the levees, he was accustomed to walking up behind any white man who was bald and calling him Daddy.

Now many of his playmates from the court were dead or imprisoned in basement dungeons and old hotbox metal truck bodies. Chewing his beard here in Khartoum, he read missionaries' manuscripts and dusty diaries in the archives of the Verona Fathers—

who might not have permitted an Arab to examine them, for fear they would be confiscated. He was studying the nineteenth-century slave trade in the area between the Nile and Abyssinia, not a subject that his Sudanese colleagues much liked to see explored. Meanwhile he avoided the internecine cliques of Ethiopians and Eritreans in the city, and worked on the transmission of his Land Rover, without which he was immobile. There were sites to visit —jebels near the border where the blacks had battled the slavers —and lost file cabinets in some of the district missions where the escapees had fled and which had not been pored through for forty or fifty years. It was scholarship of the loneliest sort, his teaching load was onerous, and the sandstorms of the city were maddening. Because the university was switching away from the English system of giving year-end examinations, the students had been staging strikes; they were also confused and unhappy because the language of instruction in the secondary schools had been shifted from English to Arabic and back. My friend Peter looked at the dancing-harlequin shape of the Nile's upstream legs on the map, the trunk and neck curving gaily toward Egypt, and remembered riding on top of a pillowy lorryload of ostrich feathers for three hundred miles. Now he found himself stock-still, like poor Haile Selassie, overthrown by Il Duce and rotting in this same Pink Palace.

I used to meet a friend of his from time to time, a gloomy, conspiratorial white cleric who insisted that we huddle in the lobbies of obscure hotels as if the walls had ears, while he told me about various jailings, mail openings, incidents of Muslim hostility to Christians, and the embarrassment of trying to introduce an Arab extremist to a Dinka gentleman at a party and have the Arab stare straight through him, as a point of principle. Recently a mob of hundreds of Southerners marching through Khartoum North, carrying a cross, beating drums and waving an Anglican church banner, had stopped the car of the British ambassador, to his discomfiture, to cheer and salute him. However, in the summer of 1976, after the failure of the Mahdist coup attempt and Sadiq al-Mahdi's return to exile in Great Britain, an Arab crowd had shouted in Khartoum's Martyrs' Square, "Down, Down, British Crown!" Major Abul Gassim Ibrahim, in a fiery speech on British collaborationist imperialism, had vowed at another rally in Heroes' Square in Omdurman, "We shall reach Sadiq anywhere!"

A man of niceties, the cleric found it exquisitely disturbing, I suspect, to contemplate his black parishioners, who, as he kept saying, were mostly "the houseboys of the North." He liked being out in turban country where, scarcely ninety years ago, the Mahdi's dervishes had destroyed the armies mustered under Colonel William Hicks and General Valentine Baker. Yet, as a man of conscience, he hated snobbery, and was on pins and needles when trying to explain to me why some of the expatriate community had requested his assignment here. He didn't want to say that they had objected to being preached to by a black African, so, whirling his hands nervously, he accounted for it by saying they had wanted a person whose "frame of reference" was the same.

The Sudanese quite like the English, really, but there has been a general recognition all over the world that the English don't much like England any more. You meet the English everywhere, and over a beer the man will confide to you that going back to the Midlands makes him "feel as if I'm beating my wings against a cage."

An Arabist, a bloodless-looking but romantic fellow, fraily built, bespectacled, a diplomat who lived with his family in western comfort in a villa in the fancy New Extension of the city, used to lecture with excitement around town about General Gordon's doom, as well as the defeats of Britain's other Custers here. He was one of those people who hunger for a recklessness that is absent from their own makeup, except as a longing, and who go out on assignment to desperately poor countries to try to fill the hole. The knowledge that only twelve hours east by northeast by truck the leery Hadendowa were riding about on camels with six-foot swords, feuding with the Bani-Amer, and that not much farther in the opposite direction some of the Kababish were raiding southward to drive the Baggara away from traditional Baggara watering points, invigorated him. Yet despite all his ardor for unreconstructed tribalism, he would tell me that this vast swatch of Africa was a political democracy, its People's Assembly a voice of the people, that there was no corruption to speak of, no political police—and then urgently interrupt himself to have me pledge again not to print his name.

Another man, a friend with whom I traveled occasionally, appeared, from the way he liked to put on the dog in the evening, to be running away from his Whitechapel accent—that and the dark-ish tint which some seafarer had appliquéd to his ancestry. He was a mortarman who had gone into disaster relief work after his battalion had been withdrawn, first from the Suez Canal after the 1956 blitzkrieg victory against Egypt, and then from counterinsurgency duty on Cyprus in 1959. It was not that he objected to the politics of withdrawal, only that he didn't think you needed an army if that was going to be your policy. In the Sinai he had regularly poked his head into a tent of foreign legionnaires camped next to his unit, to shout *"Achtung"* and see those gaunt S.S. veterans of the proscribed regiments from the Russian Front spring to their feet. On Cyprus—another tale—the guerrillas on the mountain that his platoon was supposed to patrol sent word that they were going to celebrate a wedding in a little village in no-man's-land, and would fire only if fired upon. His sergeant, an unconventional type, not only accepted the proposal without requesting approval from higher up, but walked into the village at noon the day before to ask the white-bearded chieftain who pretended to act as a mere go-between whether his lads couldn't dance at the wedding as well. They did just that, stacking their weapons inside the door and dancing arm over arm to an *oud,* Greek-fashion, with the foe.

Now, with no more crown colonies to defend, my friend was organizing relief shipments for the foreign destitute and reading war paperbacks on weekends. In the meantime, he had married on another continent, but his wife had left him and he had waylaid her lover with a tire iron and beaten him nearly to death.

It's a truism that people who are misfits in their own country may flourish in another, especially a "backward" or exotic one. Rough living conditions exhilarate them and distract them from old bugaboos, much as the austerity of war might do. Clearly, more than a few of the expatriates I hobnobbed with needed all of the primitive imperatives they could find, plus the superstructure of Muslim ritual and ceremony, to damp them down and superimpose a substitute for self-control. Sometimes I find this kind of thing reassuring myself. I knew a plump, effeminate corporate negotiator from New York who would fly off the handle—turn into a harridan—if you disagreed with whatever he had to say about a subject as arcane as, let's say, John Lindsay. He had a history of nervous breakdowns in the United States, and yet in the company of ceremonious, galabiehed, god-fearing Arabs he became infinitely cheerful and relaxed. It was a pleasure to see how he relaxed.

The English, as a bright young business buccaneer used to put it to me, were "looking for a fighting chance." In London, he said, unless you happened to be able to live in "W. 1," you were going to be excluded from whatever action there was. He worked as an investment scout in offices in the New Extension, doing research for a seedy Saudi prince of immense wealth whose name has been bruited about the world in connection with corruption on the grandest scale. Also, he had been seconded by the prince to assist the Sudan government, and had got so sleek and affable, while keeping one ear to the ground, that people who remembered him from his earlier incarnation in Vientiane told me that they "hardly recognized the chap at first."

F. T. had a large cheerful nose, pink Folkestone skin, wore sleeveless twill shooting jackets, and enjoyed recounting the blunders that his patron's competitors, the Kuwaitis, had made. We met in the Indian Club, where nobody was around to observe us except for the proverbial barefoot servant padding about. With a nose for news, an agent's knowledgeability, he would spin me around to the fenced compound from which the Palestinians had operated until the year before—a place tightly shut up and padlocked now.

A lot of agenting needs to be done, and in the evening he drove out to a stable in the desert where he kept his red Arabian mare, and galloped on the sands in the sunset, through the starlight, for a while. By chance I might run into F. T. afterwards in the Hilton lobby, just in the interval between his desert ride and a party he was invited to. As we stood there one time, a Sudan Airways stewardess wandered in on business of her own—a brown Arab-Hamite girl of a beauty comparable to that of the Eurasian girls who fascinated British colonial officers in the tropics of the Orient. She was not invited to this party for the "Major" who was Minister for Youth and Sport, but she looked so pretty in a black and flowered gown that he waved her over, stroked her neck, squeezed her shoulder and suggested they connect later, while she gazed up at him.

It was very pleasant, living here, he said; he was sick of English snobbery, and liked the American way of tucking in, doing a job and judging people for themselves. "I'm not like most English in that. And I respect the way they're at least trying to 'develop' in the 'developing' countries."

Still, in this nation so pinched for foreign exchange, a friend of his who scouted for some of the local middlemen had clients who were in debt to him for as much as $40,000. And at the Excelsior Hotel—a step down from the Hilton, a step up from the Metropole—my Danish crop-duster acquaintances who drank at the bar had simply quit flying and come to roost in Khartoum because the government had fallen four months behind in paying them. A country without telephones or electricity was good terrain to fly low over, because you had no wires to slam into. But a country without lights or phones was also a country without money. Even when they got their pay, sometimes they had no fuel to fly with and no "dust" to spray.

In that madhouse Excelsior lobby, full of Trucial State princes with falcons on their wrists that they had bought at Jebel Marra, and Citibank representatives arriving from New York, Belgian sugar experts, Dutch environmental consultants up for a weekend from Jonglei in the Sudd, Italian pipeline specialists from Atbara and Port Sudan, International Union of Child Welfare and International Voluntary Service do-gooders, Austrian white hunters and French arms salesmen, there were a lot of brutish-looking faces—faces unformed, *undecided*. And of course these were mostly men who had either lost or given up their wives. In such a crowd it could be intimidating to trudge in unexpectedly, hungry, thirsty, caked with sand, lugging a backpack. Yet I usually fared pretty well, because in this garb I stood out. One of the clerks used to pretend I had reservations, turning away the next person who showed up with the explanation that the telex machine had broken. Once, the same man bailed me out of a misunderstanding at the bar with a couple of dollars from his own pocket. He was sensible, soft-spoken, and, unlike the other employees, wore an English-cut sports jacket. I think he may have been a police plainclothesman; yet I also think he did me special favors, not as part of his police job, but because work like mine—wherein I vanished, reappeared and then vanished again—appealed to him. He took an interest in the whereabouts of other foreign journalists; he liked the fact that I asked after them just before they showed up, unannounced, and, I suspect, he saw a similarity between my activities and what he thought his own work should be.

The plainclothesmen in the provinces were not as experienced, and very much less friendly. Once, at Juba Airport, I had to make believe I was an agent from the American embassy to prevent all my notes from being seized, and the bulging walletful of money in my side pocket often at first looked like a pistol, instead of a harbinger of tourism, to them. But, again in Khartoum, when I was waiting at the External Information Administration Office for another letter of accreditation, a man who seemed to be a senior police official—also in tweedy, well-cut dress, with an intelligent sort of face—and who, by his manner, regarded the Information people as paper-pushers, suddenly came in and sat down, speaking slowly but briefly. "Mr. Hoagland. I was passing. You can go where you want to. I am going to give you my name. It is a code name. You understand that? We have a police radio. It is a court of first resort in some of the towns, you might say, and if somebody asks you questions you can give them the name and they will call me even if I am traveling."

My favorite of the big-league American troubleshooters who trundled through Khartoum was John Goodrich, Citibank's manager in Cairo. I had interviewed him in that great city the previous year, and since he knew of nothing bad that had resulted, we ate breakfast together at the Excelsior. In his Michigan accent and McNamara haircut he'd ask for cornflakes, but have to settle for scrambled eggs. He would swallow a Coricidin pill for one of the colds he came down with regularly in this *haboob* (sandstorm) country, enjoy chopped mutton and rice or twisted-fish for lunch, and at night, in a tartan jacket, would duck out of the dinner segment of a state dinner to prepare his after-dinner remarks—back to his cramped, dim room at the Excelsior, which he thought "more central" than the flossy Hilton, more "part of the life of the city." Pushing open a balky elevator door, he said he liked to come down here "for the change of pace" from Cairo, although, needless to say, most officers at Citibank would have considered the pace of doing business in *Cairo* quite enough of a change.

Goodrich was amiably avuncular to Chase Manhattan's' young liaison man in the Sudan, Warren Townsend—who, in turn, found the East German commercial attaché walking up to him at diplomatic functions in a stunning silver-and-gray uniform to ask his advice about whom to contact to expedite one's paperwork.

Another American with an international company that had been courted by the government said it took him seven months just to open a "two-man, two-girl" office. No real procedures had been invented yet. Constant cross-checking was necessary between the ministries of Labor, Industry, Finance, Trade, and the Bank of the Sudan. So often the authority to sign a particular document would fall between two stools. Power didn't coincide with the titles in the chain of command, and ministers, ministers of state, undersecretaries, directors-general and directors didn't know what their responsibilities were and were afraid to ask. For weeks you chased around in a miasma of hospitality and optimism, everybody avowing whatever would please you.

A Sudanese who worked for Shell Oil Company told me, by way of making some distinctions, that the Egyptians had too much government, a top-heavy bureaucracy going back four thousand years, but no economy to govern, whereas the Saudis were bedouins, building streets of marble with their surplus billions, who had no civil service. Egyptians were "insular" in their cultural snobbery, but turned into "grabby glad-handers" and hypocrites when offered high wages in Riyadh. They were ready to stake everything upon making a satisfactory first impression, whereas the Saudis remained personally austere, but with a new-wealth arrogance, along with their pretensions to racial and religious purity. He said overoptimism was indeed the plague of the Sudan, imbalancing everybody's planning, but that the tribalism that lingered on perhaps helped keep people more altruistic and community-minded. A Sudanese, he said, expected to chat with his whole circle of friends every day or so, and if he didn't, another man would come knocking on his door well before the end of the week to discover what was wrong.

In this city with German, Hellenic, Italian, Syrian, Egyptian and Armenian clubs, Shell Oil, like the other local corporations or banks, had established its own "club" for executive personnel, where in the evenings and on the Sabbath they ate roast lamb, boiled eggs, cucumbers, onions, eggplant and raw lamb kidneys in hot sauce, content to be together after-hours as well as at work. These business-oriented Sudanese were a fairly liberal group—their more conventional contemporaries had gone into the army or a ministry—and they remarked to me, after nibbling and pushing the food away, how other people outside were batting their brains out to earn the wherewithal to eat such stuff.

Sudanese will pat each other's shoulders three, four or half a dozen times between regular bouts of shaking hands—catching, pulling the friend's fingers to rest against the heart, holding them there, patting his fingers and hand, pledging and repledging that "There is one God!" So, with expectations raised so high, it's no wonder that nobody believes anything will quite work out as planned. As early as March, Khartoum's temperature hits 105 degrees by 2 P.M., when working hours end. Whatever pep that graced the place has already slacked off by noon, though if you had wandered into a government office with an inquiry around ten you would have had to wait until after "second breakfast," facing in the meantime many among the junior staff who are palpably complacent at just occupying a chair.

But Union Carbide's manager, John Herzog, who is a clear-faced, practical man of forty, sounded sanguine. "It's a young country with upright people, a better than average start-up for us." His factory foreman, a Kenyan, added that "the learning curve was very fast," pointing out a Sudanese on the assembly line stuffing Eveready flashlight batteries into boxes "just like a machine."

Herzog had been stationed in India, the Philippines, Singapore, Costa Rica and the Ivory Coast. Union Carbide is a special case among American businesses because it pioneers in developing countries before there is much electricity around. For instance, more than ninety percent of Sudanese women cannot read, and so if the government is to evangelize and unify its people, it must reach them via battery radio. The company ventured in for a feasibility study in 1972, as soon as Nimeiri started his rightward swing, and within four years had built a $2.5-million plant employing two hundred and forty people, which operated in the black in its first year.

Herzog had received a marketing monopoly and various tax breaks, because an operation such as his, involving manufacture as well as sales, was what the government wanted. Unfortunately, all the ingredients of transistor batteries—zinc, magnesium, ammonium, carbon black, cornstarch, flour, wrapping paper and adhesives—had to be imported, with a large inventory maintained against the likelihood of transport delays. Even for what was only a modest factory, a full-time fixer had to be employed on the docks at Port Sudan, extracting these few items from the miles of rotting goods. Another fixer was needed to obtain from the Treasury enough foreign exchange for Herzog to pay his suppliers, because the competition was fierce for what little there was. He had a dozen salesmen distributing the batteries, mostly by truck, each going out with a driver for three weeks out of every month. They carried their own food and water, slept on the ground, traveled at night during the hottest season. An American traveling for Sterling Drug, another pioneering company, distributing aspirin and liver pills—which can be nearly the panacea a flashlight is—had broken down in the Darfur desert, and the driver and the American were digging in the sand for water with cracked lips and blurry eyes before another lorry happened along.

With government railroads and riverboats usually venally operated and antiquated, lorries are private enterprise at its romantic best in Africa. Also buses, as in socialist Tanzania, where two drivers will race for a hundred miles, tooting their horns, while you and the other passengers lean out the windows, pounding fists, sticks and spears against the sides to keep your candidate driving fast. Tanzania has been cross-hatched into communal agricultural settlements, which might be described either as a system of old-fashioned serfdom or as a revolutionary means of attempting to wrench the country into the twenty-first century. The snafus are colossal: a country that has been feeding itself since the dawn of time now has to import even maize. In the winter of 1976, just after my visit there, a huge stockpile of sisal, one of the nation's chief commodities, burned on the docks at Dar es Salaam simply because so much development money had been directed to the settlements that the city's water system was derelict and five of its few fire engines were out of commission. But the buses work wonderfully in Tanzania.

The Sudan, less advanced than Tanzania, has fewer roads and fewer buses. Still, the cabs of the lorries are upholstered in slick pinks and purples, with handmade tassels and cushions, like the overstuffed, low sofas in the driver's house. Merchants, teachers and doctors ride in the cabs, jammed three abreast next to the driver and paying a dollar or two extra for that privilege. A figure somewhat like a bush pilot in the Alaskan wilds, he is hostly, offering around a bottle of tea, a packet of sesame seeds or peanuts, a stick of sugarcane to suck, and will have a figurehead on the front of the hood—perhaps a winged female decorated with a beard and funny hat. The engine itself is painted yellow, pink or blue, and he has a boy in back with the mass of passengers to lift the hood and polish the engine whenever he stops. Because in America a lifted hood is a signal of distress, you think at first that a good proportion of the trucks you encounter have broken down.

In the North, where many drivers either have their own or drive a relative's lorry, accidents are uncommon. But in the South, the owner is a carpetbagging Arab—as the local people perceive it—with several other irons in the fire, or he wouldn't be living so far from home; he must hire drivers. You cannot travel any considerable distance without passing a turned-over lorry, elephantine, thrusting its rusty wheels up forlornly, while a few survivors squat in the shade of a blue gum tree, waiting for a lift or for help in getting it righted.

Trains in the desert tip over too, because the tracks run across the sand without much roadbed. You see upended locomotives; and in the season for haboobs, when the air is eerily silent, as in a snow blizzard, you stop and start, stop and start, while a crewman walks ahead of the engine with a shovel to clear away the sand.

But Herzog was a lorry lover, and paid his drivers mostly with incentive bonuses. He thought they probably did more for their country than, say, the Cotton Public Corporation, which had lost tens of millions of dollars in foreign exchange in each of several recent years through sheer bad timing in marketing the Sudan's main export. As neighbors he had biscuit and enamelware factories, and what he called a "cottage industry" in plastics. The country had "an instant craving" for floor tiles, doors, window frames and tubing for tables, chairs and beds, but a foreign manufacturer had best begin, he said, by reading the new 600-page six-year plan—which as yet existed only in Arabic—in order to calculate just where he could argue that his business fit in.

10
The Mahdists, to Now

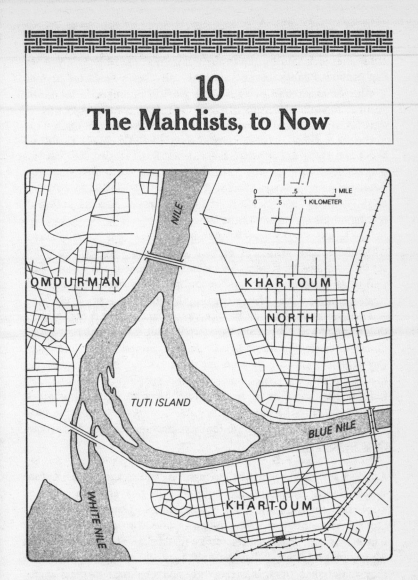

Because of the circles I moved in, I kept hearing about tomato-paste and citrus-canning factories; the hundred thousand acres to be planted to coffee and tea on the Uganda and Zaire frontiers; thirty thousand acres of rice at Aweil, and more at Malakal; seventy thousand acres irrigated by gravity-flow for food and money crops on the Peukow Plains; teak plantations and pineapple farms at Yei. The government, trying to sustain a pitch of optimism in the newspapers, announced repeatedly that U.S. Steel was prospecting in the Red Sea Hills and Chevron Oil Co. in Southern Kordofan.

But U.S. Steel must be prospecting in thirty other countries. What was going to happen, I asked a minister, if it decided that this one small venture among so many was not worth following up? After so many projects and timetables that had failed to pan out, mightn't there be a backlash against the regime and its notion of relying on the capitalism of the West?

The minister was a graceful man in his late thirties, an intellectual without hauteur, who was dressed in a light gray-blue suit that set off his blue-black skin. An idealist, a former ambassador, married to an American, he was, according to his friends, one of the inner circle who had been struggling to maintain a pro-West bent.

Looking away, he took his time about answering. Yes, he knew that some of the Americans wondered about this. What they didn't understand was that these press releases were part of a "dialogue" (by which I suspect that he meant a battle) between differing factions within the government. "Some people are cynical. They don't believe anything we're doing will come to anything at all. It is necessary that the papers print these stories so that people have some evidence that things are really happening, that there is something to hope for."

In the campaign for soft loans and technical assistance, the Sudanese have leaned toward the Russians, and talked to the Kansas Wheat Board (Nimeiri spent 1965 at Fort Leavenworth, and has a soft spot for Kansas). They have looked to German capital and Dutch engineering, and have fallen in love with the Chinese. The Chinese are a special success story in Africa. Themselves from a "developing" country, they haven't a lot of money to spend, but they materialize unobtrusively with several dozen medical teams willing to work in the back villages, and several thousand laborers and technicians who bring in their own food and machinery and sleep—including the supervising architects and engineers—on rush mats on the ground on-site when necessary while putting a bridge across the Nile at Wad Medani, or building the huge Hassaheisa textile factory that employs two thousand people.

A decade ago the Chinese made their share of mistakes in Africa and were expelled from several countries for meddling. Since then they have proven remarkably adaptive. They buy more Sudanese cotton than anybody else—and don't sell it at a profit later, like the Russians. In a town such as Juba, you meet a passel of Chinese, led by a severe-looking woman doctor, living in a compound behind the offices of the earnest Lutherans and Kuwait's robed and cryptic representatives. "We, too, unlike the Kuwaitis and Lutherans, have gone through the crucible," she tells the Africans she works with. Besides shipping in replacement parts for Russian weaponry and emphasizing quick road building, the Chinese try to do at least one prestige project in each country, such as the Tanzam Railway that links Zambia to Tanzania. In Khartoum, this has been Friendship Hall, a glass complex of conference rooms and theaters, a tall showpiece on the Nile which every visitor from the Third World admires.

But Khartoum does not enhance itself by playing up to the immediacy of the Nile, as Cairo manages to. I had come to the Sudan partly because I loved Cairo. If Istanbul and Cairo delighted me, how much I expected of Khartoum! The name means "elephant trunk," referring to the spit of land curving to the juncture of the two rivers. But instead of reverberating with the luxury of their flow, as an ancient desert city should, Khartoum turns its back upon them and looks inward. The city center lies about where the elephant's ear would be.

The original community at the Nile's grand fork was razed by the Mahdists after their ten-month siege in 1885. They founded Omdurman, across the White Nile, for their own capital, as a sort of alternative, which in fact it remains to this day. A sprawling brown town of mud walls and multicolored people all shaken up in the hopper of slavery, Omdurman is still the hub of Arab society. Khartoum was rebuilt by Kitchener soon after his reconquest in 1898. He had vengefully dug up the skeleton of the Mahdi from the wreck of the tomb which the Mahdists had constructed back in 1885—a dome said to have been visible a three-day walk away. He had thrown the remains of "the Guided One" in the river, saving just the skull, which he intended using possibly as an inkstand or a drinking cup, until British public opinion forbade it. Punitively, he laid out the city so that the principal streets took the shape of a Union Jack, as a permanent mark of the British boot upon what would become the capital once again.

Although this pattern has been obscured by now, no other character has emerged to replace it. Glassy hotels and sand-block office buildings are thrown up as if the day before yesterday with hand-mixed cement whose left-over heaps still obstruct the streets. Behind Khartoum Mosque, whose twin minarets are strung with lights, is United Nations Square—which is a bus station. The buses are mostly Mazda pickup trucks with benches fixed in back; also Bedford desert trucks and crowded Peugeot taxis. Along the north side, you can pick through bookstalls and shop among three square blocks of grocers' booths, each lit by a bare Hungarian light bulb and proffering piles of onions, oranges, limes, catfish, perch, goats' feet, calves' feet and Korean chewing gum. The poorer peddlers sit cross-legged on the broken sidewalk in front of a pyramid of bruised tomatoes or a straw-plaited basket of beans. What with the lines of beggars at the entrances to the mosque, it is a scene of exotic poverty, but lacks the seethe and tumult of Cairo's crowds, which seem to leap past mere poverty, bearing the future behind them.

You can visit the zoo and watch the desert tortoises screw, which they spent one whole afternoon, by my count, doing. The tigers are thin and the lions wrinkled, but there are fat warthogs and hyenas, and a number of plain stray dogs doing fill-in duty in cages that otherwise would be empty. Also, slim northern giraffes, and a mendicant elephant who has very long eyelashes and a Ho Chi Minh beard, a white rhinoceros with a face much too large for it, and a Nile-sized hippo in a splendid water tank.

You can stroll along the avenue that fronts the Blue Nile, under Kitchener's cool banyan trees. The sparrows are so unaccustomed to being fed that if bread is thrown to them they fly away and only find it later accidentally. A few poor men take a Sabbath bath, washing both their clothes and bodies in the river, but modestly, so that either their galabiehs or drawers remain on. They squat to urinate, instead of standing like a Westerner, then kick dirt over the wet spot.

A few boys swim across to the island of Tuti, their bobbing heads and fragments of their arms all that is visible until they reach a lovely cape of beach and run and bask. Finally they swim back, almost lost in the perspective of the river until they approach the bank once again, climb out, slip on their flip-flops, and leave —except for one boy, with a clean bandage around his leg, who notices a ragged boy sleeping in a cast-off red sweater and man's pair of long pants, and begins stoning him.

A tiny two-penny ferry slides over to Tuti. The island is part desert, part sandy truck garden, an island powered by donkeys, though it is right across from Friendship Hall. The donkeys, pacified with long-stemmed clover, ride to and fro, carrying perishables like ice and milk to the island. Half a dozen human porters with their shirts pulled over their heads lug 150-pound bags of dura or charcoal on their shoulders onto the ferry from a delivery truck, ride over and load the bags into a horse cart. Tuti also has long-tailed doves, and goats that stand on their hind legs to nibble the yellow-blossomed trees. There is a spacious little mosque, painted green and white inside, with people sitting cross-legged reading the Koran and Hadith, the horns of the crescent over the pulpit curving up like a Viking's horns, while an irrigation pump thumps steadily nearby.

Mowlid el Nabi, the birthday of the Prophet, was observed on March 2, 1977, with ceremonies in the mosques. The night before this event, as for a sort of Christmas Eve, each of the Three Towns staged an outdoor celebration, partly for the city's children but with loudspeakers preaching.

Islam puts the same emphasis as Christianity upon the necessity of sharing with the poor, and embraces the same intrinsic idea that the poor shall inherit the earth. Just as it was many of the Hebrew poor who first believed in the divinity of Jesus, so it was originally the poor who supported Mohammed against the resistance of the wealthier, established classes of Mecca and Medina.

I went to Khartoum's fairgrounds, as did the President. There, along one side of a great square, separate pavilions had been set up, representing the different sects. These tents were grandly decorated with bunting, lights, painted holy inscriptions—the Arabic lettering like smoke signals—and richly figured Oriental rugs to kneel on, while the imams and ulemas spoke one after another, competing for the crowds. Some preached a formal-sounding, reasoned sermon; others chanted in a tranced and passionate two- or three-note monotone.

For the children, vendors hawked crusty sugar cakes, red wax dolls and paper baubles. For the grown-ups, there were charred tidbits of shish kebab on bread, and a ventriloquist who was the butt of a wisecracking dummy he held on his lap. Several knots of dervishes were humbly dancing—the old-fashioned "whirling dervish" of Mahdia fame is now an individual seldom seen and rather patronized, like our Great Smokies hillbilly. Other circles sat around free-lance divines, each with a Coleman lantern and a pot of smoking incense, exchanging enthusiastic invocations with them. A great many families had come with picnic suppers and spread a cloth on the ground—three or four generations together, the women much freer in manner than usual, enjoying the lights and noise.

President Nimeiri's presence was another matter. The mounted police on prancing horses, the admirably polished limousines, the packed, murmuring masses around the pavilion where he had chosen to worship, added a particular national solemnity to the occasion—for once, a mesmerizing Cairo-type mob crush and energy, on top of the religious urgency of the fair, an urgency which in Christianity has largely been sapped away.

Politics in the modern Sudan begins with the Mahdist Ansar, who, during the years 1881–85, triumphantly threw off Turco-Egyptian-British control, and were not beaten for good until the Battle of Omdurman, thirteen years later. Although the British referred to them contemptuously as "dervishes," *Ansar.* ("Helpers") had been the plural name given to the first supporters of the Prophet; and a mahdi, a "guided," messianic holy man, a spiritual and temporal ruler, had been expected in contemporary doctrine. Neither the Mahdi himself, who died, probably of typhoid, only five months after storming Khartoum, nor the Khalifa Abdallahi, who succeeded him, employed this power overly benevolently. But with victory they became nationalists as well as religious doyens. That is, although the Ansar were defeated in their attempts to expand the Mahdia into an empire embracing Egypt, Abyssinia and all of the territory of the Nilotic blacks, they did achieve for the space of more than a dozen years a protonation almost the size of Western Europe, an amalgam of tribes that had not dreamed of such an alliance before. Even the Dinkas, who fought against enslavement and the incorporation of their territory into the Mahdi's state, incorporated the man himself into their religious beliefs.

The Mahdi had grown up in Dongola, in old Nubia, north of Khartoum on the Nile. He was a Sufi, an ascetic and a learned man, but the cutting edge of his support was not his fellow Northern sophisticates, but the Ta'isha and other tribesmen of the Baggara group, renowned for the length of their spears, in the wild and woolly west of the country. After a number of preliminary victories in Kordofan and the successful siege of El Obeid—and after annihilating the sizable Egyptian army under Colonel William Hicks that had been sent to punish them—they forged an alliance with the Hadendowas of the Red Sea Hills, seven hundred miles to the northeast, who were known for wielding enormous swords. Battling for the Mahdi under their magnificent chieftain Osman Digna, the Hadendowas butchered another Egyptian army marching under General Valentine Baker.

As the Arabist John Waterbury has pointed out, these nomads from both east and west poured into Khartoum and Omdurman after Gordon's fall like Andrew Jackson's frontiersmen taking over Washington, D.C. They ousted the effete Nile Valley bureaucrats who had so tamely served the preceding regimes. Though a killing famine and a cruel decade of administrative confusion ensued, for the first time a feeling of political unity extended over a crazy quilt of tribal homelands from the Egyptian border nearly down to what is now Juba, and from Darfur to the Red Sea. The Expected Mahdi (as he styled himself, in anticipation of his eschatological role) had visualized a Kingdom of God without borders, wherein the infidel would be conquered and converted and Islam's own purity restored. So he might be disappointed, were he vouchsafed a glimpse of Africa now, to learn that he only effected the birth of a nation.

The Ansar had hated the British, but after Kitchener's machine-gun reconquest—the Ansar charged at dawn, at Omdurman, instead of in the darkness, and, believing that supernatural aid would come to them, within range of British gunboats on the river, instead of in the desert—they began to perceive that the danger really lay not so much with the British as with the Egyptians. They might wind up being not just ruled from but annexed by Cairo. The best defense against Egyptian nationalist ambitions, therefore, was to court Great Britain. For their part, the British flourished as a colonial power because they were romantics as well as realists. They were an orderly people who knew how to keep their eye on the ball and yet, through their tolerance for eccentricity, leave plenty of leeway for individual brilliance. Everywhere, they seem, too, to have admired their old tribal adversaries, from Indian Gurkha and Kenyan Masai to the cicatrized Shilluk (whose very name in Arabic means "scar") and "Fuzzy-Wuzzy" Hadendowas. They treated the captured Osman Digna better than the U.S. army dealt with Sitting Bull, and soon started to encourage the main contingent of Mahdists to agree to a rapprochement—first pensioning and then, in 1926, knighting the Mahdi's posthumous son.

This man, Abdel Rahman al-Mahdi, proved useful to the British during World War I in countering a Turkish effort to enlist pan-Islamic sentiments on the German-Turkish side. (A victory for the Turks, after all, would only have brought back Ottoman rule.) Later he became a great landowner, and there was even talk of setting up a Mahdist monarchy under the sponsorship of the British Crown. From a British standpoint, Abdel Rahman acted as an important counterbalance to the Khatmia brotherhood, who were the second principal political and religious faction in nineteenth- and early-twentieth-century Sudan.

The Khatmia were a pious desert sect organized by a missionary from Arabia named Osman al-Mirghani (1793–1853). Although the Khatmia were comparably fundamentalist in their religiosity, they had regarded the Expected Mahdi as a spurious figure, had not, in any case, opposed Ottoman-Egyptian rule—indeed, had furnished many effendi clerks and functionaries—and had not joined with the Ansar to fight Generals Gordon, Kitchener and the rest. In fact, because they had been persecuted during the Mahdia, the Khatmia welcomed the Anglo-Egyptian Condominium which was established afterwards. Their leader, Ali al-Mirghani, was knighted in 1916.

The Khatmia also found their beginnings in the Sudan along the Dongola stretch of the Nubian Nile, where the Mahdi was born. Nubia (not to be confused with the remote Nuba Mountains and Nuba people, far to the south) had been a cultural center since the Pharaonic dynasties, and Dongola was the first rendezvous and stronghold of the nomad Arab bands who had infiltrated and gradually eclipsed Christian Nubia by around the fourteenth century. Previously it had been the capital of a Christian kingdom which for some six hundred years had succeeded in staving off, by clever treaty writing, a Muslim effort at conquest from the direction of Egypt that had begun in the year 651.

But the Khatmia, for all their wish to proselytize, did not lean to the use of the sword, and did not much concern themselves with wild tribes living hundreds of miles away from the Nile. They had a loving obsession with the river itself; Aswan was not a cutoff point for them. Sensible of the successive civilizations that had flourished along its banks, they tended to think of the oneness of the valley of the Nile all the way from Khartoum to the Mediterranean, two thousand miles downstream. Though they also possessed a vision of independence, Egypt did not frighten them.

It was perhaps a *thinner* nation the Khatmia envisaged, in other words—a country comprising the already enlightened, not a kind of God's empire enlisting barbarous peoples from Gondar in Abyssinia to the Tibesti Mountains in what is nowadays Chad. Though they wanted the British to leave eventually, they were grateful that the British had overthrown the Mahdist tyranny, and in the years between the final rout of Khalifa Abdallahi and the First World War, the British favored and leaned on them. When, however, a movement for independence from Great Britain became a threat within Egypt itself, the British naturally turned around and cultivated Abdel Rahman al-Mahdi, who could be counted on to oppose Egyptian ambitions to annex the Nile south of Aswan. Abdel Rahman seemed prepared to see the British linger on, if this would forestall an attempt to "unify" the Nile under Egyptian auspices.

To say that the Mahdists resisted and the Khatmia advocated merging with Egypt is to oversimplify. The political descendants of the Khatmia, Prime Minister Ismail al-Azhari and his National Union party, won the first parliamentary elections, held in 1953, on the strength of their opposition to British colonial authority. But then abruptly, in 1955, they dropped their cry for a union along the Nile. By linking their fortunes with those of the cosmopolitan Egyptians, they helped their nation wriggle free of Great Britain four years earlier than Nigeria and seven years before Kenya, for instance. But as soon as the opportunity presented itself, they plumped for and—like a finesse in the game of bridge—obtained independence from Egypt as well.

World War II had aroused powerful impulses of nationalism throughout the Middle East, which had been such a cockpit for the Europeans anyway. To see the Germans, British and French jockeying and battling was infectious. The colonial regimes already had foundered during the stagnancy of the Great Depression, when all around the world colonial budgets had shrunk, until even the hopes of an administrator with the best intentions for his region had failed to amount to anything.

The National Unionists were mainly a party of city people. Mr. Azhari had been a mathematics instructor at Gordon College in Khartoum; and grafted onto the original devout Khatmia faction of mystics of the Nile was a contrasting mélange of liberal civil servants, merchants, professionals, intellectuals and labor organizers, some of them educated in Cairo and few of them afraid of Cairo ideas. The Ansar supported the rival Umma party. *Umma* means "nation," with overtones of a religious or pan-Islamic "nation." This grouping was peasant and nomad—traditionalist and rural—in its voting appeal. Once independence had been attained, the conservative tilt of the Umma politicians seemed more representative of the country than the secular, vaguely progressive notions of some of the townsmen, who looked to what Gamal Abdel Nasser was doing in Egypt for inspiration.

There were obvious anomalies: reverent Khatmia imams voting with the free-thinking tradespeople and university community of Khartoum against equally reverent Umma imams. Later, many in the Khatmia camp split off from the National Union party to form the People's Democratic party, which remained attuned to events in Egypt but sometimes was in alliance with the Umma parliamentarians out of a religious identity of interest. The Kababish Arabs, however—to take another example—would logically long since have thrown in their lot with the Ansar, back during the Mahdia, to storm the fat burghers of Khartoum. Instead, they had rejected the Mahdi's overtures—their nazir was beheaded for it—and had welcomed the British victory in 1898, because the Baggara, their tribal enemies, were at the core of the Mahdi's support. Thus they voted with the National Unionists.

The Umma party had a solider base. Scarcely seven months after independence, in 1956, its leader, Abdullah Khalil, became prime minister. But the civilian parliamentarians squabbled fruitlessly and egocentrically, it seemed to almost everybody, as the civil war in the South began and spread and turned intractable. There were machinations from Egypt to contend with, too, and an economy beginning to lag so disheartening behind the Sudan's theoretical potential that the country would become known as the Sick Man of Africa. By the tacit consent of both Umma and Khatmia leaders, General Ibrahim Abboud took over in November 1958.

Though Abboud, like Nimeiri later, was Nasserist by inclination, his regime was strangely stodgy and inactive. Thus, again, the Umma were dominant in several coalitions during the four and a half years of parliamentary government which separated the end of Abboud's six-year rule and Colonel Nimeiri's May 1969 "Revolution." Under Abboud, guerrilla warfare had enveloped the South, but, with civilians again in charge in Khartoum, the worst massacres of Southern civilians occurred. Too often, the Assembly seemed only a debating society for the rival smart sets of Khartoum, whereas a good many out-of-the-way tribes had only a single candidate to vote for—their sheikh or chief. At that, they were lucky, compared to the Ngok Dinkas of Southern Kordofan, for example, who were "represented" in the Assembly by the nazir of their old slaver foes and neighbors, the Homr Arabs.

In 1944, Sudanese studying in Cairo had organized a Sudanese Communist party. In 1950, the Sudanese Workers' Trade Union Federation was formed, with leadership from the twenty-five thousand railway workers and from the Communists, as well as some egging-on by itinerant kibitzers from Britain's Labour party. Communism and trade unionism alike were suppressed with special rigor by the Abboud and Nimeiri governments, which didn't have to reckon with any widespread sympathy for them among the populace. Even today a distinction is drawn between both individuals and foreign countries which can be said to follow "a scripture," be it Muslim, Christian or Jewish, and those that don't, such as the Communists, or Southern tribes of animist persuasion. Underground, however, the Communist party still exerts a considerable pull upon some of the students at the University of Khartoum, as well as on older educated people who remember the idealism of its leaders.

It is argued across Africa that a single party, nationally based, is in a better position to champion the hinterlands, and wrestle them into an equitable relation to the national economy, than a dawdling, filibustering, multiparty parliament, which outside the cities, is unlikely to be freely elected at all, but bound to hereditary leaders and tribal or historical enmities (such as the Mahdist-Khatmia split). On domestic matters, so this contention goes, the party itself, in its councils and at the level of "village democracy," can evade the obstruction of feudal sheikhs and function as an unofficial parliament better than a supposedly unfettered body. And while we Westerners can scoff at the notion of "one-party participatory democracy" in socialist Eastern Europe, in the context of the utter urgency of Africa—malnutrition, drought, secessionist princelings, digging-stick and Bedford-lorry economies—to do so may be too facile.

President Nimeiri founded the Sudanese Socialist Union in January 1972 to replace all previous parties. He probably had in mind a locally structured model, such as Julius Nyerere's Tanganyika African National Union, rather than the top-heavy, Cairo-centered Arab Socialist Union of Nasser and Sadat. He didn't intend to go to Nyerere's extreme in Tanzania—moving his capital out of Khartoum, or centering the nation's very life within the villages. But only 11 percent of the Sudan's people are classified as urban, and 98 percent of its foreign exchange earnings are from agricultural products. By 1985, the government plans envisage that the country should provide 40 percent of the vegetables and 60 percent of the grain of the entire Arab world. A system of so-called village development committees must have seemed a natural instrument of progress.

The problem was that because the Right had tried to overthrow him in 1970, and the Left in 1971, Nimeiri inevitably conceived of his party at the same time as being another agency to protect his own power. Thus the function of the SSU became ambiguous: to sniff out discontent, like the army, as well as to dispel it. Established politicians of every stripe were told that they could belong and argue policy honestly, providing only that they joined on an individual basis, but in practice most were not allowed to do so.

What makes Nimeiri intriguing is that he did not leave it at that. Having set the stage for a military dictatorship, he kept reaching out for a civilian balance. During my visit, the First Vice-President was Rashid al-Tahir Bakr, forty-seven, a politician of some ability. A former Speaker of the People's Assembly, he had been an idealist of the Muslim Brotherhood during his university days, now was pan-Arab by inclination, and was allied with the principal commercial figures of the country. The second civilian grouping within the cabinet—and allied with politicians such as the Vice-President as a counterweight to "the Majors" —were what might be called the technocrats, led by the Foreign Minister, Mansour Khalid. He was forty-six, Ansar in his origins (as also was Nimeiri's family), and had been ambassador to the U.N. Earlier he had worked for nine years within the U.N. Secretariat. He was regarded as the technical architect of the Sudan's swing toward the West, his fortunes blooming with the American connection. A bachelor, he lived luxuriously by Khartoum standards, so that his enemies gossiped that he was the beneficiary of CIA payments, but an old classmate of his, who felt no love for him, suggested to me that it was simply money saved from his high pay at the U.N.

The toughest "Major," Abul Gassim Ibrahim, had been elevated from the Ministry of Agriculture to be the head of the SSU after his generalship during the 1976 attempted coup had proved decisive. As Minister of Health, in the 1974 emergency he had ringed the university with tanks and threatened to blow it down, and had put the Minister of the Interior under house arrest. Four years earlier, he had strafed and stormed Aba Island, earning the hatred of the Mahdists. In 1975 he had led the charge to retake Radio Omdurman, but on seizing the microphone, had screamed

"Death to the traitors! Death to the traitors!" so enthusiastically that a collective shudder ran through the radio-owning middle class. Now turned forty, he went in for mass rallies with metronomic cheering, and it was said of him by middle-class people, in the abbreviated manner necessary, that he "had not grown with his job."

Although the judiciary had been independent of the executive branch when Nimeiri came to power, it had since been bureaucratized, "made much more flexible," and purged of "the relics of the white-wig era," as a cabinet minister explained. In the absence of a prickly judiciary or parliamentary opposition, some of the senior civil servants, acting through an intricacy of official rules and procedures, occasionally exercised the type of autonomy which the People's Assembly and the judges lacked. At least, when the Ministry of Finance and Economy disagreed with the Ministry of Transport and Communication on the advisability of building a new prestige airport when money was so short, the President, in arbitrating between them, was forced to think out his priorities again.

Students of a religious turn were likely to flirt with membership in the Muslim Brotherhood, instead of with the Communists. "The Brethren" are a pan-Arab, extremist society, outlawed but influential beyond their numbers both in Cairo and Khartoum. They believe in a return to traditional dogma in an Islamic nation-state, and regard Nimeiri, like Anwar Sadat, as corrupted by secularism. They are anti-Marxist, but like the Marxists, and like the hereditary Ansar leadership, have provided a more durable rallying point for opposition to the President than the dissolved political parties could. Because they tend to be impatient young intellectuals, not peasants or nomads or landless old landlords, their attitudes are not the same as those of the Ansar. Nevertheless, because the head of the Brethren happens to be Sadiq al-Mahdi's brother-in-law, by a coupling of shared points of orthodoxy The Brethren, snuggling alongside the Mahdists, have managed to augment their clout.

Though Sadiq was criticized for losing patience in exile and taking up with mercenaries to try to overthrow the government, nearly throughout the middle class I'd found people unhappy about politics. They remembered the pleasure of reading a newspaper in the morning when the papers were in disagreement with one another, of arguing policy in public and being courted instead of lectured to by officials. Candidates for the Assembly might have to run in an SSU primary, but once the primary was over—as they themselves would tell you—their job was to roll up an overwhelming turnout for the President. In April 1977 he received 5,620,026 "yes" votes for a new term, versus only 48,377 "no's."

I talked with a prosperous physician at a party at his house in Khartoum. We drank date wine and discussed the actress Tahiya Zarruq while watching one of his friends, a black, bearlike individual in a bulky white robe and turban, dance and snap his fingers, looking incongruously androgynous. My host said that if this were a wedding party, the women, too, would appear and dance for us, responding to the music only from the neck up—except that in a traditional household the famous feature was the girl's own bridal dance, wearing a gown resembling a negligee. "Once, once in her life she has a chance to show her husband's friends what she has that they are missing."

I told the doctor that I had heard a woman complain that the bedouin wrote poetry about their camels and the Dinkas composed songs about their cattle, and that circumcision was a blight for women.

"But they do suckle their sons," he remarked with a smile, as indeed they seem to do for a long while. His own mother had embroidered religious proverbs in beads and seashells on strips of cloth tacked to the wall. He said that as a sign of love and duty he had sent her to Mecca five times.

On the wall was an oil portrait of the doctor looking doctorly, which did not succeed in disguising his mama's-boy, fun-lover's face. He was not a crusading dissenter, yet when I asked about corruption, which, though not endemic, is creeping into the highest levels of several ministries and into every level at the railway and phone companies, he listened carefully, keeping the smile Tahiya Zarruq had evoked, in case somebody else were watching. Yes, career officials at the middle echelon were likely to have remained honest, and the taxi drivers and shoeshine boys, miraculously so. "They are Sudanese!" he said.

But I described watching police in Malakal extort bribes from the drivers of a convoy of passenger lorries, under pretext of a security check.

"Yes, it comes with dictatorship, wouldn't you think?" he said quietly, before moving away. "Power corrupts."

Sadiq was Oxford-educated, could talk with The Brethren and the Communist intelligentsia, could plot in London with Sharif al-Hindi, the exiled head of the National Unionist party, and yet had inherited the loyalty of whole legions of the xenophobic peasantry of the western and north-central provinces, some of whom still wore a tag-end of their turbans hanging loose to signify their allegiance to him. In El Obeid I had seen the Ansar flag flying openly in several dooryards. Yet, despite this "dervish" backing, Sadiq had pledged constitutionally guaranteed religious freedom, had advocated conciliation toward the Southerners during the civil war, and won the support of the leader of the Nuba Mountain Christians, Reverend Philip Abbas Gabboush, for his 1976 and 1977 coup attempts. Presumably, the idea was that with a return to parliamentary democracy, the North could become all the more Muslim while the Southerners could stay autonomously non-Muslim if they chose to. Sadiq's places of residence in exile included Saudi Arabia, where he was popular for his religious conservatism, and England, where as a champion of political liberty he won friends, but Libya too.

To counter the growing influence of Sadiq, Nimeiri—who had been "looking badly," "looking pensive," "sleeping badly, even for him"—decided to move toward a more dynamic balance of military men and party regulars with heretical civilians, and invited him back. Rashid al-Tahir Bakr was replaced as First Vice-President by "Major" Abul Gassim Ibrahim, becoming Foreign Minister instead. (Mansour Khalid, the Foreign Minister, was made publisher of the party newspapers.) But now, with Sadiq himself and several other returned and skeptical exiles appointed to the SSU politbureau, with dissenting politicians of the Muslim Brotherhood, the Khatmia and National Union party winning election to the People's Assembly in April 1978, and with veterans of every coup attempt against Nimeiri, dating way back to 1970, on the street again—twelve hundred people released from prison—the pressure was on "the Majors." Could they learn to negotiate at last, and to speak softly to men of differing views, instead of always playing the role of fist? If not, waiting in the wings was Sadiq, an excellent conciliator and negotiator, and about the same age as Abul Gassim Ibrahim, but looking reassuringly older in the prayer robes that he always wore in public.

This new policy, under the rubric of "National Reconciliation," helped win for Nimeiri the chairmanships of the Organization of African Unity and the Arab Solidarity Committee in 1978,* as concern for civil or "human" rights began to wax a bit in the Third World. But in line with a continuing shift toward courting the Western countries and to a partnership with his fatherly friend, Anwar Sadat, Nimeiri started making noises presaging closer links to Egypt, too. Even with the Mahdists placated by Sadiq's return, and the blacks of the South by a housecleaning election in Juba, this was a ticklish proposition. Egypt had forty million people and six million arable acres, while the Sudan's population of seventeen million were tilling two and a half times as much land—though not as well. According to a U.N. study, by 1990 forty million acres could be under the plow in the Sudan. Obviously, a marriage of Egypt's vast, steady peasantry and cadres of agronomists with the Sudan's rain-fed and irrigable lands would create just the breadbasket of Arab fable—"Africa's Brazil." But this might be at the expense of swallowing the Sudan.

* In the fall of that year, Nimeiri lost the latter position because of his support for Anwar Sadat's negotiations with Israel. Also that fall, Sadiq won his first public test of power, forcing the resignation of the Minister of Information, Bona Malwal Ring, while "Major" Abul Gassim Ibrahim made ineffective threatening speeches.

11
Juba Rhapsody, Juba Dirge

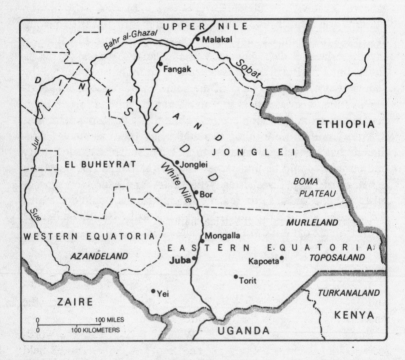

Back in Juba, my friend Bullen Alier Buttic, assistant director of Youth, Sports, Culture and Information for the Southern Region, worked in semidarkness —Juba darkness, you might say—by the light of a 25-watt bulb when the electricity was on, tapping the bell on his desk to call the messenger—in her pink servant's uniform—assigned to him, though she sat chatting outside and rarely came. During my time with him he made no direct comments about his country, merely threw me the book that was the budget, and after the day of gunfire at the airport, proffered no information, simply permitted me to extend my visa. He was acting director that week, and as I sat with him, an acquaintance now a prisoner, was brought in by two policemen, pleading to speak with him.

"I don't want to see him. This isn't at all my job," he said, but didn't refuse point-blank. The man, a civilian in turban and galabieh, importunately worried, rattling Arabic, was explaining whatever set of circumstances had thrown suspicion on him, presumably begging Buttic to intercede. Buttic picked up a radio script and began penciling through it rapidly to avoid the man's eyes. "I can't help you. This isn't my sphere," he interposed in English. The man spoke hastily, to say as much as he could while he was there, but when he ran out of explanations, Buttic nodded and he was led away.

I mentioned having heard from old Africa hands that the worst thing the Russian, American, British, French, and Israeli intelligence agencies had done here was to teach their counterparts how to compile police lists.

He liked the term "old Africa hands." "Yes," he said, changing the subject to a favorite theme, "it is a lot easier for a person from New York City to land in Juba than for a person from Juba to land in New York City."

The director's office was bigger, and boasted a 40-watt bulb, and Buttic would stretch happily as he told a friend over the phone, "Today you find me in the director's chair!"

Buttic liked to test my mettle. When I asked what the words were to the courtship songs I listened to at the Dinka dances held on the flats below town every Friday from sunset on—four or five hundred young men and women with spear-length sticks, wands, clubs and shields leaping slowly in concentric circles to a drum— he (although himself a Dinka) informed me, "They are singing the national anthem. They are practicing for the youth parade on Unity Day, like North Korea's youth parade."

Some of the dancers wore gym trunks and held flame-tree branches with the leaves still on that they had broken off as they'd walked down. They were clerks or students living in town. Others wore blue beads and gold anklets, and, if men, had daubed clay into a gray mask upon the face and washed their hair in ashes and cow urine to redden it. They may have run for forty miles in order to participate. Some had striped their legs with ochre and wore a hat of chestnut monkey hide, or a colobus monkey skin tied over the hips, or a stiff-backed, upward-pointed, blue-and-red leather sash around the waist. There was a din of talk and laughter. Two men bent over a drum standing on end and beat on its two sides.

Inside an outer ring of a couple of hundred people who clapped and jumped in place, their dancing sticks going up and down and both feet leaving the ground at the same time, was a ring of people moving counterclockwise. Inside them was a clockwise ring. Inside *them*, a handful of champions, or perhaps young men who aspired to be champions, rhythmically jumped so high that at first I assumed they must be leaping from a trampoline. The various songs served as a refrain to a four-note chant, and there were knots of people jumping independently. The men were mostly paired, holding one another by the elbow, or arm over arm. They would hit their clubs together and start jumping, then steer toward a girl whom they had selected, waggling their fingers over her head. The girls stood singly, with a bony, faraway, streamlined look; they were tall and pretended to be indifferent. Generally they allowed a little circle to form around them, eventually moving alongside their admirers to join the principal dance. If a girl wished to do more than pretend to ignore a suitor, she sat down where she was and refused to be tugged to her feet, or would go to find her proper fiancé and hold his hand.

Walking the sandy paths of Juba * among these out-of-work spearmen, I'd discover I was singing "Take Me Out to the Ballgame." Sitting on the grass bank of the Nile, I'd think *gray-green greasy Limpopo River*. You have to be lucky to see crocs or hippos right in Juba, but in Wau, on the River Jur, they are commonplace. Lizards clung watchfully above me in a tree; and kids with slingshots hunted them and the birds.

---

* A *juba* was once a dance among American and Haitian slaves, and there is a River Juba which debouches into the Indian Ocean from Ethiopia and Somalia after traveling a thousand miles. But no connection is indicated.

From Khartoum, I'd called my small daughter in New York to tell her how much I loved her. She had answered spunkily, "I know," as she always does. The day before I left, as a graduation exercise, she had pedaled her training bike around the courtyard of our building with the concentration of a little performing bear.

I should have been reading the Koran, but instead I browsed in the Bible for a familiar or soothing voice—hearing, nevertheless, a Sudanese clamor in the Gospel According to Mark. Muslim prayers are more ritualistic and the Koranic God more distant than His Christian counterpart: God is seldom petitioned or pleaded with as through the intercession of a Jesus, a Mary or a church pastor. But Juba is not Koranic, and the events in Galilee, Judea and Jerusalem seemed much more plausible in Juba than they would in present-day Jerusalem or Europe's Christendom. Here, if they happened again, it seemed to me that they would be attended, and possibly accepted, with the same pitch of fervency. A healing, miracle-working savior who would be locked in a cage within an hour if he appeared in Los Angeles or London could resurrect himself in Juba and see the populace catch fire, believe the evidence of their eyes, and make the sand streets resound once again.

Maybe for all this to happen, it is necessary that there be lepers sitting beside the road, lazy, high-horned, biblical kine, a blind albino girl with stumps for arms, a man bustling about on all fours with his thin buttocks canted as high as a baboon's because of a spinal injury that had never been treated when he was a child, and a hunter arriving on foot, carrying gazelle meat on a shoulder frame, with five spears in his hands, a brown bush hat, mud smeared on his neck and forehead to ward away the flies, and a calabash full of milk hanging from a thong around his neck. Another man stumped along on a eucalyptus stick strapped with a strip of goathide to his left hip, followed by his wife with an enormous fold of flesh which had gradually swallowed one ear and now was enveloping the whole side of her head. Miracles that wouldn't happen in New York or Jerusalem might occur in a place where the Son of God, if he were arrested, might still be killed, not entrusted to the care of social workers and psychologists.

Sadness pervades the journals of African travel written by Europeans that I am familiar with. André Gide was fifty-six at the time of his trip, and Graham Greene was thirty-one, nine years later, so that the manifest differences in temperament between them were set. And yet the sum of their impressions, when you have read *Travels in the Congo* and *Journey without Maps,* is about the same. Conditions along the line of march that each man took were simply too stark for the niceties of intellectual theory and artistic vision to operate. Alan Moorehead—like Winston Churchill in *The River War*—did charge along gaily enough when writing about the Arab Sudan, but I know of almost nothing in the literature of Europeans in black Africa which is invigorated by the exuberance of Bernal Díaz's masterpiece of travel writing, *The True History of the Conquest of New Spain.* Even in conquest, the portrait is, rather, of misery and "seasoning" illnesses for all parties concerned, including the conquerors. Joseph Conrad's "land of sorrow," David Livingstone's "open sore of the world"—overall, a place where, as Sir Samuel Baker said of the upper Nile, there were "no ancient histories to charm the present with memories of the past; all is wild and brutal, hard and unfeeling." "The strangest disease I have seen in this country seems really to be brokenheartedness," Livingstone commented, with regard to the trade in slaves. Certainly many affectionate testimonials exist, from explorers like Livingstone and Mungo Park, from subsequent missionaries, anthropologists and lay people like Isak Dinesen, but even after the slave trade a sadness suffuses most of these as well.

Diogo Cão, a Portuguese caravel captain, discovered the mouth of the Congo in 1482. Thus, just at the time of the European discovery of what would be called "the New World," this great river portal to the center of Africa was newly known. But it was never in the cards that Africa would become known as "the New World." That would have implied that Europeans wished to settle there, which, except at the fringes of the continent, they did not. Any first interest in the Congo was quickly eclipsed by the hurry of the Portuguese navigators to reach India by going on around Africa. And once the two Americas were recognized as entire continents, it was to them the colonists rushed from Northern and Southern Europe. Red Indians, needless to say, were not brought across the ocean to labor in Africa, but Africans were carried over to enrich the New World, where the colonists were. And yet, for all the sadness which Europeans felt in touring Africa—compared to the gaiety of so many diaries of "the New World"—the irony is that not the Africans but the Red Indians were largely wiped out. Today we have Black Africa, not Red America.

No firm census has been taken of Juba's population, but during the Green Monkey emergency the authorities guessed it might be about a hundred thousand. During the torpid January afternoons, nobody moves except the very poor, who have water to fetch or wood to scrounge, but at sunset, which occurs at six o'clock year round, the low-volume hubbub of the city, which a visitor has forgotten since the previous evening, begins again. Without traffic or electronic noise, what you hear is a vast, individually keyed-down village hum, lit by the cooking fires all around—everybody up and making his own sounds, visiting, drumming on a jerrycan, singing, muttering over supper, while a peddler sits selling single cigarettes, chips of soap, canned milk and strawberry syrup, with a wisp of flame from a coal lying next to his right foot so that he can see to count his change. A European might not want to walk regularly through Malakia, the enormous squatters' quarter, after dark, but elsewhere in Juba he is advised that he need only carry a flashlight to watch for vipers crossing the road, the kind called *abu ashara daquiqua,* "the father of ten minutes," in Arabic, because supposedly a man bitten has only that long left to live.

My Dutch friend had rented a house on the north edge of town, where some of the Arab storekeepers lived in patioed white houses facing a Dinka encampment of grass huts, beyond which you could start up a black-and-brown jackal sheltering under a shrub in the sun-blackened brush near the airport. We had three rooms, two screened-in porches and a walled-in yard, but at night whenever you stepped out of doors you would be aware of scores of voices softly talking—as soft as voices in a village are, originating from all directions, and commenting humorously upon you as you passed on the path—though you couldn't see anybody at all, except occasionally a figure next to a scrub fire, because your eyes were not used to the dark and because Nilotics, such as the Dinkas, are among the darkest people on earth.

Grass huts had mud walls and floors; yet in the morning you would see a pretty and immaculate Dinka girl stooped over, backing carefully out of her door so as not to muss her office pinafore —her mother humming behind her, her four-year-old son pounding a tin can with a heartbeat rhythm that one came to count on and miss if nobody was doing it, and the chickens squabbling.

Three thousand miles from Alexandria, the White Nile is more gray than white, more brown than green. With flat banks and flat brown savanna beyond, it is not straight enough to provide much of a view, not wide enough to fill the big shoes of its name, though the African Empire Air Route flying boats used to land here on their way to South Africa and Australia. The settlement called Gumba lies on the other side (if you can find it), and several copses of lovely old broad-leafed trees lean over the current from the Juba bank toward a muddy island where a few favored families raise vegetables.

Downstream six hundred miles, past the papyrus and hyacinth swamps of the Sudd, is the river town of Malakal, which still manages to turn its best face to the waterfront—a look of dark shade and even luxury, though Malakal is achingly poor. It's a proud boat town, however, whereas Juba has turned its back on the Nile, like a capital city embarrassed to remember its origins. Some wandering is required even to locate the river, which lies behind two foundries with scrap heaps outside, a tobacco warehouse, a shirt factory and a bakery with a stack of logs for firing the ovens half blocking the door. The steamers tie up alongside a sagging wharf in front of a string of sheds listing to one side, in each of which a clerk presides over some aspect of the River Service—largely imaginary, it seemed to me, as I waited a couple of weeks for the next boat to arrive from Malakal. Except for three families camped with their baskets under the trees, I was the only person eager to book passage on it. Even the poorest Sudanese prefer the back of a souk lorry, taking the boat only during the months when the roads are washed out or in order to reach a huddle of huts in the Sudd which the lorries cannot visit.

A few freight scows and out-of-service steamers were moored

there also, though it was hard to tell which were in use and which were not. They were all flat-bottomed vessels with a blunt bow and stern, a white paint job dating a decade back, and dented, blackened paddle wheels, stunted, angry and benighted-looking, like battered galley slaves partly hidden below the deck. They were not your handsome "restored" Mississippi paddle-wheelers, with whopping paddles decorated in nursery colors like a troupe of carousel horses. These paddles were split, tarred to cover the cracks, and small enough to get through the vegetation choking the Sudd—probably just as most real paddle wheels on the Mississippi and Missouri river steamers were small, to squeeze over snags and sandbars.

On deck, on each tub, was an iron box stove, sticks of driftwood to cook with, and ten or a dozen chickens stalking about before they wound up in the pot. The crew, in dirty togas, with a rag around the head for a turban, looked as if life were a good deal of fun—some of them on the sleepy side, others raffish or piratical. Around lunchtime a couple of women came by hawking paw-paws, bananas, yams, lentils, cassava flour, lulu berries—one lady as limber as a fashion plate or a dancer, balancing a basket of sesame seeds on her head like a winged hat.

Usually a bull's horns were nailed to the steamer's bridge. At the ceremony when a new boat was inaugurated into the Service, my Dutch landlord said, you'd hardly notice two bulls standing near the center of things, until at a signal the two hearties holding them whipped out pangas from under their robes and slashed the beasts' throats. Likewise, when Nimeiri arrives at the airport, an ox is sacrificed for him to touch with his foot. Such gestures are made to the Southern cattle people, but the boat crews are Arab, which is a sore point, because the storekeepers, clear to the outposts on the Ethiopian frontier, are Arab too. There are bitter rumors of collusion, bribery, fraud. It is claimed that the crews steal and resell goods which aren't consigned to another Arab, that merely out of malice they will dump overboard whole crates of stuff, that bargeloads of government fuel oil, and staples like dura, sugar and salt, are left snubbed to an island of water hyacinth among the lost sloughs of the Sudd, to be picked up when the steamer captain can't find a cargo to push to Juba more worth his while. In the meantime, a district town like Torit will go without sugar and flashlight batteries for months; no shoes of any description are displayed in the stores. Among Southerners, you hear a mumbling about "gollabas," which is the dirty word for Arab businessmen, from the galabiehs they wear.

Upriver from the wharf, several watermen ferry people across from Gumba in dugout pirogues—narrow craft burned and chiseled from a log, in which ten souls can sit in tippy fashion in single file, the women balancing a lapful of produce to sell, baskets so heavy that when they reach the slippery path on Juba's shore they help one another lift these burdens to their heads. There are lady water carriers struggling up the bank beside them, each wearing a pail for a hat. It's hot work, and the reward for stumbling is a cool slosh of water over the shoulders and neck. Donkeys are not used in the South; the head is the beast of burden here, generally a woman's head.

A madwoman with glazed, recessed, diseased eyes used to stop me on the bank and demand to know all about me. Proud of her heavy jerrycan, proud of her strength, she sang in a teasing sing-song, insulting everybody in the tribal style. She was going blind, but tossing her head to splash a dollop of water down over her dress, she would ask me in Bari if I could speak Bari. Though she was challenging me, I liked giving her the satisfaction of hearing that I couldn't. Then she would give me a dressing down and tell everybody in Bari how funny I looked. They treated both of us as funny-looking.

She hauled water for a café set under a tent in a cluster of huts, where the proprietor had tea cooking in one barrel—the milk and sugar already stirred in—and sorghum porridge in another, a boy about seven stirring it, near Manolakas the Greek's house. Cooking in such quantities, sorghum exudes an appetizing, cereally smell, but after the first plate of it you wish that it had more taste and more smell. When cooked, sorghum is the color and consistency of Cream of Wheat, if Cream of Wheat were eaten with the fingers in lumps, but lacks the fragrance of wheat.

Manolakas lived on the second floor of a disheveled stone warehouse a hundred yards from the Nile. The servant who let me in made incomprehensible sounds of the sort a man produces who has lost his tongue: the faithful servitor who cannot speak but affectionately looks after his master with a vocabulary of guinea-fowl cries and elbow and shoulder signals—nuances which Manolakas nodded to. The man had a young boy to assist him, and the tile floor was shining clean, the windows full of light. He ushered me in with an eagerness that suggested he thought Manolakas lived too alone, a sentiment I began to share. For generations the Greeks in Africa have maintained their Hellenic identity by living in this way. English explorers who wrote of themselves as the first Europeans on the scene often encountered Greek traders who had arrived before them.

It was a rare, placid roost, looking out on a view of reddish ground, mosquitoey grass, a few borassus palms and savanna trees, distant figures who were transporting head loads, and a brief undramatic turn of the river, such as Samuel Baker, Romolo Gessi, Emin Pasha, Chaillé-Long and the other original travelers who stopped at Gondoroko—as the earlier site across the river was called—would have seen. I was delighted by it, but Manolakas apologized for living in such a run-down neighborhood. He explained that he had rented his own fine white house, next to the Greek church, to a Nairobi trucking firm, and another comfortable property to a safari company, where we saw salted buffalo heads and hartebeest horns strewn on the porch when we drove past. He had led a good life here for thirty years, had married late, and consequently had babies to support, living with his wife in his other home in Khartoum. During his old age, he said, he would not be able to relax as other men did, but would need to hustle shrewdly.

I'd met Manolakas at the Greek Club, an imposing, empty, porticoed pile on Addis Ababa Avenue, in which a pathetic remnant membership gathered to play poker and gossip most evenings of the week. There seemed to be only four of them holding the fort, where thousands of English pounds had changed hands of a Saturday night back when Juba's shops had been stocked with Cadbury chocolates, Spanish sherries and fancy French brandies, and when British military and colonial officers had driven up for a gamey weekend from Kampala, nine hours away by staff car.

Manolakas's three friends, playing for piasters now, included a fellow businessman with eyes like billiard balls and a bald bullet-head, boisterous and ebullient and therefore (to my mind) "Greek"; also the gray-robed Orthodox priest, who was an ancient silently winding up his last years on earth still at his post. The fourth hand was a black-faced, slinky-looking Arab burgher in a rumpled turban, carrying his Muslim prayer beads wrapped around one wrist. "A gambler is either a born liar or a born victim," Manolakas said, and they all agreed.

The lights at the club drew the bugs—it was too hot to sit in-side—but the present police chief had been a great poker player, and they were nostalgic for the old games. Manolakas himself was Anglicized. He had an inquisitive cock to his head, a pencil mustache, an accent influenced by his service as a mortarman in a regiment of Greeks who, amalgamated with British commandos and paratroopers, had raided the Germans on the Dodecanese Is-lands from Haifa during World War II. In a Pall Mall way, he had hunted big game around here, and he told me that the fear you experience in war, "where you participate compulsorily," cannot be compared to the excitement of hunting, "which you seek."

At his home, Manolakas prepared Nescafé in a cup of boiling water for me, stirring carefully. "With my own hands I am doing this," he said, and it did seem a refinement of Greek hospitality that he did not ask his servant to accomplish the task. Because I was a bird blown by the winds from far away, he postponed a cou-ple of business appointments to tell me about Macedonia, where he had been born, and the island of Samos, where he thought of retiring with his brother-in-law to invest in a restaurant on the beach, and where I had once lived. We enjoyed a dish of *tilapia*, which is a sweet-fleshed relative of the sunfish that lives in the Nile. Another day we cruised about town while he pointed out parcels of real estate formerly owned by Greeks, and what the Greeks who were left still did own. It was peanuts, as he said, compared to property in Khartoum, yet private holdings had not been nationalized in Juba in 1970, because the government had understood that there was dissension enough to contend with dur-ing the civil war.

Manolakas asked me why I had come. I laughed and said the

Sudan was not only the largest country in Africa but also lay between Egypt and Kenya, which I had toured with pleasure the winter before. He asked if I wasn't lonely. I said I was hemorrhaging with loneliness, but that I had been lonely lately at home, though it was incongruous to spend so much money getting to a place so poor that its people could have spent ten years living on the air fare itself.

With the same wistful tone that I had heard from Greeks in the North who wondered what they ought to do—abandon their assets or somehow "steal our own money" out of the country—he told me one of his brothers had established a business in Norfolk, Virginia. However, he spoke in a gentler, more gentlemanly fashion on the subject than most of his compatriots, and, at what he called our "news conferences" (because I took notes), spoke of hunting with such sentiment that it was obvious he had loved his life here.

Like Ernest Hemingway's, Manolakas's hunting had been British in coloration, therefore not a style to be casually dropped because of the eclipse of Great Britain. At first he read from a sheet of paper—"Little did I realize that I would be asked to comment to the press on a matter on which I am only an amateur." But gradually he shed his self-consciousness. He said that lions will offer you a free shot as a point of punctilio, pausing before they retreat; that elephants, although intimidating because of their size, will sometimes sheer off if wounded, or even unwounded, during a charge, but that buffalo will not. He was a buffalo man ("Remember, there are other people who know more than me"), just as other hunters will champion the leopard, rhino, lion or "tusker" as the trophy of choice. He recounted three buffalo charges in detail, in a breathless, solemn voice—the creature always with its head high, obviating a brain shot, the head half turned to the right to keep a bead on the hunter if he tried to dodge. Buffalo, alone among the so-called Big Five that white hunters have traveled to Africa for, can see, hear and smell almost equally keenly.

Certain inaccessible pockets of the Southern Sudan, such as the Boma Plateau near Ethiopia, and parts of Dinkaland in Bahr al-Ghazal, and the tsetse-fly precincts of Azandeland near Zaire, offer a last show of African wildlife without vanloads of tourists, wardens and scientists. In crannies of Botswana and corners of Zaire, Angola, and Ethiopia recently emptied of their human beings by civil war, there are similar stereopticon scenes, a panorama forever ending—a fact that I find unspeakably sad. Partly because I had gone on safari through Kenya's parks the previous year, but partly because it was an old sad story from my own continent of which I had already written, I didn't look for encounters with wild animals in the Sudan. Instead, I squinted slightly when I saw them in passing, as one does when sighting an old friend imperiled by imminent tragedy. The U.N. had brought its best wildlife expert, a man named Blowers, from Indonesia to Juba to do a month's strenuous field survey, going places that the Sudanese in the Game and Tourism Department could not buy fuel to drive to. He had set down annotated recommendations, but when I asked the department director if he had kept a copy, he undertook an earnest, friendly search before deciding that he had not.

Manolakas's children were nearly in their teens now, so he was planning to take his son gazelle-hunting in the spring, early in the rainy season, when the grass was only knee-high, the soil not yet mud but soft enough for a quiet stalk and for finding the spoor. It would be the first hunt for one of them, maybe the last for the other, though only his tone said so. Yet the flowers were so pretty then on the Boma Plateau that he cared only that his son got something, hardly how he fared himself. There would be difficulties in procuring petrol, a permit, even bullets, for an activity the government intended to reserve for rich foreigners, and he would have to drive at least a hundred miles further to locate game that had ranged ten miles outside of Juba not so long ago. He lived a scaled-down existence in many ways, with so many friends gone.

We examined his collection of prize sporting guns. He had probably picked up these relics from Englishmen going home in 1956, or from Greeks who had transplanted themselves to Vancouver in the years since, and the police kindly let him keep them, despite their aversion to having any loose guns around town. The best was a beautifully tooled John Rigby .450 with two short black barrels and two triggers—a knock-down gun for snap shots in heavy cover, if the hunter was forced to creep after a wounded beast. Its short length made it maneuverable in the brush, and if two bullets weren't enough, you would be dead anyway, said Manolakas. "Feel it, feel how heavy. You hold on to that if you're trembling. It steadies you." Another, a twenty-five-year-old .375 magnum Holland and Holland, was graced with a longer, lighter barrel for nicer accuracy and penetration power in shooting plains game. The blueing had worn off, so that the metal looked "like a gas pipe," as he put it, but the stock had been carved to last. He also owned a .270 Belgian F. N. rifle and a .243 Austrian Steyr for killing soft-skinned antelope—smaller calibers for a smaller puncture —and a twelve-gauge W. W. Greener shotgun, for birds. Classic sporting weapons, yet inevitably I thought how little help they might be to him in independent Africa.

As an investor in a safari company, Manolakas was acquainted with the professional hunters living in Juba. There was a rough-stuff German named Werner, very competent, who had worked in Kenya until the government had regulated the fun out of hunting; people seemed to drop their eyes when speaking of him. Also two Englishmen who had transferred their energies from Zambia, when hunting there, as in Kenya, declined. The customers—Mr. and Mrs. Francis Macomber, he a sallow, workaholic Chicagoan of forty-seven turned out in khaki togs, she a boyish, touched-up blonde, ten years younger—one didn't see overmuch of. It was an expensive proposition to be here at all, and they had no reason to linger in Juba before flying north to the lechwe and reedbuck and kob of Lake No. When they left the bush, they stopped only to register their kill. For a day or two, you saw them driven about in a safari truck, holding their guns in leather cases like golf bags, the truck striped for camouflage and screened over to protect the black gunbearers—who bounced on the benches bolted in back— from a lion's charge.

I met a Spaniard who said he had written a book about how to hunt elephants, who Manolakas claimed was the best white hunter in Africa. He was middle-aged, with a high forehead, a severe but expressive mouth, watchful, emotionless eyes, the irises startlingly blue, and a little pot-curve to his belly. He was a tall, dominating, skeptical figure, cultivated and all the more formidable for being so. A specialist at shooting elephants, he was waiting at the airport for his next client, having seen off the last one the day before. He too had recently shifted his operations from Zambia, spoke the King's English like a British colonel, and was used to the four-hour waits of an African airport, with egrets and nanny goats stalking about. But he had watched so many elephants die with those wide, ironical eyes that while we talked I wondered if his expression would change if, say, my abdominal aorta happened to rupture right there and I bled to death on the floor.

The rarest antelope are hunted in special localities—bongo in the Azande country around Yambio, Nile lechwe in Dinkaland near Aweil and at Lake No. The river exists as an odd barrier, Manolakas said. On its east bank live zebra, black rhino, white-eared kob and lesser eland. (Lesser eland were his favorite meat.) On the west bank were greater eland and a few white rhino—a square-lipped species gentler, bigger and more endangered than their black cousins. Of course the river separates tribes such as the Shilluk from those such as the Nuer, as well.

I fell in with a rich, angry, loutish, overgrown German youth with a tiny mustache, who told me he was spending the equivalent of $20,000 for what would wind up as twenty shoulder-mounted trophies. I imagined this cheap, when you considered that he was counting both the taxidermy and the round trip from Frankfurt, but he did not. He had extended his stay, however, by making himself useful to the hunter named Werner, helping to guide the next party. Angrily, in English broken by German, he said that a foreigner like himself who was pouring so much money into the economy, was not allowed to kill a leopard—but that "the niggers in the villages" speared them secretly and indiscriminately. Then the pretty hides rotted because, although they wanted to smuggle them out to the skin dealers in Nairobi, they had no salt even to flavor their food, much less in such quantities as could preserve a valuable pelt.

Another riverfront character was a Portuguese, a swarthy, heavyset charmer, a ladies' man and white hunter kicked out of Mozambique by the new government, although his son had gone back to live in Maputo again. He was sure he would break down and cry if he ever did that, having left behind his house and forty years' worth of possessions. The deep-sea fishing, the seaport with its boulevards, villas and restaurants—how he missed them! He was a refugee and his prospects would become what he made of them, which was not a cheerful prospect for a man nearing sixty. New country, new weather, bitterly sweaty, new languages, a line of work exigently physical. As a newcomer, he had been given the job of ferrying safari vehicles down from Khartoum, and laying hold of eight or ten horses for a party of Texans who insisted that they wanted to ride while they hunted—no easy assignment in the Southern Sudan, where people do not own horses. "My son's blood is African. You understand? But I was born a European."

Still, because I was standing there with a young woman, he began to grin cheerfully at her as we chatted. Softening his bitterness, he sat down and said that one thing he knew about *anywhere* was lions. He rolled up his pant-leg to show us the four tooth marks left by a lion that had expired leaning against him, grasping him. These looked deep and big, though he had already shot the creature and broken its jaw. The scars of its claws were fainter because with his second shot he had blown out its chest.

"Who got the skin?" I asked.

"My client," he said, with the flat sort of look worn by professionals in any field when they mention the ironies they live with.

12
Boghosian Rampant

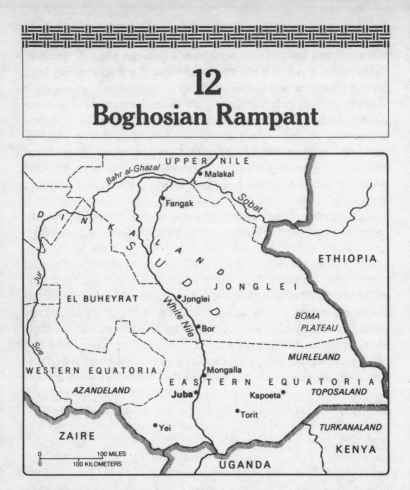

A Bari *askhari* (guard) sat round the clock under a mango tree outside the Arab compound where my Dutch landlord Willem lived. For about five dollars a week and the use of a tiny garden plot fenced with thornbush, he kept thieves away. In addition, we had the services of a Congolese, paid twice as much, who spoke French to us and Arabic to the Dinkas and Baris. He was part of a colony of several thousand refugees from one of Zaire's doomed rebellions who were situated seven miles back from the Nile's opposite bank, and who supported themselves by charcoal-burning and scavenging. He walked there on his day off. We never did know his real name, only the houseboy name "Boni," because our kitchen French was wretched, but we learned that he had been making bridal payments amounting to $200, and that in the week just after he had paid the next-to-last installment, the girl in question was suddenly poisoned by an enemy. That was all we knew—not whether he had loved her passionately, whether the poisoner had been identified, whether his quarrel had been with Boni or her family, what measures of revenge Boni might be considering, what would become of his investment, or even how bad conditions were among this pocket of exotics. If they had actually been starving, I doubt that anybody in Juba would have been the wiser. He was extremely considerate, but it was Stanleyville he had come from, where a good many whites had been massacred by rebels like him.

My Dutch friend had stiff black hair combed straight back, round, sailorly, faintly simian eyes that made his face look wizened when he was tired, and—below his cheeks and alongside his mouth—the marks of knitting his lips together in what he called "ropy" situations. Like other relief experts, Willem had witnessed Africa's worst—Biafran children so starved that they had had twelve-inch "tails," which were really their intestines sticking out. You sat them in a circle and spooned in watery milk for ten days, and then just as they had turned into people, every tenth child keeled over from heart failure. I had met him in an embassy lobby, where he was playing some kind of a waiting game. He had started giving me advice, and ended up blurting an invitation to visit. Edna, his wife, was Irish, a willowy, blasphemous girl who had sewn a double-closetful of billowy dresses from kanga cloth bought in Nairobi. She changed these bright creations several times a day, and expressed herself always in strong, rakish opinions—either "shoot all the elephants," or *none* of the elephants. The bougainvillaeas with red flowers and frangipanis with syrupy-smelling white blossoms in the patio, she said, almost made up for the rats in the outhouse. I had thought they were frogs because they made such a plop when they dived in the bucket, but her husband had caused a hole eighteen feet deep to be dug alongside the house for a proper toilet. This had bogged down as a *bukra* (tomorrow) project, and in the meantime his friends tumbled in when they got drunk.

As Edna was indubitably the most stylish European in town,

and Willem, too, possessed a certain flair for society, mixed with his Rotterdam itch to spit on his hands and knock a few heads together, they had become the center of the squash and Tusker beer set that met at the Juba Hotel as soon as the sky cooled in the evening. This group was a dotty, coed commonwealth of people from the U.N. residential compound and miscellaneous Canadian and English manpower experts who lived at the Multi-Purpose Training Center. I never saw any actual training undertaken at the latter—indeed, never saw any Africans on the grounds at all except for the secretarial staff—but we heard rumors of the $70,000 printing plant a British Kenyan was building, under another aid program, to publish schoolbooks in seven languages, so that the Sudanese would be able to choose a text other than donated *David Copperfield*s for teaching English, for example. And a social anthropologist was working ahead of a Norwegian team of well drillers to remedy a pattern of mistakes an American team had made, drilling just anywhere in the villages they came to. If it occupied ground historically allotted to a single family, or taboo ground, the well was not usable.

Every man's favorite squash opponent was Karen Stevens, a hippie stray from Toledo, Ohio, whose "vest," as the English described her T-shirt, was unraveling at the seams. It was very old, very dirty, and offended the sense of propriety of people who were earning a good salary for being overseas but often were more concerned with the proprieties than people at home who hadn't had to sign on to an overseas project in order to earn a good salary. Some wanted her to put on something else; some wanted her to wear it till it fell off, and threatened retaliation against anybody who remonstrated with Karen.

Then there was Father John, a Maryknoll missionary, popular for his sympathy and toughness, with nearly a decade in Tanzania and the Sinai behind him. Willem's best friend, Peter Lewis, a white Kenyan, wore a beard that grew clear around his big chin to mingle with his head of hair on either side, like a sea godling's. He was a trucking contractor, and the only white man that the Ugandans currently were letting across from our side of the border. He went back and forth a dozen times during the winter, when his drivers broke down or got into trouble. I don't think it was because of his business interests that they permitted him to do this; they could easily have forced him to hire a black assistant. What must have won them over was that godling's beard growing up into his head of hair and mixing with it, and the reckless, racy way he had about him, looking to the side from the corner of his eye, blunt and honest, yet sly and amused, indifferent to what people thought of him, with utter physical confidence. He lived well, slept well, worked extremely hard if there was a reason to, or loafed and pleased himself more thoroughly than the Europeans who were his drinking buddies were able to. There was a sign on his porch that said WATER, with an arrow pointing to a jug of water, and NO DRIVERS ALLOWED INSIDE, but he entertained plenty of visitors who were black but were not drivers. Various white hippies knocked at his door, begging for a bed, a meal, a ride, and he helped them on the basis of whether he liked their style of approach, rather than need.

Some of these dispossessed white Kenyans were better at operating than the best of the Europeans, no matter how much the Europeans had knocked around. They were Africans, and as Africa hands, could swim like a fish through the continent. Not being so far from where they'd been born, they hadn't the same apprehensiveness about dying, about living on borrowed time here in this legendary, menacing land, that secretly afflicted the rest of us. Although for hours at a time they were effectively color-blind, as second nature they constantly employed their white coloring to great advantage the way an equilibrist manipulates his balancing pole. They were attuned to many vibrations that were African, yet, unlike both the traveling Europeans, who feared death at the next turn in the road, and so many black Africans, who remained fearfully fatalistic, they really expected to live out a normal lifespan.

Sickness is the way people give up in Africa. Probably the most common observation the European explorers made was that the Africans they met who had not been Europeanized seemed to surrender themselves to death almost immediately when they fell seriously ill. Our expatriates, on the other hand, often appeared to fall sick in order to give up. They "lost heart," as the antique accounts express it. You heard about two Jesuits struggling against obstacles to establish a seminary in Wau, and the one who had struck his acquaintances as being most discouraged was the one invalided home. In Juba, every European had a bona fide case of malaria, suppressed though it was with medication, so he could simply skip a week's chloroquine and find reason to feel sorry for himself: a crashing headache, soaring fever, vertigo.

In Malakal, Juba's stepchild, inaccessible by land for eight months out of the year, Egil Nilssen, the director of the Lutheran World Federation outpost, made muffled reference to those of his co-workers "who create more problems then they have come to solve." The clay in the dry season was almost "too hard to dig a grave," but in the interminable wet season it was mortally slick and slippery to walk on. Just to reach their own boat landing on the Nile, they sometimes had to wade chest-deep across the fields. The wind in the fall blew fifty miles an hour and would reverse until gradually it had jimmied off the strongest roof which had eaves. Hardly anything except grass cupcake huts could be built anyway because there was no sand or stone.

All that water, but the local people were short of food, and lacked wood to keep warm. From many villages it was an all-day expedition to the nearest copse of trees, so during pneumonia season it was a hero's job for them to forage for fuel. Now, however—in the midst of the dry spell—the Africans could be told to wash their children's fly-sucked eyes (the flies were thirsty too), but they did not have even enough drinking water, Nilssen said. In a Dinka village, as I zipped by in a lorry, I had seen a gallant-looking hunter wearing an antelope's scalp on his head, a red blanket looped over one shoulder, with a ball of wood on the point of his spear as a signal of peace. He stood on one leg, the other foot angled to rest against his knee, in an insouciant pose. He was so tall that his small face seemed perched high in the air, the upper lip pushed out by little Dinka buckteeth to contrast appealingly with his martial air. He looked straight and grand as a stork, yet, across the path, one of his mates was hacking with a mattock at the muck bordering a skim of water still left in a mudhole. The mud was a mishmash of cattle tracks. The water, half urine, shone with sickly colors like oil. They had gourds which they hoped to fill when moisture seeped over into the new hole.

Down in Torit, not quite so grim a town, at the isolated headquarters for Norwegian Church Relief in the Southern Sudan, the acting chief—an army chaplain whose last posting had been north of the Arctic Circle—kept mentioning to me the incidence of bronchitis among his band of eighty Scandinavians. Of course there was bad bronchitis among the Africans as well, but his people ate kippers, bacon, oatmeal, honey and biscuits, pâté and cheese for breakfast alone, and flew regularly to Nairobi in their own Cessna to rest and recuperate. It may have been the milieu of suffering which disheartened them, he said.

The regional Minister of Agriculture in Juba, Dr. Gamma Hassan, had a weakness for dropping by incognito on a European freshly assigned by the U.N. to his domain, and, if he didn't like the cut of his jib, firing the chump, giving him twenty-four hours to get out of the country entirely. His other welcoming trick was to give a task to the fellow, as in the case of a German carpentry instructor who arrived and was ordered to make eight coffee tables, shaped, planed, glued and lacquered, for a wedding reception the next afternoon. "Why couldn't one of my people have done something like that?" said Gamma Hassan. His constituents voted him out of office in the next election.

The representative of the World Bank was a Scotsman who drank his tea as weak as his tongue was tart, and who was accused of not disposing of the Bank's money as quickly as scheduled. Some Danes were helping on fishery problems, several Dutch with irrigation, some American Baptists with the training of teachers and blacksmiths. And occasionally we had the hapless brand of international air traveler. A Boeing from Britain had glided over Khartoum, only to discover the city completely smudged over by a haboob. This is a fairly standard occurrence in the spring. Up in the bright skies that Boeings inhabit, the procedure had been to turn toward the city of Addis Ababa on its high plateau, not too far away. Addis boasted a Hilton Hotel, several Italian restaurants dating from Mussolini's brief era, and other amenities. But Sudan Airways had stopped diverting its flights to the Dergue's airport. Now these witty English radar salesmen, Japanese traders, seedy intercontinental connivers and fast-buck men were routed to Juba. There were heads of households from the Persian Gulf, whose wives wore those mutilating nose-boards under their veils that destroy even the frailest shadow of beauty; and a bony Frenchman humped up as unhappily as a tar-soaked heron. For two or three days every spare chair and prayer mat at the hotel was occupied, under the quick piping bats dodging the slow-turning blades of the fan in the ceiling.

The airport and Nile bridge were the routes out of town, and both were shut off periodically. Yet, when you came right down to it, for an expatriate without investments to worry about, with money in his pocket, nothing could be easier than to be a white man here in Africa. Outside of the several civil-war zones, the laws of gravity didn't really apply to you. Like Tarzan with his oscillating holler, off you could swing with your walletful of money by jeep or Fokker Friendship on whatever trip you were thinking of. Nobody else moved as freely as you, and the Africans, anyway, knew you would never die. Even in Ethiopia, if you came down with guillain-barre syndrome, somehow an iron lung would be found for you, though the Minister of the Interior himself would have been allowed to die of it. All the other Tarzans around would set up such a ululating holler across the world that by converted crop duster and VC-10 you would soon be launched on the long flight home.

Such is the case; yet I hardly ever met any whites except the Kenyans who acted as though they believed it—the Kenyans, and Cornelius Boghosian. Boghosian befriended me outside a Juba ministry where the chief inspector had been giving me the runaround.

"You thought that man was stupid?" he demanded to know. "He wasn't stupid. He was ridiculing you."

I never understood why Boghosian took a fancy to me; indeed, he himself may not have known. He didn't credit at all the reports that I was a writer. I was only "an observer," he said—he himself being so much more vivid a likeness of Hemingway. He was another instance of the Hemingway of "The Green Hills of Africa" crossbred with an Oxbridge model for show, although in reality he was a proud Armenian and one of the peerless wholesalers of this world. He had been "close to," as the saying goes, Ngarta Tombalbaye, Chad's former dictator, in Ndjamena, the capital (as I later heard from the Egyptian journalist at the bar mitzvah in Khartoum), until Ngarta Tombalbaye had been overthrown. Having lost that sugarplum, he was looking for new ventures, perhaps importing and job-lotting in Khartoum, combined with a safari lodge near Juba. He was a free lance, at any rate, cut from a mixture of patterns, as was natural for a man whose own people had been all but wiped off the face of the earth. At first his advocacy of me had about it the character of a white man standing foursquare in favor of another white man, which I was used to. Later on, though, during an evening's excursion we took up the Nile by Land Rover, when the rest of us teased him about being "a white hunter," he took decided exception.

"Not at all. I'm a brown hunter! You gentlemen are white hunters. I am a Sudanese, which you are not. I am an African. I can go into Idi Amin's country on my passport and he will not arrest me, as he would you." This statement, although not necessarily true, was to indicate to us that his view of Idi Amin might be different from ours.

As in most of my jaunts, I had about fifteen minutes to grab my gear and get into the green Land Rover if I wanted a free trip upriver toward Mongalla, a tour which, even for the few hours we spent, would have cost me $120 if I had gone to a safari agency. Boghosian, as sanguine as he was, had given me to understand that we might be gone for a night or two, so I'd brought my sleeping bag, a can of tinned beef and a can of fruit salad.

"Mr. Hoagland came prepared," he said. "And I am fat enough to live on my flesh for a while quite comfortably if we stay out for a few days. But I don't see what you gentlemen are going to do. The moon is full tonight, you know. It will be so beautiful we may not want to come back anytime very soon."

Boghosian was to be our guide, but our benefactors were two Italians, part of a team of both sexes of that nationality who were surveying Juba from the air and on the ground for the purpose of planning the city that it might become. Our two were photographers, and they were providing the vehicle, and, still more precious, the fuel, which had been trucked from Nairobi. We also had a commercial traveler by the name of Hans along for company, whom Boghosian called "mein Fräulein Hans," because they had been forced to share a room at the overcrowded hotel, and because of Hans's fastidious timidity.

Boghosian wore a bristly gray mustache and safari jacket, with a suitably clipped manner that showed he had been an officer with one of Montgomery's divisions. Yet behind these familiar emblems, this protective coloration, was an Armenian insistence upon a life of infinite possibilities: that we might stay out in the moonlight forever, that he might fall into another cushy berth with a dictator, that we might all die this evening, or become banner friends. He said that whenever he met an adolescent boy he told him not to pay any attention to what his mother said, but to masturbate "all you can, *while* you can!" He was in his sixties, and thirty-five years ago, he said, he had gone to a whorehouse in Kassala and screwed all seven girls there. "Is that everybody?" he had asked the madam. Everybody except the watchman, she said. "Then bring the bloody watchman—let's have him too!" And he would have, he claimed, except that all the girls screamed that it was a sin. "They do bugger each other around here, you know. But they don't want it ever said they do."

The Italians wore khakis and bright silk foulards around their throats, and carried movie cameras. The younger one was lean and sensitive-looking, like an avant-garde film-maker; the older man, his boss, was balding and practical-looking in the manner of Carlo Ponti. Both were sporty and alert, like European tourists, and once we reached the Mongalla savanna, took turns climbing on top of the car while Boghosian drove, to shoot their pictures at any cry of game ahead.

Hans watched fondly—as we all did—when animals appeared, but spoke with drawling irony on worldlier matters, usually from the position of a "sensualist," protesting the posture too much. In English, a language which almost all international travelers now speak with the same competence they employ in driving a rented car, he betrayed only the faintest of accents.

I wore a crumpled green wool hat to indicate that I was an American who summered in Vermont. I had my countrymen's air of trust, optimism or goodwill as a sort of national emblem—which was a different commodity from Boghosian's belief in an infinity of possibilities. Optimism is mere hopefulness, whereas his Armenian exuberance implied, if I read it right, the plausibility of holocaust and genocide as well as nights under the full moon.

Boghosian despised my American ignorance of other languages, and apologized to the Italians because their gracious tongue was one Romance language that he didn't know. He commenced learning it right then and there, as he swerved the car around chuckholes. Apart from Armenian, he was most fluent in Arabic, English and French, and he continued to refer to me as "our observer—not a writer," because of my lack of panache. But although it was perhaps partly my stutter that displeased him, this impediment may also have touched some soft spot in him. Therefore Hans was his primary target.

"It's warm and dry this time of year. I'm quite used to stretching out in the grass and listening to the night sounds, aren't you? Do you have matches?" he inquired.

Hans felt nervously through his pockets to be sure he did.

"Good. We may need them. Maybe we will wind up eating each other before we are through." Though he was playing the African again, in fact we had brought no water—only two cases of Camel beer—which might not be such an amusing omission. We had crossed the Nile on the narrow jerry-built bridge, shaking under the tires, which a Dutch crew had put up towards the end of the civil war. In breezy style, we had sped past the army checkpoint without stopping. But there was said to be a 9 P.M. curfew for use of the bridge; after that hour you slept in your car until sunrise on the far bank. We knew Boghosian was mocking us when he said that the soldiers were trigger-happy; on the other hand, they might well *be* trigger-happy. Once the sun went down, he kept suggesting to Hans every twenty minutes that he scratch a match and see what time it was, so that we wouldn't miss curfew.

Boghosian pointed at a muck-hole and reminded us that we might wind up grateful for a sip of the scum left from the last rainfall two months ago. "I have thanked God for a drink from a place like that. As some of you gentlemen know, there are many people who make do with no water at all except what they can paw out of a hole like that."

In his bullying of Hans as a greenhorn, his condescension to all of us, his dubious, catbird attitudinizing as an African, there was just enough poignancy and truth that we could never exactly take offense.

"This is the Cape-to-Cairo Highway. Yes!" he insisted, as we bumped north on a dirt track several hundred yards east of the Nile. I didn't believe him, naturally, until, the next month, I was on the same path farther north, and indeed it was the Cairo-to-Capetown thoroughfare. The dry creekbeds we plunged in and out of he called "Irish bridges," because of course there was no bridge. It would be a four-day drive to Khartoum. "But your balls would swell up like peaches from bouncing up and down."

On these Mongalla plains Boghosian had shot fourteen elephants during the years 1950 to 1955. "That was like your screwing the seven girls," I suggested.

"You think it was too many? Today it would be too many, yes, but not in 1950." He spoke of the time, here on Mongalla Plain, when he and a friend had watched two lionesses toying with a cornered warthog, but the friend "was very naughty and shot them both. The male that was with them got away."

We consumed some of our Camel beer, thinking how thirsty we were going to be if we ran out. Boghosian located the water hole where in his heyday he had camped on a hunt. It was choked with water hyacinth now, as is the Nile itself, though elephants had trampled a gap in the matting in order to drink. There was a heap of giraffe bones and a beheaded buffalo. "Very naughty to leave it like that and not take the meat. Those Baris we passed down the road are hungry people. They would have been grateful for a meal of that meat. They would have held a wedding with that heap of meat."

Hans agreed, but with a twist: they would have married the meat. He was living in the enclave of Djibouti, which was still under the protection of the French Foreign Legion, and a good place for a man of business to be, as he explained—"a place where you can make things disappear." Both European goods that Africa wanted, and African staples such as coffee that Europe wanted, floated through. When the French finally pulled out, the smuggling might or might not continue, but the Issa tribe would eat up the Afar tribe and, safe in Europe again, he would read about it in the newspapers. "We have a saying in Africa: White man makes, black man breaks."

The older Italian liked driving racing cars at home. He asked Boghosian's okay to take over the wheel for some strenuous practice at dodging termite mounds and aardvark holes. The sensitive-faced younger man, who was always either climbing out the window onto the roof with his camera, or hurriedly down inside again to save his skin when we rammed through a thornbush thicket, objected to Hans's cynicism. In fact, he pointed out politely in English, the company Hans represented had been accused in the world press of certain malpractices in Africa, leading to actual loss of life.

Hans answered this imputation with talk of the futility of socialism, radicalism or anarchy. Only money was worth working for. He argued the futility of marriage too. "Love is pain." When, on this subject as well, the cameraman avowed the ethical-liberal position, Hans at last frankly confessed that he had been married, had been hurt in his marriage, had left Germany, deciding to believe in nothing, and, beaching himself in Djibouti, had found just the right spot for it. He was living with an Eritrean refugee girl who was his chief cook and bottle-washer. All for the one low price, he said, he had trained her to make every move in their sex together, so that he could lie perfectly still, never stir or lift a finger, and be brought to his climax effortlessly by her.

In the sedentary fashion of tourists, we watched reedbucks flee, whistling in fear of us, and long-headed, crooked-horned Lelwel hartebeests, and Mongalla gazelles, and little fawn-brown oribis, and the usual succession of warthogs with their tails straight up as they dashed away. Another buffalo carcass had been eaten from inside out by small animals and was streaked with whitish droppings left by the kites that had scavenged at it, but had not been visited by lions.

"Should be more lions. Oh, I won't deny to you that I and not you have had the best of Africa," Boghosian agreed.

Hans remarked that black kites leave white droppings, whereas white men leave brown or black droppings. The sunset spread violet and saffron across the sky. We saw a secretary bird profiled against it, standing high in a tree, like the insignia of the Sudan that it has become. (White rhinos, the symbol before, have grown too scarce.) We caught sight of a serval cat, a white-tailed, black-legged mongoose, numerous Franklyn partridges and sand grouse, fire finches, which Boghosian called "flying plums," some colonies of weaverbirds in selected thorn trees, an aardvark, and various pelicans and storks.

Another giraffe corpse—shot, not a lion kill—prompted Boghosian to remember the Arabs making pack straps from the skin on a giraffe's back in Bahr al-Ghazal. Whenever we saw an animal or a common bird he would tell us its Latin name if he could, with an air of delight that he was recalling his natural history so well. There were tamarind trees hanging with fruit, "elephant-foot" trees with poisonous berries, heglig trees, whose wood is used for camel saddles, its fruit for soap and its juice for killing bilharzia-bearing snails, and the tree known as "the traveler's friend," a species planted by both Turks and Arabs because its seed makes a savory tea. "You could call it the slavers' tree," he said.

Apropos of Christians' distrust of Muslims, I remarked that in my country dogs and gangsters in books were often called "Turk," never "Greek," which didn't seem fair—forgetting that he was an Armenian, until he grinned at me.

When we encountered large living animals, we hushed up, peering at them as if this were a moment of sweet communication outside the boundaries of our ordinary lives. Hans, Boghosian, the Italians and I were all excited in the same way. At first it was fun to see them all running: the predators built for tearing after a target, in a crouch; the grass-eating beasts in a flatter, freer style, simply reaching for speed. Then it seemed repetitive and disturbing to have them invariably streak off, fleeing for their lives at the very sight of us, as if we were cutthroats and thugs—a feeling we didn't like. I, and probably the others, wanted to shout to them, *I won't hurt you;* but all too often, both at home and abroad, I had been the death of wild animals in many direct and indirect ways.

"It's too bad your watch doesn't shine in the dark," Boghosian exclaimed, making Hans scratch another match. After a beautiful blue dusk, it was almost dark. He had appropriated the wheel and was rapidly getting drunk, making Hans open and hold the cans for him while he expounded on the subject of other brews. The Ugandans had named their best beer "Economic Warfare"; Zairean "Primus" and "Makasi" were also smuggled to Juba by "bicycle men" along footpaths a hundred miles long.

Hans did as he was told about opening Boghosian's beer, talking of the purposeless pain of marriage all the while, though he was not alone in wondering whether our friend might not soon be too drunk to find his way back. He said he was from Hamburg, but there were no hamburgers in Hamburg, only schnitzel.

I mentioned that the Sudan had been a world power in the eighth century B.C., when the Cushites moved north from the Fourth Cataract of the Nile to create Egypt's twenty-fifth dynasty.

"Yes, that's right," said Boghosian, who was listening out the window for hyenas and lions. "There was once an Armenian governor in Khartoum, too, and he was an improvement on all the Turks."

No landforms stuck up by which the rest of us might navigate—just a crisp sky full of stars. "This is a sight you don't see every day," Boghosian muttered, getting out. In the light of the moon his face looked sometimes youthful, sometimes old; the bushy eyebrows contradicted the effect of his Trafalgar mustache and Bakerloo tones. I told him how gloomy I'd found the Norwegian well drillers, road builders, lady nurses and doctors at the town of Torit, not far from here—that the blond giant in charge of building the road and the tense stringbean nurse who tended his two hundred workers would have nothing to do with each other, as far as I could tell.

"The Norwegians are not afraid to be gloomy, even out in a place like Torit. The British would be, you see. The British think they will be finished if they ever get gloomy. The Norwegians do not, but on the other hand they don't stay as long as the British can."

Hans urged that the white hunter should think about taking us home.

"I am an African, *mein Fräulein*. You do not see ashes and cow piss in my hair, but I am an African. Idi Amin would cut your balls off and cut off a strip of your hide around the small of your back so that he could wear them around his neck. But he would not cut off mine."

I said that I knew a black Kenyan whose father had been killed by Idi Amin.

"I must agree with you, Mr. Hoagland, that we were wrong to

shoot so many lions, and that as Africans we were wrong to take a sneaking liking to a strongman such as Idi Amin when he materialized," Boghosian said.

I mentioned my theory about how nicely some of the white Kenyans were doing. We both knew a contractor in Juba whose vehicle had foundered in the dry desert bed of a seasonal stream about midway across the no-man's-land between Kapoeta in the Sudan and Lokichoggio in Kenya. He had walked eight miles back to a Toposa cattle camp which he had passed, to ask them to come and help him extricate the car tomorrow. Returning to guard the car, he discovered the stream boiling with rain from a storm on Morongole Mountain in Uganda many miles away. Trying in a panicky moment to reach the roof of the Land Rover, he was swept downstream. But next day three or four Toposas helped him dig out and saw him off toward Lokichoggio, a walk of fifty miles, one of them volunteering to stay with the disabled car no matter how long it took, if he would bring back a pair of walking shoes made from a rubber tire, in the Nairobi manner, and a blanket and a sack of sugar.

"All right," Boghosian said pleasantly. "But what did being a Kenyan have to do with that?" He was driving around the expanse of plain without confiding to us whether he knew where we were.

The older Italian pointed out that the man had been able to talk to the Toposas.

I said he had recognized that they were Toposas, not Turkanas, who were to be feared.

"All right," said Boghosian. "What else would a nice American like you not have known how to do?"

The gentleman—white-haired, generous-faced—had doubled the bounty agreed upon, I said. I would have ended up paying in money, out of ineptness; would not have known where to dig for water, in the meantime; would have wasted a lot of energy and lost a lot of sleep from fear of the animals—of which he met mostly wild camels and hyenas, which betray their approach at night with a telltale snuffle.

"Very good, and very good of him," Boghosian assented. "But you are leaving something out. What happened then? His brother had an airplane. His brother flew to help him when he radioed from Lodwar for help. His brother's airplane crashed in the clouds against the wall of the Rift Valley on the way and his brother was killed."

I had mentioned my idea of Tarzan as the traveling white man, so Hans ventured a comment. "His *vine broke.*"

Boghosian had stopped the car at the water hole once again, stepping out to listen. Then he tried to set the grass on fire. He claimed the tribesmen would want to burn it over before the rainy season. However, because he was drunk and we no longer trusted his judgment, because his gesture seemed so artificial, and because the water hole had nourished a lovely stand of trees (which had no doubt survived countless fires), the rest of us stamped out the flames. He was offended, the more so when we picked up the beer bottles that he was tossing out of the car. "A Dinka would have prized that bottle if you had left it for him. He would have used it to carry water. You are an observer, Mr. Hoagland, but you are not a good observer."

The older Italian tried to mollify him.

"This isn't Hampstead Heath," Boghosian repeated. But singing "Knees Up, Mother Brown" and "Tipperary," he brought us onto the Cape-to-Cairo Highway when he was ready to, and determinedly grasping the wheel, began crossing Irish bridges faster than he had with the daylight to help him. The Italians were silent, perhaps realizing that in their stint of a couple of weeks in the Sudan, this might be the high point.

Hans had visited the government motor pool in Juba and seen that legendary repository of broken toys. From the vantage point of Djibouti he had been watching the political convulsions in Ethiopia. Beginning with the Killing of the Sixty, as it was called, in the fall of 1974, the prisons of the revolutionary government had bulged so full that the police went out with wreckers to the auto graveyards of Addis Ababa to pull in old black Marias and truck bodies and put them on blocks in the prison yard, stuffing another dozen prisoners into each one. The reek of so many souls so closely confined, the crying from inside the trucks that people heard if they were allowed to visit—that is, to stand alongside and shout through the vent in the box—was too grievous to dwell on. Even his German friends with business in the country needed to wangle a passage through eighteen or twenty roadblocks to get to the airport, because each neighborhood in the city had established a separate militia and its own jails—democracy at the block level, which is to say, the roadblock level. "It's insane."

We passed a tipped-over lorry, like a defunct hippo in the moonlight, legs outthrust. Boghosian, who when drunk remained clipped, but who when hearing of a massive tragedy looked more Armenian than British, was reminded of a woeful incident on the road to a town called Opari. A lorry that was delivering petrol had rammed a tree and slid off a little bridge. This rendered the lorry inoperative. Unfortunately, it also suffered a broken spring, which pierced the bed of the truck and a 55-gallon fuel drum. There was a settlement around the bend, and the people came rushing with bottles and tins to catch what was dripping. "They assumed this was paraffin, naturally. The driver wasn't fluent in Madi. He couldn't convince them to the contrary. They knew from his Arabic that he was telling them to leave it alone, but they needed it for those little lamps they make from a pot and a bit of wick, and they are not easily persuaded in Arabic. You can imagine the blighter getting into a huff when they wouldn't listen. He was alone there, and when he couldn't scare them, he took himself off somewhere. Nighttime. The people light their little lamps. One by one the little huts explode in flames."

We raced toward the Nile bridge, only two hours past curfew, barreled right across without slowing down at the checkpoint, and were not shot at.

Back at the hotel, we all, except Hans, ate cutlets from a huge Nile perch that hadn't been in the kitchen for more than a couple of days, to judge by its taste.

"I am beginning to dislike you, Mr. Hoagland!" Boghosian shouted when I offered to pay for my own fish instead of letting him treat me.

Hans imbibed three bowls of soup and two rice puddings in order to recover his fluids, with lots of extra salt poured in the soup because he had sweated, as well as pepper "to make the testicles work," he said.

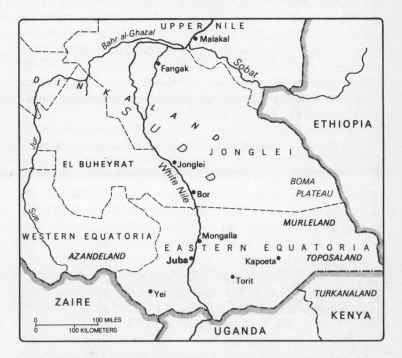

"Here you all are," Marlow cries out exasperatedly at his companions during a break in the telling of *Heart of Darkness*. They are comfortable London shipping-company executives enjoying an evening aboard a yawl anchored on the Thames. "Here you all are, each moored with two good addresses, like a hulk with two anchors, a butcher round one corner, a policeman round another, excellent appetites, and temperature normal—you hear—normal from year's end to year's end."

It's the cry of a homeless adventurer, with his shabby intestinal ailments and threadbare bank account, meeting the condescension of homebodies who believe he is roaming the world only because he is maladjusted or professionally second-rate. Now, however, an African sojourning in London would be more likely to voice Marlow's complaint. The Norwegian Church Relief people and U.N. expatriates turn their early attention to constructing verandaed living quarters and swimming pools for themselves, each dealing in only oddly circumscribed patterns with the surrounding ocean of need. Yet, looking at their haunted and tentative faces, one can't fault these individuals—for their mixed motives and healthy stools—who have come halfway down the curve of the earth to help people who are drinking water the color of burned plastic and which smells like a goat's bladder.

"Africa is less than meets the eye," a newspaperman from Paris kept telling me. To which I rejoined that sometimes not much did meet the eye: the watering rhythms, sugarcane every six days, camels every thirteen. The tribesmen who objected to having their picture taken for fear you might thereby possess them were like an American who would never disclose his bank balance, lest somebody think he could "buy me and sell me." "Oh, yes," the Frenchman said, agreeing that America was the same.

Willem, my landlord, had wanted to be a bridge builder, but there were too many bridges in Holland already; had wanted to be a forester, but could find no forests. He had gone to Surinam as an X-ray technician, but had slipped on a wet palm leaf on the steps of the post office in Paramaribo and broken his back, an injury which had hampered him in his adventuring ever since. Traveling was a tic, he said. Discovering that he had business in Yei, he piled me and the beauteous Edna in his truck to visit their friend Dr. Conn, a German forester in the Kagelu Forest, next to Zaire.

Conn was light-haired, light-boned, sunny-spirited, a brisk, slight man who had worked in Brazil and Panama. He had gone over the handlebars of his motorcycle the night before, and said that holding his swollen arm was "like sleeping with a dog in the bed." He introduced us to a pretty Kakwa girl, wearing a pretty dress, who was his housekeeper, softening the isolation of the place.

She had postponed her marriage to see him through to the end of his tour, he said.

Being a resilient fellow, Conn roused himself to show us the cashew, rubber and mahogany trees he was raising experimentally, the grafts of Indian onto local mangoes, the oil palms from Nigeria, with a small plantation of coffee shrubs situated in the shade of these. Teak was his main concern—a Burmese and Indian tree introduced into this queer indigenous forest of twisty, low, knotty-wooded species that superficially resembled apple trees, a "fool's orchard," as he said, that the Belgians had tinkered with at the turn of the century, then the British, then the Southern Sudan Liberation Movement. We saw baboons, colobus monkeys, the sole elephant left around after the firepower of the war, and a Kakwa hunter with a feather in his hair and two dik-diks slung on one shoulder, carrying a few paw-paws and leaves from the same tree for a meat tenderizer.

We saw shea "butter" trees, whose seeds when roasted, pounded and boiled produce a cooking oil, and the borassus palm, whose hanging nuts contain a pulpy layer that people chew before planting the stone, which grows rootstocks that are a hunger food. Conn maintained a small pit-sawing operation to give employment—the logs laid over a pit in which the lower man stood, digging wood dust out of his eyes between pulls on the saw.

Despite poor Conn's banged-up arm, he had English visitors as well. They were growing a short-season maize and a new, oilier peanut, for possible adaptation into the economy. Their chief was a lanky Harrow type who exclaimed "Precious!" or "Lovely!" in a choking voice after every joke, so long as it wasn't about Africans, in which case he didn't think it appropriate to laugh. His Scottish mechanic, however, had a way of whirling his hands above his head as if he were a medicine man before repairing an engine coil or starting the electric generator. "Many hands make light." Since this was a tsetse area where livestock could not survive, the vegetables people raised ought to be the best. There were other accents from the British Isles, other horticulturists hard at work, though my crude American ear could not always detect the distinctions. Upon hearing that I was a journalist a lady nutritionist announced with a giggle, "What a howl!" and clammed up.

On our trip of about a hundred miles, Willem had given a lift to a varied assortment of Africans, all "cousins," "sisters" or friends of the policemen at the roadblocks. A boy in a student's white shirt hugged a physics text. A Bari woman with a clay pot "cooked with much wood," and given a grain so that it wouldn't slip in her hands, held a precious sack of cassava flour with which she intended to reimburse the relatives she was going to visit. But an Arab businessman carelessly tossed his gear on top of the sack and pot, and they broke, so that the flour blew away. A woman with a bandaged head asked to be dropped at the dispensary in Lalyo. Even with as many passengers as the springs could support, we left plenty of people standing at the roadblocks. What spoiled the fun of our four-hour drive from Juba to Yei and back the next day was that we were seldom out of sight of other citizens who were trying to flag us down. Usually they beseeched us to stop, several hundred of them, not all of whom acted awed. Some shouted angrily as they ate our dust. In the rear-view mirror we would see a man shaking his fist as the distance lengthened between him and us. What he didn't realize was that around the previous bend, and the bend ahead, were other men and women, waving us down—that the road for as far as it ran presented an endless procession of people whose one hope of transportation beyond their villages that day was us. Seeing that we had Africans already riding with us did not mean his child wasn't sick with a fever too, or that his wife didn't face a twenty-five-mile walk to market because we had gone by with the back of the pickup not filled.

There was a schoolmaster who hoped for a ride. His blackboard was a debarked strip of tree painted black; his kids had sticks in their hands to practice copying the alphabet in the sand. He didn't want to run with begging motions toward the road—one or two of the boys did it for him—because he was afraid the class would see us buzz right by. Because nobody seemed to know the international thumbing signal, it was a little easier to pass them by. They waved at us, and since other people along the road were really waving only to say hello, we could wave back, pretending not to understand that this man with an urgent look, holding a child in his arms, was not just flapping his hand to welcome us to the

Sudan. It was not possible to be a good Samaritan unless one ceased to be anything else; yet sometimes the way people ran from a hut in the distance to try to intercept us, waving as frantically as if a life depended upon our stopping, as if a woman were lying in the agony of a breech birth, one had to remind oneself that maybe all they wanted was to save themselves a two-day walk.

"You shouldn't imagine that they like whites better here in Juba than where you were," a Dinka acquaintance explained to me, after we had been talking about Zanzibar and Dar es Salaam. "They haven't seen them very much. They don't know what they think of *khawajas;* they have been living in the bush."

And from a curial Italian churchman in a sun helmet, with a drawn and calculating face, who was stationed in Khartoum: "You need to bear in mind that the people down through most of the South have not fought against a European since the last century. The Arabs were the enemy. Perhaps they are deciding what they think about Europeans—if they are going to bother to think anything."

When I was feeling mildly weepy, with my nose raw from the dust of a trip like this, I would go to the rambling, white-plastered brick house of the Maryknoll Fathers on Addis Ababa Street. Father John was said to be excellent at handling severe emotional emergencies, but was too tough an Africanist to talk to when one simply had tears in one's nose. His partner, Father Tom, a gentle, owlish man—the sort who in America might have been described by his parishioners as "artistic"—was better for cases like mine.

Father Tom hailed from Albany, New York, but had spent seventeen years in Japan. He had hoped to spend the rest of his life there, and had accepted this temporary posting to Central Africa in mid-career as a way of paying his dues; afterwards he could expect to go back. Ever since its period of martyrdom during World War II, the Roman Catholic Church in Japan had been subsiding peacefully into a permanent eclipse, so considerable sadness was involved in working there. As the core of aged Christians died out, the assignment contrasted increasingly with the social struggles the Maryknolls were in the thick of in Latin America—or in a place like the Southern Sudan, where millions of souls were "uncommitted," destined to slide away from animism toward one of two world religions. But he loved the epochal ritual of Japan's ancient society and the civility, though we seldom talked of it, since I had not been there.

For different reasons, Father Tom and I didn't speak of Juba either. "It's quite a place, isn't it?" he said once, after I had enjoyed a couple of hours of silence in the cool parlor with a stack of *Newsweek*s, which I was licking through as if they were ice cream cones. I nodded, smiling, and he said no more, not only for fear of setting me off, but in order not to rock his own equilibrium, I think. He still pronounced the name of his hometown in the impatient tone he must have used when, as a seminarian, he had decided that the need was greater abroad than to serve as a diocesan priest. Now he spoke ironically of this youthful perception. Both on his trips home and when he read *Newsweek,* he saw that on the contrary, it could be argued that a Catholic priest had more practical tasks to perform if he stayed in the bailiwick of the bishop of Albany.

Like me, Father Tom admired the vast brown plains and the openheartedness he'd met with in the grass settlements he visited when he and Father John could wangle enough fuel for a trip. Besides training lay catechists, they were helping to establish a new university in Juba. When, a year after my return to America, I read in an issue of the magazine *Sudanow* that the founder of this university had been killed in the crash of a chartered plane at Malakal, along with a Maryknoll priest who had been accompanying him to a conference in Cameroon, I skimmed through the rest of the article, sick to learn who the priest was. Possibly my gentle friend had already received his transfer to Japan. But when the name finally appeared, it was not that of some replacement, nor of his partner, the veteran of the rigors of the Sinai and Dar es Salaam.

Lover of ritual though he was, Father Tom Manteca was the one who thought to introduce me to the groaning cynic of a veterinarian whom I best liked traveling with. This was a fellow whose favorite word was *beast,* who called missionaries and other leper-helpers "holy people," pronounced in a meaningful drawl. He claimed that he was "from the old breed of tech reps; we don't get emotionally involved," although he did seem to share the conviction of Conrad's Marlow that the world is everywhere "a dark place." A tech rep, he explained, was an expert, and an expert was "somebody who can tell from the wrinkles in the sheets whether it was done for love or for money." I will call him Hector.

Hector was Hungarian by birth, in his early fifties, large, soft in build, his eyes and nose partially lost in a sallow, doughy face like a gingerbread man's, and planning to retire eventually to the South of France, though not from any deep familiarity with the spot. He had spent better than a decade in Congo-Brazzaville, Nigeria, Angola and other problem sites rife with what he described as "self-help soldiering." The Sudan was the first country "where they hadn't shot at me," he said, until the Juba mutiny, when bullets from the airport did manage to hit his house. He had left Hungary during the revolt of 1956, when for a few days the border with Austria stood unguarded. His brother had chosen to stay behind, but now that Hector had established New Zealand citizenship and had dollars to spend, he could go back and forth. The two of them owned summer homes overlooking the Danube and had become close again. His brother worked as an attorney in some arcane capacity within the interstices of the Hungarian state. Hector had always wondered why his brother had balked at that particularly frenetic moment of decision in 1956, but recently, in talking with him, had come to understand that the reason had been his brother's dread at the idea of having to learn a new language.

We guffawed at that, for I would have felt the same. Hector said his father had been a pioneering pilot in the 1930's, flying commercial Fokkers from Holland to Java, a two-week round trip in a single-engine plane. In the fifteenth century his ancestors had been mercenaries in Venice, so both he, as a technical consultant who had not even troubled to pick the continent to which he was assigned, and his father had followed along in that line.

Hector had been waiting eight months for a shipment of veterinary supplies, six months for a team of two volunteer assistants to arrive, and the same amount of time for a Toyota Rover for them to drive. In the meantime, although he had been provided with a driver by his agency, he liked to chauffeur himself on field trips, the driver, who doubled as translator, sitting in back. When stuck for water, he would filter the local stuff through a clean sock and pour in iodine to kill the worms and germs, plus a dose of whiskey to blunt the bite of the iodine. He had "a concrete-mixer stomach," he said. Though he was married, and—in rooms almost devoid of furniture in the beginning—he and his Australian wife could appear chipper enough, there was a element of sorrow or longing in his makeup that I never quite wanted to fathom, maybe because we got along so well. When we shared barracks accommodations in the rest houses of the countryside, I heard the tossing of his sufferings at night.

We had insomnia in common, and a certain busywork way of hurrying about, certain memories of French food, and a similar style in talking with non-Europeanized black Sudanese—that is, of standing physically close to a man, perhaps touching his shoulder, and looking in the same direction in which his eyes had fallen, explaining frankly the reasons for any suggestion, question, or any quandary we had gotten into—a sort of emphasized patience that still left a gap, of course, but was more democratic than colonial.

"Sir, I'm sorry, I wish I could," Hector would say at the roadblocks, climbing wearily out of his car to explain once again why he could not pick up riders. "My employer has an insurance policy that tells me I can't. Do you understand?" His serious manner made it seem at least a mystery, rather than an insult, even if nobody happened to know what an insurance policy was.

Not being as much of a worrier as me, Hector was amused that on our trips I read Byzantine history for relaxation instead of Sudanese, because, although Byzantine was just as bloody, it hadn't taken place right here. Yet he sweated more in the heat, and howled under his breath at delays, complaining about all the sacred cows that should be used as plow animals or else provide more meat. Like wild creatures, they had a short lactation period and produced only a couple of quarts a day apiece, though the milk was rich in butterfat. "Too *many* animals! What they need is a butcher, not a vet!"

Butcherable animals were saved forever for fests; even so, the belief was widespread that meat was too strong a nutriment for children to eat, that they should only suck the bones and leftovers or drink the cooking water. And several Nilotic groups believe that if a menstruating woman drinks milk, the cow it came from will dry up—which, as a practical matter, means that many women stay in their villages where there are garden foods to eat, not going out to the cattle camps where the grazing is better but milk is the main fare. So sometimes the men neglect the welfare of the herds to stay at home too.

Hector toured with a tent and a bird-hunting license that enabled him to keep a shotgun and was much easier to obtain than a permit to carry a rifle. Besides affording protection, the gun occasionally furnished our meals. Guinea fowl are so plentiful in places that they run down the center of the road. He would shoot a couple, smear wet clay over them, and put them in the camp-fire that evening. When he broke open the baked covering, the feathers peeled off neatly, embedded in the mold, and the flesh was ready-roasted inside.

Hector said the Toposas' big short-horned zebus were the finest cattle in the Sudan. The Toposas are a flamboyant people who have known outside government only since the British reached them in the 1930's. Located right against the Ethiopian frontier, they are so formidable that their herds escaped being stolen from them to feed the contending forces during the South's long war. Bride prices still average around fifty cattle, for instance, versus only ten or fifteen for their neighbors the Didingas, who suffered a great deal more. (Indemnification after a case of adultery might amount to three cows and three bulls, with fifteen goats thrown in, Hector said.) But—what is rare for the Southern Region—as a consequence, their territory has become overgrazed. After the Addis Ababa Agreement was signed in 1972, the Didingas and other tribes nearby—the Boyas, the Dongotonas, the Lotukos—who had also been ravaged in the war, wanted desperately to acquire any surplus animals the Toposas would part with. They were willing to trade grazing rights, fancy ironwork, grain or labor. Inevitably, though, these grazing concessions were now not granted with as light a heart, and the land-hungry Toposas were retaliating with fierce raids upon the Lotukos and Boyas, in particular, besides reviving the traditional spear fights which they worked themselves up to with their hereditary enemies, the Turkana of Kenya.

Cradling his stomach apologetically, Hector talked often about the diet of the countryside. Feeding humans was at the heart of a veterinarian's profession, he said. If the Sudanese seldom allowed themselves a meal of meat, fortunately dura sorghum, which is their staff of life, is endowed with more protein than maize, and is even a little better in this respect than wheat. An acre will produce from five to fifteen hundred pounds of sun-dried grain. The plants make do on remarkably infertile soil if necessary, as maize cannot, resisting both dry spells and waterlogging because of their branching, silica-stiffened roots. During a drought they conserve moisture by rolling their leaves.

In Equatoria, the stalks of dura sorghum grow taller than a man, stiff enough to build tukl huts from. The heads selected for next year's seed are hung from the ceiling, where the smoke of the hut helps to preserve them. Finger millet—which is a shorter relative of dura—is frequently interplanted with it. Finger millet's special virtue is that it stores well, even in a wet climate, for years. It is also a good first crop on raw land that has been newly cleared, and by laying in a first seeding with the "grass rains" of February, two harvests can be obtained. Though it needs more rain and requires somewhat more cultivating than dura sorghum, it is hardier than maize, but skimpier than either in yield. When combined as a flour with cassava flour, however, it adds protein to the miserably deficient nutritive value provided by cassava tubers alone.

Cassava, though the staff of life in some of the countries just to the south, is a secondary foodstuff in the Sudan. Propagated by planting stem cuttings, usually on older, poorer soil, its tubers consist almost entirely of fiber and carbohydrates. But it is pest- and drought-resistant, shedding its leaves in order to survive when no rain falls. Because eating cassava insufficiently cooked can bring on prussic-acid poisoning, the tubers are peeled and roasted in ashes, or peeled, cut into disks, fermented, dried and ground before being boiled. A warm climate, with minimal labor, is required to grow cassava, but babies in cassava areas shrink in weight appallingly when they are first weaned. Sudanese children, including those of the Southern tribes, are privileged to eat more millet and sorghum, and, at least until recently, had to pay a price for what they ate. Starlings, bishop birds, queleas, and other weavers attack standing sorghum with such hungry enthusiasm that children in cultivating communities, until they began to have an opportunity to go to school, spent most of the fall on platforms out-of-doors, ringing a gong or cracking a whip whenever the flocks wheeled near.

On the road, I used to think of Father Pitya, one of Juba's black priests, who, with the advice of the two Maryknolls, supposedly had a quarter of a million square miles to cover, with a gasoline allotment that allowed him only one field trip each year. Within the city, he taught classes of two hundred children—"That's freaking, not teaching!" He had been a refugee in Uganda, then had studied in Rome, and was homey with foreigners, as were his Anglican counterparts. Both Anglicans and Catholics complained that their problem was not primarily that the Khartoum government showed bias in favor of the Koranic schools operating in the South. Rather, the foreign missionary organizations found it unfashionable nowadays to send hymnals and whatnot. They poured money into preventive medicine, social work and economic development, instead. "They work on the body. They forget man has a spirit," said Father Pitya. Indeed, the hymn books in the mud churches I visited did date forty years back. Although the *fuqaha* (Islamic village teachers), like the Christians, might need to teach under a tree until a mosque was built for them, Saudi Arabia made sure that they had plenty of books and pencils in the meantime.

Individual Christian missionaries were more versatile. On our way to Renk, Hector and I encountered a Baptist gentleman from West Virginia who was coaxing a limping lorry piled with building materials, six months' worth of gasoline and kerosene, tinned beef and vegetables and wheat flour for his family, and measles and malaria shots, toward the four villages he had assigned to himself. He spoke about the possibility of cooking with methane gas generated from cow manure when the kerosene was gone. "Why not just dung?" Hector remarked, raising his eyebrows, as he liked to do with these "holy people."

The gentleman had been traveling a week, and had crossed the roadless desert directly from Kenya, in order not to risk having his truck seized by the Ugandan army. He had broken an axle outside Lodwar, had figured out how to fix it, and had experienced the predictable customs difficulties upon entering the Sudan. The question was whether he would have to pay duty on the prayer books and cement that he had brought in. Within six short months he had established a lonely brickworks, had laid the foundations for a church and school. Now, pale and tired, he was confronted with the matter of getting his and his wife's provisionary visas renewed. He didn't dare do less than fly to Khartoum to argue his case personally before the Muslim authorities, although his slender budget made no allowance for such an excursion. Nor did he dare to leave his wife behind again, because of the chance their application would be refused; they might need to leave forthwith. He had fretted about her, alone during this trip, because of the dicey situation after the Juba mutiny. Absolutely bone-tired, he was wondering at the moment what was going to happen at the market town of Bor. Would the soldiers at the roadblock there ask him to unload his entire eight tons for inspection, and then watch him load it all back again? (In fact, to give credit where credit is due, they did not.)

In Bor we met a Swedish anthropologist, a gray little man with a funny beard who seemed preoccupied and uncharming, as so many excellent researchers do. Like some of the best, however, he was traveling with a lovely high-strung protégée, a blond countrywoman of his, who was also studying the Murle tribe, and who when they were together lent him the benefit of her good looks. She calmed him, strengthened him. They laughed about the hidden satchel of canned herring and artichoke hearts they kept for secret snacks after every tenth meal shared with the Murle.

Over a guinea fowl that evening, I remembered a story of Richard Nixon's private interregnum in the City of New York. A clever female reporter, interviewing the former vice-president, had asked whether he was enjoying the cultural advantages of the metropolis. Did he like the theater? "Oh, I love the theater," said Mr. Nixon. "I've never seen a play I didn't like."

Just so, I told Hector, I had yet to meet a missionary I didn't like. Could he show me one?

"Out here, the outhouse is your theater. Oh, do we howl sometimes. Plenty of drama. What gets up my nose," he went on, "is that most of the women have a face like a hatful of assholes. It isn't only that they have nothing better to do with themselves than come out to Africa. Their director up in London isn't about to ship his assier ladies out to where you've got all these black men lounging about. He'll send them to Chile or Hong Kong; he's got proper ideas. Otherwise he wouldn't be religious."

We met two Save the Children Fund nurses who, with the doctor they had with them, were seeing thirty or forty thousand patients a year, none over the age of five—which is a zany idea to many Africans, who know that in the next famine it will be the bread-winner's survival that is going to count. But the older woman, a widow, a Scot, with a quick, fond heart, served us hot rich Scotch broth. She liked "young people with stars in their eyes," and had with her an example, an Irish girl named Dora, who had gone home from Biafra to care for her elderly father, and now that he had died, had come back.

There was a dapper Dan named Bill Anderson, who was stationed at a hardship post at the mouth of the Sobat River near Malakal. Wearing a sport jacket and a fashionably cut beard, he looked actually debonair as you saw him go by in the cab of a souk lorry, journeying to Juba. He had been raised in Egypt, and had worked here at a Bible center before General Abboud's expulsion of the missionaries in 1963 and 1964. Yet in this classic missionary-martyr battleground beside the Sudd, where the Verona Catholics in three Pyrrhic, heroic Attempts had relied "on God's help," on "death or patience," during successive sieges of malaria and Shilluk spearmen and the Mahdists—where still the Lutherans in Malakal said that what was most disheartening was that during the rainy season you couldn't so much as *walk;* your feet flew out from under you as if the ground were one enormous banana skin—he had somehow preserved a natty look, a confidence like some sort of Californian's, which I found admirable.

There were five hundred thousand Christian parishioners in the South before the 1964 expulsion, Father John Vantani of the Verona Fathers had told me in Khartoum. From a beginning in 1848, with ventures into the slave market to buy a few "converts," and an Attempt upon the Sudd so ravaging to the first sixty-four priests of the mission that the Pope himself had called them back, this was an impressive figure. But now these Italian priests and nuns were restricted to schoolteaching jobs north of the tenth parallel. It was the free-lance Protestants whom the regional government was permitting to "trickle" or "sneak" back under cover of social aid work, an Arab of the Khartoum administration had grumbled to me afterwards.

Another man we met, Dr. Harold Laurence, an English physician-missionary who was working for an association of American churches which wished to be represented in Africa, mentioned with satisfaction the exasperated comment of an immigration official at Khartoum Airport: "So you've come right back again?" "I was able to assure him that I had never set foot in his country before," he said.

Dr. Laurence had served in several bordering nations, however. He had white hair and eyes like a local African's, eyes that under his glasses were recessed, as if they had tried to draw back into his head to escape the sun and dust and flies. They seemed not quite able to focus at the same short distances as mine. His skin was so burned that if he didn't already have skin cancer, he never would. He had five grown children, all of them born in Africa, and a center of gravity like someone not English or American, and who believes that he is, as Hector put it, "an outrider for God."

Not for security reasons but because of a bureaucratic snafu, maps of the Sudan were unobtainable. Nonetheless, having anticipated this, he had gone to the British Museum and carefully xeroxed a topographic map of Equatoria Province in the archives, pasting the sheets together afterwards. He had also looked up the appropriate anthropological reports on several tribal peoples whom he described as "my new friends," and whenever he ran into another expatriate he would unroll this xeroxed creation and painstakingly mark down every location where the Baptists, Lutherans, Presbyterians or the government's own medical corpsmen were said to be working. The rest of us on our tours might make similar inquiries so that we could spend the night near other Europeans; but when he had circled all of these hamlets, it was in a sector left over, where the last lorry track had long since petered out, that he and his wife, with their Vitamin A and Vitamin C, their diphtheria vaccine and one-shot worming capsules, set up shop.

Needless to say, Dr. Laurence kept his eye on the main chance.

Through all of his concern with sore mouths and bloody stools, he was here "to give witness," and confessed that he had encountered very few citizens in the bush "who call themselves Christians." The Troubles had come tragically soon. Had Christianity been vouchsafed another couple of decades of spadework before the repressions began, those five hundred thousand converts would have become millions.

I said I'd been told that as soon as the Arab Sudanese had sense enough to send in black Africans from the Muslim communities of Nigeria and Tanzania, they would make quick progress in converting the South, but that the same cultural arrogance that had already cost them so heavily in the region would delay this.

He nodded, all eyes and ears in his new territory, though he knew a good deal more about it than I did—listening in that vivid manner of a person who believes that he is an agent of God. We were sitting over tea near the town of Fangak, and Dr. Laurence spoke about the beauty in the faces of the Nuer children, and about the marvelous cloudbanks overhead. An old friend of his, a missionary in the Ogaden Desert in Ethiopia who had served in Africa for half a century, had been shot a few months earlier. Somali rebels had walked into his camp, interviewed him in Somali for a minute, and pushed him against the wall. For a moment it must have been like countless visits he had received from Somali and other tribesmen over a span of fifty years. He had turned and greeted them with the same alert smile—except that this time, almost before he had had time to recognize the difference, he was dead.

Hector said he had heard of a parcel of missionaries in Ethiopia, at a school for the blind, who had resisted evacuation from a war zone because they were waiting for a sign to appear in the sky.

"Ah, well, you see, they probably didn't want to leave the children," explained our acquaintance. "They couldn't tell the soldiers that, so they told them *this*."

Dr. Laurence spoke repeatedly of "blessings in disguise." Hardly any development could fail to be such. He referred to the fact that Khartoum's handsome tan Anglican cathedral, on the People's Palace grounds, had been sequestered by the authorities ever since the coup attack of 1971, when Communists had put a machine gun up in the belfry that commanded the front lawn. Naturally, they had wanted to close the cathedral anyway because of its awkward placement, but now instead of one congregation existing in the city, "you have three, meeting at three churches."

In Kenya, he had worked with mirror-adversaries, like the Turkana and Samburu, crossing "like a war correspondent" between them. There was no doubt of his admiration for them, or that he wasn't simply condescending when he spoke of seeing most of his patients only once, before their relatives carried them off to some inaccessible cattle camp. He gave the one-shot shots because there was no use in handing over any pills for the patient to carry away; they would go to his personality ox and to his friends, if he thought they were helping him.

Because of the reinforcing effect of his own dramatic beliefs, it was a private, medieval magic land that our man of the cloth traveled in—very like the combination of dragon myths and living beasts from their home villages that Attilio and Ilariyo had evoked for me, back in Gilo. He spoke inflectionlessly of stints in Uganda and the Central African "Empire" of Life President, Field Marshal, Emperor Jean-Bedel Bokassa—a place that most of us in Juba mentioned with mocking but fearful hoots—as if the Emperor were present himself. But he allowed me to catch a flicker out of the corner of his eye as he said "empire" to indicate that this term was "rendering unto Caesar."

When Laurence asked why we were going to Renk, Hector announced with a groan that he was the latest representative of an ancient line of mercenaries. Even in New Zealand, he had worked on North Island or South Island according to where he was *sent*. I said that last year I had been at an FAO conference in Rome and had talked for a while with the Sudanese representative, named Babiker; I had found him so subtle, so "Levantine"—as I had conceived this foreign corner of the world—that when he described his country it had caught my imagination.

"And how does it strike you now?" asked our physician.

I said I'd met nobody as subtle as Babiker since arriving in Khartoum, not even Babiker himself, when I'd looked him up.

I also said that in Cairo last year my guide to the city had been a Coptic woman, plump, green-eyed, not conventionally good-look-

ing, whose angry dilemmas as a woman, as a Copt and as a proud
Egyptian were so complicated—

"That you wanted to try the missionary position," Hector interrupted.

"That I wanted to hear more about them."

Somehow the plumpness represented to me a potential for kindness, as straight "Levantine" fat would not have, and hinted at
other indulgences besides a sweet tooth, although the clumsy, self-
consciously risqué jokes Lilah told on herself indicated an inno-
cence, instead. Like a fox in a net, she had snapped at me and everyone else, afraid she was losing her mind. She believed she needed
psychiatric help, but couldn't obtain it in Cairo, and because of
the currency regulations couldn't afford to go elsewhere. I had pitied
her painfully when I heard later that she had been killed in a car
crash—wondering whether she had been driving alone or riding
in the passenger's seat with a friend.

By education Lilah was a European, but was passionately loyal
to Egypt, though hopelessly mired in the two-hour traffic jams and
three-day red tape of Cairo in her work as a cicerone. She made in
a day what a laborer with a family would work for two months to
earn, and so she gave much of her money away in tips, chatting
with ordinary people she met, as a Muslim woman could not. At
thirty, she still lived with her parents and her old nanny, sleeping
on the couch in the living room, and yet she was being shadowed
by the morals police because of her habit of falling in love with
foreigners and visiting them at their hotels. She said she had thereby
made herself unmarriageable to most of her countrymen, including
those who wanted just such "a plump wife with whitish skin who
plays the piano and speaks French," and yet had been stood up by
those same foreign lovers when they went home to Milan or Rio
de Janeiro or Paris and decided that marrying an Egyptian woman
might not be so good an idea after all. In Arabic, at the Estoril
Restaurant, a pal of hers had jeeringly cooked my goose one afternoon by comparing me at length to her Brazilian, her Italian, her
Frenchman, whose "long-haired dictionary," as she finally explained in English, she had become.

Lilah wore a green scarf or sweater and green eye shadow to
set off her large eyes and flushed skin. She had big teeth, bold, dis-

approving lips, a majestic pout, a temper that could be alarming even apart from the boost given it by her bad nerves—a continual edge of impatience, but then, a rather bright smile. She was a witch at palm reading (at least, I liked what she said), but very businesslike in manner afterwards. Her shoulders were queenly, but her stride was earnest and dumpy, like the busy career woman in her country's foreign service that she ought to have been, but couldn't be, as a minority Copt.

Though her chin was round and receding, Lilah was blessed with that wonderfully forceful, fastidious, disdainful nose which Copts, who are descended from the original Egyptians, tend to have; it dominated and centered her face, as in Pharaonic art. With a fox's fierce joy, she defended me in dragoman's slang from the dragomen at tourist traps like the night Pyramids, yet otherwise often had a breakable air, because of her hawking cough, tense, plaintive voice and harried expression, as she worried more and more about herself. A diplomat's *haute* French interspersed her Oxford English, but in a voice only thinly authoritative, as she lectured on tourist buses (on their sides was emblazoned the word MISR, which is Arabic for "Egypt," but which toward the end read like "misery" to me). Here was I, another visiting fireman, ignorant, needy, at sea, and sometimes it absolutely infuriated her. They picked her brains—these married professors on five-month sabbaticals, journalists, junior diplomats—and then tamely returned to their wives.

"The leaves need a washing," Lilah would say, in her green sweater, her smile flashing, as we set out on a walk on the winter days. She knew her city's history from its founding as the tent encampment of the conqueror Amr, who had plunged from Syria with four thousand bedouin and swept through Christian Egypt in the year 641. So we played that favorite lovers' game where one person leads and the other closes his eyes for the fun of following blindly.

She had a jittery way of "saluting" when saying goodbye, or of putting up her hand to warn me off, but sometimes murmured instructions as to what was permitted by custom in Cairo—holding hands in a taxi but not kissing, holding hands when crossing the street but not when walking on the sidewalk. Ardently patriotic, she was driven to distraction by the suffocating difficulty of placing a telephone call or getting around the city quickly, by the pigeon-holes women (and Copts) were put in, by the poverty and defeated gallantry of so many Egyptian family men whom she met in the course of her roamings as a tour guide. Worse, it was "terrifying" to live in a country medically primitive and to want medical help.

"We must be careful. We can hurt each other," Lilah told me. People unhappily married in America liked to pretend that it was the same as not being married, but she had learned to be cautious. When she left me, however, it was not for an Egyptian, but for a European, an ambassador's son who crashed his car on the road to Faiyum and killed both of them.

"And what about Lilah? Was *she* here?" our missionary-physician asked me after I had told the story.

"No, she certainly was not. Nobody nearly so complicated."

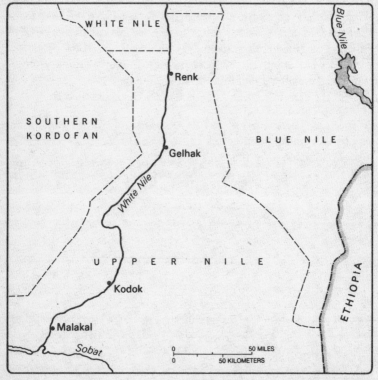

Renk is a river town about sixteen hours south of Khartoum by fast truck. Hector and I never added up the time it took us to get there from Juba, because our car broke down after three days near Malakal. We left the driver to watch over it, and caught a bus-truck (a bus body on a truck bed) north. Sitting five abreast, with a man in a gold-and-blue hat and a brown, red-trimmed robe, holding a ceremonial umbrella, on the bench facing us in front, we were far more comfortable than in the average lorry, until I realized that it was really constructed as a sort of cage proposition—the windows barred, both doors opening on the same side—and that if we tipped over, we might spend the rest of our short lives inside.

The passenger so colorfully dressed was West African, I presumed, and had with him two veiled wives, whose faces we saw only when they nursed their babies. Then we saw both their pert faces and their breasts. I slept as I sat, dreaming of Joe DiMaggio slapping two home runs, and of a fox leaping high to catch a guinea fowl. The man in the seat ahead of me woke me once to look at my watch because, as he said, he had one himself. He spat out the window in the heat every few minutes, regardless of the direction of the wind, though in the course of many hours I never saw him drink anything.

The track became not a road but a succession of rutted attempts, side by side and a hundred yards broad, which our own and other lorries had made after the rains to get across a series of mud bogs. This was the same slick, self-sealing, fecund Nile clay that will be the engine of the Sudan's prosperity in twenty years, but in the meantime is so slippery in the bad season that even people riding a bull or a camel need to dismount and walk, clinging for support to the halter of the beast.

Like a caravan, we stopped every thirty miles with five or six other lorries to rest or to be looked over at the police posts. At one of these two-room establishments, the door of the jail cell was open and a young man in striped pajamas stepped out. I thought he was a prisoner until he started shouting at us to stand up, feeling each man's sleeve for the sheathed dirk sometimes concealed there —officious, menacing-looking in his spectacles, like a university graduate among peons. He slapped the ones who were slow about raising their arms, and exacted from our driver the bulb from our right headlight to replace a broken bulb in the police truck, and— with a wheedling, insulting expression, as if he were propositioning a "lioness" (prostitute)—a Sudanese pound.

Hector and I unrolled our sleeping bags next to a hut, where we wouldn't be stepped on, and woke up at dawn to a gray horizon and caravan stirrings. All around, people were emptying their lungs of phlegm, and squatting modestly, clutching their galabiehs close around them, then lighting a cigarette—"the grass of the ancestors," as the Shilluk call it.

Up to now we had passed both thatch villages and mud-brick ones; this was one of the latter, its dogs of an ancient coursing breed, like dogs on a frieze. They were actually coursing; somebody had started a fire to burn the old growth off the plain, and rabbits and other small beasties were fleeing. A half-dozen kites swooped in front of the flames, catching mice. Several pied crows, wagging their tails, were gobbling charred grasshoppers. The fire in the wind lent a smoky taste to our tea. From a ten-year-old girl we bought sesame seeds.

A sheep that had traveled on one of the lorries was being loaded again, hauled up by a leg. When the motor started, the animal leaped off and lay broken-kneed, till a man with a spear with a ball of wood on the point, like the button on a fencing foil, jumped down and hoisted it up.

"Meat!" Hector said mournfully. Then, "Keep cheerful. Lean into a trip. We are leaving the Kingdom of the Shilluk and entering the Kingdom of the Fung, as it was—who were also Shilluk to begin with, some people say."

A strip of trees marked the Nile, with camels occasionally browsing on them. We saw women carrying bundles of firewood on their heads, their smooth skin purple-black, the color of eggplant. At the agricultural settlements were stacks of bagged cotton, and one boasted an open-air slaughterhouse, hooks hanging from a scaffold and three maribou storks stalking around, waiting for offal. The butcher lugged a squalling kid by its front feet while the mother goat trotted anxiously after them, trying to comfort it.

At Gelhak, we parked under the palms for two hours and ate baked mincemeat in dough, which a doctor from Malakal insisted upon paying for. He wore a gray skullcap, a gabardine traveling gown, and, speaking perhaps a hundred words of English, would translate for us at the police posts when he wasn't sitting cross-legged on the ground telling his prayer beads. When Hector offered him a swig of vodka, he quoted the Muslim injunction that what will harm you in quantity will harm you "even a little."

We saw two crocodiles in the grass by the river, yet many cattle watering. There were donkey water-carts, lambs wallowing in the greenery of the irrigation ditches, plovers in flocks, black and white ducks, and cormorants and herons. Next to each grazing sheep stalked a white egret, on the watch for bugs routed up by its feet. The lambs had their own birds, of a smaller species. At the irrigation pumping station, a green and brass donkey engine thunked, looking as if it dated back to the Condominium.

We saw a man with a monkey's nose; and a woman whose feet were reversed, her toes pointing backwards. More turbans and tarbooshes now, more Arabs, as well as the eggplant-black Dinkas, and purple Nuer with carved stripes that circled their foreheads under the hairline, and Shilluk with beadlike cicatrices stretching from ear to ear just over the eyes—sometimes wearing a ring through the top of one ear. By Gelhak we were seeing both the large humpless long-horned cattle that the Dinka and Nuer keep, which Hector said were brought to Africa about 5000 B.C., and the short-horned humped zebu ("brahman" cattle in India), which are herded mostly by Arabs in the Sudan, and which arrived around 1500 B.C. in the company of Semitic tribes.

Big pigs scavenged the streets in Renk, a rare sight in the Sudan. Generally a small boy trotted alongside to supervise. Renk is an administrative center, but the light plant was out. So was the supply of Pepsi-Cola and Khartoum beer. The telegraph line to Khartoum was down, and the riverboat was delayed by a week. There was no sign of Hector's Sudanese or agency colleagues at the government rest house or anywhere else. Naturally, no wire advertising our own appearance had been received; the rooms were booked full.

In the sandy square, a defunct gas station with broken windows functioned as the lorry depot. We sat on a cracked block of concrete next to a professional scribe, who, posted at a portable writing desk with his feet drawn up under him, appeared to be writing a love letter, to judge by the taut face of the young man dictating to him. Hector, his lumpy valise crammed with alarming farrier's forceps, hypodermic syringes, and needles and medicines, rubbed his big, slow, pessimistic hands together and surveyed the starving dogs and sacred cows that surrounded us—"like a doctor in

Calcutta," as he remarked. He was fond of saying that our expatriate friends in Juba belonged in a sanatorium instead of in Africa; feeling teary, I was reminded of this. The five or six days of brown savanna land lay like a blur behind us, less immediate than my homesickness and my thoughts—sharp as grief—of my daughter in New York City. I thought of other people, too, and the streets of Greenwich Village, all much more clearly in focus than Renk, Gelhak and Malakal.

A taxi drew up. A dead dog lay on the roof—to be deposited outside town, the driver told us. Fuel was scarce, but he could take us anywhere at double the usual rate.

"I have told him this is illogical," our traveling companion, the doctor from Malakal, said disapprovingly as he boarded a lorry headed for Rabak, six hours north, which would be the next leg of his trip to Khartoum.

We had nowhere to take the taxi to, anyway. I felt a panicky yearning to desert my friend, climb onto the truck and hurry on toward the metropolis, with its transatlantic telephone lines, lights, magazines, Penguin paperbacks, ready-made clothes, Greek food, Arab pharmacies, its feline English fixers in third-story offices on the side streets, and German Fräuleins at the airline ticket counters. But the truck was already loaded with dura, and there was no more space on top. I would have flipped off when we hit the first bump, and no second truck was leaving till 2 A.M., the doctor said.

I had stood up, but Hector did not. "We'll wait a day. My esteemed associates may turn up. At least we can say that we waited a day."

My irresolute figure provoked the sympathy of a burly, light-skinned army sergeant who was on his way to report for duty at Rabak. He climbed off the truck, clapped me on the back, said *Ma'alesh* (Never mind), *Ba'allah* (with God), another one would be along, or (in sign language) maybe they could fit me on top of the load. He waved over another fellow in uniform, a spiffy-looking Shilluk game warden. This stringbean divined that it was not necessarily a place on the truck I wanted. I put my hands pillow-fashion against my cheek.

"We'll find somebody who can put you both up," he said in

English, having gone to the mission school at the mouth of the Sobat. He translated for the Arab sergeant, and for a couple of small boys who dashed off to locate a friend of his. In no time, through the kindness of the game warden and the sergeant, Hector and I found ourselves being entertained by two young Nuer civil servants and an Anglican Dinka of about twenty-five named Gabriel Ring, in a two-room cement house, screened by a high grass fence, off the square.

A roofed terrace separated the rooms. We sat there, and Gabriel poured "Khartoum sherry," date wine, for us. "This is your bottle," he said. "Each of you will have a bottle. We will drink the other. Be at home. Please be at home. This is your home. You are not my friends, you are my brothers!" He turned to his housemates, who spoke English less well. "They are our brothers!"

Gabriel was a name from the Bible, he pointed out. "Be at home." He apologized in advance for the accommodations and for what he called the "jungle toilet" in back, though it was simply an Arab-style squat-toilet.

Hector asked whether we couldn't invite him and his friends for supper at the restaurant on the square.

"I have ordered supper. I live as a bachelor and cannot cook, but I have ordered supper for us." He said that he hoped to go to Holland to study agriculture, and surely the Dutch would return any hospitality he showed us. He had a way of screwing up his face slightly as if suffering a twinge of pain, and kept urging me to drink my sherry faster so that he could refill my glass. "Do you fear it?"

The truth was that I was thirsty only for water, but did fear *it*. Our canteens were dry, and I was waiting for a private minute to drop a purifying tablet into a cupful from their pail. I had a headache from the heat of the day and from lack of sleep, and the liquor was acridly heavy and sweet, so I tried to beg off.

Gabriel explained that it was his duty as my host to make me want to share with him whatever he had. I suggested that it was foolish for us to argue about the nature of hospitality in our two countries—in America, guests were cruder—when I was so comfortable, lolling like a prince in this chair in the shade, with no further worries about where I was going to spend the night. This sufficed for a while, but because I was not drinking my share of the sherry, he became agitated again that I was not participating in the ritual of being his guest. I didn't know whether the way he knitted his forehead was from a host's unease, from empathy with my discomfort with the headache, or from real twinges of a kind of pain of his own. He wanted to hear more about my country. Unfortunately, Hector's New Zealand didn't interest him as much.

"There's a lot to tell," I said, sighing.

"Yes. We have so few visitors. We are cut off." From June to December even the lorries could not get through.

I went inside, apologetically, to the cot intended for me, taking some water along, explaining that the purifying tablet I put into it was medicine for my headache.

"Yes, you must rest," he agreed; his was a hard country.

I pulled up the blanket, and he sat on the bed beside me. In America this might have signaled a sexual advance. Here, though, he was hungry for news, information and food for thought, and concerned that I, as his guest, rest comfortably. He had no other place to sit except his own bed—we were sharing the room. Would I excuse him for asking questions when I was tired? How did I travel at home? Did I go around by train or car—did I have a car of my own?—or by boat or airplane? What crops were raised? Did we have cows? Where did the cows graze in a country so full of skyscrapers and people? Or did the cowboys keep cows in the Rocky Mountains? Did the sheepmen still battle the cowboys?

I answered drowsily in broken sentences, almost drifting off. "Mainly I'm homesick," I said. "I miss my daughter. Just before she goes to bed like this she shines her flashlight at the four corners of the ceiling to make certain that no monsters are hiding there. Her favorite words are Philadelphia and February."

"Yes, I have a son too." He got up and showed me a set of photographs pasted to the wall, which I could barely make out in the dim illumination. Two were of himself with the baby in his arms, one was of his father, and one, of the Dinka statesman, William Deng, who had been assassinated on a bush road during the civil war. There was no picture of his wife or mother.

Gabriel said that his village was two hundred miles southwest of Renk, and that lions still roamed there. He had pinned up some drawings done by his younger brother: a rhino standing under a thorn tree, a lion charging a spearman. His wife was staying with her mother in Malakal because so far he had been able to pay only half of the bride price of forty cows. He had married her when she was seventeen and he twenty-four, but the custom was that until they had had a second child and until he had paid for her, she would continue to live with her mother. He said his relatives were prepared to chip in with extra animals, or money to purchase animals, but that arrangements were difficult to make because so often he had no way to reach Malakal except by boat. "You fix with your boss a week when he promises you that you can go, and you write to her to be ready to expect you, and you wait for the boat to come, but it is so late in coming that by the time it does come, your holiday is over and you cannot go. Anyway, she didn't receive your letter, so she never knew, and maybe she could not have made babies that week, so it would not have mattered."

He had stopped asking me questions. As I fell asleep he was telling me that he had spent part of the civil war in Liberia; that the civil servants in Renk like himself had received no pay for three and a half months; that President Nimeiri had good intentions, which were sabotaged at the second level by officials who meant the South ill.

Hector woke me for supper. They had enjoyed a fine sunset and now sat outside with a single candle, the black sky arching spectacularly above them, as it had for the ancient astronomers, the stars the "celestial herders" of Masai legend. To Hector and me, the sight was monumental, but it was depressing as a steady condition of life for our three hosts, who would have preferred to be able to read, play cards or write letters. We could hear the buzz at the dry-goods and food stalls across the square, where several prosperous merchants had each managed to proffer the shopping public the hissing white light of a Coleman lantern. We also heard a great deal of barking. All night, indeed, dog packs raced past the fence, quarreling. At dawn, Renk's many roosters were to join them in crowing, as the muezzin in his minaret called the faithful: *"Come to prayers; come to salvation."*

Now a black man appeared, bearing a round tin tray, with a black feather and a gold coin affixed to his hair. The tray held a miracle of crowded dishes—delicious charcoal-cooked Nile perch that we picked apart with our fingers, a roasted wild-tasting chicken, onions, cucumbers, bread, eggplant, rice and tomatoes. A doubly brave feast, when I remembered that poor Gabriel had not been paid for nearly four months and must have financed this out of his shrinking bank balance. By now it had been ascertained that we had missed Hector's associates, so he had bought fruit for our journey tomorrow. Since, in effect, he was our translator, there was no way that we could revise the finances of the situation. We could leave some money where we hoped he would find it, and hope that the Dutch men and women at his college in Holland would somehow repay him. But with the best will in the world, I could not stay awake long enough to tell him all that he wanted to know about my own country.

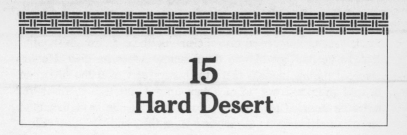

15
Hard Desert

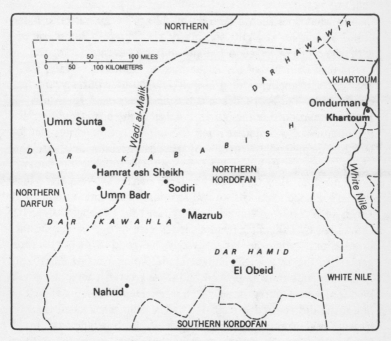

In Khartoum lived Frederick Hamilton March, one of the world's premier sergeants major. He was an Australian of ninety-six who boasted a whole raft of medals, ranging from the Serbian Eagle and the Africa Star to the Croix de Guerre and the George Cross. During World War I he had swum the Dardanelles at night with Brigadier (later, Lord) Bernard Freyberg to cut minefield anchor wires before a British landing, and had distinguished himself at the battle of Beersheba as a flight sergeant. Joining the Cairo police force in 1920, he was chauffeur to Sir Lee Stack, the British sirdar of the Egyptian army and governor-general of the Sudan, when

Stack was assassinated in Cairo. Gunning the car through shouting crowds, he had got him to the hospital before he died. He was "king of the nightclubs" there for many years, and the first man, he told an interviewer, to race a motorcycle more than a hundred miles an hour. Then, during World War II, he won five more medals, and received still another from the hand of Queen Elizabeth in 1957.

And what does such a hero do in old age? Why, retire to Khartoum, inevitably, at eighty-six, marry his Ethiopian housekeeper—with whom he conversed in Italian—and await events.

Another Britisher of my acquaintance, named Ott-Craig, was a one-time tea rancher booted out of Uganda after thirty years' residence, under the Properties and Business Decree of Idi Amin. He liked to stand outside the V.I.P. Lounge at the airport and inquire ingenuously of a Sudanese what the initials meant. After the fellow had explained, "What?" my English friend would exclaim, "Very Important People in the *Democratic* Republic of the Sudan?"

He liked needling Sudanese he met at parties by comparing their People's Palace, with its twelve-foot-high, half-mile-around wall (even so, President Nimeiri did not feel safe sleeping inside, but commuted by helicopter from a pied-à-terre in one of the military installations) with the Palace when the good British governor-general of the 1940's, Sir Hubert Huddleston, oversaw Khartoum. "This may look most impressive, all these guns of yours," he would mention with a pursy smile. "But when Huddleston lived in that house, he didn't need a wall. He had a little black chain as high as your ankle running around the place to keep people from treading on the lawn. When you visited a principal town, the military consisted of a sergeant, a bugler and just six troopers. And Huddleston, when he traveled, used to have only his aide-de-camp, a driver and a guard, whereas you can see for yourself how these African heads of state go about with a regiment of soldiery to protect them!" Then he'd whoop with a ringing, old-man's laugh, touching his sparse, white hair—which is why they put up with him.

Ott-Craig had arrived in London from Kampala in 1972 in a planeload of Asians, refugees under a parallel Amin decree. He had the sagging brown shorts and short-sleeved tan tea rancher's shirt that he was wearing, his hyphenated name and nothing else. So he got into a queue with the Asians, at the head of which sat a tableful of bloody lady liberals, dispensing emergency aid. When his turn came, he told them he had spent his life growing tea near Mbale and now had nothing.

"But you're English!" said one of the ladies. "You don't belong in this queue."

He repeated what his condition was.

"Oh, well," the lady said. "Then you've been living off the sweat of the blacks for thirty years!"

Now he was back in Africa. He had obtained a sinecure in Darfur Province, a "watchdog position," as he said, managing a corporate outpost. He said that in London an orange peel would catch his eye and he would think it was a piece of paw-paw lying in the street. He had even missed the blasted drums at bedtime. "They say it reminds you of your heartbeat."

"It reminds me of fucking," said Hector.

Hector and I had had a week in Khartoum, Hector with his witty wife. I had been sick for two days in the Hotel Metropole after ordering a plate of tasty hors d'oeuvre to celebrate another return from the bush. Now we were on the train to Northern Kordofan, where Hector was to look at the veterinarian situation ("camels—I know nothing of camels") with a view to future funding. I was tagging along, as usual, and old Ott-Craig, after sharing our compartment for sociability's sake, would continue by rail from El Obeid to Nyala in the company of a young lady, the daughter of an American official of the corporation which employed him, who had embarked upon a winter of adventure, touring Africa. Although I felt a bit wistful in her presence, she was a familiar type, a Tulsa girl in her late twenties, an American princess becoming an American hostess, murmuring sotto voce comments about the Sudanese—indeed, about all of us—that I sometimes wished I hadn't heard. To the Sudanese, however, she was *Nefissa* (Precious One), Dove of the Moon, Moon of the Night, and other love-diminutives—an educated, unmarried woman who was happy to talk with them on terms of equal footing and was not bound to bridle at compliments and other verbal intimacies which if addressed successfully to a woman of their own country would have amounted to a conquest.

Except for ours, the six-bunk compartments in first class were segregated by sexes, and, as we rattled along, the women, too, lying abed in yoke-bodiced dresses wrapped around with the feminine taub, doing their nails and suckling their comely sons, admired her American independence. They smeared lamb oil on her neck and hair when she let them, and one of them, richer, older, offered her money for sweets when we stopped at the town of Kosti and vendors and lepers came scrabbling along the platform. The men, of course, practiced their English on her. "That was a good jest," I heard one say.

Our wooden car, half a century old, had been painted yellow a decade before. It was nearly full, with a dozen more people riding on top for free and about a hundred others on top of the rest of the train. We were traveling with caution because of a sandstorm which blew intermittently and which even indoors, induced a sensation of chalk in our noses, mouths and finally our brains. Like snow in the air, it smothered most sounds except for the thump of the wheels under us, and laid a muffling covering on the ground as we stretched our legs when the train stopped. If we stayed at a station for long, most of these precariously balanced souls on the roof climbed down to spit, cough, walk about, kneel and pray, facing back along the track—the direction itself lending universality to the religion, just as the use of Latin once did for Roman Catholicism. When the engineer tooted a warning, the trainmen waited considerately for the last individual to boost his body up over the couplings onto the roof before signaling the engineer to pull ahead slowly again.

The engine—steam, with a coal car and a flickering furnace—was blue with gold numerals, and streamed water under the tanks at the fueling stations. After Sennar, eleven hours south of Khartoum on the Blue Nile, we had turned west, past Jebel Moya, Jebel Dud, Jebel Biyat, to Kosti, on the west bank of the White Nile. Next came Umm Koweika, Tendelti, Umm Ruaba. At each of these hamlets there was a radio tower, several low, cement-roofed brick houses where the police and railway officials lived, and perhaps a row of margosa trees that the British had planted. People rode over on zebus, donkeys or camels to stare at us, and at Kosti, some twenty dervishes paraded in costume, waving a green flag for Mohammed's birthday, just past.

Our companions in first class draped their turbans around their necks like a towel, walking in semi-undress down the aisle. The ladies' compartments looked like veritable harems of lounging women. They had nowhere to sit—they could only lie down—but the women's quarters of most Sudanese houses also are furnished with cots rather than chairs. A woman complained that her four-year-old son sucked his thumb. Again and again she drew it out of his mouth and squeezed his head against her wrapped breasts, where she also kept her money in a purse on a thong.

At either end of the car stood a jug of drinking water, and the steward prepared excellent omelets, bean and scallion salads, and English tea served with jam and biscuits. Wherever we stopped, the peddlers hawked mangoes, roasted pigeons, rugs, trinkets, cooked rice, bananas and boiled eggs to passengers both inside the train and on top, while behind them trailed a bobbing congregation of dogs and goats. The goats ate the banana skins that were tossed down, and the dogs the egg shells.

We had each paid $26 for a twenty-six-hour ride, as it turned out. The shrubby brown desert turned red, and back to brown. Ott-Craig quoted the proverb "When Allah made the Sudan, He laughed." He said that twelve thousand Britons had run the whole country after World War II, but that now at the airport the soldiers barged into the transit lounge and started going through the luggage of people who had already passed through customs and immigration, and stood by the gangplank to intercept any spies who might still try to board "under a big hat," as the saying goes. Once they had stopped an Austrian mechanic who had packed his grease gun, along with other tools, to take home. They informed him that he ought to have obtained a firearms permit, and that since he was in violation of the laws of a sovereign nation, he could be imprisoned for as long as three years. "Their captain was a proper chap, but until he came, I told them in Dinka, I told them in Arabic, I told them in Fur, that a grease gun could be better compared to a particular appendage of the anatomy."

For all his sturdiness—the strip-searches and cat-and-mouse stuff he had endured in Kampala—Ott-Craig was a bit prim, a bit of a bigot, and began to grate on me in that narrow compartment. So did the mushy American acceptance of my young countrywoman, who, without entertaining a notion of cultural reciprocity, was given a valuable *taub,* a carved teak monkey, and a four-year-old's handcrafted toy automobile as we rode west on the train. It seemed doubtful that Sudanese hospitality could invent any present she wouldn't accept.

I was homesick, disgruntled, unfairly critical. Already I was anticipating the view of the desert from a British Viscount—a rumbling map-eater—en route to the U.S. In two or three hours, Cairo; then over the crinkly, satiny Mediterranean, with ships' tracks on the glisten; the robust toe of Italy; Mount Aetna, where I had once lived with my first wife; then Swiss snow peaks, with appropriate turbulence; and the circling descent through scary fog to the macaw-green of Heathrow.

My groaning friend Hector, too, most of whose humor was directed not against Africans but against his fellow expatriates—that "walking sanatorium"—displeased me. I suppose at that moment, I would have called him emotional but leaden.

I asked why he didn't become an ordinary dairy doctor in New Zealand, and he said something about his mercenary ancestor who had fought for Venice, and the way that a Dalmatian dog always jumps into the fire truck at the sound of the bell. "Foot rot, endless foot rot, is what you treat in that wet climate. When the cow is bred, you check to see whether the breeder did his work correctly. If she takes a trip, you inoculate her for shipping fever. If she dies in the field, you look to see if it was lightning, so that the bloke can get his insurance. But of course it's always the rich guy with the big high field, who collects, not the little farmer down in the sticks of the slough, whose cow has choked on a crab apple."

El Obeid means "the White," for the white donkey one of the founding settlers rode out of the brown desert into the green oasis. Ott-Craig and company had changed trains for Darfur. Hector and I proceeded to police headquarters for our traveling papers, which entailed a wait because I was an unknown quantity, unpredictable like a live asp, and although this was a city of a hundred and ten thousand people, their phone line to the ministries in Khartoum was down. The police were concerned because Dar Kababish, where Hector and I were headed, led straight to the Libyan border. The security chief, in a razor-creased green uniform, with a spit-shine on his shoes that was incongruous for these sand streets, flourished a swagger stick. His colleague, the deputy provincial commissioner, was a brown, tough man, a cross between a hanging judge and a tank officer by his expression, who looked as if he had risen through the Prison Service and looked prepared to play hardball.

"Good sir, do you know what the Libyans would do to this gentleman if they caught him around their border?" asked Hector.

There was also a third Sudanese in the room, a bearded illustrator who was drawing election posters to earn the stipend with which the government sometimes subsidizes young artists. He spoke not at all. His beard marked him as a nonconformist—beards are customarily reserved for venerable patriarchs—and he wanted nothing to do with either policemen or foreigners who chatted pleasantly with policemen.

El Obeid is yellow and white, with walled, prosperous housing. We wandered about to the museum and gum-arabic market while waiting for the Khartoum Information Ministry to vouch for my character by Telex or passenger pigeon.

In the Muslim hell—said a woman selling goats' ears and black honey—you drink only hot water and eat only fire. She drew her scarf close to her cheek, as if to conceal her beauty-scars but really to emphasize them. Many older Arab women bear these slanting tribal cuts, and I had been here long enough to get over my first surprise and to recognize how they could perhaps enhance rather than disfigure the face—"like rivers in the cheeks," as a friend had described them. Rivers of tenderness, rivers of sorrow —one's tongue in them at night—depending on how the events of the marriage itself might run. As fleshly jewelry, even to a Western eye, they lent a worldliness to women often unworldly, and for the past millennium had kept the eyes of the men of the tribe from straying to women not so marked.

We were staying in a school building dedicated by the Right Reverend Llewellyn H. Gwynn, bishop of Egypt and the Sudan in 1932, the year of my birth. Now it was overhung with the camel flag of Northern Kordofan and the broadcast prayers and harangues of the minarets. At least to a listener ignorant of Arabic, there is a fanatical ring to these loudspeakered declamations. The sound system itself is a new plaything to many a muezzin, and in Kordofan not only the rare tourist but everybody remembers the Mahdi. Religiosity brought about the astonishing conquests of the Mahdia, but also its bloodbath defeats—eleven thousand dead in the daylight assault on Kitchener's machine guns at Omdurman, as against forty-nine killed among the Anglo-Egyptians. The Baggara Arabs, who fought at the core of the Ansar, still have a formula which a young man repeats to the girl he is courting, as he stands at the door of her tent: "May I bring in my spear? I am afraid the dogs will eat it" (because it is so blood-soaked).

Both Hector and I were sick from eating tainted fish, and were being fed chicken soup by the cook at the rest house without having had to ask for it. For much of the night, in celebrations connected with Mohammed's birthday, the noise of drumming, roaring, dancing and wailing was broadcast, besides many emphatic hours of prayers. When you are lying alone, hallucinating quietly, not always sure which continent you are on, such noise is company at the same time that it is depressing.

"Why is it that I *like* that screeching?" I asked Hector after we were on our feet again. "The long prayers, the puritan bowing and kneeling, when I can't understand the words and don't even kneel to the God I was brought up to believe in? Is it wistful? Is it wanting to believe, do you think? Or is it like my liking marches and band music and my eight weeks of infantry training?"

"I think you don't realize that he is saying, 'Dearly beloved, we are gathered together . . .' "

We went out to El Banjediid, an oasis village a few miles away in the desert, with our new driver, whose mistress lived there. Though the natural surface springs were dry in March, water to irrigate the squash and tomato gardens and lemon and guava trees could be obtained only twenty feet down, which cast an air of luxury over the place. Nobody native to El Banjediid need ever go thirsty or starve.

We were invited to drink carcady-flavored water in the house of the chief landlord. Its several rooms were built of mud, dung and dura straw, painted blue and white inside, and furnished alike with iron beds and rugs on the dirt floor in the men's and the women's half. He had pictures of Gamal Abdel Nasser—the great Arab socialist—on the wall, though he was a capitalist himself, soon to go off to Abu Dhabi to try to increase his fortune.

I dropped in at the cathedral in El Obeid—concrete painted like red-and-white marble—to meet Father David, a pastor of the slow, solicitous variety. "*Ay-wa, ay-wa,*" he said—"Yes, yes." A Bolognese with a feminine wrist and masculine shoulder, he conducted services in Arabic, and grade-school classes in English, and said that his ten years in the Sudan "seem like a day." Arabic pervaded his English, though probably not yet his Italian. He claimed that it wasn't missionary zeal but his friendships which kept him here, and that he'd aimed for Africa straight from the seminary, "maybe because it was the closest." A man of obvious tenacity, he said the city's imams appeared to regard him with a certain degree of alarm or distaste, when he visited them on Islamic feast days, but not so much so that they were ever uncivil. Ordinary people did not, and at his last Christmas party the district commissioner had made a friendly speech saying that a true Muslim accepts "the mission from God of Jesus and of Moses," of the Gospel and the Torah.*

"Are you his brother?" a Muslim boy asked me as I left the church. My confused ear did not immediately apprehend that he meant co-religionist.

In the more tolerant atmosphere of the police office after my *bona fides* had been attested to, the fist-faced deputy commissioner told a joke he said he'd heard in Ireland. A father, it seems, came back dispirited from a visit to his daughter in London. "She is a Protestant?" cried the poor mother. No, no, no, it was only that she had become a prostitute. "Oh, thank God! I thought you said a Protestant!"

Next morning the muezzins started their song half an hour ahead of the roosters. Half an hour after the roosters had chimed in, we hit the sands in a slick sky-blue Ford Ranger pickup truck, our

* The Koran itself is of two minds. The Medina suras say at one point: "All . . . who do that which is right, whether they are Jews, Christians, Sabeans or Muslims, shall have their reward from Allah, who will take away from them all fear and grief." Yet, at another: "No one who follows any other religion than Islam will be accepted by God or saved from perishing in the life that is to come."

driver, Ahmed, weaving at high speed in the deep lorry ruts—the moon still white over us—and Mohammed, his thin, put-upon assistant, holding down the leaping fuel drums and water cans and veterinary equipment cases in back.

Hector, although he was a "gingerbread man" in his doughiness and coloring, was also exceedingly durable. He had a stomach stronger and a mind more self-contained than mine, besides a rear end to sit on so stout that it could have carried him across all of Africa in comfort. We were trying to navigate first to Sodiri, an eight-hour journey if all went well. Though one could steer partly by where the various lorries had preceded us, if we followed them too closely we would get stuck in the ruts, so it was best to parallel them. We headed in the direction of a jagged jebel that resembled a craggy face gazing up toward the clouds. As the sun rose, heat began to shimmer off the jebel, and when we lurched, *it* lurched and jumped.

Ahmed drove in the heroic style, pulling the wheel to capture the proper angle to attack each dip or rise. He never let up on either himself or the truck, and remarked that it was "very intense" of me to be writing my eighth book, but that I should have had more children; something was wrong there. Ahmed was a motoring man. He informed Hector with some satisfaction that he had "never laid my hand on an animal." He was well-fleshed and tireless, and such a good driver, he said, because he had been employed by an oil company. Never out of gas, he had had more practice. My stutter fascinated him, not so much its mechanics as the conundrum of why Allah had strapped me with it; he eyed me speculatively.

He was probably about forty, so Mohammed, at thirty, could expect to have a long apprenticeship to serve. Mohammed was prone to weep and rub the tears away with the knuckles of one hand if he was hurt and angry—as once when Ahmed shouted at him for pouring cold water into the hot radiator with the engine turned off. Yet Mohammed bounced on the bed of the truck until he hit the canvas roofing and didn't complain, whereas I felt sick to my stomach after riding for an hour in back.

There was a special reason for Ahmed's style of driving, his continually revving the accelerator as our tires spun in a thick patch of sand or we plunged through a thicket down into the dry bed of a stream and up and out again: our battery was dead. Hector and I didn't realize this until we stopped at a thatched hamlet of Hamid Arabs to fill a jar with sesame oil and Ahmed took considerable pains to park on a slope. "We can push. Four strong men." He said auto supplies in El Obeid were short and he had not been able to lay hands on a new one.

We saw a few camels, and periodically a rain-fed dura field, now harvested and dry, where birds with zebra stripes and blue-and-black birds scoured the ground for grain. We passed a water lorry, which was ferrying that precious elixir about. Most of the time we had no jebel in sight to hold a course by, but since our passage was the event of everybody's day—the children ran as far as they could to keep us in sight—people walking or riding an animal happily directed us. The landscape was often yellow steppe rather than proper desert, dotted with bunchgrass and occasional huge baobob trees—like "upturned carrots," in David Livingstone's phrase—as well as the stumps of littler trees that had been cut for firewood, until we reached Mazrub around lunchtime.

The town of Mazrub consists of a square of zinc-roofed mud shops enclosing three or four large mango trees, which throw some pools of shade. There are not many houses, because so many of the customers are nomads who come in only in order to trade. Not much thatch around any more for roofing material in the wastes of sand, but still enough thornbush to build cattle corrals. The citizenry wore slippers, instead of open sandals, against the thorns. Their white robes had yellowed from the force of the sun, and their faces possessed a clearer point or focus from the precision of desert life. They met your eye with certainty when you talked with them, as though it could not possibly be intimidating to look into the face of any man after so many years under the eye of the Sahara sun. The ritualized Koranic greetings—gripping the shoulder, patting the heart, as God's name was repeated half a dozen times—seemed a device to tame into humane dimensions the harsh self-sufficiency, to soften the hardened hearts which people otherwise would have brought with them into town.

At the teahouse, next to the camel saddlery, we ate cheese with a flat loaf of bread and a dish of *ful* beans—brown beans the English call "tick" beans because they swell when cooked from a raisin's to an acorn's size. In front of the fabric stalls, like a harbinger of industry, sewing machines rattled, but a man limped by peddling waterskins which he had crafted from goat stomachs, waterproofed with a liquid distilled from bitter-melon seeds, as in "the time of ignorance," before the Prophet, Ahmed announced.

Hector suggested to me that I was "running out of power. Out of oomph. Out of oompahpah. I can see the signs in you."

"Maybe so," I agreed.

"You expect more, I think. I am not so lonely as you. I'm a member of the passing parade. I watch the parade."

"Oh, I don't know. I hear you grind your teeth at night."

"Sure you do. Right down to the dentine. Tell me, though," he said quietly, with a laugh. "You didn't really expect to find that there would be a woman in the Sudan or in Cairo who had more interesting problems in her head than the sophisticated women you must already know in New York City? You must know plenty of people who are worth paying closer attention to than that Copt was."

"Yes, I suppose I do."

"Like your wife; or not?"

"My wife is very much like she was, except that they would have hated each other on political grounds."

He didn't say anything, and neither did I for a moment, irritated because, in fact, I'd already decided before that the first fancy he had taken to me had been in part homosexual.

"I didn't come this far to meet a lady friend," I said.

"No, but you've run out of power, and you were probably tired and lonely even when you got here."

"Why not be tired and lonely? Life is short. Why shouldn't it be busy?"

Hector replied that some people are inclined to look for what they're never going to find—which might have seemed a wiser thought if I had known how to interpret it. I didn't answer except to point out that I didn't spend all night grinding my teeth.

"I am a refugee from totalitarianism. I'm not an American. Americans shouldn't grind their teeth." He laughed. "Shall we press on?"

Five miles north of Mazrub we passed a resting party of Majanin nomads, like figures in a diorama, their dozen camels hobbled, the loads laid in an easy circle. Five or ten miles further, a wedding celebration was in progress at a clutch of huts in the desolate sand. A boy beat on a pot-shaped drum. A row of five or six women stood in front of an elderly but vigorous man, who shook a herder's stick over their heads. Another man held out his arm above them and snapped his fingers to the same rhythm, whereupon they closed their eyes, bent back their heads, and, otherwise standing stock-still, undulated their necks with an erotic push-pull movement, as if the libidos of all of us were concentrated there. The women on the sidelines ululated as they watched.

Pitching like a dinghy in the troughs of sand, we had two jebels to steer by for an hour or more. One was bulky and complex enough in its topography to have concealed gazelles or a leopard, perhaps a lion, until the years after World War II. Because of our dead battery, our drive was dramatic. It was essential that we not stall, and Ahmed, gunning the gas pedal, did not.

By midafternoon we had reached Sodiri, the administrative center for Dar Kababish. It is situated in a slight hollow in a dry reddish expanse of desert with tussock grasses. Dar Kababish itself extends in a sort of rectangle lying north of El Obeid, from Darfur nearly as far east as Omdurman—fifty thousand square miles. Seventy-five thousand people are at present confederated into the Kababish tribe, and they have mildly unfriendly minority neighbors such as the Kawahla, who share some of this land. Thousands of Hector's "beasts"—sheep, camels, cattle, goats—were bivouacked at Sodiri around the government's bore well. There was a little hospital, and six stone school buildings with shining roofs, one each for boys and girls at each of three grade levels. Shops formed three sides of a square, in the center of which was the meat market and grinding mill, and hitching posts for the riding camels. The village mosque, like a tiny stone castle, boasted stairs winding up a small round tower. The Rural Council had office buildings and a garage, and at the police station the prisoners pushed to look through the bars, as interested as the lieutenant to know whether our traveling papers were in order, or whether we might not be spies fleeing toward the sanctuary of Libya. The register at the rest house indicated that only four other foreigners had visited Sodiri within the past three years.

Because the nazir of the Kababish had been beheaded by the Mahdi, and many of his tribe had died of disease and famine while being held in virtual detention by the Mahdists near Omdurman, the British, when they returned in force in 1898 to the Sudan, naturally looked kindly upon those who had survived. The son of the dead nazir, Sheikh Ali at-Tom, was appointed nazir in his stead. He turned out to be a brilliant political manipulator: "the *beau idéal* of a nomad sheikh under the Condominium," in the words of a recent writer. Within a year he was collecting his splintered peoples together in a village forty miles west of Omdurman (according to Talal Asad's account, in *The Kababish Arabs*). Two years later he was operating halfway out toward El Obeid. Within ten years he was still further west, to about our present longitude at Sodiri.

He proved readily obedient to British wishes in the regulation of his own Kababish, curtailing their propensity for raiding nearby tribes that were also receptive to British rule, but lending the scouting expertise of his bedouin irregulars to punitive expeditions against any bands that weren't compliant. In a famous scene of defiance, the nazir of the Kawahla had plucked the pen out of the hand of a British district commissioner as the latter was about to sign an order affecting his tribe, and broke it. Immediately he was dismissed as nazir—a hero to his tribe—but the result was that the Kawahla increasingly were dispossessed of their land by the British in favor of the Kababish.

Ali at-Tom, more than acting as a mere collaborator, however, soon discovered that westward, beyond the frontier of British penetration, he could do as he liked if he didn't advertise it. His aggressive ventures and counter-reprisals—when word filtered back—would only be regarded as softening up such "wild" or "unadministered" tribes as the Sanusi religious sect, who had been riding to watering points in northern Darfur from eastern Libya, and whom the Italian colonial authorities had not yet subdued, or the Bedayat and Gura'an of Chad, who were not yet in a state of subjection to the French. Darfur proper was supposedly an independent entity under the rebellious Sultan Ali Dinar, until the British succeeded in overthrowing and killing him in 1916. But they tacitly supported

Sheikh Ali in any forays that he undertook against the subjects of the sultanate, "loaning" him more than two hundred rifles, in the meantime.

So trusted was Ali at-Tom by the British that later he unofficially picked for them a new nazir of the Baggara Arabs (according to Reginald Davies, in *The Camel's Back*), although the Baggara had been the most formidable tribal enemies the Kababish had. And (says Davies) he did a good job of this.

We went to see Sheikh Hassan at-Tom, Sheikh Ali's grandson. Here was a middle-aged man in a brown jibba and orange skullcap with a harem smile and a drinker's eyes but with the habit of command. Though the prerogatives of all of the nazirs have been curtailed since independence, "merciless"-looking, practical, calm, in his two-room mud townhouse, he gave directions for our refreshment with a wave of the hand. A rifle in a leather case leaned against the wall—a sight you rarely see in the home of a private citizen in the Sudan. Both in public governmental sessions and privately, Sheikh Hassan still heard many petitioners. Bored but savvy, cynical and hedonistic, he had attended the University of Nottingham, and asked Ahmed in Arabic whether I always jerked my head when talking. *"Inshallah"* (by the will of God), he answered to Ahmed's response.

The mud houses had mud walls outside, grass huts had grass fences, and the new bureaucrats' brick houses, concrete barricades curving around. We were a hundred and twenty miles out of El Obeid, but a hundred and thirty-five miles short of Umm Sunta, where Sheikh Hassan's herds watered and where his wife's tent was. Looking more sheikhly that evening—less like a nazir whose wings had been clipped by the May Revolution—he shared our tea while we stewed vegetables over a charcoal fire. The Arabs drink tea loudly for good manners, to show that they are enjoying it, whereas Hector and I sipped it as quietly as possible; but loud is easier when it is hot. When we remarked on this difference in custom, a boy repeated through the marketplace what we had said.

At dinner we were visited by an old campaigner from the wars in Eritrea and Sicily in World War II. With his mouth knitted, he said that American weapons had turned the tide then, that Nimeiri had been a fool to imitate Nasser and at first ask for arms from the Russians, who had never been as industrialized as the Americans. He had come to call on us because he wanted to see another American. He told us that three years ago a German had ridden a camel from here to Libya and back, killing the animal, and then had bought another, riding on to Egypt in training for some obsessive feat of hermitry he hoped to perform in the Arabian desert. "He was as hard as us," the campaigner laughed.

I lay in my sleeping bag, cleaning my toes with my toes.

"I think you are running out of vim," Hector called in my direction, to see whether he couldn't ruffle my feathers again. But I didn't envy the German, and laughed with them.

The next afternoon we headed over to Umm Kherwaa, an hour away, to meet Sheikh Fadlallah, who is an actual son of Ali at-Tom's by one of his younger wives. Along the way we passed caravans of donkeys loaded with waterbags, and desiccated, loping dogs and flocks of desert doves. Nowhere in Dar Kababish is there any permanent running water. After a quick blue sunset the bats emerged.

Fadlallah, a less politic fellow than Sheikh Hassan—with muscular cheeks, eyes less bloodshot, fewer burps and yawns, an early riser with a sturdy chin, and hundreds of ewes and camels to look after—more resembled a rural leader. He lived on a sand knoll within a thornbush zariba guarded by three or four rugged dogs, looking over a lower settlement and out at distant jebels. In the compound he had his mare and stallion, and four favorite riding camels, each with its left leg tied under it, and several chickens that sheltered in the lee of the camel out of the cold wind. Also several starved and several well-fed donkeys. The fattest donkey ate from a feed bag which a pet milk goat nuzzled from at the same time, while a kid suckled at its other end. The tent faced east, its roof woven camel's hair, its sides goat's-hair carpeting. A waterskin hung inside, the skin legs tied together for easy carrying. The canopied bed, made from palm-leaf ribs tied with camel-leather thongs on a collapsible arrangement of pedestals and poles, was the principal item of furniture. The cooking fire was outside, surrounded by a brushwood fence into which sacks of food, gourds of milk, and utensils were stuck, out of reach of the dogs.

Hector and I and the camp bachelors sat outdoors at another

fire while supper was prepared and laid for us on a woven mat lit by a kerosene lamp in a satellite tent occupied by an itinerant game inspector. "Do you have good fires like this in America?" one of the herders asked.

In the night chill, after such heat, it seemed no accident that Arabic is harsh-sounding, but the handsome sky, the tradition of utter hospitality and the refrain, "Praise be to God," "There is no god but God" soon soothed us. I was used to people trying to read my notes over my shoulder to figure out what I was saying about them. Here, though, they clustered behind me approvingly to watch the very process of writing English, Ahmed shining his flashlight on it. A boy who had been to school sketched in the sand some words in his language. Much tremolo yodeling and emotional argumentation, clicks of the tongue and the lips to agree, the method of catching one's attention being first to snap the fingers loudly, which I found irritating.

Supper was dura porridge flavored with a sticky sauce containing bits of gazelle meat that had been dried last year after a hunt. We drank lemon squash. Incense burned in a pot. As we washed our right hands before beginning, Sheikh Fadlallah remarked on everybody's good health, saying that good health wafts through the air. "The air is the doctor." I remembered that the Sharia punishment for thieves was to cut off the left hand. Therefore they would have no clean hand to eat with, only what would now be the toilet hand.

Sheikh Fadlallah had a pickup truck, but complained of the absence of gasoline: "It disappears." He had a big, triumphant, upward smile that suddenly lit his face, like a war sheikh's. During the news report from Radio Omdurman, he improved his time by telling his prayer beads and reading the Koran. Coffee was served, with a twist of straw in the mouth of the pitcher to keep the grounds in. The sheikh's wife, whom we met briefly afterwards and thanked, wore paint on her fingernails and a painted square cross on each cheek. She had lips that had been tattooed gray-black when she was a girl, six cheek scars and the "large, black, pearl-like eyes" of the women of Paradise, of whom the Prophet speaks.

By nine-thirty, Hector and I were asleep in a stick hut down the hill, on wooden cots the sheikh had walked down to inspect for our comfort, next to a strip of burlap where a row of his swaddled bachelor dependents curled like white caterpillars in the illumination of the moon. The Sudanese sleep just as much at night as if they didn't also sleep during the afternoon, and enjoy four leisurely meals a day, even though sometimes among the poor more courtesy than food is consumed.

Breakfast was porridge with a sour goat's-milk sauce as good as the gazelle sauce was, though it depressed me to see the starved, tethered donkeys outside suffering while the fat ones ate, and the thirsty chickens dashing for a chance to peck at our spit. Siphoning gas, Mohammed caught a spurt in his eye, but only laughed at the pain.

Real desert, now, as our foursome set out with a guide for Hamrat esh Sheikh, the home settlement of Ali at-Tom's clan of the Kababish. No kites or black-and-white crows because we were too far from water: we saw a donkey carcass awaiting their return with the rains of July. Also a dying, abandoned baggage camel, cut loose miles from anywhere.

Deep sand, then rocky spots, red bare-bone tracts and raceways of hard ground. "Sore-ee," Ahmed apologized, for the bumps. We got stuck more than once, but he managed to keep the engine roaring all the time as we dug out. In Sodiri we had noticed him pouring dirty water into the battery, and had wondered whether this wasn't why it was dead—that all his ace driving might stem from errors like that. Back near Mazrub, the motor had boiled over when we'd driven through the dura fields and chaff had blocked up the radiator, but in the desert there were no leaves or chaff.

We remembered the luxuries of Mazrub and Sodiri: Chinese china, canned mango juice and mackerel and peas, a shoemaker, school supplies, a plastic flute we had bought to give as a toy. Nevertheless, even out here, every half-dozen miles we were likely to glimpse a grass hut (there being no clay or water to make mud from), a lean child skipping out, a dog voicelessly making a run for us. We saw a girl with hoop earrings and a ring through one wing of her nose, helping to drench a camel with medicine, to the tune of its sea-lion groans. Along with our guide, Mohammed sang in the back of the truck. Occasionally we passed a baobab tree— its fruit medicinal, its bark used for weaving rope; a few holes were dug close around to catch the quick rains in puddles which could be scooped through a hole in the trunk into the cistern inside.

But next to the Wadi al-Malik, a veritable river of trees flowed northeast toward the Nile at Old Dongola. There were ground squirrels diving underground, and huts galore at the well fields. The water was twelve or fifteen feet down, each well a dimple in the sand, spaced twenty yards away from the next, and walled with sticks so that it wouldn't tumble in. Usually a couple of dark-clad women with reddish-black faces presided over it, hauling up water in a leaky skin bucket on a threadbare rope running over a grooved log. The camels groaned, the cattle lowed. Sheep and goats were also being watered in manageable bunches. There was so much water that the people stood about smiling and relaxed, no matter how far they would have to march the herds afterwards to find grass for the cattle and thorns for the goats. A trader had spread a cloth under a tree, with pots of perfume and razor blades for sale. Somebody offered us merissa in a pail, and bread baked in an eight-foot-tall beehive oven. We dickered for a sheep, but Ahmed insisted that the herders would have to be thirstier than they were here to give us a bargain.

Red desert, yellow desert. We saw a jackal. Ahmed told us that he was already gaining weight driving for us. He couldn't wedge his finger inside his belt. But, after the two meals of porridge at Fadlallah's camp, which had been prepared by the game inspector's wife, I had been approached by her son. She had pains in her stomach, he said. Could I give her any pills? Now *I* had a pain as well. I could envision her grinding the dura, kneading the porridge in her hands.

Though lorries occasionally did travel this way, a sandstorm had filled in the ruts. Our guide was confused for a while, until we heard what sounded like our first airplane engine since leaving El Obeid; it turned out to be the straining motor of a bogged lorry.

Because my stomach is the weakest link in my body, I was starting to worry, wondering how many days we would spend in Dar Kababish before turning back. I was weary of the whole African calliope—that nagging, pulsing musical din that has been reverberating strongly without letup for thousands of years before you arrive and will be continuing without any respite for sickness or fatigue long after you have left the earth. There was pathos in it, and endless, repetitive joy, but I was too tired for poignance or joy.

Thirty miles beyond Wadi al-Malik, we pulled into Hamrat esh Sheikh. The grande dame of the place, the mother of Sheikh Hassan, a large, noble woman of eighty-four with long beauty scars and much jewelry around her neck, emerged from a hut remarkable only for its thatch-roofed porch, to see who we were. She was lovely still, even her round neck, which she didn't bother to cover until after I had seen that it was unmarred. She looked twenty years younger than she was, just as Mohammed, lifting the hood of our pickup so that the motor could cool, looked so weather-worn that he might have been forty, instead of thirty.

We must have reminded this great lady of visits the British inspectors had made, friends of her husband and father-in-law and the tribe half a century ago. She had a sheep slaughtered for us. Wagging its tail nervously, it bled into a bowl as it died, and was hung up on a Y-shaped pole by its Achilles tendons, the servant carrying away its stomach for his share. We napped on beds made of peeled wood poles and strips of goat hide with the hair still on, as the meat roasted; and then went with her to see Ali at-Tom's whitewashed, mud-brick tomb, whose roof was falling in. Two schoolteachers were delegated to show us around more. They hefted bamboo-butt, hippo-hide whips, just as the herders did, and pointed out a thatched dovecote, with kite wings hanging up to scare the kites away, and a proud heglig tree, whose sweet fruit the children loved, but which also made soap, and whose flowers were used as a poultice for wounds. It stood at the village's center like a tree of life. Both the girls' and boys' schools were practically unfurnished: broken benches, scarcely a blackboard on the wall, a torn book or two strewn. The teachers lived in a stone hut without furniture, except for what they called a "donkey rack" for clothes and two boards on the floor to sleep on.

At the widow's instructions, Hector and I, with the schoolteachers for company, were served shoulder of mutton with giblet stew and sorghum pancakes with a piquant gruel—orange pudding topped off the feast. After thanking her profusely, we struck off to the south for two hours to the Kawahla town of Umm Badr, where we planned to spend the night at a government rest house.

The desert was red and gray, with trees but no grass and old birds' nests in many of the bushes, between egg-shaped stones ten feet high. We topped a last rise and gasped at the sight of the shimmering miraculous little permanent body of standing water which Umm Badr overlooks. With its large-limbed trees in a dry wadi stretching south, its deep yellow sand contrasting with red rock formations, its sparse, self-effacing housing, including another castle-mosque, it was the most beautiful village site I had seen in Africa.

In the morning, we bought dates and snuff and Indian tea from a lonely Egyptian merchant, talked with him, toured a bit, and watched a boy's circumcision celebrated. There was a parade, the boy sitting on a donkey ritually shaking a whip, while half of Umm Badr's women accompanied him, chanting and singing and clapping, and lots of children ran ahead. His father walked next to the imam, accepting congratulatory shakes of the hand. Afterwards, as the donkey nibbled straw, you could see its powerful horse-head—flawed, like the heads of all horses and burros, by the tragic horse-cleft in the jaw.

We saw nomads with swords in their scabbards on stately-gaited camels—the two right legs, then the left ones swinging out. Even at a trot, when the legs stick forward in front of the camel like a duck's, the length of the leg and its own height lend it special dignity. Unlike a giraffe, it is never so tall as to look ridiculous.

Heading for Umm Sunta, Sheikh Hassan's own family *dar*, we met two parties of baggage camels led by men riding donkeys, with dogs that coursed after us for want of a gazelle. The addax and oryx are probably extinct in Dar Kababish and in Darfur, and the small sand-colored desert dorcas gazelles are at best a threatened species, several Kababish having told us that they must make long trips by truck to reach a possible hunting ground. Nevertheless, we were lucky enough to see two, and then five, gazelles among wispy dead tussocks in the expanse of white and red sand. These little creatures, only about two feet tall, a pale sandy fawn color, with lyrate horns, appeared as though in tracery form, as if they were mere wishful thinking, outlines that still needed filling in, even as they dashed from us in light bounds. Once we sighted a sand fox.

Umm Sunta was a charmless flat stretch of sand ringed by

scraggly trees. *Sunt* acacias were no longer among them, the people told us; it had become too dry. "It is a very hard life now with camels. A lot of what you do see is dead," the Kababish representative to the People's Assembly told us. In the dry climate, dead trees and shrubs take years to rot and fall over. He had just ridden thirty miles in twelve hours from where his herd was pastured, and, looking over the country with a fresh eye, after months in Khartoum, was feeling somber.

We heard a suffering bellowing, so we didn't have to ask where to find the government bore well. The engine had broken down three days before, and hundreds of miserable cattle, standing in gaunt postures or lying in despair on the ground, protested their thirst, never ceasing to bawl; by now, it was simply a cry for survival. The government veterinarian, a young man from Southern Kordofan who had been stationed here among the Kababish for three months on an experimental basis, threw up his hands when he saw Hector. Because of the appalling noise we couldn't talk, or even sit and enjoy a cup of coffee in the dismal stone hovel of a cottage assigned to him and discuss veterinary measures. *What* veterinary measures!—as Hector signaled with his hands. Even before this temporary disaster, the man had been counting the days until he left. None of the local herd owners had consulted him or even acknowledged his presence.

Between three hundred and five hundred people lived around Umm Sunta in season, and grass huts and square, flat-roofed cotton tents were distributed at polite intervals of fifty or a hundred and fifty yards in family conclaves. The store, built of grass, had an ostrich egg on top. The tents were man-high, with a square little hole in the spread of canvas more like the entrance to a cave than a house door—black, low, always open, like a work of nature; crickets sang inside. Sheep and goat skins were draped in the trees, and boys hounded the living animals. Six tents of soldiers were posted in town, people said—the first time ever—because of the danger of an invasion from Libya, although the Kababish themselves, as hereditary enemies of Sadiq al-Mahdi's family, would have opposed any force that was allied with him.

As we inquired for the tent of Sheikh Hassan's wife, we met both the usual mood of frank exhilaration at the freedom of God's desert which we were used to encountering in the Northern Sudan and a feeling of dogged, ragged apprehension at unforeseen changes. To suggest to a nomad that because of the southward creep of the Sahara, he must try to limit instead of forever increasing his herds, that he should hope that they *not* multiply, is to turn topsy-turvy the very order of living.

The sheikh's wife was a large lady, hips rolling in fat, less lordly and cultivated than his mother had seemed. But when she waved her hand, a black servant girl with the top of her dress tied around her waist set to work grinding dura on a rock for us. I was vomiting at intervals now, and any food that didn't immediately come right back up emerged quickly the other way, still looking exactly like sorghum, goat ribs, kidneys in hot sauce, or whatever it might have been. Because the lady and our other well-wishers were under no obligation, except for their own wonderfully stylized sense of honor, to provide us with anything at all, it is only as the weak sister in camp that I mention my problems at meals. But in the first place, Hector and I were at some disadvantage in the group of men we always ate with because we could not finger hot food as well. The rhythm of the meal was for everybody to pick steadily, though never greedily, from each bowl from the minute that it was brought, and so, even if we burned our hands, we lost several turns. Also, we weren't accustomed to chewing tough meat as fast. And though our hosts exerted themselves to provide the best they could offer, there was seldom enough for me to stop feeling hungry despite my digestive upset.

At a certain point one was supposed to express fulfillment, to praise the food and the wall hangings from Libya and Saudi Arabia, and leave a sufficiency in the bowls for the women and children, as well as for the younger sons, who, according to custom, had served. If I felt too sick to eat, then it was a matter of watching the rest of them licking and sucking their fingers between courses of liver and courses of ribs, while five or ten staggering dogs, just able to wobble back out of reach of the clubs the men kept at hand, waited and fought for what niblets of hooves, ears, spittle and sorghum wads we threw to them—these tall hunting dogs, with their tails curved permanently under their ribs, snapped up altogether perhaps enough protein for one American cocker spaniel to have eked a meal from. Hungry as I was from losing my meals, I began to feel like the dogs.

A constant wind from the northeast cooled the air 10 degrees. The few household cattle wandered home in the evening quite of their own volition, though the children harried them, and curled separately into two knots of bodies against an isolated thornbush, allowing an extra thorn barrier to be tucked tightly around them. Considering that bare white sand lay nearly everywhere, flecked with dead blades of straw but no other forage, the amount of manure on the ground was extraordinary. Puppies and little birds lived on it. Maybe the climate preserved it.

The thorn trees bore sweet tiny fruit that the kids knocked down with sticks, and, as firewood, snaked out sparks like fireworks. Across the space between tents the men talked in whups, whoops and shouts. All had a whip, most a sword, some a rifle tucked away behind the tin trunks full of clothes and cans full of clarified butter next to their curtained beds. The women were wordless with Hector and me, shaking hands with both hands—like a vassal—sometimes offering to kiss our hands. But besides being pretty, they tended to have intelligent and forceful or sensitive faces. They wore an enamel medallion on the right nostril, and hung amulets around their sons' necks—sewn leather scrolls containing a holy verse to ward off bad spirits. The small girls didn't have these, but their hair had often been braided laboriously like strings of minute black beads, as many as a hundred individual braids.

The boys beat the donkeys to make them buck for our entertainment, never giving less than a wholehearted whack. The boys' mothers beat *them,* too, with their own donkey sticks, even if they were as young as three years old, if they let a donkey drink before it was supposed to at the sheikh's hand-dug well. This went down for ninety feet. Two camels, ridden by boys, pulled up the pails by means of shrieking pulleys attached to forked sticks, while two women of what would be called "slave origin" in anthropological circles dragged up a third pail for domestic needs. The water for the animals ran into a shallow cement pit with tree limbs in it to prevent the creatures from climbing right in. All day every day, sheep were released in batches of twenty or thirty from successive herds that had been driven from far-off pastures and then held back a couple of hundred yards. Urgently running, drinking frantically at first, after two or three minutes they stood aside, looking as indifferent as if they had never been thirsty at all.

On our second day at Umm Sunta two policemen in yellow turbans rode up in high-canted, two-horned saddles to check us out. When made to kneel, their camels showed their teeth in snide, snobbish mouths, expostulating through slitted nostrils with snarls, whines and whuffles, although later they slept as meekly as turtles, with their necks stretched out. The officers laid their hands on their hearts between handshakes. One wore a bandolier studded with rifle bullets; the other wore shotgun shells. The rifleman, who was in his seventies, told me with signs of the hands that here, as elsewhere, most police drove about in jeeps, but that he on his camel was a better policeman than they. He could ride anywhere silently, see everything, and fire his gun.

I was up all night emptying my gut. At least Hector had quit teasing me about my loss of vim. The donkey engine at the big well had been fixed, but he said he was going to shorten his visit anyway. He suggested I watch the sheikh's camels being watered, a spectacle that would consume much of the next night. I rested in the tent and went over before sunset.

"The pump is not in good health," said the gloomy Sudanese veterinarian, though it nattered away now in its tin housing sufficiently for water to flow. "They don't take care of their animals, they don't take care of their machinery, and they don't take care of themselves." The army detachment commander, too, was counting the days until he could leave Kababishland.

Umm Sunta was certainly no place for cattle, but the herds of female camels (*niyag*) were a happy sight. A thousand strong, they stood divided into eight or ten compact bands, drawn up in a line facing the corral at the well. With the foals suckling, the few hairy-eared sires grimacing like a dog or a sheep when sniffing a tempting vagina, there was a great deal of bending of necks and stamping of feet—roars, belches, growls, death-rattle approximations, loud, complicated, broken-off noises, such as whales or elephants give voice to. Though intensely impatient and poised to race for the corral when the herders permitted it, they were not in any anguish from thirst. They were still absorbed in the flow of herd life, like a school of fish.

The herders—black men in torn clothes with direct, noncommittal faces—kept watch with their whips. Some of them played a game called *Umm al-Banat*, "Mother of Daughters," with forty-eight bits of camel dung tossed into twelve scoops in the sand. Among the Kababish, a different vocabulary is used to talk to camels from that used for sheep, and, poor hired hands though they were, they moved with the self-assurance of men still practicing the ideal of the tribe, resisting the shift from camels to sheep and from desert to town.

Hector and I took seats behind the shield of the well-master's cubicle within the corral, to watch the event and wind up my sojourn in Africa. It was efficiently executed, as established routines so often are. Fifty in a clump, the camels charged through the gate, all heads and humps against the dark sky. They were enormous; the ground shivered. Anyone in their path would have been crushed. This was to be a "two-week drink," now in March, and the water was salted for each new group. With cracks of the whip, the herders caused them to mill about as they drank, so that the troughs weren't trampled apart and the weaker animals could get to the water. When they felt replete, they drifted out, their motions willowy, frivolous, sleepy again, with the next alert bunch poised against the shortening horizon to tear towards the corral.

When it grew darker, we could no longer see the herd as a whole, or even the heads, necks and humps whirling in front of us around the corral. What we saw in the small hours were the big legs, each like a separate person, so that crowds of thumping, nickering human beings seemed to be milling before us, imbibing the water until all had been satisfied.